Contents

The White Guard

Mikhail Bulgakov

Translated by Roger Cockrell

ALMA CLASSICS LTD
3 Castle Yard
Richmond
Surrey TW10 6TF
United Kingdom
www.almaclassics.com

The White Guard first published in full in 1966
First published by Alma Classics Ltd in 2012
This new edition first published by Alma Classics Ltd in 2016

© by the Estate of Mikhail Bulgakov

Translation © Roger Cockrell, 2012

Cover © nathanburtondesign.com

Extra Material © Alma Classics Ltd

Printed in Great Britain by by CPI Group (UK) Ltd, Croydon, CR0 4YY

Typeset by Tetragon

ISBN: 978-1-84749-620-1

Mikhail Bulgakov (1891–1940)

Afanasy Ivanovich Bulgakov,
Bulgakov's father

Varvara Mikhailovna Bulgakova,
Bulgakov's mother

Lyubov Belozerskaya,
Bulgakov's second wife

Yelena Shilovskaya,
Bulgakov's third wife

Москва.—Moscou. № 322.
Садовая Тріумфальная д. Пигитъ.—Sadovaya Maison

Bulgakov's residences on Bolshaya Sadovaya St. (above) and Nashchokinsky Pereulok (bottom left); an unfinished letter to Stalin (bottom right)

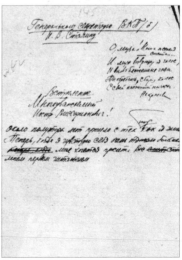

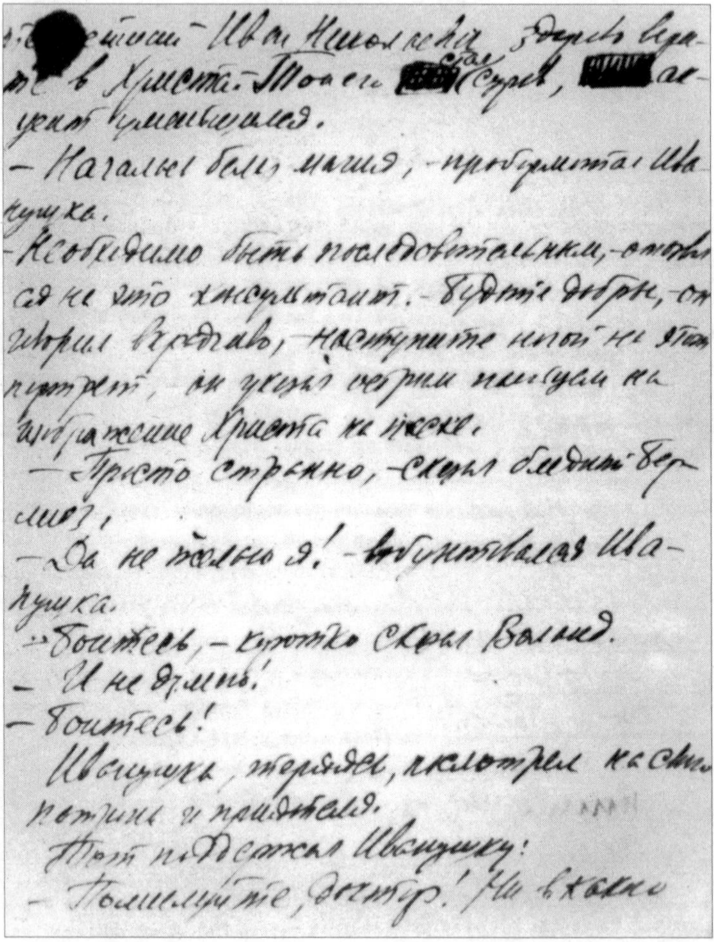

[illegible] [redacted] [illegible] [redacted] [illegible]

— Начальник был магом, — пробормотал Иванушка.

— Необходимо быть последовательным, — отозвался на это консультант. — Будьте добры, — он говорил вкрадчиво, — наступите ногой на этот портрет, — он указал острым пальцем на изображение Христа на песке.

— Просто странно, — сказал бледный Берлиоз.

— Да не хочу я! — взбунтовался Иванушка.

— Боитесь, — коротко сказал Воланд.

— И не думаю!

— Боитесь!

Иванушка, теряясь, посмотрел на своего патрона и приятеля.

Тот поддержал Иванушку:

— Помилуйте, доктор! Ни в каком

An autograph page from *The Master and Margarita*

Introduction

It is an evening in mid-December. The tiles of the Dutch stove are blazing with heat, and the outside world lies concealed behind cream-coloured curtains. On the table with its starched white tablecloth and vase of slightly faded flowers stand plates of food and bottles of vodka. In one corner of the room there is a piano with an opera score lying open. One of those present, the youngest of the family, the seventeen-year-old Nikolka, is strumming quietly on a guitar; the others, including Nikolka's brother and sister – Alexei and Yelena – are sitting round the table engaged in animated conversation. Every so often, a fierce argument breaks out, only to dissolve in banter and laughter. The room is bathed in the pink glow of the lamplight, filtering through the cigarette smoke. Next door there is a library lined with books and journals in many languages, evidence of a rich cultural heritage.

This is Bulgakov's portrayal, in his novel *The White Guard*, of the Turbin family at home, seemingly secure in their first-floor apartment and striving to recreate, now that Alexei has returned from military service, the environment of cosy domesticity that they have all known since early childhood. It is an apparently timeless and strangely innocent picture. Yet time and history have caught up with the Turbins, threatening to destroy not only them, but an entire culture and way of life. For at the point the novel opens – a week or so before Christmas in the "terrible year" of 1918 – the world beyond the cream-coloured curtains has become fractured, fraught with menace and confusion. The immediate environs are relatively quiet, with only the occasional sledge swishing along the street on which the Turbins live. But the wider city, with its shops, bars, clubs and schools that are all so familiar to them, stands on the edge of an abyss.

The *White Guard*, written for the most part in the early 1920s, but remaining unpublished in full in Soviet Russia until 1966, is set in Bulgakov's native city, the Ukrainian capital of Kiev. The narrative spans a period of less than two months during the exceptionally harsh winter of 1918–19. With the withdrawal of German troops from Kiev after Germany's defeat on the Western front in November and the consequential abdication of Kaiser Wilhelm II, the situation of the Ukrainian puppet government under its Hetman, Pavlo Skoropadsky, has become untenable. Now, in December, the city is under attack by the forces of the Ukrainian nationalist Symon Petlyura, resisted only by scattered and disorganized units of officers and cadets, including the Turbin brothers and a group of their close friends (the "White Guard" of the title). Everyday life for the city's population has deteriorated, with circumstances suddenly becoming frighteningly arbitrary and fragile.

Although their lives are to be profoundly affected by these events, the Turbin family remains at the still centre of this whirlpool throughout the novel. Despite their differences in character, behaviour and temperament, the three of them, together with their close circle of friends, are united by their love for pre-revolutionary Russia, the Tsar and autocracy, and by their anti-Ukrainian sentiments embodied in their hatred for Petlyura. Their most vitriolic contempt, however, is reserved for the treacherous behaviour of the Hetman and the general staff officers, including Yelena Turbin's husband Sergei Talberg, who abandon their posts and flee to Germany. Meanwhile, waiting in the wings for the opportunity to strike, are the "grey hordes" of the Bolsheviks under Trotsky.

The story that Bulgakov tells is a largely authentic reconstruction of these historical events. Many of the details relating to the setting and the characters, furthermore, possess a strongly autobiographical element, an evocation of Bulgakov's own family circumstances. Yet his use throughout of the term "the City" to refer to Kiev reminds us that *The White Guard* is primarily neither autobiography nor history, but a visionary novel springing from a highly original and creative imagination. As in his short story *The Fatal Eggs* (1925), the last of Bulgakov's prose works to be published during his lifetime, facts jostle with fiction to portray an alternative universe that diverges from historical reality in seemingly random and therefore unsettling ways. The novel's essentially fictional quality is further emphasized by its abundance of literary allusions, both direct and indirect. Among the most resonant and pervasive of these are the allusions to Tolstoy's *War and Peace*, the two novels sharing a central theme: the contrast between the concerns of the individual and the family on the one hand, and wide-reaching and destructive historical events on the other. The parallel can be extended to include at least some of the characters. Alexei Turbin, for example, has much in common with Tolstoy's equally sceptical and world-weary Prince Andrei Bolkonsky. And his younger brother Nikolka shares a number of attributes with Petya Rostov; both are guileless, impulsive young men, and both idealize war, anticipating a "glorious and heroic" death in battle – until, that is, they come face to face with its reality. Additionally, there is more than an echo in *The White Guard* of Tolstoy's derisive attack on the pomposity and hubris of so-called "great" men – the generals and politicians – who imagine that they are able to shape the course of historical events. In reality, however, they are merely puppets, their decisions shaped by forces of which they are unaware and which they are unable to control.

Whereas Tolstoy tells his story rationally and lucidly, Bulgakov's narrative unfolds far less evenly: episodes of family life intersperse with accounts of military action, punctuated by songs, poems, dreams, fragments of thoughts, swirling rumours and snatches of conversation (often of uncertain provenance). The novel's first epigraph, a quotation from Alexander Pushkin's historical novel *The Captain's Daughter* describing the onset of a disastrous blizzard, plunges us into a world of darkness and elemental chaos, a world in which people's minds become unhinged and the usual social norms governing human behaviour no longer operate. Suffering and tragedy are portrayed on both an individual and a grand scale, with scenes depicting barbaric acts of primitive savagery perpetrated by members of Petlyura's armed forces and frequently motivated by the crudest kind of anti-Semitism. The second epigraph, taken from the Book of Revelation, anticipates the apocalyptic theme that manifests itself in various ways throughout the work, including references to the Bolshevik leader Trotsky as the Antichrist, with his armies characterized as legions of the Devil. Here Bulgakov's world intersects most closely with that of Dostoevsky; it is not by chance that the book languishing open at the foot of Alexei's bed is Dostoevsky's most apocalyptic novel, *The Devils*.

Despite the undoubted bleakness of much of *The White Guard*, this is not the whole story. We note that the "red, quivering" Mars of the opening paragraph is counterbalanced by Venus, the goddess of love. Through the Turbin family we are made aware of the resilience of the human spirit and of the virtues of loyalty and steadfastness of principle – qualities that are thrown into strong relief when contrasted with the self-serving banalities of their landlord Vasilisa Lisovich skulking with his wife Vanda in the apartment immediately below the Turbins'. Although, with the arrival of the Bolsheviks in the City at the end of the novel, the Turbins' eventual fate remains as uncertain as ever, one of the final scenes shows them at home together, laughing and singing. And, in the penultimate paragraph, we see young Petya Shcheglov, from the neighbouring family, "uninterested", we are told, "in the Bolsheviks, or Petlyura, or the Devil" and dreaming he is walking across a large, green meadow towards a glittering diamond globe that showers him with coloured lights when he reaches it; he bursts out laughing from happiness.

In the light of Father Alexander's injunction to Alexei that despair is forbidden, such scenes acquire a particular significance. But the novel's clearly religious dimension is not confined to the need for optimism. Every so often the veil of fog and despair lifts to reveal a providential and mysteriously interconnected universe in which the course of people's lives can be shaped by the apparently miraculous, rather than the logic of brutal reality. Nikolka somehow manages to escape from an impossible situation; Alexei is rescued, quite out of the blue, by a total stranger, who unselfishly acts to help save his life, and he is later resurrected from the dead through, we are led to believe, the intercession of Yelena with her impassioned prayer to the Virgin Mary. Both brothers are linked, in circumstances that transcend the merely coincidental, by the labyrinth of houses and the "white, fairy-tale terraced garden" on Malo-Provalnaya Street: it is here that Alexei finds Julia, and that Nikolka meets the sister of his idol, the heroic Colonel Nai-Turs, whose horrific death he has witnessed, and whose body he has helped to bury.

There is an unexpected final twist. Bulgakov directs his readers' attention away from purely earthbound concerns – away even from the City, with its abundance of beautiful parks and gardens, and the mighty river Dnieper, overlooked by the towering statue of St Vladimir and its gigantic illuminated cross. The novel concludes as it began: with an image of the night sky. Since, as Bulgakov assures us, nothing will remain of value other than the stars, why then do we stubbornly continue to ignore their existence? This final paragraph is no mere rhetorical flourish, for it forces us to consider an aspect of the novel that has been present throughout: Bulgakov's implied criticism of the blinkered lives that the Turbins lead. How far, however, is such criticism counterbalanced by Bulgakov's sympathy for a family and a way of life that were so close to his own heart? As in the conclusion to Chekhov's *The Cherry Orchard*, in which there is a similar tension between conflicting emotions, we cannot be certain on which side Bulgakov intended to tip the scales. Whatever we may decide, the fact remains: if people choose to live behind cream-coloured curtains they may be able, at least for the time being, to shut themselves away from the outside world, but they will certainly deny themselves the opportunity to see the stars.

– Roger Cockrell

The White Guard

To Lyubov Yevgenyevna Belozerskaya*

It began to snow… lightly at first, but then in large flakes. The wind started to howl; it was a snowstorm. In an instant the dark sky merged into an ocean of snow. Everything disappeared.

"We're done for now, sir," shouted the coachman. "It's a blizzard!"

Pushkin, *The Captain's Daughter**

…and the dead were judged out of those things which were written in the books, according to their works.

Book of Revelation 20:12

Part One

I

G REAT AND TERRIBLE was the year of Our Lord 1918, the second year after the revolution. The summer was abundant with sun and the winter with snow, and two stars stood especially high in the sky: the shepherds' star – the evening Venus – and red, quivering Mars.

Yet, whether times are peaceful or bloody, the days fly past like arrows, and the young Turbins did not notice the onset of white, hoary December. Oh, Santa Claus, glistening with snow and happiness! Oh, mother of ours, glittering queen! Where are you?

A year after her daughter Yelena had married Captain Sergei Ivanovich Talberg, and in the very same week in which her elder son, Alexei Vasilyevich Turbin, had returned home to the Ukraine, to the City,* after a disastrous period of military service and heavy fighting – that very same week the white coffin containing the body of their mother had been carried down the steep St Alexei's Hill* to the little church of St Nicholas the Good in Podol, on the Embankment.

It was May when they conducted the funeral service for their mother, and the arched windows of the church were overhung with the branches of cherry trees and acacias. Father Alexander, stumbling from grief and strong emotion, sparkled and shone in the golden lights, and the deacon, his face and neck the colour of violet, the forged gold gleaming from his head right down to the soles of his boots, sorrowfully intoned the words of the funeral service for a mother who had left her children behind.

Alexei, Yelena, Talberg, Anyuta, who had been brought up as one of the family, and young Nikolka, stunned by the death, with a lock of hair falling over his right eyebrow, stood at the foot of the ancient brown icon of St Nicholas. Nikolka's light-blue eyes, on either side of his long, birdlike nose, wore a lost, shattered expression. From time to time he looked up at the iconostasis, at the arch of the altar, barely perceptible in the semi-gloom, and at the sad, enigmatic figure of an ancient God towering above them and winking. Why had this insult been inflicted upon them? What an injustice! Why had it been necessary to take their mother away from them, just when everyone had come together and started to feel a sense of relief?

Flying away into the crack in the dark sky, God said nothing in reply, and Nikolka was as yet unaware that everything that happens, whatever it might be, is always as it should be and always only for the best.

When the service was over, they went out onto the ringing flagstones of the church porch and accompanied their mother the whole way across the huge city to the cemetery, where their father had long since lain under a black marble cross. And there they buried their mother...

How many years before their mother's death, at No. 13 on St Alexei's Hill, had little Yelena, the elder son Alexei and tiny Nikolka been warmed and nurtured by the tiled stove in the dining room! How often had they sat by its glowing tiles, reading *The Shipwright of Saardam*,* with the clock playing its gavotte! At the end of every December the air had been filled with the scent of pine needles, the multicoloured paraffin candles glowing on the green branches. The black clock on the dining-room wall had chimed in response to the gavotte played by the bronze clock standing in their mother's – now Yelena's – bedroom. Their father had bought these clocks long ago, when women still wore comical sleeves, puffed up to the shoulders. These sleeves had disappeared, time had sped by, their professor father had died, everyone had grown up, but the clocks remained, continuing to chime just as they had always done. These clocks had become so familiar that if, by some strange chance, they had vanished from the walls, everybody would have been affected as much as if a familiar voice had died, creating a gap that nothing could fill. But clocks, fortunately, live for ever, just as the Shipwright of Saardam lives for ever and, like some wise, ancient rock, the tiled Dutch stove continued, even in the most difficult times, to radiate warmth and life.

And these tiles, together with the old red-velvet furniture, the beds with their shiny brass knobs, the worn rugs – some multicoloured, some red – depicting Alexei Mikhaylovich* with a falcon perched on his arm, the portrait of Louis XIV reclining languorously on the shores of a silken lake in some heavenly garden, the Turkish carpets with their stunning Oriental curlicues that entered the young Nikolka's delirious dreams when in bed with scarlet fever, the bronze lamp and lampshade, the finest bookshelves in the world, smelling mysteriously of old chocolate, with Natasha Rostova* and the Captain's Daughter, the gilt cups, the silver, the portraits and the drapes, all seven dusty, cluttered rooms that had nurtured the young Turbins – all this the children had inherited from their mother at the most difficult of times. With her final breaths she had clutched at the weeping Yelena's hand and enjoined them all to live together in friendship.

But exactly how were they to live? How?

The elder brother, the young doctor Alexei Vasilyevich Turbin, was twenty-eight, Yelena, twenty-four, her husband, Captain Talberg, thirty-one, and Nikolka, seventeen and a half. Their lives seem to have been shattered just as dawn was breaking. The winds had long since started to blow from the north, to blow and blow without ceasing, and the more they blew the worse it all became. The oldest Turbin had returned to his native city after the first gusts had blasted the hills above the river Dnieper. Now, at last, one might have thought, it would all stop, and the way of life depicted in those books smelling of chocolate would begin; but instead, it simply grew more and more terrible. The blizzard in the north howled and howled, while, close at hand, they could hear the dull rumbling of thunder, and an anguished growling from the depths of the earth. As the year 1918 flew towards its end, life became more threatening and bristling with the passing of each day.

The walls would fall, the frightened falcon would fly from the tsar's white sleeve, the light in the bronze lamp would fade, and the Captain's Daughter would be burnt in the stove. And, although the mother had told her children to live, the time would surely come when they would suffer and die.

One day, at dusk, shortly after their mother's funeral, Alexei Turbin went to Father Alexander and said:

"We're all feeling so sad, Father Alexander. It's hard for us to forget about our mother, especially when times are so difficult... After all, I've only just got back from the fighting, and I thought we could put everything right, and now this..."

He fell silent. Sitting at the table in the twilight, he looked pensively into the distance. The priest's little house was overhung with branches from the trees in the church courtyard, so that the walls of the cramped, book-lined study seemed to mark the edge of a mysterious, tangled spring forest. Filled with the scent of lilac, the evening air hummed with the muffled sound of the City.

9

"What can you do?" the priest muttered a couple of times. (He was always embarrassed whenever he had to talk to anyone.) "It's the will of God."

"Do you think that perhaps all this will come to an end? That maybe things will be better in the future?" Turbin asked, addressing no one in particular.

The priest shifted uneasily in his chair.

"Times are unquestionably hard," he muttered, "but you must not be downhearted."

Then, suddenly, freeing his pale white hand from the dark sleeve of his cassock, he placed it on a pile of books and opened the top book at the page in which there was already a coloured, embroidered bookmark.

"Despair must not be permitted," he said, still sounding embarrassed, but now with a note of conviction in his voice. "It is a great sin… even though there will be trials and tribulations to come, I think. Yes, yes, major trials and tribulations," he said, speaking in an even more assured tone. "Lately, you know, I have been sitting at my books, mostly theological, of course…"

Raising the book a little to allow the last rays of light from the window to fall upon the page, he started to read:

"And the third angel poured out his vial upon the rivers and fountains of waters; and they became blood."*

2

A ND SO THE FROSTY, white December raced towards its halfway point. There was already a feeling of Christmas in the snowy streets: 1918 would soon be at an end.

The Turbins' apartment was situated on the first floor of No. 13, overlooking the street. No. 13 was a two-storey house of strikingly unusual design, with the ground floor adjoining a sloping and compact little courtyard. Above the house was a garden, clinging to an extremely steep hillside, the drooping branches of the trees reaching almost down to the ground. The hill and the little outbuildings were covered in snow, turning them into one gigantic sugarloaf. The house itself was topped by a covering of snow resembling a White general's fur cap. At the front, the lower floor looked out onto the street, whereas, at the back, it formed a basement abutting the courtyard, beneath the Turbins' veranda. Here the cowardly engineer and unpleasant bourgeois Vasily Ivanovich Lisovich had just lit his feeble, yellow lights. Upstairs, by contrast, the Turbins' windows were cheerfully ablaze with lights.

At dusk Alexei and Nikolka went out to the shed to fetch some logs.

"Oh look at that! Practically all gone, damn it! They've been at them once again."

By the blue cone of light from Nikolka's torch they could see that some planks on the shed wall had been ripped away and hastily replaced from the outside.

"By God, they should be shot, the devils! Tell you what: why don't we keep watch tonight? I know who it is: it's those shoemakers in No. 11. They've got more logs than we have, damn them!"

"Oh, to hell with them... Come on, let's go."

The rusty lock squeaked and a pile of logs crashed down. The two of them carried the logs into the house and, by nine o'clock that evening, the tiles of the Dutch stove had become too hot to touch.

The gleaming exterior of this extraordinary stove bore the following historical notes and sketches, the work of Nikolka's hand, done in black ink at various times during 1918, and full of the most profound meaning and significance:

If anyone tells you that the Allies are hurrying to our rescue, don't believe them. The Allies are bastards.
He's a Bolshevik sympathizer.

A sketch of Momus's face,* signed "Lancer Leonid Yuryevich".

There's terrible news, so they say:
The red hordes are on the way!

The painted sketch of a head with a drooping moustache and wearing a fur cap with a blue tassel, with the inscription: "*Thrash Petlyura!*"*

And the following notes, in paints, Indian ink, ordinary ink and cherry juice by Yelena and the Turbins' oldest and dearest childhood friends – Myshlayevsky, Karas and Shervinsky:

Yelena Vasilyevna loves us all so...
But to some she'll say yes, to others no.

*Lenochka, I have a ticket for Aida.**
Seat 8, dress circle, right-hand side.

Noon, 12th May 1918: have fallen in love.
You're fat and ugly.

After saying this, I shall shoot myself. (Accompanied by a very life-like sketch of a Browning automatic pistol).

Long live Russia!
Long live autocracy!

June. A barcarolle.

The whole of Russia remembers
*The day of Borodino.**

Then in Nikolka's hand, in capital letters:

I HEREBY DECREE THAT ANY COMRADE RESPONSIBLE FOR WRITING UNAUTHORIZED MATERIAL ON THIS STOVE SHALL BE LIABLE TO BE SHOT WITH DEPRIVATION OF ALL RIGHTS.
   SIGNED: COMMISSAR, PODOL DISTRICT COMMITTEE, LADIES', GENTLEMEN'S AND WOMEN'S TAILOR,
ABRAM PRUZHINER.*
30TH JANUARY 1918

The stove's decorated tiles glowed with heat and, just as thirty years ago, the black clock ticked on: *tonk, tank.* The older Turbin brother, clean-shaven, fair-haired, having noticeably aged and become sunk in gloom ever since 25th October 1917,* was sitting in his favourite pose with his legs on the armchair. He was wearing an army jacket with huge pockets, blue riding breeches and soft new shoes. Nikolka was sitting by his brother's feet on a little stool, his forelock flopping over his eyes, his legs stretched out towards the sideboard – it was not a large dining room. He was wearing buckled boots, and he was strumming gently on his beloved guitar... *twang... twang...* a little absent-mindedly, however, since everything seemed uncertain at the moment. Things were bad in the City; anxiety and confusion were everywhere...

Nikolka was wearing the epaulettes with white stripes of a junior officer. On his left sleeve there was an acute-angled tricolour chevron. (Infantry, First Detachment, Third Squad. Formed four days ago, in anticipation of impending events.)

And yet, despite these events, everything in the dining room, it has to be said, was wonderful: warm, cosy, the cream-coloured curtains drawn, and the brothers wrapped in languorous warmth.

Alexei dropped his book and stretched himself.

"Come on then, play us 'On the March'."

Twang, ta tum… twang, ta tum…

"Their boots and caps so smart,
The young engineers look the part
As they march along!"

Alexei joined in the singing. There was a spark in his eyes, as well as sadness, and his blood quickened with life. But softly, gentlemen, softly.

"Hello there, summer residents,
Hello there, all you folk…"

The guitar began accompanying the engineers as they marched along… left, right, left, right! Nikolka's eyes were full of memories of the military school with its cannon and its peeling classical columns. The cadets crawling on their stomachs from window to window, returning fire. The machine guns in the windows.

The school had been surrounded by a large group of soldiers, a whole crowd of them. What could they do now? But General Bogoroditsky had taken fright and surrendered, given himself up with all his cadets. What a disgrace!

"Hello there, summer residents,
Hello there, all you folk,
The survey lads are here."

Nikolka's eyes clouded over: the columns of heat rising over the red Ukrainian fields; the companies of cadets marching along, covered in dust. At one time it had all been so real, but now it had all gone. The nonsensical disgrace of it all!

Yelena pulled back the heavy drapes over the doorway, and her auburn-golden hair was silhouetted against the dark gap. She looked tenderly at her brothers, and then cast a very worried look at the clock. It wasn't hard to understand why: where on earth had Talberg got to? She was anxious. She wanted to hide this by joining in the singing with her brothers, but suddenly she stopped and raised a finger.

"Wait! Did you hear that?"

All seven strings of the guitar and the engineers' march came to an abrupt halt. The three of them listened intently. It was gunfire – distant and muffled, but clearly heavy gunfire. *Boom!* There it was again. Nikolka quickly put down his guitar and stood up, followed, with a grunt, by Alexei.

The sitting room was totally dark. Nikolka bumped into a chair. Outside, with all the snow, noise and twinkling lights, it looked like a scene from the opera *Christmas Eve*.* Nikolka pressed his face to the window. The heat and the training school had disappeared from his eyes, to be replaced by an expression of intense alertness. Where was the gunfire coming from? He shrugged his junior officer's shoulders.

"God only knows! Could be coming from somewhere near Svyatoshin.* It's strange, though: shouldn't be that close."

Alexei stayed back, in the darkness, but Yelena was closer to the window, her frightened black-rimmed eyes clearly reflecting her anxiety. Why hadn't Talberg come? What did that mean? Sensing her agitation, Alexei remained silent, although he very much wanted to say something. Yes, Svyatoshin: there wasn't any doubt about it. That meant the firing was coming from only eight miles or so away. What was going on?

Nikolka gripped the window latch with one hand and pressed on the glass with the other, as if he wanted to push it and climb out. His nose was flattened against the pane.

"I want to go and find out what's happening."

"Yes, you go ahead, you're all they need right now…"

That was Yelena, motivated by anxiety. This was a disaster. Her husband should have been back by no later than three that afternoon for heaven's sake, and it was now ten.

They went back into the dining room in silence. The guitar, too, was now glumly silent. Nikolka brought the samovar from the kitchen and it began to sing and splutter. On the table there were teacups, decorated with delicate flowers on the outside, but with special little gold figures on the inside. During their mother's – Anna Vladimirovna's – time this tea service had been reserved for special family occasions, but now her children used it every day. Despite the gunfire and all the anxiety, alarm and nonsense going on, the tablecloth was white and starched. This was thanks to Yelena, who could not have done otherwise, and also to Anyuta who had grown up in the Turbin household. The floors were gleaming and, even though it was December, there were a few blue hydrangeas and two rather sorry-looking sultry roses in a tall, matt vase on the table – asserting life's beauty and permanence, despite the fact that, at the gates to the City, there was a cunning enemy capable, perhaps, of destroying its snow-covered beauty and trampling on the rubble. The flowers had been brought by Yelena's faithful admirer, Guards Lieutenant Leonid Yuryevich Shervinsky, the friend of the saleslady in La Marquise, the famous confectionery shop, as well as of the saleslady in the snug little flower shop Les Fleurs de Nice. Beneath the hydrangeas there was a blue-patterned plate, some slices of sausage, some butter in a glass dish, sugar lumps in a bowl and a long, white loaf. If only things weren't so awful outside, how wonderful it would have been just to enjoy it all! Goodness, how wonderful!

There was a brightly coloured tea cosy in the shape of a cockerel covering the teapot, and the distorted reflections of the three Turbin faces could be seen in the gleaming side of the samovar, with Nikolka's cheeks resembling those of Momus.

Yelena's eyes had an anguished expression, and locks of hair touched with gold drooped mournfully down.

The evening had been ruined: Talberg and his train with its consignment of the Hetman's money* must have got stuck somewhere. What could have happened to him, damn it?... The brothers listlessly ate their bread and sausage. In front of Yelena lay her cup of cold tea and a copy of 'The Gentleman from San Francisco'.* Her eyes, misted over and unseeing, were fixed on the words "gloom, ocean, storm..."

But Yelena was not reading.

Finally Nikolka could hold out no longer.

"I'd really like to know why the firing is so close. It can't be that close, surely..."

He interrupted himself, his reflection in the samovar being distorted as he moved. Pause. The hand on the clock crawled on past ten and... *tonk, tank*... on towards a quarter past.

"They're shooting because the Germans are bastards," Alexei blurted out unexpectedly.

Yelena looked up at the clock.

"But surely they wouldn't just leave us to our fate, would they?" she asked dejectedly.

As if by command, the brothers looked the other way, and started lying to her.

"Nothing is certain," Nikolka said, chewing at a piece of bread.

"I was talking hypothetically. It's just rumours."

"No, it's not just rumours," Yelena replied stubbornly. "It's a fact, not a rumour. I saw Mrs Shcheglova today and she said that two German regiments had withdrawn from Borodyanka."

"Nonsense."

"Think about it," said Alexei. "Would it make any sense for the Germans to allow that sly devil to come anywhere near the city? Think about it! I cannot begin to imagine how they could coexist even for a single minute. A totally absurd idea: the Germans and Petlyura! They themselves call him nothing but a bandit. Just a laughable idea."

"What are you on about? I've got to know the Germans now; I've seen some of them myself, in red armbands. And I saw a drunk warrant officer with some woman or other. The woman was drunk as well."

"So what? You'll get individual cases of misbehaviour just like that even in the German army."

"And so Petlyura won't enter the city, in your opinion?"

"In my opinion, that will never happen."

"*Absolument*. Pour me another cup of tea please. Stop worrying. Remain, as they say, calm."

"But where is Sergei, for goodness' sake? I'm sure his train has been attacked and—"

"Stop it at once! That line he's on is completely clear, I know it is."

"Well, why isn't he here then?"

"Good God! You know yourself what travel is like; I bet they've had a four-hour delay at every station."

"That's revolutionary travel for you: one hour on the move, two at a standstill."

Sighing deeply, Yelena glanced up at the clock.

"But, Good Heavens," she continued after a pause, "if the Germans hadn't behaved so abominably, everything would have been fine. You only needed two of their regiments and this Petlyura of yours would have been crushed like a fly. No, the Germans are clearly playing some despicable double game. And what about the wonderful Allies? Where are they? The scum! They promised and promised…"

The samovar, silent up to this point, suddenly started to sing, and a few coals covered in grey ash tumbled out onto the tray. Involuntarily the brothers glanced at the stove. That was its answer perhaps: "The Allies are swine."

The hand of the clock reached a quarter past. With a distinct wheeze the clock struck once, to be answered immediately by the quiet high-pitched ring of the doorbell on the hall ceiling.

"Thank God, that must be Sergei," Alexei said joyfully.

"Yes, it's Talberg," agreed Nikolka, who ran to open the door.

Yelena stood up, her face flushed.

But it wasn't Talberg at all. Three doors slammed shut, and Nikolka's astonished voice could be heard indistinctly on the staircase. Then someone's reply, followed by the clatter of hobnailed boots and a rifle butt on the floor. The door into the hallway let in a draught of cold air, and in front of Alexei and Yelena stood a tall, broad-shouldered figure in a full-length army coat with khaki epaulettes, with the three stars of a lieutenant drawn in indelible pencil. The coat hood was covered in hoar frost, and the heavy rifle and brown bayonet filled the whole hallway.

"Hello," piped the figure in a hoarse tenor voice, as he clutched at his hood with numb fingers.

"Vitya!"

Nikolka helped the figure untie the ends of the drawstring, and the hood slipped down to reveal an officer's cap with a faded badge, and then, above the huge shoulders, the head of Lieutenant Viktor Viktorovich Myshlayevsky. It was a very handsome head, strangely sad and beautiful, its attractiveness the result of many centuries of good, if somewhat degenerate breeding, also reflected in his long eyelashes and the fearless expression in his eyes, each of a different colour. The nose was aquiline, the lips proud, and the forehead white and smooth, without any distinguishing marks. But one corner of his mouth drooped sadly, and his chin slanted slightly, as if a sculptor had begun with the intention of carving an aristocratic face, but had then conceived the wild idea of chipping off a chunk of clay to create a small, irregular chin that was more feminine than masculine.

"Where have you come from?"

"Yes, where've you been?"

"Careful," Myshlayevsky answered in a feeble voice, "don't break the bottle of vodka."

Nikolka carefully hung up the heavy coat. The neck of a bottle wrapped in newspaper peeped out from one of its pockets. Then, rocking the antler stand, he hung up the heavy Mauser in its wooden holster. Only then did Myshlayevsky turn to Yelena, kiss her hand and say:

"I've come from the Red Tavern area. Let me stay the night here, Lena; I won't be able to make it home."

"My God, of course."

Myshlayevsky suddenly gave a groan and tried to blow on his fingers, but his lips wouldn't obey him. His white eyebrows and velvety trimmed moustache tipped with hoar frost had begun to thaw, and his face ran with moisture. Alexei unbuttoned his service jacket, running his hand down the seam of his dirty shirt as he started to pull it away.

"I knew it: crawling with lice."

"I know what," Yelena said, suddenly stirring herself, momentarily forgetting about Talberg in her anxiety. "There are some logs in the kitchen, Nikolka; run and light the boiler. Oh, it's so awful! Why on earth did I have to give Anyuta the evening off? Quick, Alexei, take his jacket off."

In the dining room Myshlayevsky, by now giving full rein to his groans, slumped down on a chair by the stove. Yelena bustled about, her keys jingling. Alexei and Nikolka knelt down and tugged off Myshlayevsky's tight-fitting dapper boots buckled at the calves.

"Hey, gently... gently..."

Then they unwound his disgusting, filthy leggings to reveal his lilac-coloured silk socks. Nikolka immediately took the jacket out to the cold veranda; the lice can all die out there. Sitting in his dirty linen vest, black braces and blue-striped breeches, looking ill, worn and thin, Myshlayevsky cut a pathetic figure. He clapped his blue hands together and rubbed them along the tiles of the stove... *terr... new... hor... way... love... May...*

"The bastards!" exclaimed Alexei. "They might at least have given you proper felt boots and warm sheepskin coats."

"Felt boots," repeated Myshlayevsky mockingly, the tears in his eyes. "Felt boots..."

The warmth inside the apartment was inducing unbearable pain in his frozen hands and feet. When Yelena's footsteps in the kitchen were no longer audible, he cried out angrily and tearfully:

"What an utter shambles!"

Twisting and turning, breathing hoarsely, he slumped down again and jabbed a finger at his socks:

"Take them off, take them off…"

There was a revolting smell of methylated spirits, and a mound of melting snow lay in the basin. With a glassful of vodka inside him, Lieutenant Myshlayevsky had suddenly become inebriated; all sense had gone from his eyes.

"I hope to God they won't have to be amputated…" he said bitterly, rocking in his chair.

"No, they're fine; they'll be all right. The big toe's frostbitten, that's all. It will come back to life, just like everything else…"

As Myshlayevsky put his stiff, wooden arms into the sleeves of a shaggy bathing robe, Nikolka squatted down by his feet and pulled on a pair of clean black socks. Hunched up, in clean underwear and bathing robe, the frozen Lieutenant Myshlayevsky returned to the land of the living; red spots had appeared on his cheeks. Swear words started leaping violently about the room like hail on a window sill. With unfocused eyes, he began to direct a torrent of obscenities at the general staff in their first-class railway carriages, at a certain Colonel Shchetkin, at the frost, Petlyura, the Germans and the blizzard, finishing by referring to the Hetman of all Ukraine himself in the basest and foulest terms imaginable.

Alexei and Nikolka looked at the lieutenant as he sat there thawing out, grinding his teeth. Every so often they made sympathetic and understanding noises.

"The Hetman, eh? The motherfucker!" roared Myshlayevsky. "And what about the Horse Guards? Where were they? In the palace! How about that? But we were sent off to fight as we were. How about that? Whole days and nights out in the snow and the frost… Good God! We thought we wouldn't get through, fuck it! Nothing but a few officers strung out every couple of hundred yards. Do you call that a defensive line? Could have been slaughtered like a lot of chickens."

"Wait a moment," Alexei said, reeling from the coarse outburst. "Tell us who it was in the Red Tavern area exactly."

"Pouf!" Myshlayevsky gestured dismissively. "Absolutely no idea! Do you know how many of us there were there? For-ty of us. Then that old witch Colonel Shchetkin arrives and says" – at this point Myshlayevsky screwed up his face and, speaking in a repellently thin lisp, attempted to mimic the hated Colonel Shchetkin – "'Gentlemen, the entire hope of the City rests on you. Be worthy of the trust of the dying mother of Russian cities, and if the enemy should appear, then attack. God is with us! You will be relieved in six hours. But use the ammunition sparingly.' And off he swishes in his car with his adjutant," continued Myshlayevsky, now speaking in his normal voice. "It's dark as an arseho—! And the frost jabs into you like needles."

"Yes, but who was it there, for Heaven's sake? Petlyura can't be anywhere in that area, surely."

"Who the devil knows? By next morning, believe me, we've practically gone out of our minds. Ever since midnight in fact, waiting to be relieved. All feeling in arms and legs has gone, but no sign of any relief. We can't light any fires, of course – there's a village less than a mile away, and the Red Tavern's even closer. During the night you begin to imagine things: the field seems to be moving, could be people crawling. All right, I think, what shall we do? You fling up your rifle, wondering whether to shoot or not; it's very tempting. You stand there and howl like a wolf. You shout, and someone farther along the line answers. In the end, you dig yourself a hole in the snow with your rifle butt, settle down, and try to stay awake. Sleep, and you're done for. Just before daybreak, I can't hold out any longer: I can feel myself dozing off. What do you think saved me? Machine guns! As the sun comes up, all hell breaks loose, perhaps a couple of miles away! And, can you imagine, I don't want to get up! Then a field gun starts blasting away. I stand up. I feel as if I have heavy weights on my legs. That's just brilliant, I think – Petlyura's here. Our line closes up a little, and we start to call across to each other. We decide that, in the event of an attack, we'll close up and form a single group, return fire, and move back in the direction of the City. If they overwhelm us, then they overwhelm us. At least we'd be together. And then, can you imagine, everything goes quiet. During the morning, groups of three of us at a time run to the tavern to thaw out. When do you think our relief arrives? Two o'clock in the afternoon – that's two o'clock this afternoon. Two hundred cadets from the First Detachment. All properly equipped, as you can imagine, in fur caps, felt boots, and with a machine-gun unit. Led by Colonel Nai-Turs."

"Ah, one of ours!" shouted Nikolka.

"Wait a moment, isn't he with the Belgrade Hussars?"*

"Yes, that's right. Anyway, when they see us, they're horrified, of course. 'We thought there were two companies with machine guns here,' they say. 'How on earth did you manage to hold out?'"

"It turned out that those machine guns we'd heard at daybreak had been part of a motley group of about a thousand attacking Serebryanka. Luckily, they didn't know just how thin our line was; otherwise, as you can imagine, the whole lot of them would have been in the City. And lucky, too, that the others just had time to inform Post-Volynsky, which meant that some battery or other could shell the enemy. Anyway, they lost the will to carry on the attack and melted away into thin air, God knows where."

"But who were they? It can't really have been Petlyura, can it?"

"Who the hell knows? I think it was local peasants – God-bearers straight out of Dostoevsky!*... The motherfuckers!"

"Good God!"

"Yes," Myshlayevsky continued hoarsely, drawing on a cigarette. "We were relieved, thank the Lord. When we counted up there were thirty-eight of us. So there you are, you see: only two of us had frozen to death. Finished. But there were two others taken away to have their feet amputated..."

"What, two of you died?"

"Well, what did you expect? One cadet and one officer. But things were even more fun in Popelyukha, a village near the Red Tavern, where I'd gone with Lieutenant Krasin to get a sledge for those who'd been frostbitten. So here we are in the village – seems absolutely dead, not a soul. We look around and finally spot some old bloke in a sheepskin cloak hobbling along on a crutch. When he sees us he's really happy. Can you imagine? There's something going on that's not quite right here, I'm thinking. Why's this silly old codger shouting at us so ecstatically? 'Hey, lads!' he called out in Ukrainian. So I launch into Ukrainian as well, using my sweetest voice: 'Hello, granddad, we need a sledge, quickly.' And he goes and answers: 'There ain't no sledges; them officer lot have taken them all off to Post.' So I wink at Krasin and say: 'Officer lot, eh? So where's everyone else then?' 'Them's run off to join Petlyura,' he blurted out. How do you like that, eh? The blind old fool hadn't spotted the epaulettes under our hoods and had taken us for Petlyura's men. So, as you can imagine, I can hold back no longer... I see red, what with the frost and everything. I grab the old boy by the front of his coat and shout at him so loudly he almost dies from fright. 'Run off to join Petlyura? I'll shoot you on the spot! That will teach you how to run off to Petlyura! You'll run off to kingdom come, you swine!' At this, of course, our saintly son of the soil" – a whole avalanche of abuse poured from Myshlayevsky – "sees the light in a flash, falls to his knees and starts shouting: 'Oh, Your Honour, please forgive me, I was joking; I'm just an old man, can't see very well. I'll get your horses right away, many as you want, only please don't shoot me!' So we get our horses and our sledge.

"Anyway, we get to Post-Volynsky by dusk. You simply can't imagine how awful everything is there. On our way there we come across four batteries, but none of them ready for action; no ammo, it seems. Countless staff officers. Nobody knows a thing, of course. But our main problem is to know what to do with the dead bodies. In the end we come across a mobile first-aid unit, but they just dump the bodies on the ground. Would you believe it! Not interested in them, simply say we should take them to the City. At this we become really angry. Krasin wants to shoot some staff officer who tells us we're behaving as badly as Petlyura's men and then vanishes. It's not until dark that we finally find Shchetkin's railway carriage. First-class carriage, electric light… And what do you think? We're refused entry by some lickspittle orderly. How about that?! 'He's asleep,' he says, 'and not to be disturbed.' Well, I start bashing against the side of the carriage with my rifle butt, and everyone else joins in. People immediately pour out of every compartment, like peas from a pod. Then Shchetkin himself appears. 'My God, yes, of course,' he says ingratiatingly. 'Hey, orderlies, soup and cognac for these officers! We'll find you somewhere immediately, and you can have a complete rest. You're all heroes. Terrible losses, I know, but what can you do? Sacrifices are necessary. I've been through so much…' You could smell the cognac a mile off." Myshlayevsky suddenly yawned, and his head began to nod. Then he started muttering, seemingly in his sleep.

"They gave the group a separate carriage with a stove. But I was lucky: he decided to get rid of me after all that racket. 'I order you, lieutenant, to go to the City and report to General Kartuzov's headquarters.' Got a lift on a locomotive… freezing… Tamara's Castle*… vodka…"

Myshlayevsky's cigarette dropped out of his mouth; he leant back in his chair and immediately started snoring.

"Well, that's terrific, isn't it?" said Nikolka, totally confused.

"Where's Yelena?" asked Alexei anxiously. "He'll need a sheet. Take him for a wash."

All this time Yelena had been in the room off the kitchen, weeping. A fire of dry cut birchwood crackled in the boiler behind the gauze curtain, next to the zinc bath. The ancient kitchen clock wheezed as it struck eleven o'clock. The image of Talberg lying dead came into her head. Obviously the train carrying the money had been attacked and the escort intercepted. Blood and brains in the snow. She sat there in the semi-gloom, the light from the fire glowing through her tangled hair, the tears pouring down her cheeks. Dead… dead.

Then the doorbell rang. It was very soft, but audible throughout the apartment. Yelena raced through the kitchen, through the darkened library and into the dining room, where the lights were brighter. The black clock struck the hour, then resumed its slow progress.

But the two brothers' outburst of joy faded very quickly. Indeed, any joy was reserved more for Yelena. When they saw the wedge-shaped badges on Talberg's epaulettes, denoting the Hetman's War Ministry, they reacted very negatively. Ever since the day of Yelena's wedding, in fact, it was as if a crack in the vase of the Turbins' life had formed, and any good water inside had imperceptibly been draining away. The vase was now dry. Perhaps the main reason for this was the double-layered expression in the eyes of Staff Captain Sergei Ivanovich Talberg...

Be that as it may, at this moment at least, the upper layer could be read perfectly clearly: the natural, happy expression of someone reacting to light, warmth and a feeling of security. A little deeper, however, was the sense of plain fear, which Talberg had brought with him into the house. But deeper still, of course, everything was hidden from view. In any event, Talberg's figure revealed nothing at all outwardly. His belt was broad and firm. The white surfaces of both his badges – the academy and the university – gleamed equally brightly. His lean, wiry figure moved around above the black clock like an automaton. Although he was frozen to the bone he smiled at everyone with equal benevolence. But there was anxiety in this smile as well. Nikolka, his long nose twitching, was the first to notice this. In a slow but light-hearted drawl, Talberg described how the train, which he had been escorting and which had been carrying money to the provinces, had been attacked near Borodyanka, some twenty-five miles from the City. But nobody knew who the attackers were. Yelena grimaced with horror and clung to him tightly, while the brothers again made soothing noises, and Myshlayevsky lay there snoring the sleep of the dead, revealing the three gold crowns in his teeth.

"Who could it have been? Petlyura's men?"

"If it had been Petlyura's men," said Talberg in a superior tone, but with an anxious smile, "I'd hardly be here now... er... talking to you. I don't know who it was. A mixed group of Ukrainian nationalists, possibly. They burst into the carriage waving their rifles around and shouting: 'Whose lot are you?' 'Ukrainians,' I replied. They tramped up and down the carriage, then I heard the command: 'Everyone off, lads!' And they all disappeared. I suppose they were looking for Russian officers, probably thinking that the escort hadn't been Ukrainians, but Russian officers." As he said this, Talberg glanced meaningfully at the stripes on Nikolka's uniform, then he glanced at the clock and said unexpectedly:

"Yelena, I'd just like a word or two…"

Yelena quickly followed him into the bedroom in the Talbergs' half of the apartment, the room where the falcon sat perched on the tsar's white sleeve, where the green lamp glowed softly on Yelena's desk, and where the bronze shepherds stood on the mahogany pedestal supporting the clock that played the gavotte every three hours.

It cost Nikolka a superhuman effort to wake Myshlayevsky. The latter stumbled to the bathroom, clutching at a couple of doors as he crashed into them. Once in the bath, he fell asleep, with Nikolka keeping watch to make sure he didn't drown. In the meantime Alexei, without knowing exactly why, made his way to the darkened living room, pressed his ears to the window and listened intently: once again there was the seemingly inoffensive sound of distant gunfire, muffled as if the guns had been wrapped in cotton wool.

Golden-haired Yelena had suddenly aged and become less attractive. Her eyes were red. With her hands hanging at her sides, she was listening sorrowfully to Talberg. Towering above her in his crisp, dry staff uniform he was saying implacably:

"There is no other course of action, Yelena."

"All right, I understand," Yelena said, reconciled to the inevitable. "You're right, of course. Five or six days, yes? Maybe the situation will have improved by then, yes?"

At this point Talberg found himself in difficulty. Even his permanent, patented smile disappeared from his face. It, too, had aged; every line in it demonstrated that his mind was firmly made up. Yelena… Yelena. Oh, her hope was so fragile, so treacherous… five or six days…

"I have to go now, this very minute," he said. "My train leaves at 1 a.m."

…Half an hour later everything in the room with the falcon was topsy-turvy. The suitcase lay on the floor, its inner stripy lid wide open. Yelena, looking thin and severe, and with lines at the corners of her mouth, was silently packing his shirts, underwear and sheets. Talberg was kneeling at the bottom drawer of the cupboard, fiddling with the key. And then… then, however unpleasant a room in which the chaos of packing is taking place, it's always much worse when a shade is removed from a lamp. Never ever remove a shade from a lamp! A shade is sacred. Never scuttle like a rat into the unknown and away from adversity. Sit by the lampshade and doze or read. Let the storm howl outside and wait for people to come to you.

But Talberg was indeed scuttling away. He stood up straight, treading on the scraps of paper lying near the heavy suitcase, its lid now closed. He was wearing his long army coat, his neat black cap with earmuffs and blue-grey hetman's badge, and his sword belted to his side.

At the long-distance platform of the City's Passenger Railway Station No. 1 the train was already waiting. As yet, it had no locomotive, so that it resembled a headless caterpillar. There were nine carriages, all dazzlingly lit with electric lighting. This was the train that was transporting the headquarters staff of General von Bussow to Germany. They were taking Talberg with them, for Talberg had connections... The Hetman's regime was an idiotic and banal comic opera – just like the Hetman himself, it had to be said. (Talberg was fond of using such direct, but trivial expressions). Even more trivial, since...

"The Germans are abandoning the Hetman to his fate, you understand," he whispered to Yelena. "And it's perfectly possible that Petlyura will enter the City and that... you know..."

Oh yes, Yelena knew all right! She knew perfectly well. In March 1917, Talberg had been the first – the first, you understand – in the military training school to wear a broad red armband on his sleeve. This was in the very early days, a time when all the Russian officers in the City, on hearing the news from St Petersburg, totally clammed up and went off into a dark corridor, unwilling to listen to anything further. As a member of the revolutionary military committee it had been none other than Talberg who had arrested the famous General Petrov. When, towards the end of that famous year, the City had witnessed a whole succession of marvellous and strange events, and when people had begun to appear on its streets without boots, but wearing wide baggy trousers under their grey military coats, and when these same people had started to declare that they wouldn't leave the City for the front line under any circumstances since there was nothing for them to do there, and that they would remain here, in the City, Talberg became annoyed, drily observing that this was just a comic opera – not at all what was needed. And it turned out he was partly right: what had transpired had indeed come to resemble a comic opera, but a far from simple one – one that entailed considerable bloodshed. In no time at all, the people in baggy trousers had been chased out of the City by various irregular groups of soldiers who had appeared from somewhere out of the forests and from the broad plain leading to Moscow. Talberg said that the people in baggy trousers were merely opportunists; the real roots lay in Moscow, even if these roots might be Bolshevik.

One March day, however, columns of Germans, dressed in field grey and wearing rusty metal helmets to protect them from shrapnel, arrived in the City. They were accompanied by hussars, and when Talberg saw their beautiful fur caps and horses he immediately understood where the roots actually lay. After a few salvos of heavy gunfire from the German guns on the outskirts of the City, the troops from Moscow vanished somewhere beyond the grey-blue forests to eat carrion, while the people in baggy trousers followed the Germans and shambled back into the City. This was a big surprise. Talberg smiled in some confusion, but decided there was nothing to be afraid of since, with the Germans there, the baggy trousers behaved extremely placidly, not daring to kill anybody, and even walking about the streets a little warily, behaving as if they were guests at an event, but not certain they'd been invited. Talberg said that they lacked proper roots and had not served in any post for a couple of months. One day, however, Nikolka had to smile walking into Talberg's room. Talberg was sitting at his desk writing out grammatical expressions on a piece of paper. A slim volume printed on inexpensive grey paper lay open in front of him: Ignaty Perpillo, *Ukrainian Grammar.**

In the April of 1918, at Easter, the electric arc lights hummed cheerfully, and the circus arena was packed to the top of the dome with people. Talberg's tall military figure stood in the centre of the arena counting the votes on a show of hands: this meant the end of the baggy trousers and the beginning of a Ukraine – not just any Ukraine, but a "Hetman's" Ukraine. They were electing the "Hetman of all Ukraine".

"We are now protected from that bloody comic opera in Moscow," Talberg said, as he stood at home, gleaming in his unfamiliar hetman's uniform, looking incongruous against the background of the familiar old wallpaper. The clock wheezed derisively on – *tonk, tank* – and the water continued to drain from the vase. Nikolka and Alexei had nothing to say to Talberg. And, indeed, it would have been very difficult to say anything, because Talberg became very angry at any mention of politics, especially whenever Nikolka tactlessly broached the topic of what he, Seryozha, might have said in March. At this, Talberg would become agitated and bare his unevenly spaced but firm white teeth, his eyes sparkling with a dangerous yellowish glint. As a result, such conversations quickly died a natural death.

Yes, a comic opera… Yelena knew what this meant when uttered by puffy Baltic lips. But now the operatic portents no longer boded well – not for the baggy trousers, nor for Moscow, nor for any old Ivan Ivanovich, but for him personally, for Sergei Ivanovich Talberg. Everyone has their own star, and it was not for nothing that, in the middle ages, the court astrologers had compiled horoscopes, predicting the future. How wise they had been! For Talberg's star, you see, was extremely unlucky. Had everything proceeded in a single straight line, he would have been all right, but at this moment in time events in the City were proceeding not in a straight line, but in astonishing zigzags, and Sergei Ivanovich's attempts to predict the future were unsuccessful and totally fruitless. Still some distance away, perhaps a hundred or a hundred and twenty miles from the City, a brightly lit Pullman railway carriage was waiting in the sidings. A clean-shaven man lolled in the carriage, like a pea in a pod, dictating orders to his secretaries and adjutants. Woe to Talberg should this man enter the City – and he could well do so! Everybody had read the edition of the *News*, featuring the name of Captain Talberg as someone who had voted for the Hetman, as well as the article he had written that said that Petlyura was "an opportunist who threatened to destroy the region with his comic-opera tactics…"

"Yelena, I can't take you with me, you do understand, don't you? We would just be wandering about in the dark."

But Yelena was too proud to say anything.

"I'll be able to get to the Don* by going through Romania and the Crimea without too much trouble, I should imagine. Von Bussow has promised to help – the Germans think highly of me. The German occupation has become an absurd comic opera, and they're already leaving. And I calculate that Petlyura" – he continued in a whisper – "cannot last very long either. No, the real force will come from the Don. And you must understand that I simply have to be there when the army representing justice and order is being formed. My career would be in ruins otherwise – you know, don't you, that Denikin was my divisional commander?* I'm sure that in three months' time – well, by May at the very latest – we'll be entering the City. You have nothing to fear, nobody will touch you under any circumstances, and in any case, if the worst comes to the worst, you have your passport in your maiden name. I shall ask Alexei to make certain you come to no harm."

Yelena suddenly recollected herself.

"Wait a moment," she said. "You will warn my brothers at once, won't you, that we are being betrayed by the Germans?"

Talberg's face reddened.

"Yes, of course, absolutely… but why don't you tell them yourself? Not that it will change things very much, of course."

A strangely disturbing thought flitted through Yelena's mind, but she had no time to express it: Talberg was already kissing his wife. Just for one moment there was a look of tenderness in his double-layered eyes. Yelena could stand it no longer and began to cry, but only very quietly – she was, after all, her mother's daughter, as well as being a remarkably strong woman. Then it was time to say goodbye to the brothers in the living room. The bronze lamp illuminated one corner of the room in a pinkish glow. Above the piano's familiar white keys, the score of *Faust* lay open at the page of the densely black, rippling passage where the ginger-bearded and magnificently costumed Valentin sings:*

> Please, I beg you, for my sister's sake:
> have pity and take care of her.

And even Talberg, never one to indulge in any sentimental feelings, remembered the dark modulations and tattered pages of the immortal *Faust* once more. Goodness! Never again will Talberg hear the aria 'Oh, Almighty God', or listen to Yelena accompanying Shervinsky! And yet, long after the Turbins and Talberg have departed this earth, pianos will be played, the magnificently costumed Valentin will come onto the stage, the scent of perfume will be redolent in the theatre boxes, and in domestic living rooms women, bathed in lamplight, will play the accompaniment – for *Faust*, just like the Shipwright of Saardam, will never die.

Talberg said all that he had to say, standing by the piano. Out of politeness, the brothers remained silent, trying not to raise their eyebrows. The younger out of pride, the elder because he considered Talberg to be worthless. Talberg's voice trembled.

"Be sure to look after Yelena," he said, an anxious and pleading expression reflected in the upper layer of his eyes. Lost for words and not sure what to do, he glanced at his watch. "Time to go," he said anxiously.

Yelena embraced her husband, made a hasty sign of the cross over him, and kissed him. Talberg pricked the faces of his brothers-in-law with the bristles of his black clipped moustache. He anxiously checked the documents in his wallet, counting a thin bundle of Ukrainian notes and German marks. Then, smiling tensely, he turned and left the room.

There was the sound of footsteps on the floor, the light spluttered on in the hallway, then the rumble of a suitcase on the stairs. Leaning over the banisters, Yelena saw the sharp peak of his hood for the final time.

At 1 a.m. an armoured train, resembling some grey toad, rumbled out of a darkened Track 5 and into the graveyard of empty goods wagons. Hooting like a wild beast and spitting hot sparks from its furnace, it quickly picked up speed. Within seven minutes it had covered the five miles or so to Post-Volynsky. Without slowing down and with its lights flashing, it rattled and crashed across the points and away from the main line, instilling in the hearts of the frozen cadets and officers huddled together in their carriages and trenches at Post-Volynsky a vague feeling of hope and a sense of pride. Totally unafraid of anything or anybody, the train boldly curved away in the direction of the German frontier. It was followed ten minutes later by a passenger train with scores of brightly lit windows and pulled by an enormous locomotive. Solid-looking, massive German sentries, wrapped to the eyes against the cold and standing on the platforms at the end of each carriage, flashed past, their broad black bayonets glinting in the light. The signalmen, their faces fitfully illuminated by the lights from the windows, watched as the long Pullman carriages clattered across the points. The train disappeared, leaving the cadets' hearts filled with envy, anger and alarm.

"The bastards!" someone shouted, as the carriage was buffeted by a gust of driving snow – that night was a particularly stormy one for Post-Volynsky.

Talberg was sitting opposite a German lieutenant in the third carriage from the front, in a compartment furnished with striped covers. He was speaking German with a polite and ingratiating smile on his face.

"*Oh, ja,*" drawled the fat lieutenant from time to time, chewing on a cigar.

The lieutenant fell asleep. With the compartment doors closed, the warm, dazzlingly lit carriage was filled with the monotonous hum of casual conversation. Talberg went out into the corridor, where he pulled up the light-coloured blind bearing the transparent letters "SWR"* and stood for a long time staring out into the gloom. Sparks and snowflakes danced around in the air, while the locomotive up front emitted such threatening, unpleasant howls that even Talberg felt a sense of unease.

A T THIS VERY SAME HOUR, in the downstairs apartment belonging to the owner of the house, the engineer Vasily Ivanovich Lisovich, there was total silence, broken only by the occasional sound of a mouse in the small dining room. The mouse was busily and doggedly gnawing away at a piece of old cheese in the sideboard, cursing the miserliness of the engineer's wife, Vanda Mikhaylovna. The object of the mouse's curse, the bony and jealous Vanda, was fast asleep in the dark bedroom of the damp, cool apartment. The engineer himself was awake in his cramped little study, hung with curtains and stuffed with books, which gave the room a remarkably cosy feel. A standard lamp, in the form of an Egyptian princess, topped by a green, florid, umbrella-shaped lampshade, filled the entire room with a soft, mysterious light, a mysteriousness that was shared by the engineer himself, sitting in his deep leather armchair. The mystery and ambiguity of the uncertain times in which they lived was above all reflected in the fact that the person in the armchair wasn't Vasily Ivanovich Lisovich at all, but simply Vasilisa… He called himself Lisovich, it is true, and many of those he came across called him Vasily Ivanovich. But this was only to his face; behind his back, everyone just referred to him as Vasilisa. The reason for this was that, ever since the beginning of the truly unusual events in the City in January 1918, he had become afraid that he might be held responsible for something or other in the future. Instead, therefore, of neatly appending his usual name of "V. Lisovich" on questionnaires, forms, certificates, orders and ration cards, he had started writing "Vas. Lis.".

On 18th January 1918, Nikolka had been queuing for sugar on the Kreshchatik* with a ration card given to him by Vasily Ivanovich when, instead of getting any sugar, he had been struck with terrible force in the back by a stone, and had spent the next two days spitting blood. (A shell had burst right over the heads of the people who had been bravely standing in the sugar queue.) Back home, although green in the face and clutching at the wall, he even managed a smile so as not to alarm Yelena. But when he spat up a whole basinful of blood she cried out in horror:

"My God, what's happened?"

"It's all Vasilisa's fault, damn him, him and his sugar!" Nikolka replied. Then he turned white and collapsed onto his side. He was on his feet again within two days, but by this time Vasily Ivanovich Lisovich was no more. At first it was only his immediate neighbours, but later the whole city began to refer to the engineer as Vasilisa, with the exception of his wife, who continued to introduce him as Chairman of the Housing Committee Lisovich.

Once he was sure that it had become totally quiet outside, with not even the occasional swish of a sledge going by, and that, from the whistling sound coming from the bedroom, his wife was still soundly asleep, Vasilisa went out to the hallway and carefully checked that the bolts, lock, latch and chain were secure, and then returned to his little study. He took out four safety pins from the drawer of his massive desk, placing them on top. Then he tiptoed somewhere into the darkness and returned carrying a sheet and a rug. Once again, he stood for a moment, listening carefully, and even put his finger to his lips. He took off his jacket, rolled up his sleeves, and reached up to the shelf for a pot of glue, a neat roll of wallpaper and a pair of scissors. Then he pressed his face close to the window and, shielding his face with the palm of his hand, looked out onto the street. He hung up the sheet over the bottom half of the window on the left-hand side, then attached the rug to the other window with the safety pins. He carefully arranged the sheet and the rug so that no chinks were visible. Then he climbed on a chair and, groping around for something above the topmost bookshelf, he took a knife and made a vertical cut in the wallpaper, followed by another at right angles to the first. Inserting the knife under the slit, he uncovered a neat little hidey-hole, two bricks wide, which he himself had made the previous evening. He removed the thin zinc cover and placed it to one side. He then got down from the chair, glanced apprehensively at the windows and checked the sheet once more. With two jingling turns of the key he then opened the lower drawer of his desk to reveal to God's world, at the very bottom of the drawer, a sealed packet covered in newspaper, neatly tied both ways. He buried the packet in the hidey-hole and replaced the cover. He then spent a long time measuring and cutting out strips of wallpaper on the red tablecloth until he was certain they were the right size. He glued the strips over the slit so expertly, and managed to match the little squares and flower patterns so precisely, that he was delighted with the result. When the engineer finally got down from the chair, he was satisfied that the hidey-hole was completely invisible. He rubbed his hands in glee, scrunched up the wallpaper cuttings and burned them in the stove. Then he stirred the ashes and hid the glue.

Outside, in the dark and empty street, a grey, unkempt, lupine figure climbed silently down from the acacia branch on which he had been sitting for the last thirty minutes. Although frozen to the bone, he had eagerly been observing all that the engineer had been doing through a giveaway gap at the very top of the sheet; it had been the contrast between the white sheet and the green-painted window frame that had first fatally attracted the stranger's attention. Springing lightly down into a snowdrift, he went on up the street, and then continued making his way down alleyways, all traces of him being swallowed up and obliterated by the blizzard, the dark and the snow.

Night-time. Vasilisa in his armchair under the green lampshade, looking the very image of Taras Bulba.* Drooping, bushy moustache – by God, this isn't Vasilisa, but a real man! There's another gentle jingle of keys in the drawer, and a wad of oblong notes designed like green playing cards appears on the red tablecloth in front of him. The notes bear the following legend, in Ukrainian:

STATE BANK CERTIFICATE
50 Karbovantsy*
Parity with All Credit Notes

The front of the notes depicted a peasant with a drooping moustache armed with a spade, together with a peasant woman carrying a sickle. The reverse side featured the same couple, their reddish faces magnified within an oval frame, the man sporting the same drooping moustache, in the Ukrainian style. The top of the note carried the warning:

The penalty for forgery is imprisonment
signed: *Lebid-Yurchyk*, Director of the State Bank

A bronze Alexander II on horseback, sporting a ragged metal foam of side whiskers on either side of his face, looked irritably down at Lebid-Yurchyk's work of art and, more indulgently, at the Egyptian princess on her lamp. On the wall, an official with the Order of St Stanislav* round his neck – an oil painting of one of Vasilisa's ancestors – stared in horror at the notes. The spines of books by Goncharov and Dostoevsky* glowed softly in the green lamplight, and the gold and black row of Brockhaus and Efron* stood to attention like Guards on parade. Domestic bliss.

Safely tucked away in the cache in the wall were five-per-cent bonds, together with fifteen hundred roubles from the time of Catherine the Great, nine hundred "Peter the Great" roubles, one thousand "Nicholas the First" roubles, three diamond rings, one brooch, one Order of Anna* and two Orders of St Stanislav.

In cache no. 2 were another two thousand "Catherine" roubles, another thousand "Peter" roubles, twenty five silver spoons, a gold watch and chain, three cigarette cases (inscribed "To our dear colleague", although Vasilisa was a non-smoker), fifty ten-rouble gold coins, salt cellars, a canteen of silver cutlery for six people and a silver tea-strainer. This large cache was to be found in the woodshed: from the doorway, take two steps forward, one to the left, and then one more step from the chalk mark on a plank in the wall. Everything was in Einem biscuit boxes,* wrapped in oilcloth with tarred seams and buried to a depth of nearly five feet.

There was a third cache to be found in the attic, hidden in clay under a beam and reached by taking two quarter-steps in a north-easterly direction from the chimney stack. Here there were the sugar tongs, another one hundred and eighty-three ten-rouble gold coins and bonds to the value of twenty-five thousand roubles.

The Lebid-Yurchyk was for current expenses.

Vasilisa glanced round, as he always did when counting money, licked his finger and started to check the Ukrainian notes. He had an inspired expression on his face. Then he suddenly went pale.

"That one's a forgery... and so's this," he growled angrily, shaking his head. "This is a disaster!"

Vasilisa's blue eyes darkened murderously. One of the notes in the third batch of ten was forged; two more in the fourth and sixth batches; and, in the ninth batch, there were three notes in a row for which Lebid-Yurchyk would indubitably threaten imprisonment. Out of a total of one hundred and thirty notes, eight, if you please, looked clearly to be forgeries. The peasant had a sullen expression, when he should have been looking jolly, the hidden quotation marks and colon next to the sheaf were missing, and the paper was of a better quality than Lebid's. When Vasilisa held one note up to the light, the watermark of Lebid's portrait clearly showed through on the wrong side.

"Right, one of these will be for the cabby tomorrow evening," he said to himself. "I'll have to take a cab anyway, and then there's also the market."

Carefully setting the forged notes intended for the cabby and the market to one side, he locked the bundle of money away with a jingle of keys. He jumped, as the deathly silence was broken by the sound of someone running in the room above, and he could hear laughter and muffled voices.

"There you are, you see," he said, addressing Alexander II. "Never any peace."

Everything went quiet again. Vasilisa yawned, stroked his bristly moustache, took the sheet and the rug down from the window, and switched on the small lamp in the sitting room. There was a faint gleam of light from the gramophone loudspeaker. Ten minutes later, and the apartment was completely dark. Vasilisa was asleep next to his wife in the damp bedroom. There was a smell of mice, mould and querulous boredom. And Vasilisa dreamt that Lebid-Yurchyk arrived at the house on horseback, accompanied by thieves who opened up the cache with screwdrivers. Then the knave of hearts climbed up on the chair, spat at his moustache and shot at him point-blank. Vasilisa leapt up with a yell, bathed in cold sweat. The first thing he heard was the family of mice in the dining room, gnawing away at a bag of biscuits. Then the sound of laughter, and the strumming of a guitar that was being played with unusual tenderness coming through the ceiling and the carpeted room above.

Then, in the room above, a voice started singing with extraordinary power and passion, and the guitar struck up a march.

"There's nothing for it; I'll have to kick them out," said Vasilisa, tossing and turning in bed. "This is torture; no peace, day or night."

"The cadets are singing
As they march along
With their arms a-swinging
As they march along."

"And yet, maybe… just in case… after all, these are terrible times, and you never know who you might have in their place. As officers they would be some sort of protection if anything happened… Scram!" he shouted at the enraged mouse…

And the guitar played on and on…

Four lights burning in the chandelier in the dining room. Wreathes of blue smoke. The glass doors onto the veranda hidden behind cream-coloured curtains. The clocks are inaudible. Fresh vases of hothouse roses against the whiteness of the tablecloth. Three bottles of vodka and some slender bottles of German white wine. Lafitte wine glasses, apples in gleaming cut-glass vases, slices of lemon, crumbs all over the table, tea...

A crumpled page from the humorous newspaper *The Devil's Plaything** on an armchair. Minds clouded by the fog of uncertainty, with thoughts now rising to sunlit uplands of irrational joy, now plunging into dark valleys of anxiety. Random sentences and snippets of nonsense verse floated around in the fog:

"Best not sit on a hedgehog without any clothes..."

"Load of old nonsense... but at least the guns have stopped... what a laugh, damn it!
Vodka... vodka... my mind's gone blank. Come on, how about a twang on the guitar?"

"No point in baking melons on a bar of soap.
The Americans have won – so don't lose hope."

Hidden behind a wall of smoke, Myshlayevsky, now quite drunk, roared with laughter.

Breitman's wit is pretty good, as everyone knows.
But where are the Senegalese, do you suppose?

"Yes, right, where are they? Where are they?" asked Myshlayevsky, slurring his words.

"Sheep give birth when they're in a tent,
and Rodzyanko'll be our president."*

"But they're talented those bastards – you have to give them that!"

Presiding over all of this was Yelena, sitting in an armchair at the narrow end of the table. Since Talberg's departure she had not been allowed to have a moment to herself, and white wine does not take the pain away completely; it merely blunts it. Opposite her, at the other end of the table, sat Myshlayevsky in a dressing gown, unshaven, white-faced, covered in blotches from the vodka and devastating fatigue. His

35

eyes were ringed with red from the extreme cold, the shock of events, the vodka and anger. Alexei and Nikolka were sitting along one side of the table. Opposite them sat Leonid Yuryevich Shervinsky, former hussar lieutenant in the Life Guards, and now adjutant on the head-quarters staff of Prince Belorukov.* Next to him was Second Lieutenant Fyodor Nikolayevich Stepanov of the artillery, universally known since his grammar-school days as Karas, or Carp.

Karas – small, compact and, indeed, looking extraordinarily like a carp – had bumped into Shervinsky right at the entrance to the Turbins', some twenty minutes after Talberg had left. Both turned out to have bottles on them: Shervinsky a package of four bottles of white wine, Karas two bottles of vodka. In addition, Shervinsky was laden with the largest imaginable bouquet of flowers hidden in three layers of wrapping paper – roses, for Yelena Vasilyevna, of course. Standing by the entrance, Karas lost no time in telling Shervinsky about the gold artillery insignia on his epaulettes. He had run out of patience, he said; everybody would be needed to go and fight. In any case, what they had been taught at college would be irrelevant, particularly if Petlyura were to enter the City. Everybody had a duty to fight, and all artillery-men had to join the mortar battalion. The commanding officer was Colonel Malyshev, and the battalion itself was a remarkable one, full of students from his college. But the fact that Myshlayevsky had gone off to join that idiotic detachment filled him with despair. Goodness knows where he was now; he'd probably gone and got himself killed, somewhere near the City.

But when they got upstairs, who should be there but Myshlayevsky! In the semi-gloom of her bedroom, golden Yelena hastily powdered her face in the oval, silver-leafed mirror and went out to receive the roses. Wonderful! Everybody was there! Compared with Shervinsky's pale-coloured cavalry epaulettes and immaculately pressed blue breeches, Karas's crumpled artillery insignia looked far less resplendent. Shervinsky's eyes danced with malicious glee when he was told about Talberg's disappearance. The little hussar immediately sensed that he was in exceptionally fine voice and, in the pink glow of the lamplight, the sitting room became filled with an overwhelming cascade of sound as he sang a hymn of praise to the god of marriage. He sang with such power and passion that you might be forgiven for thinking that a voice such as Shervinsky's was the only thing on earth that made any sense. For the time being, of course, there was his staff job and this idiotic war – and, besides, the Bolsheviks and Petlyura had to be confronted as well (not to mention his duty). But afterwards, when everything had returned to normal, despite his St Petersburg connections (and what connections they were, too!), he would give up his military career and go on the stage. He would sing at La Scala, and at the Bolshoi in Moscow, while the Bolsheviks were being hanged on lamp-posts on Theatre Square. When in Zhmerinka he had sung an A rather than an F during a rendition of the Epithalamium, Countess Lendrikova had fallen in love with him. And he had held the A for five bars! At this Shervinsky hung his head a little, and looked round the room as if he had been telling someone else's story rather than his own.

"That's right, for five bars... All right, let's go and eat."

And so, the wreathes of cigarette smoke...

"Well, where are the Senegalese troops then?* Come on, staff officer, let's have an answer. Lenochka, my beautiful golden girl, have some more wine. Everything will work out; leaving when he did was the best thing he could have done. He'll make his way to the Don, and then he'll be back here with Denikin's army."

"They'll come!" boomed Shervinsky. "They'll come, I'm certain of it. And now, if I may, some important news: I saw Serbian billet officers today, on the Kreshchatik. The day after tomorrow, in two days' time at the latest, two Serbian regiments will be arriving in the City."

"Really? Is that true?"

Shervinsky frowned.

"Hmm, that's a little strange: if I say I saw it, then such a question seems out of place."

"Two regiments, you say?... Two regiments..."

"All right, then; be so kind as to listen to this: the prince himself told me today that troop transports, with Greeks and two divisions of Senegalese on board, are already being unloaded in Odessa. We just need to hold out for one more week, and then we can tell the Germans to go to hell."

"Traitors!"

"Well, if all that's true, then we'll catch Petlyura and string him up! String him up!"

"I'll shoot him myself."

"Another drop, gentlemen? Your good health!"

Suddenly the fog takes over completely. Fog, ladies and gentlemen! Having drunk three glasses of wine, Nikolka dashed to his room for a handkerchief. Running through the hallway he crashed against the coat stand (you can always be yourself when you know no one's watching).

Shervinsky's curved sabre with its gleaming gold hilt, the gift of some Persian prince. A Damascene sword. Actually, it hadn't been a gift from a prince, and the sword wasn't from Damascus, although it was certainly an expensive and fine-looking blade. A grim-looking Mauser on a strap in its holster, Karas's Steyr automatic pistol, with its burnished muzzle. Nikolka grasped covetously at the cold wooden holster and, running his fingers over the Mauser's lethal barrel, almost wept from excitement. He wanted to leave immediately and fight in the snow-covered fields around Post-Volynsky. He felt ashamed and awkward: here he was in a warm room, with plenty of vodka, but out there it was dark, a blizzard was blowing and the cadets were freezing to death. What were those staff officers thinking of? The unit was unprepared, the students untrained and the Senegalese still hadn't come. Almost certainly as black as boots, they'd freeze to death here, wouldn't they, for Heaven's sake? They were used to a warm climate, weren't they?

"Well, I'd string up your Hetman first!" shouted Alexei. "For the last six months he's just been laughing at all of us. Who was it against the idea of a Russian army being formed? The Hetman! And now, when things have got really bad and the enemy is at the gates, they've started to form a Russian army, but it's simply staff officers and a few independent units. What do think of that, eh?"

"You're just panic-mongering."

"Me? Panic-mongering? Why do you simply refuse to understand me? I'm not panic-mongering at all: I just want to get everything that's been boiling up inside me off my chest. Panic-mongering? Don't worry, I've already decided to go to that battalion tomorrow, and if your Malyshev doesn't want to take me as a doctor then I'll enlist as an ordinary private. I'm so fed up with all this! I'm not panicking!" A piece of cucumber stuck in Alexei's throat, and he started coughing and choking. Nikolka began to thump him on the back.

"Right!" agreed Karas, banging the table. "Private, you say? Nonsense! We'll get you in as a doctor."

"We'll all go tomorrow, together," Myshlayevsky mumbled drunkenly. "All of us, together. The entire Alexandrovsky Imperial High School.* Hurrah!"

"He's an absolute swine," Alexei continued scathingly. "He doesn't even speak our language! What do you think of that? Two days ago I was talking to that swine, Doctor Kuritsky. Apparently since last November he's forgotten how to speak Russian. He's even changed his surname so that it's Ukrainian rather than Russian... Anyway, when I ask him what 'cat' is in Ukrainian, he replies '*kit*'. But since '*kit*' means 'whale' in Russian, I ask him what 'whale' is in Ukrainian? He pauses, stares at me for a moment, and says nothing. And now he won't even acknowledge me."

Nikolka roared with laughter.

"It's not at all surprising there isn't a word for 'whale', because they don't have them in the Ukraine, whereas Russia has masses of them – in the White Sea, for example."

"As for mobilization," Alexei continued venomously, "it's a pity you didn't see what was going on in the police stations yesterday. Every one of those currency speculators knew about the order to mobilize three days before it was given. How about that? And they all either had a hernia, or some patch on their lung, or they'd simply vanished into thin air. And that, my friends, is a very ominous sign. If you have people gossiping in the coffee houses just before mobilization is announced and then nobody joins up, things are in a very bad way! The bastards, the absolute bastards! If only he'd started forming the officer corps in April we would have taken Moscow by now. You realize he could have formed an army of fifty thousand men? And what an army, eh?! Picked troops, the very best, as they would all have been officers and cadets, graduates from the training school. There are thousands of such people in the City, and all of them would have joined up with enthusiasm. Not only would we have annihilated Petlyura here, but we would have squashed Trotsky* like a fly in Moscow. And precisely now would have been the right time to attack: they say they've started eating cats there. The Hetman would have saved Russia, the son of a bitch!"

Alexei's face was covered in red blotches, and the words were gushing out of his mouth, accompanied by thin streams of saliva.

"Listen to you… you should have been minister of defence, rather than a doctor," said Karas. He smiled ironically, but he had liked and been inspired by what Turbin had said.

"Alexei's your man at any meeting," said Nikolka. "He's an orator."

"Nikolka, I've told you more than once that your so-called witticisms are not very funny," Alexei said. "Have some more wine instead."

"But you realize that the Germans wouldn't allow an army to be formed," said Karas. "They'd be afraid of it."

"That's not true," Alexei exclaimed in a thin voice. "It just needed someone with a head on his shoulders to come to some sort of an arrangement with the Hetman. And then it would only have been necessary to explain to the Germans that we weren't any threat to them. It's over; we've lost the war! But we are faced with something else, something that's even more terrible than war, or anything else: Trotsky. This is what we should have said to the Germans: you need sugar and bread, don't you? All right, take whatever you need to feed your troops. Exploit us if you want, but help us and let us form an army. You must know that it will be to your own benefit. We'll help you keep order in the Ukraine to ensure that our Ukrainian holy men don't get infected with the Moscow disease. And with a Russian army in the City we'd be protected from Moscow by a wall of steel. And as for Petlyura... *kch*..." Turbin drew his finger across his throat and broke into a violent coughing fit.

"Hold on a moment," said Shervinsky, standing up. "I've got to speak up in the Hetman's defence. There've been mistakes, it's true, but his plan was a sound one. He's a diplomat, all right. First, a Ukrainian state, to be sure, but then he would have done exactly as you've been saying: there would have been a Russian army, no argument about it. How do you like that?" Shervinsky gestured solemnly in the vague direction of the City. "The Russian tricolour is already flying on Vladimirskaya Street."

"They've taken their time about it!"

"Yes, it is a bit late, it's true, but the Prince is sure the mistake can be corrected."

"Well, I hope to God he's right." Alexei turned to the icon of the Virgin Mary in the corner and crossed himself.

"The plan was as follows," Shervinsky declaimed solemnly. "As soon as the war was over, the Germans would have reorganized in order to assist us in the struggle against the Bolsheviks. And then, once Moscow was occupied, the Hetman would have laid the Ukraine at the feet of His Imperial Majesty Tsar Nikolai Alexandrovich."

This utterance was met by the silence of the grave. Nikolka's face turned pale from grief.

"The Tsar is dead," he whispered.*

"What, you mean Nikolai Alexandrovich?" Alexei asked, stunned, while Myshlayevsky, reeling from the news, looked askance at his neighbour's glass: Shervinsky had clearly had too much to drink and was now too drunk to talk any sense.

Yelena, her head in her hands, looked up at the hussar officer in horror.

But, in actual fact, Shervinsky wasn't particularly drunk. He raised his hand and said in a stentorian voice:

"Not so fast. Just listen. But I would ask you, gentlemen, to keep what I am about to say entirely to yourselves." Nikolka went red in the face, then he turned pale again. "All right, then: do you know what happened when the Hetman and his entourage were presented to Kaiser Wilhelm?"*

"Not the faintest idea," Karas said, his interest quickening.

"Well, I know what happened."

"Pff... yes, of course he knows everything," mocked Myshlayevsky. "You should just—"

"Gentlemen! Let him speak!"

"After the Kaiser had graciously spoken to the Hetman and his suite, he said: 'I will bid you farewell, gentlemen. And now here's someone to talk to you about the future...' The curtain across the door swished back and our Emperor walked into the room. 'Gentlemen,' he said, 'go to the Ukraine and mobilize your regiments. As soon as the moment arrives, I will personally lead our army into the heart of Russia – into Moscow.' And, as he said that, his eyes filled with tears."

His eyes shining, Shervinsky looked round at the assembled company, downed a whole glass of wine at one gulp, and grimaced. Five pairs of eyes stared back at him. No one made a sound until he had sat down and started eating a piece of ham.

"Yes, but that's just a fabrication," said Alexei, screwing his eyes up from the pain of it all. "I've heard it before."

"They were all killed," Myshlayevsky said. "The Tsar, the Tsarina and the Tsarevich."

Shervinsky glanced at the stove, took a deep breath and said:

"If you believe that, you're wrong. The news of His Imperial Majesty's death—"

"—is somewhat exaggerated," interrupted Myshlayevsky, with a drunken attempt at a witticism.

Yelena, trembling with indignation, rose above the haze of smoke. "You should be ashamed of yourself, Vitya. You're an officer."

Myshlayevsky ducked back into the haze.

"...the news of His Imperial Majesty's death is a lie, dreamt up by the Bolsheviks themselves. The Tsar managed to escape with the help of his loyal tutor... sorry, I meant to say his son's tutor, Monsieur Gilliard...* and a group of officers who spirited him away to... er... Asia. From there they made their way to Singapore and then by sea to Europe. And now the Tsar is the guest of Kaiser Wilhelm."

"But they've got rid of him too, haven't they?" Karas interposed.

"They are both the guests of Denmark. And with them is Her Most August Majesty the Dowager Empress, Maria Fyodorovna. And if you don't believe me, you should know that I heard all this from the Prince himself."

Torn in two by what he had heard, Nikolka groaned inwardly; he wanted to believe it so much.

"If that's the case," he said solemnly, suddenly jumping up and wiping the sweat from his brow, "I would like to propose a toast: to the health of His Imperial Majesty!" His glass flashed, and the golden arrows on its cut-glass side pierced the white German wine. Spurs clattered against the chairs. Myshlayevsky stood up, swaying and clutching at the table. Yelena too stood up. The golden crescent of her hair had fallen loose and now hung over her temples.

"Even if he is dead, I don't mind!" she shouted hoarsely, her voice cracking. "So what! I'll drink to him all the same!"

"He will never be forgiven for abdicating at Dno.* Never. All the same, bitter experience has taught us that only the monarchy is capable of saving Russia. So, even if the Tsar really is dead, long live the tsar!" shouted Alexei, raising his glass.

"Hurrah! Hurrah! Hurrah!" The dining room resounded with cheers.

Down below Vasilisa leapt up in a cold sweat. Still half-asleep, he let out a blood-curdling yell and woke Vanda Mikhaylovna.

"My God... my God..." Vanda mumbled, clutching at his nightshirt.

"What on earth's going on? It's three o'clock!" Vasilisa shouted, weeping, addressing the blackened ceiling. "That's it, I shall certainly complain!"

Vanda started to whimper. Suddenly they both froze. A massive oily wave of sound crashed down on them through the ceiling. Riding the crest of the wave was a rich, powerful baritone voice, ringing out like a bell:

"All-mighty, all-powerful,
Reign over us."*

Vasilisa's heart missed a beat, and even his feet broke into an excessive sweat. Speaking as if through cotton wool, he muttered:

"No, that's too much, they've gone out of their minds... They could cause us so much trouble we'd never get out of it. Everyone knows the national anthem's forbidden! My God, what do they think they're doing? It can be heard outside, for goodness' sake!"

But Vanda had already collapsed like a stone into sleep again. Vasilisa himself lay down again only when the final chord, accompanied by muffled shouts and cries, had died away.

"Russia can be sustained by only two things: the Orthodox faith and autocracy!" shouted Myshlayevsky, swaying unsteadily.

"That's right!"

"A week ago I was at a performance of *Paul I*,"* Myshlayevsky mumbled, slurring his words, "and when the actor declaimed those words, I could not stop myself shouting out my approval, and what do you think? There was applause all round the theatre. Except for some swine or other in the upper circle who yelled out 'Idiot!'"

"Yids!" shouted Karas darkly, also the worse for drink.

Fog, fog everywhere... *tonk, tank, tonk, tank*... Senseless to have any more vodka or wine – hearts are full to overflowing, can take no more. In the narrow little lavatory the lamp leapt and danced about on the ceiling as if bewitched, everything became blurred as the room spun round and round. With a pale and tortured expression, Myshlayevsky was violently sick. He was supported by an equally drunk Alexei, looking terrible, his cheeks twitching, his wet hair plastered to his forehead.

"Ugh..."

Myshlayevsky finally leant back from the bowl with a groan and, struggling painfully to focus on his surroundings, clung to Alexei like an empty sack.

"Nikolka," somebody called out through the haze and the dark streaks. It took a few moments for Alexei to realize that it was his own voice he had heard. "Nikolka!" he called out again. The white lavatory wall swayed and turned green. "My God, how disgusting, how revolting! I swear I'll never again mix vodka with wine. Nikol..."

"Aaa..." groaned Myshlayevsky hoarsely, slumping onto the floor.

A black gap widened to reveal Nikolka's head and chevron.

"Nikol... help me... take him by the arm."

Nikolka made sympathetic noises and, shaking his head, reached laboriously down to help. The body, more dead than alive, slithered around in every direction, the legs jerking about like a puppet on a string, the head lolling inertly on the shoulders. *Tonk, tank*. The clock jumped off the wall and leapt back again. The flowers danced around in their vases. Yelena's face was blotched, a lock of hair bouncing over her right eyebrow.

"Right. Put him to bed."

"You could at least get him into a dressing gown. It's not very nice for me, with him in that state. You damned idiots, you're hopeless when you drink. Vitka! Vitka! What's wrong? Vit—"

43

"Leave him, Nikolusha, it's no use. Listen: in the cupboard in my room, on the shelf, you'll find a little bottle marked 'Liquor ammonia'. You'll see it: one of the corners on the label is torn... smells of ammonia."

"Right. I'll get it straight away."

"Look at you... and you're a doctor, too..."

"Yes, yes, all right."

"What? Isn't there any pulse?"

"No, it's nothing, he'll get over it."

"Basin, quickly!"

"Here you are."

"Aahh..."

"Oh, look at you!"

There was a sudden reek of ammonia. Karas and Yelena held Myshlayevsky's mouth open, while Nikolka supported him and Alexei twice poured the cloudy white liquid down his throat.

"Arr... er... pfff..."

"Get some snow... snow."

"Christ Almighty! Have to do it like this, though."

The liquid dripped down from the damp rag covering his forehead. Below the rag the bloodshot whites of his eyes could be seen rolling around under half-closed eyelids, and his sharp nose was marked by bluish shadows. Jostling each other, the three of them busied themselves over the stricken officer for a quarter of an hour until he opened his eyes.

"Go away," he croaked.

"Oh, all right; let him sleep here."

Lights shone in every room, as they bustled about the apartment making beds.

"Leonid Yuryevich, you can sleep here, next to Nikolka."

"Right."

Shervinsky, his face a copper-red colour, but still cheerful, bowed, showing his parting. Yelena's white hands fluttered over the pillows on the settee.

"You don't need to do that... Let me."

"Go away. Why are you tugging at that pillow? I don't need your help."

"Allow me to kiss your hand."

"What for?"

"To thank you for all your trouble."

"It can wait... Nikolka, are you in bed? How is he?"

"Not too bad; he's on the mend. He'll sleep it off."

In the room leading to Nikolka's, two beds had been made up behind two bookcases that had been pulled close together. Both bookcases were full of books: this was the room known in the professor's family as the library.

In the library, in Nikolka's room and in the dining room, the lights had gone out. From Yelena's bedroom a dark-red patch of light crept out through the narrow gap in the dining-room door. Finding the light tiring, Yelena had thrown a dark-red theatre bonnet over the lamp on the bedside table. At one time she used to go to the theatre wearing this bonnet, her arms, furs and lips smelling pleasantly of perfume, and her face delicately powdered. She looked out at the world from under this bonnet like Liza from *The Queen of Spades*.* But, in the course of the past year, the bonnet had rapidly become strangely tatty, the folds had shrunk and faded, and it had lost its ribbons. And, like Liza from *The Queen of Spades*, golden-haired Yelena sat on the bed in her housecoat, ready for sleep, her hands on her knees, and her bare feet buried in the ancient, worn bearskin rug. Her brief spell of intoxication had completely gone, and her head was enveloped as if by a bonnet of dark, overwhelming grief. From the next room, muffled by the cupboard that had been placed against the door, she could hear Nikolka's gentle whistling and Shervinsky's loud, hearty snoring. From the library, where Karas and the poleaxed Myshlayevsky lay asleep, there was silence. Alone in her room, in the dark-red lamplight shining through the bonnet, and the windows forming two black holes in the wall, Yelena felt uninhibited, able to talk to herself, now silently, and now in an undertone, hardly moving her lips.

"He's gone…"

Musing and muttering to herself, she screwed up her dry eyes. She couldn't understand her own thoughts. He'd chosen to go at this particular time. But all right; he was a very sensible person and by going now he'd done the right thing… it was for the best, wasn't it?

"But at such a time…" she muttered, and sighed deeply.

"What kind of a man is he?" She loved him, it seemed, and had even become attached to him. And now, sitting there alone in her room, with the windows looking like black tombstones, there was this overwhelming sense of grief. And yet, at this moment, her heart was not filled with that feeling which is so essential for every marriage if it is to survive – not even when it is a marriage between beautiful, golden-haired Yelena and a cautious, ambitious general staff officer from the

Baltic, a marriage with bonnets, perfumes and spurs, unencumbered by children. Nor, indeed, during the entire eighteen months that they had lived together, had she ever had that feeling. And so what kind of a man was he then? What exactly was it that was missing, the absence of which made her feel so empty inside?

"I know what it is," said Yelena to herself. "There's no respect. You know, Seryozha, I don't respect you," she said gravely, raising her finger as she addressed the red bonnet. And, horrified at what she had just said, she shuddered at the thought that she was now on her own, and wished that he were there with her. Even without that essential feeling of respect, she nonetheless wished he could have been with her at this difficult moment. He had gone. And her brothers had kissed him. Did they have to do that? But what am I saying, for goodness' sake? What could they have done? Stopped him from going? Of course not. Perhaps, in any case, it was better that he had gone at this difficult time, and that's fine. But on no account should they have stopped him from going. On no account. Let him go if he wants to. All right, they kissed him when he left, but deep inside they hate him, for Heaven's sake. You lie and lie to yourself, but as soon as you start thinking about it you realize they hate him. Nikolka is a kind person, but his elder brother... No, no, that's not quite right: Alyosha is also a kind person, but he just seems to hate him more. Lord, what am I saying? "And Seryozha, what am I saying about you? What if we're cut off... with you having to stay there and me here...?"

"My husband," she said with a sigh, beginning to unbutton her housecoat. "My husband..."

The bonnet listened to this with interest, its cheeks suffused with a deep-red colour.

"And what kind of a man is your husband?" it asked.

"He's simply a bastard, that's all there is to it!" said Alexei Turbin to himself, alone in his room across the hallway from Yelena. He had similar thoughts to Yelena, and he had spent the last few minutes in torment. "Yes, he's a bastard, but I'm a useless specimen. If I couldn't kick him out, I could at least have left the room without saying anything. But anyway, he can go to hell! He's not a bastard because he left Yelena at such a time – when all's said and done that's just trivial rubbish. It's for quite another reason. But what, then? I can see right through him, damn it! He's just a bloody puppet, lacking even the slightest concept of honour. Everything he says, whatever it is, makes him sound like a balalaika without any strings. And he's an officer, a graduate from a Russian military academy – supposed to be the finest that Russia can produce…"

The apartment fell silent. The strip of light emanating from Yelena's bedroom went dark. She had fallen asleep, unconscious to the world. But Alexei remained at his desk in his little room, tormented by his thoughts. The combination of vodka with German wine had disagreed with him. He sat there, looking at a page in the first book that had caught his attention, his inflamed eyes returning again and again to the same words:

For a Russian, the concept of honour is merely an unnecessary burden…*

He got undressed and fell asleep only towards morning. And, as he slept, his dream turned into a nightmare with the appearance of a little man wearing broad-checked trousers.

"Best not sit on a hedgehog without any clothes," sneered the apparition. "Holy Russia is a country that's wooden, poor and… dangerous. And, for a Russian, the concept of honour is merely an unnecessary burden."

"To hell with you, you contemptible little man," yelled Alexei in his sleep. And, still dreaming, he fumbled around in his desk drawer for his revolver, pulled it out and chased after the apparition, attempting to shoot it. Then it vanished.

He slept for the next couple of hours, a black, turbid, dreamless sleep. And then, with the timid, pale light of dawn glimmering through the veranda windows, Alexei began to dream of the City.

4

THE CITY WAS ALIVE; it steamed and roared like a multilayered beehive, glistening in the frost and mist on the hills above the river Dnieper. Day after day smoke curled up out of innumerable chimneys into the sky. The streets were hazy with smoke, and the gigantic mounds of fallen snow crunched underfoot. Blocks of houses rose five, six, seven storeys high. During the day, the windows were dark, but at night their serried ranks could be seen glowing on the dark-blue surface. Electric lights shone like precious stones, perched high on curlicues on the tall lamp-posts that stretched into the distance as far as the eye could see. In the daytime the trams, their seats padded with straw in the foreign manner, rumbled easily and smoothly along. Cabs screeched up and down the hills, and the faces of ladies, framed in the dark silver and black fur collars of their coats, seemed especially mysterious and attractive.

Covered in white, virgin snow, the parks stood silent and peaceful – and there was no city in the world that had as many parks as the City. They were everywhere – huge areas, with alleyways, ravines, chestnut trees, maples and limes.

The beauty of the hills above the Dnieper was enhanced by many lovely parks. But the queen of them all was the immortal Imperial Park, broadening out as it climbed upwards in terraced steps, now sparkling with a million flecks of sunlight, now half-hidden in gentle twilight. The rotten beams of the ancient parapet formed no barrier to the terrifying drop over the sheer cliff beneath. The steep walls of the cliff, covered with a sprinkling of snow, plunged down onto the terraces far below. Above the road that wound its way along the bank of the great river, the broad terraces, in turn, stretched into the distance, where they merged into the woods along the bank. The dark ice-bound river flowed onward into the haze, continuing on to the white Dnieper rapids, the stronghold of the Zaporozhian Cossacks,* the Chersonese* and on to the distant sea, out of sight even to anyone standing on the heights of the City.

In winter, as in no other city in the world, calm descended on the streets and alleyways of both the Upper City on the hills, as well as the Lower City that was bathed in the light emanating from the frozen Dnieper. Swallowed up by the stone buildings, the roar of the traffic turned into a gentle, muffled hum. All the City's energy that had accumulated during the sunny and thundery summer had now been transformed into light. From four o'clock in the afternoon, the lights began to glow in the windows of the houses, in the round electric lamps, in the gaslights, in the lights of house numbers and in the uninterrupted glass windows of the electricity stations, giving rise to thoughts of the vain and terrible electric future that awaited mankind: through these uninterrupted glass windows, the machines with their madly, ceaselessly rotating wheels could be seen as they shook the earth's very foundation to the core. Throughout the night, the City played and danced as it glittered and glowed in the iridescent lights – until the morning when everything was extinguished, and the City became shrouded once more in haze and mist.

But outshining everything, visible from miles away, was the electric glow of the white cross held by the gigantic figure of St Vladimir on the top of Vladimir Hill.* Often, in the summer, boats on the age-old Dnieper, trapped in dark mists or lost in willow thickets in the river's numerous creeks and backwaters, would see this light and be able to find their way to the City's jetties. In winter, the cross would shine in the black expanse of the heavens, casting its cold, even light on the far, gently sloping bank of the river. At this point the river was crossed by two bridges: the first, Nikolayevsky bridge, a weighty chain structure, led to the suburbs on the far bank; the other, tall and slender as an arrow, carried the trains from far, far away – from sprawling, mysterious, multifaceted Moscow.

And now, in the winter of 1918, the City lived a strange, unnatural life, a life that very probably will never be repeated in the twentieth century. Behind the stone walls of the buildings every apartment was full to overflowing. Those people who had lived there for ages – the original inhabitants – had crammed and continued to cram themselves into their apartments more and more tightly as, voluntarily or involuntarily, they admitted all the newcomers streaming into the City – all those, in fact, who had crossed the tall, slender bridge on their journey from the mysterious grey-blue haze to the east.

On the run were greying bankers with their wives, talented businessmen leaving behind assistants in Moscow entrusted with the task of maintaining contact with the new world that was being created in the Muscovite kingdom, landlords leaving their houses in the care of clandestine, trusted managers, industrialists, merchants, lawyers and political figures. They were joined by corrupt, greedy and cowardly journalists from both Moscow and St Petersburg; ladies of leisure; respectable ladies from aristocratic families with their delicate daughters; pale, depraved women from St Petersburg with scarlet painted lips. On the run too were the secretaries of departmental heads; young, docile pederasts; princes and misers; poets and pawnbrokers; and policemen and actresses from the Imperial theatres. All these masses of people were crowding into the City, squeezing themselves into a tiny gap.

Throughout the spring, immediately after the Hetman's election, the City filled up more and more with new arrivals. In the apartments they slept on settees and chairs. Huge groups sat down to dinner in the wealthier apartments. Countless small cafés opened up, trading far into the night, with coffee and women for sale, together with new, tiny little theatres on whose boards paraded an ever-increasing number of well-known actors who had fled the two capitals and who were now entertaining the populace. Also opening its doors was the famous theatre The Lilac Negro, together with the magnificent nightclub on Nikolayevskaya Street, Ashes to Dust, frequented by poets, producers, actors and artists, where plates clattered until the early hours. New newspapers sprang out of nowhere, carrying sketches by some of the best writers in Russia, savaging the Bolsheviks. The whole time, every day, cabs ferried people from restaurant to restaurant, string orchestras played in cabarets, and the pale, exhausted, drug-ravaged faces of prostitutes shone through the tobacco smoke with an eerie kind of beauty.

The City expanded and swelled, like leavened dough escaping from a pot. The gambling clubs were filled with the rustle of cards being played by leading figures from St Petersburg and from the City itself, together with arrogant, self-important German lieutenants and majors, whom the Russians both feared and respected. Also frequenting the gaming tables were Arabs from Moscow clubs and Ukrainian-Russian landowners, their lives already hanging by a thread. In the café Maxim a stocky, charming Romanian, with velvety hair and wondrously sad and languorous blue eyes, soared like a nightingale on his violin. The room was lit by two different colours from the lamps, which were wreathed in gypsy shawls: white below, and orange above and to the side. Dusty blue silk was spread like starlight across the ceiling, and large diamonds and rust-red Siberian furs glittered and glistened in the blue alcoves. And everywhere there was the smell of burnt coffee, sweat, spirits and French perfume. Throughout the summer of 1918 the pompous cabbies in their quilted caftans roared recklessly up and down Nikolayevskaya Street, and the rows of car headlights glowed until daybreak. In the shop windows whole forests of flowers were displayed, smoked sturgeon hung down in slabs of golden fat and stamps with two-headed eagles glistened on the bottles of wonderful Abrau champagne.*

Throughout the summer more and more newcomers crowded into the City. Among them were men with gristly, white faces or with a greyish stubble on their cheeks, tenor soloists with gleaming patent-leather boots, members of the State Duma wearing pince-nez, and whores with resonant surnames. Billiard-players escorted whores into shops to buy lipstick, women's cambric drawers with monstrous slits and hair lacquer. Letters were sent off by the only possible loophole, through troubled Poland – although, incidentally, nobody had any idea what sort of country this new Poland was* and what was going on there – to Germany, that great country of honest Teutons, letters requesting visas and transferring money, with people sensing that maybe they would need to travel on farther, to some place where under no circumstances would there be any terrible fighting or the thunder of Bolshevik regiments on the march. People dreamt of France and of Paris, but they became depressed at the realization that getting there would be extremely difficult, maybe even impossible. And, while they spent sleepless nights lying on strange settees thinking such terrible, not always totally lucid thoughts, they were struck by an even more depressing idea:

"What if? What if? What if the steel cordon were suddenly to break... and allow the grey hordes to crash through? That would be a catastrophe!"

Such thoughts occurred to people whenever they heard the distant, muffled thump of gunfire – all through that glittering hot summer, firing could inexplicably be heard in the vicinity of the City. Throughout the City itself, the metallic Germans were able to ensure peace and calm, but on the outskirts the constant dull sound of gunfire was heard.

The shelling took place at night, and who was firing at whom nobody knew. But during the day, people calmed down, as every so often they saw a regiment of German hussars marching along the main street – the Kreshchatik – or along Vladimirskaya Street. And what regiments! Proud faces crowned by fluffy fur caps, with rocklike jaws supported by scaly leather straps and stiff ginger moustaches that pointed skywards. Squadrons of horses advanced in strict formation, powerful chestnut horses seventeen hands high, and the grey-blue army jackets sat on the six hundred hussars, looking like the metal uniforms adorning the massive figures of their leaders on the statues in Berlin.

Everybody was so happy to see the Germans that they all calmed down. Grinning gloatingly, safe behind the protection of the barbed wire on the border, they taunted the distant Bolsheviks. "Come on then, if you dare!" they shouted.

They hated the Bolsheviks. But it wasn't a straightforward hatred – the kind of hatred that simply wants to fight or to kill – but a hissing, cowardly kind of hatred, a furtive, hole-in-the-corner type of hatred. They hated during the night, as they fell into a vaguely troubled sleep; they hated during the day, sitting in restaurants reading newspapers which carried descriptions of Bolsheviks shooting officers and bankers in the back of the neck, and of shopkeepers in Moscow selling horsemeat infected with glanders. Everybody, without exception, hated: merchants, bankers, industrialists, lawyers, actors, landlords, ladies of leisure, State Council members, engineers, doctors and writers…

Then there were the officers – officers fleeing from the former front line in the north and the west, all of them heading for the City. There were large numbers of them, and the number was growing all the time. Because they were largely penniless, and because it was impossible to disguise the fact of their profession, they were risking their lives. The most difficult thing for them was to acquire false papers and then make their way across the frontier. They managed, however, to make their way to the City, unshaven and ridden with lice, with hunted expressions and without their epaulettes. Once in the City they began to organize their lives so that they could find something to eat and somewhere to live. Among them were old City residents, such as Alexei Turbin, who were on their way back home from the war, returning to their familiar nests with just one thought – to rest and relax, and to start life again, not as an army officer but as a normal human being. But there were also hundreds and hundreds of others, not from the City, who had found it impossible to remain either in St Petersburg or in Moscow. Some of them – cuirassiers, cavalry officers, horse guards and hussars – found it easy to float to the top of the turbid foam that characterized the City during these troubled times. The Hetman's bodyguard walked around with their outrageous epaulettes, and up to two hundred people with oily partings sat down at the Hetman's tables, flashing their decaying, yellow, gold-filled teeth. Anyone who could not find a place in the Hetman's bodyguard became the guest of women wearing coats with beaver fur collars and owning luxurious, oak-panelled apartments in Lipki, the best part of the City; or else they found themselves a place in restaurants or hotel rooms.

The other officers were staff captains from army regiments that had been disbanded, or hussars from the regular army, such as Colonel Nai-Turs, who had fought their way through the war, hundreds of subalterns and second lieutenants, former students, such as Stepanov-Karas, their normal lives interrupted and broken by war and revolution, and other lieutenants, like Viktor Viktorovich Myshlayevsky, also former students but who would never return to their studies. On their arrival in the City, such men, in their tattered grey uniforms, with their wounds still not entirely healed and their peeling epaulettes, slept on chairs in their own or other people's apartments, using their greatcoats as blankets, drank vodka, and dashed about the City in a frenzy of activity. And it was this group that hated the Bolsheviks with an uncomplicated and passionate hatred, the sort of hatred that can lead directly to a fight.

And then there were the officer cadets. By the beginning of the revolution there had been four military academies remaining in the City: an engineering academy, an artillery academy and two infantry academies. All of them had stopped functioning, shattered in the cross-fire between rival groups. And the cadets who had just enrolled, straight out of high school, were thrown out onto the streets, dysfunctional, neither children nor adults, neither military nor civilians – people, in fact, just like the seventeen-year-old Nikolka Turbin.

"That's all very well, of course: the Hetman is in control of everything. But, as God is my witness, I still don't know and, very probably, will never know, what sort of person this invisible ruler really is, with a title that is more appropriate for the seventeenth century than the twentieth."

"Yes, who exactly is he, Alexei Vasilyevich?"

"He's a cavalry general and a very rich landowner called Pavel Petrovich…"

By some strange quirk of fate and history his election, which had taken place in the April of that famous year, had been held in a circus. Future historians will no doubt look on this as a rich source of humour. But the citizens, especially those who had settled in the City and who had already experienced the first explosive stirrings of civil war, had no time for humour, or even for any deliberations whatsoever. The election had taken place, thank goodness, with stunning rapidity; the Hetman's reign had begun, and that was splendid – just so long as meat and bread were available in the markets, there was no shooting in the streets, the Bolsheviks were kept at bay for the Lord's sake and there were no robberies. And indeed, under the Hetman, all this had more or less been achieved, even perhaps to a considerable extent. It is true that those who had fled to the City from Moscow and St Petersburg, together with the majority of its inhabitants, laughed at the strange set-up which the Hetman had created, calling it a comic opera and an unreal kingdom, like Captain Talberg. Yet their praise for the Hetman was nevertheless genuine… "May God grant it continue for ever."

But whether or not it would continue for ever nobody could say, not even the Hetman himself. No sir, not even the Hetman.

The fact was that the City, with its police force, military guard, ministries, regular army formations and newspapers with various different names, was like other cities. Yet what was going on in the wider world outside the City, in the Ukraine proper, which was bigger in size than France, with a population of tens of millions of people, nobody knew. Nobody knew anything, not merely about faraway places, but, absurdly, about villages that were only some thirty miles away from the City itself. But although nobody knew anything, people still hated with all their heart. And when vague stories about that mysterious region, the "countryside", began to circulate, stories of Germans robbing peasants and ruthlessly punishing them by shooting them with machine guns, not only was there not a single voice raised in the peasants' defence, but people sitting in their comfortable drawing rooms under silk lamp-shades and baring their teeth like wolves could be heard muttering:

"Serves them right! Serves them right – but it's not enough! I'd be even fiercer. They'll remember the revolution all right! The Germans'll teach them – they didn't want their own people, let them try others!"

"Yes, but that's so stupid, so stupid."

"What on earth do you mean, Alexei Vasilyevich? They're simply scum, nothing but wild animals. The Germans will show them, and quite right too."

Germans!!

Germans!!

And everywhere, Germans!!

Germans!!

Right: the Germans are here, but out there somewhere beyond the cordon are the grey-blue forests and the Bolsheviks. Just the two forces.

5

BUT THEN, totally unexpectedly and unforeseen, a third force appeared on the gigantic chessboard. A poor, not very clever chess player, having put in place a defensive line of pawns to ward off a threatening opponent (and, by the way, the Germans in their basin-like helmets are not too dissimilar to pawns), will group his other major pieces around his king. But his opponent's wily queen suddenly makes a flanking move to reach the back rank and launches an attack on his pawns and knights from the rear, placing the now very alarmed king in check. The queen in turn is followed by a rook in a dashing move up the board, the knights fly up to join the attack in a series of cunning zigzags, and the poor player is done for – his helpless king is checkmated.

This all happened very quickly, but not totally unexpectedly: the ensuing events were heralded by a number of signs.

One day in May, when the City had woken up to greet the morning, glittering like a pearl in turquoise, and the sun had appeared over the horizon to shine down onto the Hetman's kingdom, when the City's inhabitants had already started to move about their business like ants and the sleepy shopkeepers were beginning to open the clattering blinds in the shop windows, it was shaken by a terrible and ominous sound. Nobody had heard anything like it before – it was unlike either gunfire or thunder – but it was of such strength that many casement windows opened of their own accord and every window shook. Then the sound was repeated, ripping through the whole of the Upper City, crashing down in waves on to Podol, the Lower City, then across the lovely blue Dnieper and farther on towards the vast plains and Moscow. Citizens were woken up, and there was total confusion on the streets. It was followed instantly by people pouring down from Pechersk, the Upper City, howling and yelling, their clothes torn and covered in blood. And then the sound was heard a third time, and with such force that the windows shattered in the houses in Pechersk and the ground shook underfoot.

Many people saw women running about in just their nightdresses and shouting wildly. People soon discovered that the sound had come from outside the city, from Bald Hill right by the Dnieper, where there were vast warehouses containing shells and gunpowder. It was there that the explosion had taken place.

For the next five days the City lived in fear, expecting the influx of poisonous gases from Bald Hill. But the explosions ceased, there was no influx of gases, the people covered in blood disappeared and all parts of the City reassumed their peaceful appearance with the exception of one corner of Pechersk, where a small number of houses collapsed. It goes without saying that the German high command conducted a thorough investigation of the incident, and it goes equally without saying that the citizens remained none the wiser concerning the cause of the explosion. There were various different opinions:

"The explosion was the work of French spies."

"No, it was Bolshevik spies."

The upshot of it all was that people simply forgot about it.

The second sign occurred in the summer, when the City was covered in an abundance of dusty greenery, when the thunder crashed and roared, and when the German lieutenants drank an ocean of soda water. And this second sign was genuinely monstrous!

In broad daylight, on Nikolayevskaya Street, just where the cabbies were waiting to ply their trade, none other than the commander-in-chief of the German army in the Ukraine, Field Marshall Eichhorn, was assassinated.* Field Marshall Eichhorn – the untouchable and proud general, someone who wielded terrible power, second only to Kaiser Wilhelm himself! The assassin was a factory worker and a socialist of course. Within twenty-four hours of the death of their countryman the Germans had hanged not only the assassin but even the cabby who had brought him to the scene of the crime. This, it is true, did nothing to bring the famous general back to life, but it nevertheless set clever people thinking remarkable thoughts about the event.

One evening, sitting with a glass of tea and lemon by the open window, struggling for breath and undoing the buttons of his linen shirt, Vasilisa was talking to Alexei in a conspiratorial whisper.

"Putting all these events together, I cannot but arrive at the conclusion that our lives have become very uncertain. It seems to me that there's something unstable beneath the Germans," said Vasilisa, waving his stubby fingers in the air. "Think about it... Eichhorn... and where it all happened... eh?" Vasilisa rolled his eyes fearfully.

Alexei heard him out in gloomy silence and left the room, his cheek twitching.

One more portent occurred on the very next morning, directly impacting on Vasilisa himself. Early, very early, when the first cheerful finger of sunlight appeared in the dark underground passageway leading from the yard into Vasilisa's apartment, Vasilisa looked at the ray of sun and saw a vision. She was incomparable in the bright glow of her thirty years, in the dazzle of the necklaces on her swan-like neck, in her slender bare legs and resilient, quivering breasts. The vision's teeth gleamed white, and her eyelids cast a lilac shadow onto her cheeks.

"Fifty, today," said the vision in Ukrainian in a hypnotic voice, pointing at the churn of milk.

"What do you mean, Yavdokha?" whined Vasilisa. "For goodness' sake! The day before yesterday it was forty, yesterday it was forty-five, and today it's fifty. It can't go on like this."

"What can I do about it?" replied the vision. "It's expensive. It's a hundred at the market, it seems."

Her teeth flashed once again. For an instant Vasilisa forgot about the fifty, he forgot about the hundred, he forgot about everything, and he had a deliciously cool and daring feeling in the pit of his stomach, something that he always felt whenever the beautiful vision appeared before him in the ray of sunlight. (Vasilisa always rose earlier than his wife.) He forgot about everything, beginning, for some reason, to imagine a forest glade and the scent of pine leaves…

"See here, Yavdokha," Vasilisa said, licking his lips and cocking a glance to see if his wife had appeared. "You've become quite a loose woman since the revolution. But just take care: the Germans will teach you a thing or two."

"Should I pat her on the shoulder or not?" Vasilisa wondered in torment, but could not bring himself to do it.

A full stream of milk, the colour of alabaster, poured foaming into the jug.

"Let 'em try and teach us a lesson. We'll teach 'em a thing or two in return," the vision suddenly replied. The gleaming churn rattled and crashed on the yoke as it rose up out of the passageway, a ray within a ray, and up into the sunlit yard. "My God, just look at her legs," groaned Vasilisa to himself.

At that moment he heard his wife's voice. Turning to look, he found himself face to face with her.

"Who was that you were talking to?" his wife asked, darting a glance upwards.

"Yavdokha," Vasilisa answered imperturbably. "And guess what? Milk's gone up to fifty today."

"What?" shrieked Vanda Mikhaylovna. "That's a scandal! The cheek of it! The peasants have gone totally mad… Yavdokha! Yavdokha!" she shouted out of the window. "Yavdokha!"

But the vision had disappeared, and did not return.

Vasilisa looked at his wife's ugly, bent posture, her yellow hair, bony elbows and dry unattractive legs, and life on this earth suddenly became so intolerable that he wanted to spit at the hem of Vanda's skirt. Restraining himself with a sigh, he went back inside, into the semi-darkness, not fully understanding himself what it was that was nagging him. Maybe it was Vanda – he suddenly pictured her, with her protruding collarbones looking like the shaft of a horse's harness – or maybe it was something awkward connected with what the ravishing vision had said.

"We'll teach 'em? How do you like that, eh?" he muttered to himself. "Damn those blasted peasant markets! No, really, what would you say to that? Once they stop fearing the Germans, then that's it… we're finished. We'll teach 'em, eh? But her teeth… her magnificent teeth…"

For some reason he suddenly pictured Yavdokha naked, like a witch on a mountain.

"The cheek of it... Teach 'em, indeed! But her breasts..."

And the thought was so disconcerting that Vasilisa suddenly felt ill, and he went off to douse himself with cold water.

And so autumn crept up on them imperceptibly. The sumptuous, golden summer was succeeded by a bright and dusty September. And it was in September that a real event, rather than just a sign, occurred. And at first glance it was an event of total insignificance.

This is what happened: one fine September evening a document arrived at the city prison signed by the appropriate Hetman authorities and authorizing the release of the prisoner held in cell no. 666. That was all.

That was all! But, oh my goodness! It was precisely, and without any doubt, this document that was to be the cause of such misery and disaster, so many alarums and excursions, so much bloodshed and conflagration, so many pogroms, so much despair and horror...

The prisoner who had been released bore the simplest and most insignificant of names: Semyon Vasilyevich Petlyura. He himself, together with the City's newspapers during the period between December 1918 and February 1919, called himself Simon, adopting somewhat the French manner. Simon's past was buried in impenetrable gloom. Some said that he was a bookkeeper.

"No, he was an accountant."

"No, he wasn't: he was a student."

On the corner of Nikolayevskaya Street and the Kreshchatik stood a large, fashionable tobacco shop. On a long sign above the shop hung an exceedingly fine representation of a Turk in a fez smoking a hookah. The Turk was depicted wearing a pair of soft, yellow slippers, with upturned toes.

There were some who could be found who attested to the fact that they had recently seen Simon in this very same shop, elegantly serving behind the counter, selling tobacco goods that had been produced in Solomon Cohen's factory. But there were others who maintained that it was nothing of the sort, and that he was the official representative of the Union of Municipalities.

"No, not the Union of Municipalities, but the Rural Assembly," replied a third group. "A typical rural hussar."

Yet a fourth group of people, visitors from elsewhere, closed their eyes in concentration and muttered:

"Just hold on a moment, if you please..."

And they began to tell everyone how they'd seen him one evening in Moscow walking along Malaya Bronnaya Street. It must have been ten... no sorry... eleven years ago. He was carrying a guitar under his arm, wrapped in black calico. And they even added that the reason he was carrying a guitar was because he was going to a party of fellow nationals from the Ukraine. Yes, that's right: he was on his way to a lively party with a group of red-cheeked, fun-loving Ukrainian girl students, with plum brandy, direct from the bountiful Ukraine, and songs, including the song about the marvellous Grisha...

"...No, please don't go..."

Then their account began to lose its way, with dates, places and descriptions of his appearance becoming confused.

"Clean-shaven, you say?"

"No... just a moment... he had a beard, I think."

"But hold on; he wasn't from Moscow, surely, was he?"

"No, he was just a student there... he was—"

"Nothing of the sort! Ivan Ivanovich knows him. He was a village schoolteacher in Tarashcha!..."

Damn it! Maybe it wasn't Bronnaya Street he'd been walking along: Moscow is a large city, Bronnaya is often foggy and dark, and there can be hoar frost there. A guitar... a sunlit Turk... a hookah... the guitar twanging away... foggy, can't see much... oh, my God, it's so foggy, like a nightmare...

"...The guards cadets sing..."

...bloodstained shadows, ghosts flitting past, young girls with their plaits flying in the wind, prisons, gunshots, frost and the cross of St Vladimir shining at midnight.

"The guards cadets sing as
down the street they pound.
The trumpets and drums
and the cymbals resound."

Cymbals crashing, bullets whistling like nightingales, men being beaten to death with ramrods, black horsemen on the march on their fiery steeds.

The prophetic dream crashes up to Alexei Turbin's bed as he lies asleep, his face pale in the pink glow of the lamplight, a damp lock of hair plastered to his hot forehead. The whole house is asleep. From the library comes the sound of Karas snoring, and from Nikolka's room, of Shervinsky's whistling breath... Dark... night... on the floor by Alexei's bed a copy of Dostoevsky's *The Devils* lies open, filling the room with the sound of mocking, desperate voices... Yelena is quietly asleep.

"Well, here's what I think: there was no such person! This Simon never existed. None of it existed: neither the Turk, nor the guitar in the lamplight on Bronnaya Street, nor the Rural Assembly, not a sausage... It's all simply a myth, concocted in the Ukraine in the fog of that terrible year 1918."

And there was something else as well: sheer, undiluted hatred. The Germans numbered four hundred thousand men, but around them were one hundred and sixty times that number of Ukrainian peasants, their hearts burning with an unquenchable feeling of malice. Oh, yes: so much had been accumulating in their hearts: the lash of lieutenants' whips on their cheeks, the random shelling of recalcitrant villages, backs criss-crossed with stripes from ramrods wielded by Hetmanite Cossacks, and receipts written on torn pieces of paper by German majors and lieutenants:

To a Russian sow for the purchase of 1 pig, 25 marks

All those appearing at army headquarters in the City bearing such receipts were greeted by loud, scornful laughter.

And then there were the requisitioned horses, the pilfered bread, the fat-faced landowners returning to their estates under the Hetman, and the spasm of hatred at the very mention of the word "officers".

Yes, sir, that's how it was!

Then there were the rumours of land reform that the Hetman was planning to carry out. But alas, it was only in November 1918, when the guns were already thundering on the outskirts of the City, that clever people such as Vasilisa realized that the peasants hated this Hetman as if he were a rabid dog, considering such a dastardly plan to be totally unnecessary. Instead, what they needed was the age-old, longed-for peasants' reform:

All land to the peasants.

Three hundred acres per man.

The total abolition of landlords.

The assignment of each hundred acres to be accompanied by a stamped, official title deed attesting to the permanent entitlement of the land to be handed down from grandfather to father, father to son, son to grandson, and so on.

No crook to come from the City to requisition grain. The grain belongs to us, and no one else can have it. What we can't eat, we'll bury in the ground.

The City to keep us supplied with kerosene.

"But then, sir, no Hetman, however respected, or anyone else for that matter, could ever have carried out reforms of that nature."

There were some melancholy rumours flying around that only the Bolsheviks could deal with a disastrous situation such as the one created by the Hetman and the Germans. But the Bolsheviks were no better...

"Nothing but a bunch of Yids and commissars... the Ukrainian peasants are in a pretty miserable situation: nowhere to look to for any salvation!"

Scores of thousands of people had returned from the front line, knowing how to shoot, having been taught how to do so on the orders of the high command.

Buried in the ground and hidden in haylofts and barns were hundreds of thousands of rifles that had not been handed in, despite hastily set up German military field tribunals, whippings with ramrods and shootings. Along with the rifles, millions of rounds of ammunition were buried, in every fifth village there were three-inch guns and machine guns in every second, and each little town had its warehouses full of shells, and its stores of greatcoats and fur caps.

And in these same little towns there were schoolteachers, medical orderlies, smallholders, Ukrainian seminarists who by a twist of fate had become army subalterns, burly beekeepers' sons and staff captains with Ukrainian surnames, all speaking Ukrainian, all carrying in their heart the idea of a magical, imaginary Ukraine that was without landowners or those bloody Muscovite officers. In addition, there were thousands of Ukrainian prisoners of war who had returned from captivity in Galicia.*

Then, on top of this, the tens of thousands of peasants? Oh, my God!

Then there was this prisoner, the guitar... beset by rumours, terrible rumours...

Hey, Nikolka, that's right, twang away!

The Turk, the rural hussar, Simon. Ah, but he didn't exist, did he! So it was all nonsense, legend, a mere mirage.

And that notorious November it was pointless for clever Vasilisa to clutch at his head and exclaim: "*Quos vult perdere, dementat*",* and to curse the Hetman for releasing Petlyura from that foul city prison.

"It's all nonsense. If it's not him, then it will be someone else. If not, then someone else again."

And so all the signs ceased, to be replaced by the onset of real events. The second real event wasn't a trivial matter such as the release of some mythical person from prison. Oh, no! This one was of such import that mankind will doubtless speak of it for a hundred years to come: in far-off Western Europe the Gallic cockerels in their red trousers pecked the thickset, steel-clad Germans to within an inch of their lives. It was a terrible sight to see these cockerels in their Phrygian caps bearing down on the armour-plated Teutons with guttural screams and ripping out pieces of flesh and armour. The Germans fought back desperately, gritting their teeth and thrusting their broad bayonets into the feathered breasts of their opponents, but they were unable to hold out, and the Germans – the Germans! – begged for mercy.

The next event was closely linked with this and flowed from it as a direct consequence. The whole world, now stunned and shaken by what had happened, learnt that the man, whose name and handlebar moustache, the size of six-inch nails, were familiar to everyone, and whose body was probably fashioned entirely from metal, with no sign of any wood, had been deposed. Turned into dust, he ceased to be emperor. Then, when everyone in the City saw for themselves the colour fade from the German lieutenants, and the shining nap of their grey-blue uniforms become the colour of drab matting, a shiver of dread ran through them all like a whirlwind. And this happened there and then, in front of their very eyes, in the course of a few hours. And within just a few hours, the light in the lieutenants' monocled eyes faded, and then disappeared altogether, leaving nothing but a look of poverty-stricken despair.

Then it was as if an electric current flowed through the minds of the brighter of those people who, with their solid yellowing suitcases and their plump wives, had leapt across the barbed wire of the Bolshevik encampment and made their way to the City. They realized that their fate was now linked with a vanquished nation, and their hearts were filled with horror.

"The Germans have been beaten," said the snakes.

"We have been beaten," said the clever snakes.

The City's inhabitants realized this as well.

Ah, yes, but only those who have been beaten know the real meaning of the word! It is like night-time in a house without electric light. It is like a room in which a green mould, infested with harmful germs, is creeping down the wallpaper. It is like demon children with rickets, or rancid cooking oil, or women using foul language in the dark. In short, it is like death.

That's it, then. The Germans are leaving the Ukraine. What does this mean? It means that some will flee, whereas others will remain in the City to come face to face with its new, uninvited and unpredictable guests. And it means that some will inevitably die. If those who flee the City don't die, who, then, will?

"Dying not child's pray." It was the unmistakable voice of Colonel Nai-Turs, confusing his Rs and his Ls, as always. He had suddenly appeared from nowhere in Alexei Turbin's dream.

Nai-Turs was very strangely attired: he was wearing a coat of chain mail, with a gleaming helmet on his head, and he was leaning on a sword, the sort of long sword that had not been part of the weaponry of any army since the crusades. Behind him hovered an aura of heavenly, radiant light.

"Are you in paradise, Colonel?" asked Turbin, a tremulous feeling of ecstasy coursing through his body – the sort of feeling experienced only in dreams.

"In paladise," Nai-Turs answered in a pure, totally transparent voice, like a stream in an urban forest.

"That's very strange," said Turbin. "I always thought that paradise was simply a dream. And that's a very weird-looking uniform. May I ask, Colonel, whether you have retained your officer status in paradise?"

"The colonel's in the brigade of crusaders now, doctor," observed Sergeant Major Zhilin, someone who Turbin knew for certain had been killed in 1916 in the fighting around Vilna, together with his squadron of Belgrade Hussars.

The sergeant major towered up like a medieval hero, and his armour radiated light. His somewhat coarse features, which were extremely familiar to Doctor Turbin, as he had been personally responsible for bandaging Zhilin's lethal wound, were now unrecognizable. And the sergeant major's eyes were just like those belonging to Nai-Turs: pure, bottomless and shining with an inner light.

Above all else, Alexei Turbin's melancholy heart loved female eyes. Oh, yes, the Lord God had wrought a piece of magic when he had created a woman's eyes! But they were nothing like Sergeant Major Zhilin's eyes!

"And how about you?" Turbin asked curiously, with a sense of unaccountable joy. "You're in paradise, and yet you're wearing boots and spurs. So that means you've got horses, carts, pikes here?"

"Believe me, doctor," said Sergeant Major Zhilin in his deep, resonant, bass voice, warming the heart with the expression in his light-blue eyes as he looked directly at the doctor, "the whole squadron's there, in cavalry formation. And we've got our accordion. It's all a little awkward, it's true... Everything's spotlessly clean, you know... church floors..."

"Well, what happened?" asked Turbin, impressed.

"Well, the apostle St Peter is waiting for us. He's an old man in civvies, but dignified and courteous. I report our arrival of course: the second squadron of Belgrade Hussars has safely made it to paradise and so on and so forth; where would you like us to be? There I am reporting our arrival, but all the time I'm thinking..." – the sergeant major put his hand to his mouth and coughed modestly – "...I'm wondering what he, St Peter, is going to say. Perhaps he's going to tell us to go to the Devil. You see, as you can probably understand, it's a question of what to do with the horses, and then..." – the sergeant major scratched the back of his neck in embarrassment – "...and then, between us, there's the women who waylaid us on the way. That's what I tell St Peter, anyway, but I wink at the lads, as if to say, 'We'll get rid of the women for the time being, and then we'll see; they can go and wait behind the clouds for a bit, and then we'll see how things work out.' St Peter may be his own master, but he's a positive sort of person. His eyes open wide, and I can see that he has spotted the women on the carts: their shawls, of course, are clearly visible a mile off. Here's a pretty kettle of fish, I think. It's curtains for the whole squadron.

"'Aha,' he says, shaking his head. 'So, you've got some women with you, have you?' 'Yes, sir,' I say. 'But please don't be concerned, Mr Apostle, sir; we'll box them on the ears at once.'

"'No you won't,' he says. 'You keep your hands to yourselves.'

"So, what are we to do now, eh? He's a kind-hearted old man. But as you can understand yourself, doctor, a cavalry squadron can't go on the march without women."

And the sergeant major gave a sly wink.

"That's very true," Alexei was forced to agree, looking down at the ground. For an instant, in the dark recesses of his dream, two dark eyes and birthmarks on a smooth cheek flashed across his mind. He grunted in embarrassment and the sergeant major continued his story:

"'Right, sir,' St Peter says at once, 'I must report this.' So off he goes. When he comes back he says, 'All right, we can sort something out.' And it's not possible to describe how happy that makes us. But then it turns out there's a little problem. The apostle tells us we have to wait. But in fact we don't have to wait for more than a minute. I look up and who should I see?" And the sergeant major pointed at the silent and proud figure of Nai-Turs walking out of the dream into the mysterious darkness, without leaving a trace. "I see the squadron commander trotting up on his horse, Thief of Tushino.* And then, a little behind him, comes an unknown young cadet on foot." At this point in his story, the sergeant major gave the doctor a sideways glance, then looked down at the ground for a moment. It was as if he wanted to hide something from the doctor, but it was clearly not anything sad. On the contrary: it was a wonderful secret that made him very happy. Then, recollecting himself, he went on with his story:

"So Peter looks at us, shielding his eyes with his hand and says, 'Right, that's everything!' And immediately the door is flung open and he orders us to ride off by the right in threes. And suddenly, as if in a dream, the air is filled with the sound of metallic voices singing in chorus, accompanied by an Italian accordion...

'Oh, Dunka, Dunka, Dunka!
Dunya, my darling girl...'

"'Keep in step!' shout the troop commanders in various different voices.

'Oh, Dunya, Dunya, Dunya!
Love me Dunya, love me do!'

"And the chorus of voices dies away in the distance."

"So you managed to get in, with the women?" gasped Turbin.

The sergeant major burst out in excited laughter and waved his arms about in joy.

"Good God, doctor! There's just so much space there, you know. And it's all so clean. At first glance you might say you could accommodate five whole army corps there, together with their reserve squadrons. Then you realize it could take ten corps, not five. And then, gracious me, the church ceilings are so high there you can't see them. So I say: 'May I ask who all this is for?' Because everything's so unusual: the stars and the clouds are red, something like the colour of our shakos. 'All this,' answers apostle Peter, 'is for the Bolsheviks, those killed at Perekop.'"*

"What do you mean 'killed at Perekop'?" Turbin asked, his mere earthly brain finding this all too difficult to grapple with.

"This is because they know about these things in advance, Your Honour. In 1920 masses of Bolsheviks will be killed taking Perekop. So they have prepared accommodation to receive them."

"Bolsheviks?" Turbin exclaimed indignantly. "You must be mistaken, Zhilin, that can't be right: they wouldn't be admitted there."

"That's just what I thought, doctor, sir. Just what I thought. So, confused, I ask God—"

"God? Oh, Zhilin!"

"You must believe me, doctor, I'm speaking the truth. Why should I lie to you? I have spoken to God more than once."

"What's he like?"

Zhilin's eyes radiated light, and his face adopted an expression of pride.

"For the life of me I can't explain. His face is like aspen, but more than that, it's impossible to say... At times you look at him, and you grow cold. It seems that he is exactly like you or me. You're seized with such a feeling of terror that you wonder what's happening. And then, suddenly, it's all right, you're back to normal. His face varies. But there's such a sense of joy, of happiness. And then there's this blue light... hmm... no it's not blue..." – the sergeant major thought for a moment – "I don't know what it is. Anyway, it goes right through you six hundred miles away. Well, anyway, I report to him and tell him that his priests say that all Bolsheviks will go to hell. I ask him why they say this. 'The Bolsheviks don't believe in you,' I say, 'and you have cheered them up by promising such accommodation.'

"'So they don't believe in me?' he asks.

"'My true Lord God,' I say, afraid, you understand, to be saying such things to God. But when I look at him, he's smiling. What a fool I am! Why am I bothering to tell him such things when he already knows everything better than I do? Yet I'm curious to find out what he'll say. And he says:

"'Well, if they don't believe in me, there's nothing you can do about it. Let them believe what they like. Either way, it leaves me indifferent, neither hot nor cold. That applies to you as well as to them. I neither gain nor lose from your belief in me. Some people believe, others not, but everyone behaves the same; at the moment you're all at each other's throats. As for the accommodation, Zhilin, you should understand that, in so far as I am concerned, everyone killed on the field of battle is equal. You need to understand that, Zhilin; not everyone does. But, in general, Zhilin, don't concern yourself with such questions. Just live, and enjoy yourself.'

"A full explanation, eh, doctor? 'But what about the priests?' I ask. He makes a dismissive gesture. 'It would be better, Zhilin,' he says, 'not to remind me about the priests. I won't spend sleepless nights wondering what to do with them. There's no more idiotic group of people on earth than these priests of yours. In confidence, Zhilin, they're a disgrace, not priests at all.' 'Well, Lord,' I say, 'you should dismiss the lot of them. Why bother to feed such parasites?'

"'The fact is, Zhilin, I feel pity for them,' he replies."

The aura of radiance around Zhilin turned blue, and the sleeping Alexei's heart was filled with inexpressible joy. Stretching out his arms towards the radiant sergeant major, he started groaning in his sleep.

"Zhilin, oh Zhilin, could you not somehow organize it so that I can serve as a doctor in your brigade?"

Zhilin waved his hand in greeting, and gently and firmly shook his head. Then he began to back away and move out of Alexei Vasilyevich's dream. Alexei woke up, seeing in front of him not Zhilin, but the outline of the window growing gradually pale in the dawn light. The doctor wiped his face with his hand, feeling it moist with tears. He lay there in the dawn light for a long time, sighing. Soon, however, he was asleep again, and this time it was an uneventful, dreamless sleep…

No, sir, death was not slow in coming. As autumn turned to winter, it came along the Ukrainian roads, together with the dry, drifting snow. It began to show itself in the woods with the rattle of machine-gun fire. Death itself remained invisible, but it was clearly preceded by an outburst of unbridled peasant fury, running howling and out of control through the blizzards and the cold, wearing torn bast shoes, and with hay in its unkempt hair. In its hand it carried a huge club, without which no enterprise in Russia is undertaken. The red roosters started to crow and, in the dying crimson sunset, the genitalia of

Jewish innkeepers were hung up for all to see. And in Poland's beautiful capital, Warsaw, a vision of Henryk Sinkiewicz* appeared, standing in the clouds with a spiteful smirk on his face. Then all hell simply broke loose, with bubbles expanding everywhere and leaping around in the air. The priests rang the bells under the green cupolas of endangered little churches, and revolutionary songs could be heard coming from nearby schools, their windows shattered by bullets. And along the roads came the ghost of old man Degtyarenko, reeking of home-made vodka and croaking terrifying words that formed on his dark lips, seeming to suggest something extraordinarily like a declaration of human and civil rights. And then this prophet Degtyarenko was lying on the ground howling, while men with red ribbons on their chest were lashing out at him with ramrods. And even the subtlest mind could not cope with this paradox: if it's red ribbons, then ramrods are out of the question; but if it's ramrods, then red ribbons are impossible.

Yes, you could definitely suffocate at such a time and in such a country. Never mind, let it go to hell! It's all a myth, anyway. Petlyura's nothing but a myth. He never existed at all. It was a myth every bit as remarkable as the myth concerning the non-existence of Napoleon, but far less pleasant. Then something else happened. That very same peasant fury had to be induced to travel along a certain road, for things are so magically organized on this earth that no matter how far fury travels it always ends up by finding itself at the same fatal crossroads.

It was all very simple: there would be chaos, but people would be found who would be able to deal with it.

And then, from out of the blue, Colonel Toropets appeared.* Toropets had apparently served with none other than the Austrian army.

"How is that possible?"

"I assure you it's true."

Then the writer Vinnichenko* appeared on the scene, famous for two things: for his novels, and for the fact that it was only the magical wave of early 1918 that had thrust him to the surface of the seething Ukrainian ocean. Not wasting a second, the St Petersburg satirical journals called him a traitor.

"Serves him right."

"Perhaps, I don't know. And then there's that mysterious prisoner released from the town jail."

Back in September, nobody in the City could have imagined what three individuals, possessing the talent to be in the right place at the right time, could be hatching up – even in such an insignificant little place as

Belaya Tserkov. By October, however, people had a strong idea of what might be happening. Trains, their hundreds of windows blazing with light, began to leave the City's Passenger Railway Station No. 1, taking the new but still broad-gauge railway line through newly established Poland and on to Germany. Telegrams flew everywhere. Away went diamonds, shifty eyes, slick partings and money. People fled southwards, too, to the seaport of Odessa. And alas, by November everybody had become very familiar with the name "Petlyura"! It was everywhere, jumping out at you from every wall, from grey telegraph messages. In the mornings, it dripped down into the coffee from newspaper pages, and the divine, tropical beverage immediately turned into the foulest stinking slops in one's mouth. It tripped around on everyone's tongue and was tapped out on keys by operators on Morse telegraph machines. The City became witness to strange and wonderful events connected with this strange, enigmatic word, which the Germans had taken to pronouncing as "Peturra".

There were individual cases of German soldiers who had acquired the lamentable habit of roaming around the City's suburbs and disappearing at night. They disappeared at night and, during the day, it became clear that they had been murdered. As a result, the Germans started patrolling the streets in steel basin-shaped helmets. They marched about, telling everyone to behave themselves in the glow of the street lamps. But no street lamp could disperse the chaotic mess that was inside people's heads.

Wilhelm. Wilhelm. Yesterday three German soldiers were murdered. Are you aware that the Germans are leaving for Heaven's sake? Trotsky arrested by workers in Moscow! Some sons of bitches have waylaid a train near Borodyanka and helped themselves to everything. Petlyura has sent a mission to Paris. Wilhelm, again. Black Senegalese troops in Odessa. The unknown, mysterious name of Consul Enno. Odessa. Odessa. General Denikin. Wilhelm, again. The Germans will leave, the French will come.

"It's the Bolsheviks who'll come, old chap!"

"Keep your trap shut, old man!"

The German have this contraption with a pointer – place the contraption on the ground, and the pointer will tell you where a weapon is buried. That's something, isn't it! Petlyura has sent a mission to the Bolsheviks. That's something else again, isn't it! Petlyura. Petlyura. Petlyura. Petlyura. Peturra.

*

Nobody, not a single person, knew what this Peturra actually had in mind for the Ukraine, but absolutely everyone knew that he was a mysterious and faceless figure. (Every so often, however, the newspapers published a photograph of a Catholic prelate they were sent, each one different, but each signed Simon Petlyura). And people knew for sure that this mysterious and faceless figure wanted to conquer the Ukraine and that, in order to be able to do that, he would enter the City and take it.

6

MADAME ANJOU'S BOUTIQUE, Chic de Paris, was situated on the ground floor of a huge multi-storeyed house in the very centre of the City – on Theatre Street, behind the opera house. Entrance into the boutique was gained through a glass door at the top of three steps leading from the street. On either side of the glass door were two windows hung with dusty tulle curtains. Nobody knew the whereabouts of Madame Anjou, and as a consequence her boutique was being used for purposes quite other than commercial. In the left-hand window someone had drawn a picture of a colourful lady's hat, with the words CHIC PARISIEN written in gold letters, while in the right-hand window there was a huge yellow cardboard poster depicting two crossed Sevastopol cannon, similar to those on the epaulettes of artillery officers, with the following words written above:

"You might not be a hero, but you are obliged to enlist as a volunteer."

And underneath the cannon:

"Enrolment of volunteers in the Mortar Battalion, named after the commanding officer, now taking place."

At the entrance to the boutique there was a blackened and partially dismantled motorcycle and sidecar. Every other minute the entrance door, which was on a spring, banged shut, and each time it opened again the doorbell rang magnificently... *rrring, rrring...* reminding people of recent and happier times, when Madame Anjou was in charge.

Alexei Turbin, Myshlayevsky and Karas got up at practically the same time after their night of drinking with, to their astonishment, completely clear heads – although, it is true, they all got up fairly late, around midday. Nikolka and Shervinsky had clearly already left the house. Nikolka had hastily wrapped up a mysterious little red bundle and, muttering to himself, had gone off to join his unit. A few minutes before, Shervinsky had left for army headquarters.

Myshlayevsky stood stripped to the waist in Anyuta's cherished little room behind the kitchen, with a washbasin and bath hidden by a curtain. He doused his back, neck and head with icy-cold water and shouted out with a shriek of horrified delight:

"Hey... that's wonderful," he yelled so loudly that it could be heard for many yards around. Then he dried himself with a rough towel, dressed, brilliantined and combed his hair, and said to Alexei:

"Alyosha... umm... be a good chap and lend me your spurs. I won't have time to go home, and I don't want to turn up without any spurs."

"You'll find them in the study, in the desk, right-hand drawer."

Myshlayevsky went to the study where he clattered around for a bit, then came out again, his spurs jingling. Black-eyed Anyuta, who had returned that morning after spending her day off with her aunt, was busy dusting the chairs with a feather duster. Myshlayevsky cleared his throat, gave a sideways glance at the door, and started to adopt a more circuitous route, making a detour towards Anyutochka.

"Hello, Anyutochka..."

"I'll tell Yelena Vasilyevna," Anyuta whispered quickly and mechanically, without a second thought, and closed her eyes like an intended victim waiting for someone to stab her.

"You silly little—"

At that moment Alexei unexpectedly poked his head round the door. His face was as dark as thunder.

"You see that brush, Vitya? Right. It's lovely, isn't it? I would get out of here now if I were you. And you, Anyuta, you need to bear in mind that if he starts talking about marriage, don't believe a word of it."

"Good God, can't a fellow simply say hello to someone!"

Smarting from the undeserved insult, Myshlayevsky puffed out his chest and left the sitting room, his spurs clattering. In the dining room he went up to lovely golden Yelena, his eyes expressing a certain alarm.

"Hello, Yelena, my beautiful girl, may I wish you... er... a very good morning..." He spoke in a hoarse baritone voice, instead of his usual clear and strong tenor. "Lena, my beautiful girl," he exclaimed, his voice full of emotion, "don't be angry with me. I love you, and you must love me. Don't pay any attention to those boorish remarks yesterday. You don't really think I'm a bastard, do you Lena?"

Saying this, he flung his arms round Yelena and kissed her on both cheeks. In the sitting room, Anyuta's brush, in the form of a cockscomb, fell on the floor with a gentle thud. Strange things always happened to

Anyuta whenever Myshlayevsky made an appearance in the Turbins'
apartment. Household objects started spilling out of her hands: knives
would crash down and, if she was in the kitchen, dishes would fall off
the stand on the sideboard. Annushka would become distracted, suddenly running out of the kitchen, and busy herself with the galoshes,
wiping them with a rag until she could hear the clinking of short
spurs set well down on the heels. Then, when Myshlayevsky's broad
shoulders, sloping chin and blue breeches appeared, Anyuta would
close her eyes and sidle out from her cramped, cunning little hiding
place. And now, in the sitting room, having dropped the brush, she
stood for a long time lost in thought, looking through the patterned
curtains at the grey cloudy sky in the distance.

"Vitka, Vitka," Yelena said, shaking her head, with its shining crown
of hair resembling a theatre prop. "Just look at you – a perfectly healthy
young man – and yet, your behaviour last night! Sit down and have
some tea; perhaps you'll feel better."

"Do you know how absolutely gorgeous you look today, Lenochka?
And I swear, your housecoat fits you so well," Myshlayevsky said ingra-
tiatingly, glancing into the mirrored depths of the sideboard. "Look,
Karas: what a fantastic housecoat! Such a beautiful green, isn't it?"

"Yes, Yelena Vasilyevna, you're looking very beautiful," Karas
answered seriously and sincerely.

"It's actually electric blue," clarified Yelena. "Anyway, Vitya, why
don't you get straight to the point and tell me what's wrong?"

"The fact is Lena, my beautiful girl, that after what happened to me
yesterday, I'm liable to have a migraine, and nobody is able to fight
with a migraine."

"All right then... look in the sideboard."

"Thank you, thank you... just one little glass... better than any
aspirin."

Screwing up his eyes from the pain of it all, Myshlayevsky downed two
tumblers of vodka one after the other, taking them with limp gherkins
left over from the evening before. Then he declaimed he felt as good as
new and expressed the wish for some tea with lemon.

"Don't worry about me, Lenochka," Alexei said hoarsely. "I'm just
going to enlist and then I'll be straight back. And don't worry about
any possible military action: we'll just wait in the City and repel any
attack by that so-called president, the bastard."

"Yes, but won't you be sent somewhere?"

Karas shook his head reassuringly.

"No, don't worry, Yelena Vasilyevna. Listen: in the first place, under no circumstances will the battalion be ready for action for at least two weeks – we still don't have any horses or ammunition. And secondly, even when it is ready, we shall definitely stay in the City anyway. The entire army, which is now in the process of formation, will be the City's garrison. Maybe, a little later, when we have to advance on Moscow—"

"But that may never happen…"

"We shall need to join up with Denikin rather earlier…"

"You don't need to console me, gentlemen; I'm not afraid of anything at all – on the contrary, I approve of your intentions."

Yelena, indeed, sounded cheerful, and the expression in her eyes indicated that her interest had already turned to matters of domestic concern. "Sufficient unto the day be the evil thereof."

"Anyuta," she shouted. "Out on the veranda you'll find Viktor Viktorovich's washing. Take it, will you, give it a good brushing and then wash it straight away."

Most reassuring of all from Yelena's point of view was the small compact figure of blue-eyed Karas. The assured Karas sat there in his light brown army jacket, his eyes screwed up slightly, smoking and looking calm and nonchalant.

They said goodbye in the hall.

"May God keep and preserve you," Yelena said solemnly and made the sign of the cross over Alexei, then over Karas and Myshlayevsky. Myshlayevsky embraced her, and Karas, his greatcoat belted tightly round his waist, blushed as he tenderly kissed her on both hands.

"Permission to report, Colonel, sir," Karas said with a salute and gentle click of his spurs.

The colonel sat at a small desk in a low green lounge chair raised up on a kind of dais in the right-hand side of the shop. Behind him towered piles of blue cardboard boxes bearing the inscription "Madame Anjou. Ladies' Millinery", somewhat dimming the light coming from the dusty window hung with a patterned tulle curtain. The colonel had a pen in his hand – in actual fact he wasn't a full colonel, but just a lieutenant colonel with broad gold epaulettes, two stripes, three stars and crossed gold cannon. The colonel was a little older than Alexei Turbin, about thirty years old, certainly no more than thirty-two. His sleek, clean-shaven face sported a black moustache, trimmed after the American fashion. Although he was clearly tired, the expression in his eyes was lively, thoughtful and aware.

The colonel was surrounded by primordial chaos. A couple of yards away a fire was crackling in a small black stove with a black, knobbly flue, occasionally dripping globules of black gunge as it snaked away over the partition and disappeared into the depths of the shop. Scraps of paper and red and green material cuttings littered the floor, not only on the raised platform, but also in the rest of the shop extending into the recesses at the back. High up, right above the colonel's head, someone could be heard clucking away at a typewriter like the alarm call of an anxious bird. When Turbin looked up he saw that the sound was coming from behind a railing suspended right under the shop's ceiling. Someone's feet and rear in blue riding breeches could be seen behind the railing, but the head was invisible because the ceiling intervened. To the left, another machine was clattering away, in an invisible pit in the floor, revealing only the bright epaulettes and blond head of a volunteer, but neither his arms nor his legs.

A multitude of faces and gold epaulettes with cannon flitted around the colonel. Nearby stood a large box with telephone receivers and wires, and next to the piles of hatboxes lay several coiled machine-gun belts and a number of hand grenades, looking like tins of preserves with wooden handles. A sewing machine with a treadle stood under the colonel's left elbow, and by his right foot protruded the snout of a machine gun. Somewhere in the depths and semi-darkness, behind a curtain hanging from a gleaming rail, a voice could be heard on the telephone, clearly under pressure: "Yes... yes... speaking. Yes... yes... I'm telling you, yes..." *Rrring, rrring* went the bell, and what sounded like a small bird tweeting came from the invisible pit, as a young bass voice mumbled:

"Battalion headquarters here... yes, yes."

"How can I help you?" the colonel asked Karas.

"Permit me to introduce you, Colonel, sir, to Lieutenant Viktor Myshlayevsky and Doctor Turbin. Lieutenant Myshlayevsky is serving at present in the second infantry unit as a private, and wishes to transfer to the battalion under your command as an artillery officer. Doctor Turbin requests appointment as a battalion medical officer."

When he had finished speaking, Karas lowered his hand from the salute position, whereupon Myshlayevsky saluted. "Damn it, I wish I were in uniform," Alexei thought irritably, feeling awkward without a cap, dressed like some dolt in a black coat with a lambskin collar. The colonel's eyes flitted over the doctor, then across to Myshlayevsky's face and greatcoat.

"Right, that's excellent," he said. "And what unit were you with, lieutenant?"

"A heavy battalion, Colonel," answered Myshlayevsky, referring to his position during the war with Germany.

"A heavy battalion, you say? That's very good indeed. The Devil knows what they're doing shoving artillery officers into the infantry. What a mess."

"Not at all, Colonel, sir," Myshlayevsky replied, masking his challenging tone of voice with a little cough. "I myself volunteered to join the infantry detachment when there was an urgent demand for troops to go to Post-Volynsky. But now that the detachment is fully up to strength…"

"Very good… that meets with my complete approval," the colonel said and, indeed, the expression in his eyes as he looked at Myshlayevsky was one of complete approval. "I'm pleased to have met you… so… ah, doctor, you'd like to join us too?"

Turbin silently inclined his head, so as to avoid having to say "Yes, sir", dressed as he was in only his coat with its lamb collar.

"Hmm…" the colonel said, glancing out of the window. "That's a very good idea, you know. Especially since, sooner or later, we may… Right…" he suddenly broke off, screwing up his eyes slightly, and then continued more quietly. "It's just that… how can I put it? There is one little matter… social theories and all that… umm… you are a socialist, aren't you? Like all members of the intelligentsia?" The colonel's eyes slid sideways. His whole manner, his lips and his honeyed tone of voice expressed just how much he indeed wanted Turbin to be socialist, rather than anything else. "Our battalion is called the students' battalion," the colonel said with an emotional smile, averting his eyes. "A little sentimental, of course, but I myself am a university man."

Turbin was extremely disappointed and astonished at this. "What has Karas been saying, damn it?" he thought, sensing at that moment Karas standing to his right. Without looking, he realized that Karas urgently wanted to communicate something, but it was impossible to know exactly what it was.

"I regret," Turbin suddenly blurted out, his cheek twitching, "that I am not a socialist, but a… monarchist. And, I have to say, the very word 'socialist' is anathema to me. And of all socialists I hate Alexander Fyodorovich Kerensky* most of all."

From behind his right shoulder he heard a sound coming from Karas's lips. "It would be very sad not to be with Karas and Vitya," he thought, "but the Devil take this 'socialist battalion', damn it!"

The colonel glanced down fleetingly, and there was a sparkle in his eyes. He gestured to Turbin, as if to indicate politely that he should keep his mouth shut.

"That's a pity," he said. "Hmm... a great pity... achievements of the revolution and so on... I have orders from above not to accept any monarchist elements: the population as a whole needs restraint, you understand. Moreover, the Hetman, with whom we are in the most immediate and direct contact, has, you know... a pity... a great pity."

As he said this, the colonel's voice not only did not contain any note of regret but, on the contrary, he sounded positively pleased, and his eyes expressed the exact opposite of what he was saying.

"Aha," thought Turbin, understanding the position perfectly. "I am an idiot, and the colonel is far from stupid. Judging by his face, he's probably a careerist, but I don't mind that."

"I don't know now what's the best thing to do. At the present moment, as you know," said the colonel, particularly emphasizing the word "present", "I repeat, at the present moment, our most immediate task is to defend the City and the Hetman from Petlyura's gang, as well as, possibly, from the Bolsheviks. We'll just have to wait and see... Where did you serve, doctor, before this, may I ask?"

"In 1915, after graduation, I worked as a junior doctor in a clinic for venereal diseases, and then as a medical officer with the Belgrade Hussars, and after that in a mobile field hospital. At the present moment I am demobilized, and have my own private practice."

"Cadet!" the colonel ordered. "Ask the senior officer to report to me."

A head disappeared down into the pit, followed by the appearance of a young, dark-skinned, lively-looking and eager officer, wearing a lambskin fur cap with a purple striped top and a grey greatcoat *à la* Myshlayevsky, with a tightly fastened belt and a revolver. His crumpled gold epaulettes indicated that he was a staff captain.

"Captain Studzinsky," the colonel said to the young officer, "be so kind as to send a message to headquarters requesting the immediate transfer to me of Lieutenant... er..."

"Myshlayevsky," said Myshlayevsky, saluting.

"...Lieutenant Myshlayevsky, from the Second Infantry Detachment, as an artillery officer. And with it, a message concerning Doctor... er..."

"Turbin."

"...Doctor Turbin. I would very much like him to become battalion medical officer. Please request that he be appointed immediately."

"Yes, colonel, sir," answered the officer in a foreign accent, and saluted.

"A Pole," thought Turbin.

"You, lieutenant, should not return to your infantry unit," the colonel said to Myshlayevsky. Then, turning to the captain, he said: "The lieutenant will take over the fourth platoon."

"Yes, Colonel, sir."

"Yes, Colonel, sir."

"As for you, doctor, as of this moment you are a serving officer. I would like you to report today, within the hour, to the parade ground in front of the Alexandrovsky High School."

"Yes, Colonel, sir."

"Issue the doctor with a uniform immediately."

"Yes, sir."

"Yes, sir!" shouted the bass voice from the pit.

"No, do you hear! No, I'm telling you, no!" came a shout from behind the partition.

Rrring… cheep, *cheep*, chirped the bird down in the pit.

"Can you hear me…?"

"*Liberty News*! *Liberty News*! Your new daily… *Liberty News*!" shouted the newspaper boy, his hair wrapped in a woman's scarf. "Petlyura demoralized. African troops arrive in Odessa. *Liberty News*!"

Within an hour Turbin was back home. The silver epaulettes were located in the depths of the drawer in Turbin's study, next to the sitting room. The study itself was sparsely furnished and rather cramped, but nonetheless comfortable. There were white curtains on the glass door opening out onto a balcony, a desk with books and an inkwell, shelves of medicine bottles and instruments and a couch made up with a clean sheet.

"Lenochka, if for some reason I'm back late today and someone comes, tell them there's no surgery; it won't be any of my regular patients. Quick as you can, my girl."

Having turned back the lapels of Turbin's army jacket Yelena was hastily sewing on the epaulettes. She had already sewn the others – khaki green with a black stripe – onto the greatcoat.

A few minutes later, Turbin dashed out of the front door, glancing at the white board on the way:

DOCTOR A.V. TURBIN
Venereal diseases and syphilis.
606–914
Surgery hours: 4 p.m. to 6 p.m.

Sticking on the amended times of "5 p.m. to 7 p.m.", he set off up St Alexei's Hill at a run.

"*Liberty News*!"

Turbin stopped, bought a copy and continued on his way, opening the paper as he went.

Independent democratic newspaper.
Published daily. 13th December 1918.
Issues relating to external trade and, in particular, trade with Germany, compel us...

"But where on earth is it?... my hands are freezing."

According to our correspondent, negotiations are taking place in Odessa concerning the disembarkation of two divisions of black colonial troops. Consul Enno rejects any suggestion that...

"The son of a bitch, that newspaper lad!"

Deserters who turned up yesterday at army headquarters at Post-Volynsky have spoken of the increasing demoralization in the ranks of Petlyura's forces. Two days ago a cavalry regiment in the Korosten region fired on an infantry regiment of Cossack riflemen. Among Petlyura's forces a strong desire for peace has been observed. Petlyura's little adventure is clearly coming to an end. According to the same source, Colonel Bolbotun* has rebelled against Petlyura and gone off with his regiment and four guns to an unknown destination. Bolbotun inclines towards support of the Hetman. The peasants hate Petlyura for his requisitions. The mobilization orders he has published in the villages have had no success. The peasants are ignoring them in their masses by taking to hiding in the forests.

"It's possible, I suppose... oh, damn this bloody frost... Sorry."
"There's no need to push like that, my dear sir. Newspapers should be read at home."
"Sorry."

We have always maintained that Petlyura's little adventure...

"What a bastard! Oh, you bastards!

> Don't let Petlyura have his way –
> come, join the volunteers today!

"Why so glum today, Ivan Ivanovich?"

"My wife's gone down with Petlyura; she did a Bolbotun on me this morning."

Hearing this witticism, Turbin's expression changed, and he angrily scrunched up the newspaper and hurled it onto the pavement.

Then, suddenly, his attention was caught by the *boom, boom* of heavy gunfire, followed by a series of dull thuds coming seemingly from the depths of the earth, from somewhere outside the City.

"What the devil's that?"

Turbin turned abruptly, picked up the crumpled ball of newspaper, straightened it out and read through the first page again more carefully.

> In the Irpen region there have been clashes between our advanced forces and individual groups of Petlyura's bandits. All reported calm in the Serebryansk area. No change at the Red Tavern. In the Boyark area a fierce attack by a regiment of Hetmanite Cossacks has dispersed a group some 1,500 strong. Two men taken prisoner.

The roar of gunfire could also be heard in the grey winter sky somewhere to the far south-west of the City. Turbin suddenly turned pale, his mouth open. Mechanically he stuffed the newspaper into his pocket. Crowds of people were moving slowly from the boulevard and along Vladimirskaya Street. Many people in black coats were walking directly on the road, while peasant women could be glimpsed on the pavement. A horseman of the State Guard rode commandingly along. His large horse, its ears twitching, looked around nervously as it moved sideways along the road. The rider seemed rather confused. From time to time he would shout something, brandishing his whip to show who he was, but nobody paid any attention. At the front of the crowd the gold copes of bearded priests could be seen bobbing along, a religious banner waving above their heads. Small boys were dashing up from all directions.

"*News!*" shouted a newspaper boy, making a beeline for the crowd.

Sous-chefs in their white, flat-topped hats ran out from the dark interior of the Metropole Restaurant. The crowd spread out over the snow like black ink over paper.

A number of long yellow boxes were swaying along above the heads of the crowd. When the first box drew level with Turbin he was able to make out the charcoal inscription scrawled on its side: "Ensign Yutsevich".

On the second box: "Ensign Ivanov".

And on the third: "Ensign Orlov".

Suddenly there was a howl from the crowd. A grey-haired woman, her hat on the back of her head, dashed from the pavement into the crowd, stumbling and dropping various packages along the way.

"What's going on? Vanya!" she yelled. Someone turned pale and ran off to one side. A peasant woman started howling, followed by another behind her.

"Lord Jesus Christ!" Turbin heard someone mutter behind him. Someone pushed him in the back, and he could sense someone's breath on his neck.

"Lord, what terrible times we're living in. So people are being killed now? Is that it?"

"I don't know anything, except what I can see here in front of me."

"What? What? What's going on? Who's being buried?"

"Vanya!" someone yelled in the crowd.

"They're the officers who were murdered in Popelyukha," a voice boomed hastily, anxious to be the first with the news. "They had got as far as Popelyukha where they spent the night. But some peasants, together with a group of Petlyura's men, surrounded them and simply slaughtered them... yes, just like that, slaughtered. Their eyes were gouged out, and their epaulettes carved onto their shoulders. Completely mutilated."

"Oh, my God! So, that's what happened!"

Two more yellow coffins went by: "Ensign Korovin"... "Ensign Gerdt".

"What times we're living in... just think!"

"Internecine fighting."

"What on earth do you mean?"

"They fell asleep, apparently..."

"Serves them right..." someone hissed darkly behind Turbin, and he immediately saw red. Faces and caps flashed past. Turbin thrust his hand between two necks and grasped the sleeve of the man's black coat in a pincer-like grip. The man turned round with a horrified look.

"What did you say?" Turbin hissed, relaxing his grip.

"Please, sir, I beg you," the man answered, shaking with fright. "I didn't say anything; I didn't open my mouth. What do you want?" he asked, his voice quavering.

The man's beaklike nose paled, and Turbin realized at once he'd made a mistake: he'd seized hold of the wrong man. The beaklike nose belonged to a face expressing nothing but the best of intentions. Its mouth was unable to speak and its eyes were rolling from terror.

Turbin let go of the man's sleeve and, in cold fury, began looking around at everybody, searching among the seething mass of caps, heads and collars. His left hand was poised to grab, and his right hand was in his pocket, firmly holding on to the handle of his Browning revolver. The priests walked past singing mournfully, and a woman in a shawl sobbed. The man he was looking for seemed to have vanished into thin air, so there was nobody he could grab. The last coffin floated by: "Ensign Morskoy". Several sledges went past at speed.

"*News!*" somebody shouted in a hoarse falsetto right by Turbin's ear.

Turbin pulled out the crumpled newspaper from his pocket and, without thinking what he was doing, jabbed it twice into the newspaper boy's face.

"Here's your news for you," he said, grinding his teeth. "Here's your news, you little swine!"

As soon as he'd said this, Turbin's fit of rage left him. Dropping his newspapers, the lad slipped and sat down in a snowdrift. His face puckered up and he began to weep patently false tears, but the expression in his eyes was one of undiluted and far from false hatred.

"Why did you do that... what have I done?" the lad whined, in an attempt at a wail, and started digging into the snow. Someone looked at Turbin in astonishment, but he was afraid to say anything. Feeling ashamed and aware of the absurdity of what he'd done, Turbin tucked his head into his shoulders and, turning sharply, ran from the street onto the huge familiar square in the park of the Alexandrovsky High School – past the gas lamp, past the white wall on the side of the large, circular museum building, and past several pits in the ground filled with snow-covered bricks. Behind him he could still hear the shouts from the street: "*News!*" "Daily democratic newspaper!"

The huge, peaceful edifice of the school that Turbin knew so well, with its four storeys and its one hundred and eighty columns, stood along one side of the square. Turbin had spent eight years as a student there. Every spring for eight years, during the breaks between classes, he had run around that very same square, and in the winter, when the classrooms were full of choking dust and the square was covered in a cold, solid mass of snow, he used to stand at the window looking out onto it. For eight years, within these peaceful brick walls, Turbin and his younger fellow pupils, Karas and Myshlayevsky, had been educated and nurtured.

And it was exactly eight years ago that Turbin had last seen the school park. For some reason his heart contracted from fear. A black cloud suddenly seemed to have covered the sky, and a tornado had apparently appeared out of nowhere and wiped his life away, just like a huge wave washing away a jetty. Eight years as a student! How many absurdities, how much sorrow and despair had he lived through as a small boy! And yet, how happy he had been too. One grey day after another, on and on. Like Julius Caesar he had been given the lowest possible mark for cosmography, and from then on he had always hated the subject. But then there was the spring – springtime, with noisy, echoing classrooms, the girl pupils walking along the boulevards in their green pinafores, the chestnuts in May and, above all, the ever-present lighthouse pointing the way ahead – to university, to freedom and life, in other words. Do you understand the significance of that word "university"? Sunsets over the Dnieper, freedom, money, the life force and fame.

And he had lived through it all. The teachers with their inscrutable expressions, the swimming pools – still featuring in his dreams – from which the water always seemed to be draining but which always remained full, and the endless discussions concerning the difference in character between Lensky and Onegin,* Socrates's scandalous behaviour, when the order of Jesuits was founded, the dates of Pompey's campaign and of someone else's campaign, and of campaign after campaign over two thousand years of history...

But this was far from all. After eight years of school, with the swimming pools left far behind, came the corpses in the anatomy theatre, the whitewashed hospital wards, the glassy silence of the operating theatres, and then three years being tossed about in the saddle, the dressing of wounds, the humiliations and the suffering – oh, the damned cesspit of war. And here he was once again, back in the same old school grounds, running across the square, feeling ill and overwrought, clutching the Browning in his pocket, running God knows where and what for. Probably to protect that very same life, that future for whose sake he had worried himself sick over swimming pools and those blasted pedestrians, one setting off from point A and the other setting off to meet him from point B.

The blackened windows of the school seemed frozen in complete gloom. It was immediately apparent that their stillness was that of the grave. It seemed very strange that in the centre of a city, in the midst of all the chaos, bustle and commotion, there should be this dead, four-tiered ship that had once carried scores of thousands of lives onto the open sea. It seemed that nobody was looking after it any longer, and that there was neither sound nor movement of any kind in its windows and under its walls, decorated with yellow paint dating from the time of Nicholas II. A layer of virgin snow covered the roofs, crowned the tops of the chestnut trees and spread evenly over the square; only a few tracks showed that someone had recently crossed it.

But the main point was that not only did nobody know what had happened to everything, but that nobody cared. Nobody cared who was still studying here in this ship; or, if there weren't any students any more, why that should be so; or where the watchman might be. Why were there those fearful-looking blunt-snouted mortars protruding from under the line of chestnuts by the railing? Why was there a weapons store in the school? Whose was it? Who? What for?

Nobody knew the answers to these questions, just as nobody knew what had become of Madame Anjou and why there were bombs in her boutique lying beside the empty hatboxes.

"Deploy!" someone roared, and the mortars began to move and creep slowly forward. About two hundred people were busy running in various directions, squatting down and leaping about near the huge metal wheels of the mortars. There were glimpses of yellow sheepskin coats, grey greatcoats and fur caps, military, khaki and blue students' caps.

Turbin walked across the imposing square to find the four mortars in a row, gaping at him. The hurried drill procedure around the guns had ended, and the motley recently recruited soldiers of the mortar battalion stood to attention in two ranks.

"Captain," sang out Myshlayevsky's voice. "Platoon present and correct, sir."

Captain Studzinsky stepped out in front of the ranks of soldiers, took a step backwards, and shouted:

"By the left, quick march!"

The ranks swayed and marched off raggedly, the snow crunching under their feet.

As they marched by, Turbin glimpsed many familiar, typical student faces, including that of Karas, at the head of the third platoon. Still uncertain where he was going and for what purpose, he started crunching through the snow in step with the platoon.

Karas, concerned that his platoon was out of step, went out in front of his men and, walking backwards, shouted:

"Left… left… hup… left!"

The company snaked towards the dark basement entrance to the school. One after the other, the ranks of soldiers were swallowed up by its black maw.

The interior of the school was even more lifeless and gloomy than its exterior. The crashing echo of marching feet quickly brought the stone walls and eerie darkness to life. Strange sounds began to fly around under the vaults like animated demons. With the ponderous sound of marching feet came the squeak of alarmed rats scuttling about under the floorboards. The company marched along endless, dark, brick-paved basement corridors until they came to a huge hall lit by a miserly light trickling through narrow barred windows and musty cobwebs.

The silence was broken by the hellish din of hammers. People were opening boxes of shells, removing seemingly endless numbers of cartridge belts, together with round cartridge cases for Lewis guns, looking like cream cakes. Grey and black machine guns emerged, resembling evil-looking mosquitoes. There was a clattering of nuts and bolts, a ripping of pliers and, over in the corner, the high-pitched whine of a saw. Cadets were unloading piles of frozen and sorry-looking fur caps, folded greatcoats that were as rigid as iron, belts that had become stiff, cartridge pouches and water bottles wrapped in cloth.

"Look lively there!" Studzinsky could be heard saying.

A group of about six officers in faded gold epaulettes swirled around the room like clubmoss on top of a pond. Myshlayevsky's strong tenor voice was singing some song or other.

"Doctor," Studzinsky shouted from out of the gloom. "Please be so kind as to take the medical assistants and give them their instructions."

Two students appeared in front of Turbin. One of them, short and agitated, had a red cross on the sleeve of his student coat. The other was wearing a grey coat and a fur cap that he kept on having to adjust because it was slipping down over his eyes.

"The boxes of medical supplies are over there," Turbin said. "Take the shoulder satchels out and give me my doctor's bag and equipment. Make sure you give each artilleryman two of the individual medical packs, with a brief explanation how they are to open them in an emergency."

Myshlayevsky's head emerged above the seething mass of soldiers. He climbed up onto a box, took his rifle, pulled back the bolt and, slamming in a cartridge clip, took aim at the window, pulled back the bolt again, took aim, repeating the action again and again, showering the cadets with expended bullets. The basement began to sound like a factory. With a general din and the clatter of bolts being pulled, the cadets loaded their rifles.

"Anybody who can't do it, take care," Myshlayevsky sang out. "Cadets, show the students how it's done."

When everyone had pulled the straps of cartridge pouches and shoulder satchels over their heads, it was as if a miracle had taken place: what had been a motley, disparate bunch of men was now a single, compact unit with a bristling row of bayonets wavering unsteadily over their heads like a steel brush.

"All officers to me, please," Studzinsky said from out of the darkness. Studzinsky addressed them quietly in the dark corridor, to the sound of softly clinking spurs.

"Well, impressions?"

There was a stamping of spurs and Myshlayevsky, nonchalantly and adeptly placing the tips of his fingers in his cap band, stepped forward towards the Staff Captain and said:

"I have fifteen men in my platoon who haven't the first idea how to use a rifle; makes life difficult."

Studzinsky looked up, as though inspired, towards the window that was letting in the final feeble ray of light into the basement.

"What about morale?" he asked.

Again it was Myshlayevsky who spoke.

"Hmm… not helped by seeing those coffins. The students were upset; it hit them badly. They saw what was going on through the railings."

Studzinsky's dark, unwavering eyes flicked over him.

"Do all you can to raise morale."

They all dispersed to the clink of spurs.

"Cadet Pavlovsky," roared Myshlayevsky in the armaments store, sounding like Radamès in *Aida*.

The store's stone walls resounded with the shout of cadets' voices calling for Pavlovsky.

"Here, sir!"

"A student of Alexeyevsky Academy?"

"Yes, sir."

"Right then. Let's have a song that will blow the roof off. Put such force into it that Petlyura will drop dead, damn him to hell."

Under the stone vaulted ceiling a clear, high voice started singing:

"A gunner boy I was born…"

This was taken up by several tenor voices from among the forest of bayonets:

"…taught and nurtured by the brigade…"

The entire group seemed to tremble with excitement as they all quickly picked up the tune by ear, until suddenly the whole room was echoing with the elemental sound of a bass chorus exploding into song.

"…baptized by the sound of gunfire…
wrapped in lush velvet,
and the sound of gunf-i-i-i-re."

The song rang in everyone's ears and heads, as well as in the boxes of ammunition, and even some dusty glasses standing abandoned on the sloping window ledges trembled and tinkled…

"In my cradle of anchor ropes
the gun crew rocked me to sleep…"

Studzinsky seized hold of two pink-cheeked ensigns from the mêlée of greatcoats, bayonets and machine guns.

"Go to the vestibule and take the cover off the painting there – quick as you can!" he ordered in a hurried whisper. And the two of them raced off.

"The guards cadets sing as
down the street they pound.
The trumpets and drums
and the cymbals resound."

The empty stone shell of the building now thundered and roared to the terrifying sound of a march, and the rats cowering in their deep underground lairs were too petrified to move.

"Hey up!" Karas shouted shrilly.

"Come on! Put some life into it, students of Alexeyevsky Academy!" Myshlayevsky yelled in his clear tenor voice. "This isn't a funeral!"

"The seamstresses, maids and laundry girls
watch the cadets as they march away!"

Instead of a grey indeterminate caterpillar shuffling along, an organized troop of men bristling with bayonets moved down the corridor and the floor bent and groaned under the heavy tread of their feet. They marched along the seemingly endless corridor, then up to the first floor and into the gigantic vestibule, lit by the light streaming through its glass cupola. The first to arrive were already there, waiting a little restlessly.

Mounted on his rearing thoroughbred stallion, Emperor Alexander,* slightly balding and with a radiant smile, his saddlecloth embellished with imperial monograms, charged along ahead of his troops, his white-feathered tricorne hat cocked to one side. Bestowing smile after smile on them, full of a rather disingenuous charm, Alexander gestured with his baton to show them the regiments who fought at Borodino. The battlefield was strewn with piles of cannonballs and the entire background of the fourteen-foot canvas was taken up by a black forest of bayonets.

"What a battle it was…"

…Pavlovsky sang…

"…Yes, what a battle it was…"

…thundered the basses…

"…no Russian will ever forget
the glorious day of Borodino."

The dazzling Alexander galloped on and upwards towards heaven, with the cover that had concealed the painting for a whole year lying at the feet of his stallion.

"Just look at the blessed Tsar Alexander, won't you! Come on, keep in step there. Hup! Left, left!" yelled Myshlayevsky as the file of troops climbed the staircase with the heavy tread of Tsar Alexander's infantry. Once past the conqueror of Napoleon, the squadron stopped singing as they wheeled into the vast assembly hall and stood there in their dense ranks, bayonets waving. The hall was filled with a whitish, rather gloomy, light and, behind the covers over the paintings on the walls, the figures of previous tsars could be discerned, peering down like pale ghosts onto the assembled company.

Studzinsky took a step backwards and glanced at his wristwatch. At that moment a cadet ran up to him and whispered something in his ear. Those standing nearby could hear what he said:

"The battalion commander."

Studzinsky gestured to his officers, who ran to the ranks and dressed them. Studzinsky went out into the corridor to meet the commander. His spurs jingling, Colonel Malyshev was climbing the stairs towards the entrance to the assembly hall, turning to glance at the painting of Alexander on the way. His curved Caucasian sabre with its cherry-coloured sword knot dangled at his left side. He was wearing a black cap of luxuriant velvet and a long greatcoat with a huge slit at the back. He was looking thoughtful. Studzinsky went quickly up to him and saluted.

"They all have uniforms?" asked Malyshev.

"Yes, sir. All orders have been carried out."

"And?"

"They will fight, but they're totally lacking in experience. One hundred and twenty cadets are in charge of eighty students, none of whom knows how to hold a rifle."

Malyshev frowned, but he said nothing.

"I am very fortunate to have such good officers," Studzinsky continued, "especially the one who's just joined me, Myshlayevsky. We shall manage somehow."

"Right. But now I want you to see to it that the battalion – with the exception of the officers and sixty of the best and most experienced cadets, who will stay behind to guard the mortars, the ammunition store and the building generally – disperses to their homes to be back here at seven o'clock tomorrow morning."

Studzinsky's face expressed blank astonishment. His mouth open, he glared at the colonel with an extremely defiant expression.

"But Colonel, sir," in his agitation, Studzinsky started to stress all his words in the Polish way, on the penultimate syllable, "with all due respect, that will not be possible. The only way the battalion will be able to maintain its fighting readiness will be if it stays here for the night."

The colonel there and then demonstrated that he possessed a new quality: the ability to erupt into a fit of rage on the grandest scale. His neck and cheeks turned a brownish red, and his eyes flashed fire.

"Captain," he said furiously, "I shall ask that an official complaint be made against you, so that your duties as an officer will cease and you will become a lecturer whose job will be to instruct senior officers. And I will not find that at all pleasant, as I have always supposed you, of all people, to be an experienced officer and not a civilian professor. So I don't need to be lectured, and I don't need any advice from you! Listen to what I've been saying and remember it. And then, when you've remembered, you are to carry out my orders."

The two of them stood there glaring at each other.

A reddish glow crept over Studzinsky's neck and cheeks, and his lips trembled.

"Yes, sir," he said gratingly.

"Yes, sir! Now send them home. They are to sleep, without their weapons, and then be back here tomorrow morning at seven o'clock. But that's not all: they are to disperse in small groups rather than in their platoons, and they are to remove their splendid epaulettes so as not to attract any attention from idle people."

A ray of understanding flashed in Studzinsky's eyes, and his sense of outrage subsided.

"Yes, sir, Colonel, sir."

The colonel's mood changed abruptly.

"Alexander Bronislavovich, I have long known you as an experienced fighting officer. But you also know me, don't you? So, no hard feelings then? Resentment at such a time would be inappropriate. Please forget the fact that I spoke so harshly to you, but then you also..."

Studzinsky's face flooded with colour.

"Yes, Colonel, I'm sorry."

"Well, excellent, then. Let's not waste any more time, otherwise the men will lose the will to fight. Everything will depend on what happens tomorrow, when it will all have become clearer. But I'll just say this for now: don't bother with the mortars at all tomorrow – there won't be any horses or shells. Instead, you are to start by concentrating on their rifle drill. Shooting and more shooting. Ensure that by midday tomorrow the battalion is capable of shooting as well as any top-class regiment. And all experienced cadets are to be given grenades. Understood?"

Deep shadows crossed Studzinsky's forehead. He had been listening carefully to everything the colonel had been saying.

"May I ask you a question, sir?"

"I know what you want to ask me, and no, you may not. But I'll answer it anyway: the situation's terrible. It has been worse, but rarely as bad as this. Now do you understand?"

"Yes, sir!"

"So then," the colonel said, his voice considerably lower, "you understand why I don't want anybody to spend a night in this stone death trap at such a dangerous time, and I certainly don't want to be responsible for the deaths of two hundred young men, one hundred and twenty of whom don't even know how to use a rifle!"

Studzinsky said nothing in reply.

"Right, then. We'll deal with the rest this evening; there'll be enough time. Let's go and have a look at the battalion."

They went into the assembly hall.

"Officers... atten-shun!" bawled Studzinsky.

"Good day, gentlemen!"

From behind Malyshev's back, Studzinsky gestured at the men like an anxious theatre director and the grey, bristling ranks responded with such a roar of greeting that the windows shook.

Malyshev gave the ranks a cheerful once-over and brought his hand down from the salute.

"Splendid... Gentlemen," he said, "I will not waste any words. I am not a great public speaker as I am not in the habit of addressing meetings, and therefore I will be brief. We will be hitting that son of a bitch Petlyura where it hurts and, you may rest assured, we will beat him. Among you are graduates from the Vladimir, Constantine and Alexeyevsky Military Academies, and not once has any of you fine fellows from these academies ever brought disgrace on their institutions. And there are many present who were students of this famous school. Its ancient walls are looking down on you, and I trust you will not do anything to make them ashamed of you. Gentlemen of the mortar battalion! We shall defend this great City from the besieging marauders. We simply need to start firing at this wonderful so-called president with our six-inch guns and all he'll have to show for it will be a pair of dirty underpants, God rot his slimy soul!"

Encouraged by the colonel's cheerful humour, the bristling, dense ranks responded with a roar of laughter.

"Gentlemen, do your best!"

Once again, as if from the wings, there was a theatrical gesture from Studzinsky, and once again the ranks responded with a roar that disturbed several layers of dust as they raised three cheers for their commanding officer.

Ten minutes later the assembly hall, just as on the battlefield at Borodino, was dotted with hundreds of weapons in stacks. Two sentries stood in the shadows at either end of the dusty parquet floor, guarding the forest of bayonets. Somewhere far off, down below, came the hasty clatter of footsteps as the men, following their orders, dispersed. Officers could be heard shouting in the corridors, accompanied by the rumble and metallic clatter of feet. Studzinsky was himself posting the sentries. Then, suddenly, again in the corridors came the sound of a bugle call flooding through the entire school. If there was any note of anxiety in the sound it was unconvincing, and the halting, broken nature of the playing indicated that it was not warning of any real danger. In the corridor above the landing bounded by the double staircase leading to the vestibule a cadet was standing, puffing out his cheeks. Faded ribbons of the Order of St George* dangled down from the tarnished brass instrument. Myshlayevsky, his feet spread wide apart like a pair of compasses, stood in front of the bugler, instructing and testing him.

"Not so hard… no, like this… blow out, like a bellows… that old thing's not been played for ages… How about the general alarm?"

Ta-ta-tam-ta-tam, went the bugler, spreading alarm and despondency among the rats.

The light in the assembly hall was fading rapidly. Malyshev and Alexei Turbin stood among the stacks of rifles. Malyshev gave Turbin a rather suspicious look at first, but then a welcoming smile spread over his face.

"Well, doctor, how are things going? Everything all right in the medical section?"

"Yes, sir."

"In that case, doctor, you can go home. And you can tell the medical orderlies they can go too. But tell them that they must be here at seven o'clock tomorrow morning, along with the others. As for you…" here Malyshev paused for a moment, concentrated in thought, "as for you, I would like you to be here tomorrow at two o'clock in the afternoon. Until then you are free." Malyshev again thought for a moment. "And you know what? Don't wear your epaulettes for the time being." Looking a little embarrassed, he continued: "Our plans won't get very far if we draw attention to ourselves. So, then: here tomorrow at two o'clock."

"Yes, sir."

Turbin shuffled his feet. Malyshev took out his cigarette case and offered him a cigarette. In response, Turbin lit a match. Two red pinpoints started to glow, clearly indicating just how dark it had become. Malyshev glanced anxiously up at the dully shining arc lights on the ceiling, then went out into the corridor.

"Lieutenant Myshlayevsky, please come here for a moment," he called. "I would like you to be in total charge of the electric lighting. Ensure that the building is fully lit as soon as possible. Be so good as to ensure that you have such control over the lighting that you are able not only to turn it on everywhere, but also to turn it off. You have complete responsibility for the building's lighting arrangements."

Myshlayevsky saluted, and turned abruptly on his heels. There was a final squeak from the bugle. Myshlayevsky, his spurs jingling, clattered down the main staircase so rapidly that he could have been on skates. A moment later, and the thunderous sound of hammering fists and yelled commands could be heard coming up from somewhere in the depths of the building. This was followed by a sudden blaze of light in the main entranceway downstairs that led into the vestibule, dimly illuminating the portrait of the Tsar Alexander. His eyes shining with pleasure, Malyshev turned to Turbin.

"There's a real officer for you, damn it! Did you see that?"

At that moment, a small figure appeared on the staircase, slowly climbing the steps. When it reached the first landing Malyshev and Turbin, hanging over the banisters, could see it more clearly. The figure was moving with feeble, tottering steps, shaking his white head. He was wearing a wide double-breasted jacket with silver buttons and green lapels and holding an enormous key in his shaking hands. Myshlayevsky followed him up the stairs, exhorting him every so often.

"Come on, old fellow, look lively! Stop crawling along like some slow-witted beetle."

"Your… Your…" spluttered the old man, as he shuffled up the stairs. Suddenly Karas dived out of the gloom on the landing, followed by another, taller, officer, then two cadets and, finally, the pointed snout of a machine gun. Horrified, the old man stumbled, then bent down and bowed to the waist before the machine gun.

"Your Excellency," he mumbled.

With trembling fingers the old man poked around in the semi-gloom and opened an oblong box on the wall, to reveal a white spot of light shining inside. He placed his hand inside the box, there was a click, and suddenly the whole upper area of the vestibule, the entrance to the assembly hall and the corridor were flooded with light.

The darkness turned and fled into the distance, as far as it could go. Myshlayevsky immediately seized hold of the key and, placing his hand in the box began to experiment, clicking and pulling the black switches. The light, so dazzling that it appeared pink, now came on, now vanished again. The globe lights in the assembly hall flared up and then went out. Soon two lights at the end of the corridor went on and the darkness, somersaulting, disappeared for good.

"How's that down below," shouted Myshlayevsky.

"No, off," someone replied from the vestibule. "Wait, it's on again!"

After many attempts Myshlayevsky finally succeeded in turning on the light in the assembly hall, the corridor and over the Alexander painting. He locked the box and put the key in his pocket.

"Off you go now and have a sleep, old fellow," Myshlayevsky said soothingly. "Everything's fine now."

The old man's short-sighted eyes blinked nervously.

"But what about the key, Your Excellency... the key? Will you keep hold of the key?"

"Yes that is exactly what I intend to do: keep hold of the key."

Still trembling, the old man slowly began to leave.

"Cadet!"

A stout red-faced cadet snapped to attention by the box and stood motionless.

"Unhindered access to the switchbox is to be permitted to the battalion commander, the senior officer and myself. But to nobody else. In the case of an emergency, and if ordered by one of those three officers, you may break open the box, but whatever happens, make sure you don't damage the switchboard."

"Yes, sir."

Myshlayevsky approached Alexei Turbin and whispered:

"Did you see Maxim?"

"My God, yes, I did," came Turbin's whispered reply.

The battalion commander stood by the entrance to the assembly hall, a thousand lights playing on the silver edge of his sabre. He called Myshlayevsky over to him and said:

"So, Lieutenant, I'm so glad you've joined us. Good man!"

"Pleased to be of service, Colonel."

"All that's left for you now is to sort out the heating, here in the assembly hall, for the cadets on shift duty, and I'll take care of the rest. I'll make sure you have something to eat, and some vodka – not much, but enough to keep you warm."

Myshlayevsky smiled charmingly at the colonel and cleared his throat appreciatively.

But Turbin didn't listen to any more of their conversation. Leaning over the banister, he did not take his eyes off the white-haired figure until it disappeared out of sight. He was overcome by a feeling of emptiness and sadness. As he stood there, leaning on the cold banister, he remembered a particular event with especial clarity...

...A crowd of students of all ages was streaming excitedly along this very same corridor. Maxim, the thickset school beadle, grabbed at two small dark figures in the front of the crowd.

"Well, well, well," he mumbled, "the school inspector will be so pleased at the opportunity to feast his eyes upon Mr Turbin and Mr Myshlayevsky, particularly on the occasion of the school patron's visit. He will be so pleased, so extraordinarily pleased!"

These words of Maxim, it has to be said, were shot through with malicious irony. Only someone with the most perverted of tastes could have derived any pleasure from the sight presented by Messrs Turbin and Myshlayevsky, particularly on the joyous occasion of the school patron's visit.

Mr Myshlayevsky, firmly grasped by Maxim's left hand, had a split upper lip and his left sleeve was hanging by a thread. And Mr Turbin, gripped by Maxim's other hand, had lost his belt, and not only all his shirt buttons but also all his fly buttons had flown off, exposing his body and underclothes in the most scandalous way to anybody who cared to take a look.

"Let go of us, please, Maxim, be a good chap," implored Turbin and Myshlayevsky, looking up at Maxim, all expression draining from their bloodstained faces.

"That's it, Max! That's wonderful! Give him what for!" the boys behind them shouted excitedly. "He can't be allowed to get away with beating up his juniors!"

Oh, my God! What a day that was! Such sunshine, such a racket, such noise! Maxim then was quite different from the way he looked today – white-haired, melancholy and impoverished. His hair then was black and bristly, with only a few strands of grey showing through, he had metal claws rather than hands, and a medallion the size of a carriage wheel hung round his neck... Ah, yes, the wheel, the wheel, rolling on from village "B" making N number of revolutions, only to arrive finally at a stony void. God, it's so cold! We must defend now... but what exactly? Emptiness? The hollow sound of footsteps? Oh Alexander, will you really be able to save the dying building with your Borodino regiments? Come on, come to life and bring them all down from the canvas; they'd defeat Petlyura.

Turbin's legs carried him downstairs of their own accord. "Maxim!" he wanted to shout, but then he slowed down and stopped altogether. He imagined Maxim downstairs, in the basement apartment where the caretakers lived. No doubt he would have forgotten everything by now, and he would be sitting by the stove, trembling and crying. But Turbin was depressed enough without worrying about that. Enough of this stupid sentimentality: everyone had wasted their lives being too sentimental. Enough.

And yet, when Turbin had dismissed the medical orderlies, he found himself in an empty, dimly lit classroom, with blackboards looking down from the walls and desks standing in rows. Unable to restrain himself, he opened the lid of one of the desks and sat down. Everything felt so difficult, awkward and uncomfortable; the blackboard was too close for comfort. Yes, he could swear this was the classroom, or perhaps the one next door: the exact same view of the City from the window. Over there towered the lifeless mass of the university building. And yes, there was the boulevard, as straight as an arrow, lined with lamplight, the boxlike houses interspersed with dark gaps, the walls, the sky rising to infinity...

And outside it was like a performance of the opera *Christmas Eve*, with the snow and the lights dancing and twinkling... "I really would like to know what the shooting's about at Svyatoshin." It all sounded pretty harmless and distant, as if they were firing through cotton wool... *boom, boom...*

"That's enough," Turbin said to himself and closed the desk lid. He went out into the corridor, past the sentries, and through the vestibule out into the street. A machine gun was standing in the front entrance. The street was practically empty of pedestrians, and thick snow was falling.

That night the colonel was very busy. He made a large number of trips from the school to Madame Anjou's boutique, just a stone's throw away, and back again. By midnight everything was operating well and at full stretch. Hissing faintly, the arc lamps were bathing the school in a pinkish glow. The assembly hall had warmed up considerably – all evening the fires had been raging in the ancient stoves in the library alcoves along the sides of the main hall.

On Myshlayevsky's orders, the cadets had been stoking the stoves with copies of the literary journals *Notes of the Fatherland* and *Library* *for Reading** for the year 1863. Later, throughout the night, they had used old school desks, chopping them up to the clatter of axes. With two glasses of vodka inside them (the colonel had kept his promise and provided half a bucket of the stuff – enough to warm them up), Studzinsky and Myshlayevsky each kept two-hourly shifts throughout the night, taking turns to sleep on greatcoats alongside the cadets by the stove, the shadows and red glow from the fire playing on their faces. Then they would get up and check the sentry posts. Karas, together with a group of cadets manning machine guns, kept watch by the garden exits, while four cadets wearing sheepskin coats stood guard an hour at a time over the wide-barrelled mortars.

At Madame Anjou's the stove crackled away merrily, with the flues ringing and roaring. One of the cadets was standing guard by the exit, never taking his eyes off the motorcycle standing just outside in the street, while five cadets slept the sleep of the dead, having spread their greatcoats out on the floor of the shop. By one o'clock, the colonel had finally been able to settle down at Madame Anjou's. Even then, however, he did not go to bed, but was constantly on the telephone, yawning all the time. And then, at two o'clock in the morning, a motorcycle roared up to the shop and a military man in a grey coat climbed out.

"Let him through; it's for me," the colonel said.

The man handed the colonel a bulky package wrapped in a sheet and tied both ways with string. The colonel personally placed it in the little safe at the end of the shop and locked it with a padlock. The man in the greatcoat sped off on his motorbike, while the colonel went up to the gallery where, spreading his coat out on the floor and placing under his head a pile of rags, he lay down. After ordering the cadet on duty to wake him at exactly half-past six, he fell asleep.

7

PITCH-BLACK NIGHT had descended on the terraces of the finest spot on earth: Vladimir Hill, whose brick paths and alleyways were hidden under an endless downy mantle of virgin snow.

No inhabitant of the City ever sets foot on that huge, terraced prominence in the wintertime. And indeed, who would venture onto it at night, especially at such a time? It is simply a horrendous place! It's no place even for the brave. And in any case, there is nothing to do there. There is just one part that is lit: for one hundred years now the dark, metallic figure of St Vladimir has been standing on his awe-inspiring massive plinth, holding in his outstretched hand an eighteen-foot-high cross. Every evening, as soon the snowdrifts, slopes and terraces become enveloped in twilight, the cross lights up, continuing to shine throughout the night. The light is visible for some thirty miles, as far as the dark, distant plains stretching away in the direction of Moscow. But on the hillside itself very little is illuminated, just a feeble white light falling onto the dark green plinth and picking out of the darkness the balustrade and a section of the railing bordering the middle terrace. And that is all; go just a little distance away, and you'll find nothing but total darkness. The snow-capped trees have a strange appearance, like chandeliers wrapped in muslin, and you would sink up to your neck in the snowdrifts. Quite terrifying!

So you can understand why no one – even the most daring – should want to go there, mainly because there would be no point. But the City is a different matter. A night of alarm, of military activity. The street lamps shining like strings of beads. The Germans are asleep, but they're sleeping with half-closed eyes. In the darkest alleyway a blue cone of light suddenly erupts into life.

"Halt!"

Crunch... crunch... the sound of pawns in their basin-like helmets marching along in the middle of the street. Black ear mufflers... *crunch...* rifles not on shoulders, but held at the ready. There's no fooling about with Germans, at least not now... whatever you might think, Germans have to be taken seriously; they're like dung beetles.

"Documents!"

"Halt!"

A beam of torchlight pierces the dark. "Hey there, you!"

A large, black, shiny car, with four headlights. Clearly no ordinary car, for this gleaming carriage is being escorted by eight mounted troopers, proceeding at a leisurely trot. But the Germans remain indifferent to this and shout at the car:

"Halt!"

"Your name? Where are you going and why?"

"General of Cavalry Belorukov, Commander-in-Chief."

Now that was quite different, of course. Please, General, proceed. A pale moustached face behind the glass, in the depths of the car. The faint glimmer of a general's insignia on his coat. And the German basin-like helmets saluted. Deep down inside, it is true, they actually couldn't care less whether it was General Belorukov, or Petlyura, or some Zulu chief in this lousy country. But still, when in Zululand, do as the Zulus do. So the helmets saluted. Diplomatic courtesies, as the saying goes.

A night of military activity. Light streams through the windows of Madame Anjou's boutique, illuminating ladies' hats, corsets, ladies' drawers and Sevastopol cannon. The cadet on duty marches backwards and forwards like a pendulum, shivering from the cold, tracing the imperial monogram in the snow with his bayonet. And over there, in the Alexandrovsky High School, the assembly hall is lit up like a ballroom. Myshlayevsky, fortified by a sufficient quantity of vodka, is constantly on the move, glancing up at the portrait of Tsar Alexander the Blessed, as he makes his way to check the switchbox. The general mood in the school is cheerful but at the same time serious. The building is being guarded by eight machine guns and cadets – no, not students, but cadets! They'll fight, all right! Myshlayevsky's eyes are red, like a rabbit's. True, he won't get much sleep tonight, but he's had plenty of vodka, and there's a fair amount of tension to deal with. For the time being, things weren't too difficult in the City. If you're someone with a clear conscience, that's fine, please go on your way. You'll be stopped about five times, of course, but if you have your documents with you, then please, you're free to go. It's surprising you're out at night at all, but please, on your way...

But who would climb Vladimir Hill at this time? Absolute madness. Particularly with the wind howling through the snowdrifts like banshees from hell, as it does in that part of the world. If anyone were to climb the hill, then it could only be some totally desperate outcast who, in any regime on earth, would feel like a wolf in a pack of dogs. Utterly miserable, like one of Victor Hugo's characters. He would be the sort of person who should not show his face in the City – and if he were to dare show his face, it would be totally at his own risk. Should you manage to evade the patrols, then you've been lucky; but if not, you've only yourself to blame. If such a person were to find his way onto the hill, then he truly deserves our every sympathy.

You wouldn't wish it even on a dog. The wind is icy. Just five minutes in such a wind and you'll wish you were safe at home, and yet...

"Five hours out here and, my God, we'll freeze to death!"

The trouble was that you couldn't reach the Upper City by going past the lookout point and the water tower, because Prince Belorukov's headquarters, you understand, were situated in the monastery building in Mikhaylovskaya Street. And you were in constant danger of coming across a military convoy or armoured cars, or...

"Officers, damn it! Blast them to hell!"

Patrols, patrols and more patrols.

And there was absolutely no point in thinking you might be able to get down to the Lower City, to Podol, via the hillside terraces, firstly because of the tightly spaced street lamps on Alexandrovskaya Street winding its way round the foot of Vladimir Hill, and secondly because of the Germans, damn them! One patrol after another! But what if you tried just before dawn? You'd freeze to death in no time! And as the icy wind whistled along the alleyways, you imagined you could hear the murmur of voices in the snowdrifts by the railing.

"We'll freeze to death, Kirpaty!"

"Just be patient, Nemolyaka. The patrols will carry on till daylight, then they'll pack it in and go to bed. We'll slip through to the Embankment and stay at Sychika's for a bit of warmth."

Three dark shadows seemed to materialize out of the blackness and started moving along close to the railing, leaning over it to look down onto Alexandrovskaya Street immediately below. The street looked empty and silent, but at any moment two blue-white cones of light might appear and German armoured cars would come speeding along the street, or the sharply defined dark shadows of German troops in their steel helmets... And everything was so close...

One of the shadows on Vladimir Hill detached itself from the others.

"Hey, Nemolyaka..." he hissed through his teeth. "Let's risk it and go! We may be able to slip through..."

No, things are not right on Vladimir Hill.

And, believe it or not, things that night weren't going too well at the Hetman's palace, either: something rather unusual and unseemly was happening. An elderly footman with sideboards scurried like a mouse across the gleaming parquet floor of a large room furnished with dowdy gilt chairs. A distant electric bell rang fitfully, accompanied by the jingle of spurs. In one of the bedrooms, the mirrors with tarnished crown-topped frames reflected a strange, unnatural picture: a thin, greying, foxy individual with a clean-shaven face, as white as parchment, and a clipped moustache was pacing up and down in front of the mirrors. He was wearing an expensive Circassian coat with ornamental silver cartridge cases. Three German and two Russian officers were hovering nearby. One of the Russians was in a Circassian coat, like the foxy man in front of the mirrors, while the other was wearing a military jacket and riding breeches clearly indicating he was a cavalryman, although he was also sporting Hetmanite wedge-shaped epaulettes. They had been helping the foxy man change his clothes. This process had entailed helping him put on his Circassian coat, a pair of broad-bottomed trousers and patent-leather boots. He was now wearing the uniform of a typical German major and, as such, he looked no better and no worse than hundreds of similar German majors. Then the door opened and the dusty palace curtains parted to admit another man, wearing the uniform of a doctor in the German army and carrying a large number of packets. He opened the packets and, with clinically deft movements, bandaged the head of the newly born German major in such a way that all that remained visible was the latter's foxy right eye and thin lips, which were half open to reveal a number of gold and platinum capped teeth.

These unseemly goings-on at the palace continued for a little while. On his way out, the doctor, speaking in German, told the group of officers who were lounging about in the room with the dowdy gilt chairs, as well as in the neighbouring room, that Major von Schratt had accidentally wounded himself in the neck while unloading his revolver and that he needed to be taken to the German military hospital as a matter of urgency. A telephone rang somewhere, followed by a bird-like tweet from a second telephone. Then a German ambulance with Red Cross markings drove silently through the wrought-iron gates and drew up at the side entrance. Swathed in bandages and wrapped from head to foot in his greatcoat, the mysterious Major von Schratt was carried out on a stretcher. The ambulance's side door slid open, and he was placed inside. The ambulance drove off with a muffled roar and turned out of the palace gates.

Meanwhile, in the palace itself, the commotion continued right through until the morning. The lights continued to burn in the portrait galleries and in the gilded halls, telephones rang, and the servants' faces began to adopt an expression that was little short of insolent, their eyes lighting up to show their amusement at the whole business.

In a cramped little room on the ground floor of the palace, a man wearing the uniform of a colonel in the artillery regiment was standing by the telephone. Before lifting the receiver he first carefully closed the door of the small whitewashed communications room, a room that was totally unlike any other room in the palace. He asked the unsleeping operator at the exchange to connect him with telephone number 212.

Obtaining the number, he said *merci* and, frowning with anxiety, asked in a soft, confidential tone:

"Is that the headquarters of the mortar battalion?"

Alas, alas! Despite his best intentions, Colonel Malyshev was not able to sleep through until half-past six the following morning. At 4 a.m. the little bird at Madame Anjou's started tweeting with extraordinary persistence, and the cadet on duty was forced to wake the colonel. The colonel awoke with astonishing speed, his brain getting into gear and operating at full stretch immediately, as if he hadn't been to sleep at all. The colonel, furthermore, wasn't angry with the cadet for interrupting his sleep. A little after four he was whisked away somewhere by the motorcycle and, by five o'clock, when he returned to Madame Anjou's, he was frowning with anxiety, his expression exactly like that of the other colonel who had telephoned the mortar battalion from the palace communications room.

At seven o'clock the next morning, the very same extended file of men who had marched up the staircase towards the portrait of Tsar Alexander the previous evening stood by the battlefield of Borodino, illuminated in a rosy light. Huddled together from the pre-dawn cold, they were grumbling and muttering among themselves. Staff Captain Studzinsky stood among the group of officers, a little apart from his men. And strange as it may sound, his eyes reflected exactly the same anxious expression as those of Colonel Malyshev four hours earlier. But anybody who might have seen both the colonel and the staff captain during that notorious night would definitely have been able to tell the difference between them: Studzinsky's expression was one of anxiety about the future, whereas Malyshev's was one of certainty that he knew and understood exactly what the future held in store for them. Sticking out from the sleeve of Studzinsky's greatcoat was a long list of the names of the men in his battalion. Having just taken the roll-call, he was now certain that the unit was twenty men short. This would explain why the list was crumpled and bore the marks of his fingers all over it.

The air was thick with smoke from the officers' cigarettes.

At precisely seven o'clock – to the minute – Colonel Malyshev appeared before the assembled men, to be greeted, as he had been during the evening before, by a roar of welcome. And just like the previous evening, the colonel's silver sabre was belted on his waist, except that this time, for some reason, its silver blade was not reflected a thousand times by the light. A revolver in its holster hung on his right hip. The holster was unbuttoned – the result, no doubt, of Colonel Malyshev's uncharacteristically agitated state of mind.

The colonel stepped out in front of his men, his gloved left hand placed on the hilt of his sword and his uncovered right hand fingering his holster. He began to speak, as follows:

"I would ask the officers and men of the mortar battalion to listen carefully to what I am about to say. During the course of the night there have been marked and sudden changes affecting our position as a battalion, the wider position of the army and, I would say, the overall political position of the Ukraine. As a result, I am announcing the disbandment of the battalion. I would consequently like each of you to remove all insignia from your uniforms, to take from the armaments store anything you're able to carry and that you might require, and then to disperse to your own homes, where you are to lie concealed, without giving yourselves away, and await a further summons from me."

He fell silent for a moment, thereby underscoring even further the absolute and utter silence that filled the assembly hall. Even the lamps ceased their hissing. Everybody, officers and men, had their eyes fixed on one thing in the room – the colonel's clipped moustache.

"Such a summons," he continued, "will follow as soon as there is any change in the position. But the chances of this happening, I have to say, are slim. I myself have no idea how everything will work out, but I think that the best that can be expected by each... er... by the *best*" (the colonel said with sudden emphasis) "among you is that you will be sent to join the forces on the Don. I therefore order the entire battalion, with the exception of those officers and cadets who have been guarding the building overnight, to disperse to their homes immediately!"

"What's this?! What's this?!" the entire body of men started whispering incredulously, and the forest of bayonets seemed to dip and wilt. Among many there was a look of utter bewilderment but, among some others, one of apparent jubilation.

Staff Captain Studzinsky, his eyes askance and his face a bluish pale colour, detached himself from the group of officers and took several steps towards Colonel Malyshev. Then he stopped and glanced round at the officers. But rather than look at the staff captain, Myshlayevsky kept his eyes firmly fixed on Colonel Malyshev's moustache, his expression indicating, as was his wont, that he wanted nothing better than to utter a whole string of obscenities. Karas just stood there blinking absurdly, his arms akimbo, while a separate group of young ensigns could be heard whispering one damning, alarming word: "Arrest!"

"What's this? What are they saying?" said somebody in a bass voice among the ranks of cadets.

"Arrest!"

"Treachery!"

As if taking inspiration from the light overhead, Studzinsky suddenly looked up. Then he glanced quickly down at the butt of his holster and shouted:

"Number 1 Platoon!"

The front rank broke up and several grey figures detached themselves from it. A weirdly confused scene followed.

"Colonel," Studzinsky said, his voice totally hoarse, "you are under arrest."

"Arrest him!" one of the ensigns suddenly shouted hysterically, stepping out towards the colonel.

"Wait, gentlemen!" shouted Karas unhurriedly, sizing up the situation.

Myshlayevsky leapt briskly out of the group of officers, seized the impulsive ensign by the sleeve of his greatcoat and tugged him back.

"Let go of me, Lieutenant!" the ensign snarled, his mouth twisted with rage.

"Be quiet!" the colonel shouted in an unusually assured voice. His mouth, it is true, was no less twisted than the ensign's, and his face had gone red and blotchy, but the expression in his eyes was more assured than was the case with any of the officers. And everybody stood still.

"Quiet!" the colonel repeated. "I order you to stay still and listen to me!"

There was now absolute silence in the hall, and Myshlayevsky immediately looked alarmed. It was if a light had suddenly been switched on in his head and he was waiting for the colonel to say something that would prove to be of greater import and interest than anything he had said earlier.

"So then," the colonel said, his cheek twitching. "Right, so then... I can see now exactly how fortunate I would have been if I had gone into battle with the unit that the Lord God has seen fit to provide me with. Really fortunate! But although it might be possible to forgive such behaviour in the case of a student volunteer, or a young cadet, or perhaps even an ensign in extreme circumstances, this would be totally out of the question in your case, staff captain!"

As he said this, the colonel gave Studzinsky a piercing look of quite exceptional hostility, his eyes flashing with genuine irritation. Once again the room fell silent.

"Right, then," the colonel continued, "I have never in my life participated in a rally until now, but it looks as if I shall have to do so. All right then, let's have a debate! Your attempt to arrest your commanding officer shows you to be good patriots, but it also reveals your... er, how can I put it?... inexperience as officers! To put it briefly, I don't have the time to waste and, I can assure you," the colonel emphasized with menacing significance, "neither have you. Now let me put a question to you: who is it you wish to defend?"

Silence.

"I'm asking you: who is it you wish to defend?"

Myshlayevsky, burning with interest and curiosity, stepped forward from the rest, saluted, and said:

"It is our duty to defend the Hetman, colonel."

"The Hetman, you say?" responded the colonel. "Excellent! Battalion, atten-shun!" he bawled suddenly with such force that the squadron instinctively shuddered. "Well, listen to this: earlier this morning, at about four o'clock, the Hetman fled the City, thereby shamefully abandoning us to our fate! Just ran away, like a total blackguard and coward. And an hour later, the Hetman was joined by our army commander, General of Cavalry Belorukov, both of them heading for a German train that was waiting for them. And within a few hours at most we will be witnesses to a catastrophe, in which people such as yourselves, hoodwinked and embroiled in a venture not of your own choosing, will be slaughtered like cattle. Listen: Petlyura is now drawing close to the City with an army of more than one hundred thousand men, and tomorrow... wait, what am I talking about?... not tomorrow, but today," here the colonel pointed out of the window, indicating where the sky over the City was already beginning to turn blue, "scattered and broken units of unfortunate officers and cadets, abandoned by staff-officer bastards and those two scoundrels who deserve only to be hanged, will come up against Petlyura's well-armed troops, who will outnumber them by twenty to one... Listen, my children," Colonel Malyshev suddenly shouted, his voice breaking. Although he used the term "my children" to address the massed ranks standing in front of him with their bayonets fixed, the colonel himself was actually more of an age to be their older brother rather than their father. "Listen: as Staff Captain Studzinsky will testify, I am an officer in the regular army who fought against the Germans throughout the war, and I am informing you that the responsibility for everything is mine and mine alone! It is on my conscience! I am sending you home! Do you understand?" he shouted.

"Yes," they all answered, their bayonets swaying. Then one of the cadets in the second rank broke into a fit of loud, convulsive weeping.

Totally unexpectedly for the entire battalion and, no doubt, for himself, Staff Captain Studzinsky, in a gesture not fully befitting an officer, covered his eyes with his hands, allowing the list of names to fall on the floor, and burst into tears.

Following the staff captain's example, many other cadets started sobbing, and the ranks of men began to break up. The voice of Radamès-Myshlayevsky rose above the disorderly hubbub of noise.

"Cadet Pavlovsky!" he barked at the bugler. "Sound the retreat!"

"May I have permission, Colonel, to set fire to the school building?" asked Myshlayevsky, looking directly at the colonel.

"No, you may not," Malyshev replied courteously and calmly.

"Colonel, sir," Myshlayevsky said emotionally, "Petlyura will get hold of the armaments store, the weapons and most importantly…" he added, pointing at the door into the vestibule where the head of Tsar Alexander could be seen rising above the stairwell.

"Yes, he will," confirmed the colonel politely.

"But then why, Colonel?"

Malyshev turned to Myshlayevsky with a thoughtful look on his face.

"Lieutenant," he said, "in three hours' time Petlyura will be claiming the lives of hundreds of people, and my only regret will be that I will be unable to prevent their deaths by sacrificing my own life, as well as yours – far more valuable than mine of course. I would ask you never to bring up the subject of the portraits, guns and rifles again."

"Colonel," Studzinsky said, coming up to Malyshev, "on my own behalf, and also on behalf of the officers whom I incited to behave in that disgraceful fashion just now, I would ask you to accept our apologies."

"Accepted," answered the colonel courteously.

By the time the morning mist lying over the City had begun to disperse, the blunt-snouted mortars standing on the school square had had their breechblocks removed, and the rifles and machine guns, now smashed into pieces, had been flung into the recesses of the attic. Whole piles of shells had been tossed into holes dug in the snow and into the hidey-holes of the cellars, and the lights in the assembly hall and the corridors had been extinguished. On Myshlayevsky's orders, the white switchboard had been smashed by cadets wielding their bayonets.

Outside, the sky was now totally blue. And under the blue sky, Myshlayevsky and Karas – the two who had been the last to leave the school – stopped for a moment on the square to talk.

"Did the commander warn Alexei?" Myshlayevsky asked Karas anxiously.

"Of course he did; you could see for yourself that he wasn't around," answered Karas.

"Will we be able to get to the Turbins this afternoon?"

"No, that won't be possible while it's still light. There's lots to do, including hiding things away. Let's go back to the apartment."

The sun was now shining in a blue sky. The mist was lifting and dispersing.

Part Two

8

Y ES, THERE HAD BEEN MIST... together with needle-sharp frost, hoary coniferous branches and snow – dark, moonless snow – falling just before daybreak. Beyond the City, in the distance, the blue cupolas of churches dotted with tinsel-like stars were visible, while, on the far Moscow bank of the Dnieper, the illuminated cross on the top of the statue of St Vladimir rose high into the fathomless sky, shining until dawn.

With daybreak, the light on the cross went out, and the stars disappeared. But the day didn't brighten up especially, threatening to become rather grey – the Ukraine was covered with a low-lying layer of impenetrable cloud.

In the village of Popelyukha, some eight miles from the City, Colonel Kozyr-Leshko* awoke exactly at daybreak, with the meagre light trickling like sour milk through the narrow little window of his hut. His awakening coincided with the word "position".

It seemed at first that the word had simply appeared as if part of a warm dream while he was fast asleep; he had even tried to brush it aside with his hand, as if it were cold to the touch. But the word expanded and made its presence felt in the hut, together with the crumpled envelope and the revolting red pimples on the face of his batman. Taking his mica map case to the window, he pulled out a map, found the village of Borkhuny, then Bely Hai, and started tracing with his fingernail along the network of roads, dotted with little bushes on either side, like flies, until he came to the huge black area denoting the City. In addition to the smell of the strong, cheap tobacco that Kozyr himself smoked, the room was filled with the reek of strong low-grade tobacco from the possessor of the red pimples, who was under the assumption not only that he could smoke in Kozyr's presence, but also that he would not thereby be harming the war effort.

Kozyr was faced with the immediate prospect of going into battle. Reacting cheerfully to the idea, he gave a huge yawn and buckled on the intricate harness, slinging the straps over his shoulder. He had slept that night in his greatcoat, not even removing his spurs. A peasant woman came bustling in with a jug of milk, but Kozyr never drank milk and wasn't about to start now. Some young children appeared from nowhere and started crawling about. One of them, the smallest, with a completely naked behind, crawled along the shelf and clambered up to get hold of Kozyr's Mauser. But before he could get to it Kozyr had already strapped it on.

All his life, up until 1914, Kozyr had been a village teacher. In that year he went to war with a regiment of dragoons, and by 1917 he had been commissioned. And now, at dawn on 14th December 1918, Kozyr found himself to be a colonel in Petlyura's army, and nobody in the world (least of all Kozyr himself) could explain how this had happened. But it had happened because for him, Kozyr, war was a vocation, whereas teaching had been a drawn-out and major mistake. This, however, can be a frequent occurrence in our lives. For twenty whole years someone can be engaged in doing something or other – lecturing in Roman law, for example – and then, suddenly, in the twenty-first year, it turns out that Roman law has become totally irrelevant, that it is a subject he neither understands nor likes, and that he is in actual fact a keen gardener with a passion for flowers. This happens, it might be supposed, because of the imperfections in the way in which society is organized, as a result of which people often find their true vocation only towards the end of their lives. Kozyr found his at the age of forty-five. Before then, he had been a poor teacher, tedious and cruel to his pupils.

"Right, tell the lads to get outside and mount their horses," Kozyr said in Ukrainian, tightening the creaking straps around his waist.

Smoke was rising above the white huts of Popelyukha as Colonel Kozyr's column of troops, about four hundred sabres strong, rode out of the village. Wreaths of cheap tobacco smoke hung over the column, and Kozyr's fifteen-hand bay stallion trotted nervously under him. The baggage wagons creaked along, strung out for a few hundred yards behind the column. The men swayed in their saddles and, as soon as the regiment was out of Popelyukha, they unfurled a two-coloured banner at the head of the column – one yellow strip and one blue strip attached to a pole.

Kozyr couldn't stand tea, preferring more than anything a measure of vodka in the morning. He loved "Imperial" vodka – something that hadn't been around for four years, but that now, under the Hetman, had become available throughout the Ukraine. The vodka poured from Kozyr's grey flask and into his veins like a hot flame. It ran, too, through the veins of his men, poured from mess tins obtained from a store in Belaya Tserkov and, once it had taken effect, a three-sectioned accordion struck up at the head of the column, and someone started singing in a falsetto voice:

"Oh the woods, the woods, the forests of green,
that stretch as far as the eye can see..."

The song being taken up by the basses in the fifth row:

"...the young girl was ploughing the field
with a strong black ox that refused to yield;
and when the ox – oh, the ox – went its own way,
she asked a Cossack on his fiddle to play..."

The trooper carrying the banner started whistling happily like a nightingale and cracking his whip. Lances and black-braided and black-tasselled fur caps swayed along in time with the singing. Snow crunched under a thousand iron-shod hooves. A tapping drum added to the general sense of merriment.

"That's it lads! Keep your spirits up!" Kozyr shouted approvingly, as the nightingale song soared up over the snow-covered Ukrainian fields.

When they had passed through Bely Hai the mist lifted. All the roads were black with troops, the snow crunching underfoot as they marched along. At a crossroads near Hai they allowed a fifteen-hundred-strong group of infantrymen to go ahead of them. The men in the front ranks, all from Galicia, were wearing identical dark-blue jerkins made from good-quality German cloth, and their faces were more refined and mobile than Kozyr's troopers. The men towards the rear were wearing long hospital gowns reaching down to their ankles with yellow leather belts tied round the waist. On their heads, bobbing above their fur caps, they all wore battered German helmets. Their metal-soled boots pounded the snow beneath them.

All this activity had turned the snow on the roads leading to the City black.

"Hurrah!" cheered the infantrymen as they marched past the blue-and-yellow banner.

"Hurrah!" echoed the woods around Hai.

The cheers were answered by gunfire on their left flank and to the rear. During the night the commander of the besieging forces, Colonel Toropets, had sent two batteries to take up their positions in the City park. The snow-covered pine trees, tall and straight as masts, awoke to the thunderous sound of waves of six-inch shells. Two rounds landed near the large settlement of Pushcha-Voditsa, shattering all the glass in the windows of four snowbound houses. Several pine trees were reduced to splinters, sending fountains of snow cascading many yards into the air. But then the gunfire in Pushcha died down. The forest stood there, once again half-asleep; only the alarmed squirrels scurried and clawed their way up and down the hundred-year-old tree trunks. The two gun batteries were transferred from their position near Pushcha to the right flank. They moved across the seemingly endless ploughed fields, then through the wooded area around Urochishche, and turned down a narrow path until they reached a fork in the road where they stopped and deployed, now within sight of the City. Then, in the early hours of the morning, they started shelling Podgorodnaya, Savskaya and the City suburb of Kurenyovka with high-bursting shrapnel.

In the low-lying snowy sky there was a rattling sound as if someone were playing on a musical instrument. The inhabitants had been sheltering in their cellars since early morning and, in the half-light of dawn, frozen groups of cadets could be seen making their way towards the centre of the City. The gunfire, however, soon ceased, to be replaced by the animated crackle of small-arms fire somewhere on the outskirts, to the north of the City. Then that, too, fell silent.

The train carrying the commander of the troops besieging the City, Colonel Toropets, stood at a small station somewhere deep in the forests about two miles from the snowbound deserted village of Svyatoshin – still reeling from the deafening crash and thunder of gunfire. Throughout the night the electric light had been burning in all six carriages, and the station telephone, as well as the field telephones in Toropets's grimy compartment, had never stopped squawking. As soon as the snowy landscape outside had emerged into the full light of day, the guns farther up the line from Svyatoshin to Post-Volynsky started thundering away, and the little birds in the yellow receivers burst into song once again.

"We've taken Svyatoshin," the thin, nervous Toropets informed his adjutant, Khudyakovsky. "Find out, if you please, whether we can now move up to it."

Toropets's train slowly started to move between the walls of tall snow-covered trees, stopping close to where the railway line was crossed by a major road that pointed like an arrow straight into the heart of the City. Here, in his compartment, Toropets began to carry out the plan that he had devised over two sleepless nights in this selfsame bug-ridden carriage no. 4173.

Shrouded in mist, the City was surrounded on all sides: to the north, forest and ploughed fields; to the west, the captured village of Svyatoshin; to the south-west, the ill-fated Post-Volynsky; and to the south, where the railway line bordered the woods, there were cemeteries, pastures and a shooting range. And there was cavalry on the move everywhere, the horses' harnesses jingling as they crept in a black tide along the tracks and railway lines, or advanced unhindered across the snowy plains. The heavy gun carts creaked, while Petlyura's infantry, worn out by a whole month of hanging about in reserve, became bogged down in the snow.

In the apartment of Toropets's train, with its scuffed cloth floor, the telephone trilled incessantly, and the operators Franko and Haras, not having had a wink's sleep all night, began to fool about, making silly noises over the phone.

Toropets's plan was a cunning one, just as he himself – the black-browed, clean-shaven, nervous Colonel Toropets – was a cunning man. It was not for nothing that he had posted two gun batteries close to the City's forest, nor was it for nothing that his shells had crashed through the frosty air to destroy the tramline in the shabby village of Pushcha-Voditsa. Neither was it a coincidence that he had then moved his machine guns across from the ploughed fields to a position where they would be closer to the army's left flank. Toropets wanted to pull the wool across the eyes of those defending the City by pretending that he would be taking the City from the springboard of his, Toropets's, left flank (that is, from the north), and from the suburb of Kurenyovka, thereby drawing their army over in that direction. In actual fact, however, he would be striking right at the heart of the City by moving directly from Svyatoshin along the Brest-Litovsk highway, as well as by thrusting forward from the extreme right flank in the south, from the village of Demiyevka.

And so, in accordance with Toropets's plan, elements of Petlyura's army, moving along the roads, made their way across from the left flank to the right. Among them were the black-capped troopers of Kozyr-Leshko's regiment, marching, with the NCOs in the lead, to the accompaniment of pipes and accordion.

"Hurrah!" echoed the woods around Hai. "Hurrah!"

Advancing, they left Hai behind them and crossed the railway line by a wooden bridge, where they came within sight of the City. The City was still warm from sleep, and the sky was wreathed either in mist or smoke. Standing up on his stirrups and looking through his Zeiss binoculars, Kozyr could see the roofs of the huge multi-storey buildings and the cupola of the ancient St Sophia Cathedral.

On Kozyr's right flank, fighting was already under way. Less than a mile away he could hear the metallic crash of heavy guns and the rattle of machine-gun fire. Detachments of Petlyura's infantry could be seen dashing across in the direction of Post-Volynsky, while uncoordinated and assorted detachments of White Guard infantry, stunned by the intense shelling, were falling back from Post...

The City. Low, cloud-covered sky. A street corner. Houses to one side. The occasional greatcoat.

"It's just been announced that there's been some sort of agreement with Petlyura to allow all armed Russian troops to leave the City and join Denikin on the Don."

"Well? And?"

The crash and thunder of gunfire.

The whine of a machine gun.

Despairing, baffled cadet's voice:

"But doesn't that mean we'll have to stop resisting?"

Despondent cadet's voice:

"Who the devil knows?"

Colonel Shchetkin hadn't been at army headquarters that morning, for the very simple reason that the headquarters no longer existed. On the night of 14th December it had left for City Passenger Railway Station No. 1, spending the night at the hotel Rose of Stamboul, right next to the telegraph office. There Shchetkin's telephone had trilled once or twice during the night, but by morning it had fallen silent. And that morning two of Colonel Shchetkin's adjutants vanished without trace. An hour later, after rummaging around in boxes full of papers and tearing some documents into shreds, Shchetkin himself left the grubby Rose, no longer in his grey greatcoat with epaulettes, but in a civilian fur coat and a pork-pie hat. Where they had come from, no one had any idea.

Taking a cab one block away from the Rose, Shchetkin went to a small but well-furnished apartment in Lipki, rang the bell, kissed a generously proportioned golden-haired woman and retired with her to a secluded bedroom. Her eyes widened in shock as he looked directly into them and whispered:

"That's it, it's all over! I'm exhausted..." he said, and went behind an alcove, where he fell asleep after drinking a cup of black coffee prepared for him by the hands of the golden-haired lady.

The cadets of the First Infantry Detachment knew nothing about any of this. And this was a pity! Had they known, their desire to fight would have been diminished and, instead of stumbling about under a shrapnel-torn sky at Post-Volynsky, they would have made their way to that cosy little apartment in Lipki, seized Colonel Shchetkin, dragged him outside and hanged him from the nearest lamp-post right opposite the golden-haired woman's apartment.

Had they done this, it would have been really good. But they didn't do it, because they didn't know or understand anything that was going on.

And, indeed, nobody understood anything about what was happening in the City, and it was quite likely that it would be a long time before anyone did understand. There were still some metal-helmeted Germans in the City – although, it is true, they were somewhat demoralized. Maybe the foxy Hetman, too, with his trimmed moustache was still there (only very few people knew about the wounding of the mysterious Major von Schratt in the neck that morning); possibly also His Excellency Prince Belorukov; and General Kartuzov, responsible for setting up detachments charged with the defence of the mother of Russian cities. The headquarters' telephones were still trilling, although nobody was yet aware that, since early morning, these very same headquarters had begun to melt away. In general, however, the City was full of military men. There was real anger in the City whenever Petlyura's name was mentioned, and he was still being mocked by dissolute St Petersburg journalists in that morning's edition of the *News*. While cadets were walking around inside the City, out there, in the suburbs, the whistle of Petlyura's approaching black-capped cavalry could already be heard, together with the high-spirited Ukrainian Cossacks as they moved jauntily across from the army's left flank to the right. And if their whistling could be heard only a couple of miles away, then what hope was there for the Hetman? And the whistling meant they were coming to get him! Maybe the Germans would come to his rescue? But then why were those stolid Germans just sitting around at Fastov Station, grinning apathetically into their clipped German moustaches as unit after unit of Petlyura's army passed them on their way to the City? Perhaps there had been some agreement with Petlyura to allow him to enter the City peacefully? But if so, why the hell should the White officers' guns still be firing at him?

No, nobody will ever understand what was going on in the City during the afternoon of 14th December.

The headquarters' telephones were still trilling away, albeit, it is true, less and less often…

Less often!

Now only occasionally!

Rrring!…

"What's going on?"

Rrring!…

"More ammunition to Colonel… Stepanov…"

"Ivanov…"

"Antonov… Stratonov!…"

"We should go to the Don, lads, immediately… nothing's going right here, damn it."

Rrring!

"To hell with those bastards at HQ!"

"To the Don!"

The telephones rang less and less often. By midday, they had all but stopped.

All around the City, now in one place, now in another, there was the intermittent thunder of gunfire… But despite all the noise, life in the City at midday continued much as normal. The shops were open and trading as usual. The pavements were filled with a mass of scurrying pedestrians, doors slammed and the trams continued to run along the streets, their bells ringing.

But then, at midday, there was a lively burst of machine-gun fire from the Pechersk region of the City. The Pechersk hills echoed to the staccato rattle that could be heard as far away as the City centre. My goodness, that was a bit close, wasn't it? What's going on? Passers-by stopped and began to sniff the air. Immediately there were noticeably fewer people on some of the pavements.

What? Who?

Ratatat… ratatatat… atatat… ta… ta!

"Who's that firing then?"

"What do you mean who? Don't you know? That's Colonel Bolbotun!"

*

So, he'd rebelled against Petlyura, had he?

Tired of attempting to carry out Colonel Toropets's complicated staff plan, Colonel Bolbotun had decided to speed things up. His cavalry had been frozen, just hanging around behind the cemetery in the very south of the City, where it was only a stone's throw to the wise, ancient, snow-covered Dnieper. And Bolbotun had been frozen too. So with a flourish of his whip he had sent his regiment moving off in threes, spreading out along the road and onto the railway line hugging the edge of the City. Here Bolbotun met with no resistance. Six of his machine guns started firing with such force that the sound crashed like thunder around the entire low-lying wooded area near Nizhnyaya Telichka. In a flash, Bolbotun cut off the railway line, halting a passenger train which had just crossed the bridge over the Dnieper, bringing a fresh consignment of Muscovites and Petersburgers with their chic women and long-haired dogs. Everyone went crazy with fear, but just at that moment Bolbotun was too busy to be concerned with dogs. Accompanied by the whistle of shunting engines, the alarmed empty goods wagons moved from the freight depot to the passenger station, and Bolbotun's men sent a hail of bullets crashing onto the roofs of houses on Svyatotroitskaya Street. Bolbotun continued on into the City and along the street, making unimpeded progress as far as the military academy, where he sent his cavalry on ahead to scout along every little alleyway. It wasn't until he reached the peeling columns of the Nikolayev Academy that he came up against his first opposition. Here he was met by machine-gun and ragged rifle fire from isolated units. One of the Cossacks in the forward troop of the leading squadron, Butsenko, was killed, five men were wounded and two horses had their legs shattered. As a result, Bolbotun's progress was for a time delayed. He imagined, mistakenly, that he was confronted by unknown numbers of the enemy, whereas in actual fact the blue-capped colonel was faced by only thirty cadets with four officers and one machine gun.

Bolbotun quickly ordered his columns to dismount, take cover and return the cadets' fire. The whole Pechersk region was filled with the sound of gunfire echoing along the walls of the buildings. In the area of Millionnaya Street everything came rapidly to the boil.

The effect of Bolbotun's incursion into the city was immediate. The metal shutters in the shops lining Yelisavetinskaya, Vinogradnaya and Levashovskaya Streets came crashing down, the brightly lit shop windows went dark, and the pavements immediately emptied, becoming strangely resonant. Caretakers hastily closed gates.

The effect of Bolbotun's advance was also felt in the City centre: the trilling of the field telephones at army headquarters began to fall silent.

A gun battery telephones its headquarters. No answer, damn it! An infantry detachment telephones its commanding officer, and manages to get through to someone. But the voice at the other end just mutters some incoherent nonsense.

"Are your officers still wearing epaulettes?"

"What's that?"

Rrring, rrring...

"Send a detachment to Pechersk immediately!"

"What's that?"

Rrring...

The name Bolbotun crept from street to street... Bolbotun... Bolbotun...

How did people know that it was definitely Bolbotun and not someone else? The answer was not clear, but there was no doubt that people knew. Perhaps they knew it was Bolbotun because, from midday onwards, certain people wearing coats with lambskin collars began to mix with pedestrians and the usual City types lounging around. These people were everywhere, darting in and out of the crowd. They would fix cadets and gold-braided officers with long, lingering stares and begin to whisper.

"Bolbotun's in town," they would say, without any note of sadness in their voice. On the contrary: their eyes showed just how happy they were at the idea.

"Hurrah!" they seemed to be saying. "Huuuuurrrraaahhh," came the echo from the hills around Pechersk.

This was the signal for all kinds of nonsense:

"Bolbotun is Grand Prince Mikhail Alexandrovich."

"Not at all: Bolbotun is actually Grand Prince Nikolai Nikolayevich."

"No, Bolbotun's simply Bolbotun."

"There'll be a Jewish pogrom."

"No, there won't – just the opposite: they're wearing red ribbons."

"We'd better get home quickly."

"Bolbotun is against Petlyura."

"No, he's not, he's for the Bolsheviks."

"Quite the opposite, he's for the Tsar, but without any officers."

"The Hetman's gone, hasn't he?"

"Surely not! Really? Really?"

Rrring... rrring.

*

A Bolbotun reconnaissance group led by Cossack Lieutenant Galanba was trotting down a totally empty Millionnaya Street. Then, suddenly – can you imagine it? – a door opens, and none other than the famous army contractor Yakov Grigoryevich Feldman comes dashing out and makes straight for the five mounted Cossack troopers. Have you taken leave of your senses, Yakov Grigoryevich, that you should even think it necessary to come running out at such a time, when such things are going on? And certainly Yakov Grigoryevich had the expression of someone who has taken leave of his senses. His hat had toppled onto the back of his head, his coat was unbuttoned and his eyes were rolling all over the place.

Yakov Grigoryevich Feldman had good cause to go out of his mind. The moment the gunfire had started in the vicinity of the military academy, he had heard a groan coming from his wife's lovely little bedroom. Another groan followed, then silence.

"Oy vey," Yakov Grigoryevich said in response to the groan. He looked out of the window and convinced himself that things were not good at all: nothing but empty streets and gunfire.

But then the groaning increased in volume, cutting through his heart like a knife. His round-shouldered old mother poked her head round the bedroom door and shouted:

"Yasha! It's begun! Do you understand?"

And Yakov Grigoryevich's thoughts focused immediately on one place – the corner house at the very end of Millionnaya Street, next to the patch of waste ground, where there was a small rusty sign announcing in gold letters:

MIDWIFE
E.T. SHADURSKAYA

Although Millionnaya Street wasn't a major road, it wasn't particularly safe: people were firing along it from Pechersk Square towards the upper part of the City.

Just make it there, that's all he wants to do!... With his hat on the back of his head, his eyes bulging with terror, Yakov Grigoryevich Feldman slinks along the wall.

"Halt! Where do you think you're going?"

Galanba leant down from his saddle. Feldman stood there, his face black as thunder, his eyes rolling, as he noticed the green Cossack ribbons on their caps.

"I'm just a peaceful citizen, sir. My wife's giving birth and I need the midwife."

"The midwife, you say? So why are you skulking about by the wall, eh, you horrible little Yid!"

"Sir, I—"

Feldman felt the sergeant's whip curl like a snake round his fur collar and his neck. He screamed out from the hellish pain, and his face, no longer black as thunder, turned white. As he stared at the Cossacks' tassels, he had a sudden mental image of his wife.

"Papers!"

Feldman pulled out his document wallet, opened it and took out the first piece of paper. But, as soon as he had done so, he started trembling: he'd suddenly remembered something... oh God, oh God! What had he done? Why on earth had he taken out that piece of paper? But how could he possibly be worried about such trivial matters while dashing out of the house with his wife in labour? Oh, woe to Feldman! Sergeant Galanba grabbed at the document immediately. It was just a small piece of paper with a stamp, but for Feldman it meant death.

The holder of this pass, Yakov Grigoryevich Feldman, is hereby permitted to enter and leave the City freely for the purposes of supplying the armoured units of the City garrison with equipment, and to move freely about the City after 12 midnight.

Signed: Quartermaster General, Major-General *Illarionov*.

Adjutant, Lieutenant *Leshchinsky*.

Feldman's job was to supply General Kartuzov with lard, together with petroleum jelly for greasing his artillery pieces.

Please, God, let there be a miracle!

"But, sir, that's the wrong document!... Please..."

"No, it's the right document," said Galanba, grinning evilly. "Don't worry, we can read it for ourselves."

Please God, let there be a miracle! You can have eleven thousand roubles... take it all. But just let me live, just let me live! *Sh'ma Yisrael!**

But no miracle was forthcoming, and it was as well for Feldman that he died an easy death; Sergeant Galanba had no time to waste and so, with just a single downward sweep of his sabre, he sliced through Feldman's head.

9

HAVING LOST SEVEN COSSACKS and seven horses, with nine of his men wounded, Colonel Bolbotun continued to advance from Pechersk Square for another few hundred yards until he reached Rezinkovskaya Street, where he stopped. Here reinforcements had joined the retreating group of cadets, including one armoured car. Looking like an ungainly grey tortoise with gun turrets, the armoured car lumbered along Moskovskaya Street, firing three rounds from its three-inch gun in the direction of Pechersk with a noise like the rustling of dry leaves. Bolbotun quickly dismounted: he ordered the horses to be led off down a side street and his men, now on foot, to fall back a little way towards Pechersk Square and take cover. A fitful exchange of fire ensued. Firing the occasional round, the armoured tortoise blocked off Moskovskaya Street, accompanied by some sparse shooting from the end of Suvorovskaya Street, where a detachment who had fallen back from Pechersk Square under fire from Bolbotun had dug themselves into the snow. With them were the reinforcements who had joined them and who had been obtained as follows:

Rrring... rrring...

"First Infantry Detachment?"

"Speaking."

"Two companies of officers to be sent to Pechersk immediately."

"Yes, sir."

Rrring...

The reinforcements reaching Pechersk included fourteen officers, four cadets, one student and one actor from the Miniatures Theatre.

Alas! One thin line of troops on its own was not enough – even when reinforced by an armoured tortoise. There should have been at least four such tortoises. And it can be said with certainty that, had there been four of them, Bolbotun would have been compelled to retreat from Pechersk. But there weren't four of them.

There was a reason for this state of affairs: the person who had been appointed to command one of the armoured cars belonging to the Hetman's squadron of four first-class machines was none other than the famous ensign Mikhail Semyonovich Shpolyansky,* who in May 1917 had been personally awarded the St George Cross by Alexander Fyodorovich Kerensky.

With his dark skin, clean-shaven cheeks and velvety sideboards Mikhail Semyonovich bore an extraordinary resemblance to Eugene Onegin. His fame had spread throughout the City as soon as he had arrived from St Petersburg. He became particularly famous in the Ashes to Dust nightclub as a superb reader of his own poem 'Drops of Saturn', as well as being an excellent organizer of the poets' group and chairman of the Magnetic Triolet Poetry Society. Apart from having no equal as an orator, Shpolyansky was able to drive military as well as civilian vehicles, kept a ballerina from the Opera Theatre, Musya Ford, together with another lady whose name, as a gentleman, he never divulged to anybody, and possessed an inordinate amount of money, which he lent on very generous terms to the members of the Magnetic Triolet Society. In addition to all of which he drank white wine, played *chemin de fer*, bought a painting entitled *Venetian Girl Bathing*, lived at night on the Kreshchatik, spent the morning in the Café Bilboquet, the afternoon in his own luxurious room in the City's best hotel, The Continental, the evening in Ashes to Dust, and in the early morning, before sunrise, he worked on his scholarly article 'The Intuitive in Gogol'.

The Hetman's City died three hours earlier than it should have done precisely because, on the evening of 2nd December 1918, in the Ashes to Dust nightclub, Mikhail Semyonovich Shpolyansky had declared the following to the committee members of the Magnetic Triolet Society, Stepanov, Sheyer, Slonykh and Cheryomshchin:

"They're all swine – the Hetman as well as Petlyura. But Petlyura, apart from being a swine, is also a Jew-basher. But that's not my main point, which is that I'm bored because I haven't thrown any bombs for ages."

After dinner at the Ashes to Dust, paid for by Shpolyansky, all the committee members left with him. Shpolyansky was wearing an expensive fur coat with a beaver collar and top hat. They were accompanied by a fifth man – an inebriated individual in a mohair coat. Shpolyansky knew a thing or two about him: firstly, that he had syphilis; secondly, that he had written some atheistic verse which Shpolyansky with his excellent literary connections had arranged to be published in one of the Moscow journals; and thirdly, that he, Rusakov, was the son of a librarian.

Under the Kreshchatik lamplight, the man with syphilis wept into his mohair coat and, transfixed by the sight of Shpolyansky's beaver cuffs, said:

"Shpolyansky, you're the strongest person of all in this city which, just like me, is in the process of rotting away. You're such a special person that you can be forgiven for the fact that you look like Onegin. Listen, Shpolyansky… it's indecent to look like Onegin! You're *too* healthy, somehow. But you lack that little worm inside you that all members of the nobility have, and without which you'll never be able to become one of the outstanding figures of our time… Look at me: I'm rotting away and I'm proud of it! You're too healthy, but you're also tough, as tough as steel, and you should therefore break through to the top… right to the top! Look, like this…"

And the man with syphilis demonstrated exactly how it could be done. Grasping the lamp-post he began winding his way up it, managing somehow to become unusually tall and thin, like a grass snake. A group of prostitutes went by, as pretty as dolls, wearing green, red, black and white hats.

"Hey, look at you, you…" they called out cheerily. "Had one sniff too many, have you?"

Far away there was the sound of gunfire and, in the snow blowing about in the lamplight, Shpolyansky's similarity to Onegin was more striking than ever.

"Go to bed," he said to the syphilitic man of steel, averting his head a little so that the other man wouldn't cough into his face. "Go on, go to bed," he repeated, giving the front of the man's mohair coat a shove with the tips of his fingers. As soon as his kid gloves touched the threadbare material the man's eyes became like glass. They went their separate ways. Mikhail Semyonovich summoned a cab, shouted instructions to be taken to Malo-Provalnaya Street,* and left. The man in the mohair coat staggered off to his home in Podol.

That night, in the librarian's apartment in Podol, the owner of the mohair coat stood in front of the mirror, stripped to the waist and holding a lit candle. The syphilitic's eyes were dancing about, crazed with fright, his hands were trembling, and his lips quivering like a small child's.

"Oh my God, oh my God… this evening has just been so horrible! And I'm so miserable! All right, Sheyer was with me, but he's healthy, he's not infected – that's why he's happy. Maybe I should go and kill the girl, Lelka… but what would be the point of that? Can anyone explain to me what the point would be? Oh Lord… I'm only twenty-four, and I could have… Just another fifteen years and I'll be going blind, my legs will be gangrenous, and then nothing… nothing but a mouldy, rotten corpse."

With his candle held high, he peered into the dust-covered mirror reflecting his emaciated body and bare chest covered with a faint blotchy rash. The tears poured down the sick man's cheeks, and his whole body trembled and shook.

"I should shoot myself really, but I don't have the will-power. So, you there, standing in the mirror, what would be the point of lying? What would be the point?"

He took a slender little volume, printed on the most execrable grey-coloured paper, from the drawer of a small lady's desk. On its cover were the following words, in red letters:

PHANTOMISTS – FUTURISTS
Poems by:
Shpolyansky · B. Friedmann · V. Sharkevich · I. Rusakov
Moscow, 1918

Opening page thirteen, the poor sick man saw the following, familiar lines:

IV. RUSAKOV
God's Ravine

Spread out across the sky,
Heaven's misty ravine.
Like a bear, sucking its paw,
Divine essence, great father,
Great shaggy bear,
God.
In the ravine, in his lair
Strike down the bear,
Strike down the God.
The crimson sound
Of battle divine,
Has met with a prayer,
A curse of mine.

"Oh my God," the sick man groaned through clenched teeth. "Oh my God," he repeated in inconsolable agony.

His face distorted with pain, he spat on his poem and hurled the volume on the floor. Then, kneeling down and pressing his forehead to the cold, dusty parquet flooring, he crossed himself several times with nervous little gestures and started to pray. And as he prayed he raised his eyes up to the dark, cheerless window.

"Oh, Lord, forgive me and have mercy on me for writing such vile rubbish. But why have You been so cruel to me? Why? I know You have punished me, punished me so harshly! Take a look, if You please, at my skin. I swear to You by all that's holy, by all that's precious on this earth, by the memory of my departed mother, that I have been punished enough. I believe in You! I believe with my heart and soul, with every fibre of my brain. I believe in You and am turning to You, because there is no one on earth who is able to help me. My hope rests on nobody apart from You. Forgive me, and arrange things so that there are medicines that can help me get better. Forgive me for deciding You didn't exist: for if You didn't exist then I would now simply be a pathetic, mangy dog, without any hope. But I am strong only because You exist, and only because I can turn to You at any moment with a prayer for help. And I believe that You will hear my prayer for help, and that You will forgive me and cure me. Oh Lord, make me better, and forget about that vile rubbish. I wrote it in a fit of insanity, when I was drunk, under the influence of cocaine. Just don't let me rot, and I swear I will become a new man. Give me strength and rid me of cocaine, of weakness of will and, above all, of Mikhail Semyonovich Shpolyansky!"

The candle started to gutter, and the room grew cold. Towards morning, the sick man was covered in little goose pimples. In his heart he felt considerable relief.

Meanwhile, Mikhail Shpolyansky himself spent the rest of the night on Malo-Provalnaya Street, in a large room with a low ceiling and an old portrait depicting a prominent pair of rather faded epaulettes from the 1840s that had clearly seen better days. Shpolyansky was jacketless, in a white zephyr shirt and elegant black waistcoat with a deeply cut front. He sat on a narrow settee talking to a woman with a pale, smooth complexion.

"You know Julia, I've finally decided," he said. "I'm going to join the Hetman's armoured squadron, even though he is a swine."

At this the woman, wrapping herself in a grey fluffy shawl and still exhausted from the passionate Onegin's lovemaking of half an hour earlier, replied:

"I'm really sorry that I don't understand – and have never been able to understand – your decisions."

Shpolyansky picked up a brandy glass of sweet-scented cognac from the little table in front of the settee and said:

"No need to worry about such things."

Within two days of this conversation, Mikhail Semyonovich had been transformed. In place of his top hat he wore a flat military cap with an officer's ribbon, while instead of his civilian clothes he had on a short knee-length sheepskin coat, with crumpled khaki epaulettes, a pair of gauntlets like Marcel's in *Les Huguenots*,* and leggings. He was covered all over (including even his face) in engine oil and, for some reason, soot. On one occasion – on 9th December, to be precise – two of the armoured cars had taken part in the fighting on the outskirts of the City and, to give them their due, they had enjoyed considerable success. They had advanced about twelve miles along the main road and it had only needed a few rounds from their three-inch guns and machine guns to force Petlyura's units to retreat. The enthusiastic, rosy-cheeked ensign Strashkevich, the commander of the fourth armoured car, had sworn to Shpolyansky that, had all four armoured cars been deployed at once, then they could have defended the entire City. This had been on 9th December and, two days later, at twilight on the 11th, a group of men, including Shchur, Kopylov, some others (gun-layers, two drivers and a mechanic) and Shpolyansky, the officer on watch, had discussed the position.

"You know, my friends," Shpolyansky said, "it's essentially a matter of considerable importance to decide whether or not we are doing the right thing in defending this Hetman fellow. In his hands we're nothing but an expensive and dangerous toy, which he can use to impose his outlandishly reactionary ideas on the population. Who knows? Perhaps Petlyura's struggle against the Hetman is a historical imperative, and a third force will arise out of this struggle that may well prove to be the only possible correct outcome."

Those listening to Shpolyansky adored him for precisely the same reason for which everyone at the Ashes to Dust nightclub adored him: his exceptional eloquence.

"And what would this force be?" Kopylov asked, puffing at his hand-rolled cigarette.

Shchur – a clever, thickset man – winked and gestured knowingly towards the north east. The group talked a little more and then separated. On 12th December, the same group met again for a second conversation behind the vehicle sheds. What they talked about is unknown, but what is known is that, the next day, when a group of them, including Shchur, Kopylov and the snub-nosed Petrukhin, were on guard duty at the sheds, Shpolyansky appeared carrying a large packet wrapped in paper. The sentry, Shchur, let him through into the sheds, lit by a reddish glow from a feeble little lamp. Kopylov gave the packet a conspiratorial wink and asked:

"Sugar?"

"Uh-huh," Shpolyansky answered.

With a lamp flashing beside the armoured cars like an eye, an apprehensive Shpolyansky and one of the mechanics worked on the cars to prepare them for the following day's excursion.

The cause of all this was the piece of paper from the troop commander, Captain Pleshko, ordering all four armoured cars to "advance on Pechersk at 8 a.m. on 14th December."

The combined efforts of Shpolyansky and the mechanic to get the armoured cars ready for battle were to yield somewhat strange results. On the morning of 14th December the three cars that had operated perfectly well the day before (the fourth car, commanded by Strashkevich, had been engaged in fighting) were unable to leave their sheds, as if paralysed. Some alien substance had got into the carburettors and no one was able to pump it out, no matter how hard they tried. In the dim early-morning twilight people bustled about with lamps, but to no avail. Captain Pleshko, his face pale, looked around himself, like a wolf, and demanded a mechanic. But then, disaster after disaster! Firstly, the mechanic had disappeared. It transpired that, against all the rules, nobody in the troop knew where he lived. It began to be rumoured that he had suddenly come down with typhus. This was at eight o'clock, and at half-past eight, Captain Pleshko was dealt a second blow: at four o'clock in the morning Ensign Shpolyansky, after dealing with the armoured cars, had ridden off to Pechersk on a motorcycle driven by Shchur and not returned. Instead, Shchur came back with a sad story to tell. They had gone as far as Upper Telichka, where Shchur had tried in vain to dissuade Shpolyansky from embarking on any rash acts. But the latter, known throughout the squadron for his exceptional courage, had left Shchur and, armed with a carbine and a hand grenade, had set off alone into the darkness to reconnoitre the railway line. Hearing shooting, Shchur was convinced that Shpolyansky had come up against the enemy's forward troops, who had now advanced as far as Telichka, and had been killed by superior forces. Although Shpolyansky had ordered Shchur to wait there for him for no more than an hour, Shchur stayed there in fact for double that time. He then returned to his squadron to avoid putting himself and military motorcycle no. 8175 into any further danger.

When he heard Shchur's account of events, Captain Pleshko turned an even whiter shade of pale. The telephone trilled incessantly with calls from the Hetman's and General Kartuzov's headquarters requesting that armoured cars reinforce this or that position. When, at nine o'clock, the enthusiastic rosy-cheeked Strashkevich returned with his armoured car from engaging the enemy, some of the colour in his cheeks transferred itself to the squadron commander's own face. The enthusiastic young man had taken his car as far as Pechersk where, as has already been related, he had blockaded Suvorovskaya Street.

By ten o'clock, however, Pleshko's pallor had returned to his cheeks, this time to stay. Two gun-layers, two drivers and one machine-gunner had vanished into thin air. All attempts to get the armoured cars moving again proved unsuccessful. And Shchur, after riding off on the motorcycle on Captain Pleshko's orders, had not returned to base. As for the motorcycle itself, that didn't come back either, for the obvious reason that it couldn't have returned on its own! The shrill telephone calls started to become more threatening. The longer the day went on, the more calamitous the squadron's situation became. Two artillerymen, Duvan and Maltsev, disappeared, together with another couple of machine-gunners. The cars themselves looked weirdly abandoned, with nothing but a few screws, wrenches and buckets lying on the ground.

And then at midday the troop commander himself, Captain Pleshko, disappeared.

10

IN A SERIES OF UNUSUAL and intricate manoeuvres, some associated with savage fighting, others the result of telephone calls from headquarters, Colonel Nai-Turs led his troops for three whole days through the piled-up snow drifts on the outskirts of the City, along the stretch from Red Tavern to Serebryanka in the south, and as far as Post-Volynsky in the south-west. On the evening of 14th December he brought his troops back to an alleyway in the City, to an abandoned barracks with broken glass in the windows.

The troops under Nai-Turs's command were a strange group of men. Everyone who saw them was struck by the fact that they were wearing felt boots. At the beginning of the three days there had been about one hundred and fifty cadets and three ensigns.

In the first week of December, a swarthy, smooth-shaven artillery officer of medium height, with melancholy eyes and wearing the epaulettes of a hussar colonel, had reported to Major-General Blokhin, the commander of the First Infantry Detachment. The newcomer introduced himself as Colonel Nai-Turs, formerly commander of the second squadron of the Belgrade Hussars. Everyone who came across the colonel, with his halting gait and fading ribbon of St George on his threadbare military greatcoat, was so struck by the sight of his melancholy eyes that they always listened to what he had to say with the greatest attention. After a short conversation with Nai, Major-General Blokhin asked him to form a second infantry detachment, requesting that it be ready for action by 13th December. And, astonishingly, the process of forming the new detachment had been completed by 10th December, on which date Colonel Nai-Turs, always economical with words, briefly told Major-General Blokhin, who was beset on all sides by trilling telephones, that he, Nai-Turs, together with his cadets, was ready to move out, but only on the understanding that all one hundred and fifty of his men be supplied with felt boots and fur caps; otherwise any fighting would be quite out of the question. Hearing this laconic announcement, delivered in Nai-Turs's idiosyncratic Russian, Blokhin willingly wrote out the requisite order for the quartermaster's department, but warned the colonel that he would probably not obtain anything in less than a week, since the headquarters in general and the supply department in particular were in unbelievable chaos and scandalous disorder. Nai-Turs took the requisition order and, tugging at his left moustache, as was his wont, and looking neither to the right nor to the left (ever since he had been wounded in the neck he had been unable to turn his head, needing to move his whole body whenever he wanted to look to the side) walked out of Major-General Blokhin's room. On arrival at the detachment's headquarters on Lvovskaya Street he commandeered ten cadets (together with their rifles, for no apparent reason) and two carts, and set off for the supply department.

The supply department was situated in a most attractive little detached house on Bulvarno-Kudryavskaya Street. In a cosy little room, with a map of Russia and a portrait of Alexandra Fyodorovna* on the walls, left over from Red Cross times, Colonel Nai-Turs was met by Lieutenant General Makushin, a small, curiously red-faced man in a grey sheepskin sleeveless jacket with a spotlessly clean vest peeping out from under his collar, making him extraordinarily like one of Tsar Alexander II's ministers, Milyutin.*

Putting down the telephone receiver, the general asked Nai in a childish voice sounding like a clay whistle:

"What can I do for you, Colonel?"

"My detachment wishes to deproy, and I lequest suppry of felt boots and fur caps for two hundled men immediatry."

"Hmm," said the general, chewing his lips and crumpling Nai's requisition order in his hands, "you must understand, Colonel, that I am unable to supply you with these today, because we are at present making an inventory of our supplies. Please submit your request again in three days' time. But note that, in any event, I will be unable to supply the quantity you are requesting."

He placed the order in a prominent place under a paperweight in the form of a naked woman.

"Felt boots," Nai repeated in a flat monotone and, his eyes narrowing, he looked down at the soles of his feet.

"What did you say?" the general asked, staring at the colonel in astonishment:

"Felt boots, at once, immediatry."

"What's this? What are you saying?"

By now the general's eyes were bulging out of their sockets.

Nai turned to the door. Half opening it, he shouted out into the warm corridor.

"Pratoon, to me!"

The general turned a grey shade of pale, looking from Nai's face down at the telephone receiver, then at the icon of the Virgin Mary in the corner, and then back to Nai's face.

There was the sound of thudding, crashing feet in the corridor, followed by a knock on the door. Then the black bayonets and the red bands on the flat caps of a group of Alexeyevsky cadets appeared in the doorway. The general started to get up from his soft armchair.

"Never heard anything like this before in my life... this is mutiny..."

"Sign the lequistion order, if you please, Your Excerency," Nai said. "We have no time; we must reave in an hour. The enemy, they say, light by City."

"What?"

"Rook rivery," said Nai in a special sepulchral voice.

The general, his head sunk in his shoulders, his eyes bulging, pulled the paper out from under the naked woman and, with trembling hands and a spattering of ink, scrawled the word "Authorized" in one corner.

Nai took the piece of paper and tucked it up his sleeve.

"Quickry, road the felt boots," he ordered the cadets. With a crashing of bayonets the cadets left the room, leaving behind their dirty footprints on the carpet. Nai, however, stayed where he was.

"I will telephone headquarters," the general said, his face a shade of purple, "and immediately institute proceedings to have you courtmartialled. Then you'll know what's what…"

"Just you tly," Nai answered swallowing hard. "Go on, just you tly and see what happens." He lowered his hand to the handle of his gun, peeping out from the top of his holster. The general came out in a rash, quite unable to say another word.

"You pick up phone, you sirry old man, and my gun shoot you in head," Nai said with sudden emotion. "Then you rie on froor."

The general sat down in his chair again. His neck was purple and swollen, but his face had resumed its grey pallor. Nai turned on his heels and left the room.

For several minutes the general remained seated in his padded leather chair. Then, turning towards the icon, he crossed himself, picked up the telephone receiver, raised it to his ear and heard the operator's muffled but familiar voice. Suddenly the strange hussar's melancholy eyes flashed into his mind, and he replaced the receiver and looked out of the window. He saw the cadets busy carrying the grey bundles of felt boots out of the dark entrance to the warehouse. He could also see, in the background, the totally stunned expression on the face of the quartermaster, holding the piece of paper. Nai was standing, his feet wide apart, by one of the two-wheeled carts, looking at the document. The general desultorily picked up the day's newspaper from his desk, opened it and read the report on the first page:

By the river Irpen there have been clashes with enemy units attempting to force their way through to Svyatoshin.

He tossed the newspaper back onto his desk and said out loud:

"Why did I ever get involved in all this, damn it?..."

The door opened and a captain, the chief quartermaster's assistant, with the appearance of a tail-less ferret, entered the room. He looked expressively at the purple folds on the general's neck and said:

"Permission to report, sir."

"You know what, Vladimir Fyodorovich," the general interrupted, breathing heavily, his eyes rolling wearily, "I don't feel too good... the onset of something or other... I think I'll go home now... and I would ask you if you would be so kind as to look after things in my absence."

"Yes, sir," the ferret answered, a quizzical expression on his face. "But what do you want me to do? The Fourth Detachment and the mounted engineers are asking for felt boots. Did you agree to two hundred pairs?"

"Yes, yes!" the general replied in a high-pitched voice. "Yes, I did agree to that! I agreed! My decision and my decision alone! They are to be treated as an exception, as they are about to leave for the front line. Yes!"

The ferret's eyes danced with wonder and curiosity.

"But we've only got four hundred pairs in total..."

"What can I do about it? What?" shouted the general hoarsely. "Give birth to some more? Give birth? Is that it? If they ask for boots, then give them to them! Give them to them!"

Five minutes later General Makushin was driven home in a cab.

On the night of 13th to 14th December the barracks on Brest-Litovskaya Alley came to life. In the vast, dirty hall the electric lights on the walls between the windows came on again – the cadets had spent the day suspended on lamp-posts connecting various wires. One hundred and fifty rifles stood on trestles, and the cadets slept side by side on dirty plank beds. Nai-Turs sat at a rickety wooden table, piled with hunks of bread, pots of some sort of congealed liquid, cartridge pouches and cartridge clips, with a multicoloured map of the City spread out in front of him. A small, domestic lamp threw a patch of light onto the map, showing the river Dnieper in blue, branching out like a tree.

At about two o'clock that morning Nai started to be overcome by sleep. He leant forward several times, sniffing at the map, as if trying to discern something more closely. Then he called out quietly:

"Cadet!"

"Yes, Colonel, sir!" came the response from the door, and a cadet came up to the lamp, his felt boots swishing.

"I'm going to rie down now," said Nai. "Wake me in three hours. If there is a terephone message wake Ensign Zhalov, and he must wake me, or not, depending on what the message says."

But there was no telephone message. Indeed, Nai's detachment remained generally undisturbed that night. The next morning, at dawn, the detachment set off with three machine guns and three two-wheeled carts, spreading out along the road. The little houses on the outskirts of the City seemed devoid of life, but when they emerged onto the broad stretch of Polytechnic Street they came across a lot of activity. In the early light of dawn they caught a glimpse of baggage wagons rattling past them, and of the grey fur caps of troops trudging along. Everything and everybody was heading back into the City, looking a little fearfully at Nai's men as they went by. As it slowly but surely became lighter, the mist hanging over the gardens of the official government dachas and the rutted and potholed road began to lift and disperse.

That day Nai's detachment stayed in the area of Polytechnic Street until three o'clock – a cadet from his signals unit had ridden up on a fourth two-wheeled cart with the following pencilled note from headquarters: "Maintain defence of Polytechnic Street. Engage enemy on sight."

Nai-Turs first saw this enemy at three o'clock, with the appearance of numerous mounted troops way over to his left, on the snow-covered parade ground of a military barracks. These were Kozyr-Leshko's men attempting to come out onto the main road, along which they could penetrate into the heart of the City in accordance with Colonel Toropets's plan. In actual fact, right up to the Polytechnic Street area, Kozyr-Leshko had not encountered any resistance at all. He was not so much attacking the City as simply entering it in a broad, triumphant sweep, knowing full well that he was being followed by Colonel Sosnenko's regiment of Ukrainian Cossack cavalry, two regiments from the Blue Division, a regiment of riflemen from the south and six gun batteries. As soon as the distant dots of horsemen appeared on the parade ground, shrapnel started bursting high in the heavy snow-laden sky, like a flock of cranes. The horsemen formed into a single line that darkened and swelled as they galloped towards Nai-Turs. All along the lines of cadets the snap of rifle bolts could be heard. Nai-Turs took out his whistle, gave a piercing whistle and shouted:

"Take aim at cavary ahead!... Lapid... fire!"

Flashes sparked along the grey lines of cadets, as they fired their opening shots at Kozyr. Then the sky resounded three times as shells hurtled as far as the walls of the Polytechnic and, three times, Nai-Turs's men responded with a thunderous roar. The dark line of horsemen broke up, scattered and disappeared from the road.

Meanwhile, a change had been taking place in Nai-Turs. Although, as a matter of fact, no one in the detachment had ever seen Nai-Turs to be afraid of anything, now it seemed to the cadets that he had become aware of danger – maybe in the sky, or maybe he'd heard something in the distance… In short, whatever it was, Nai gave the order to retreat back to the City. One unit remained, firing deafeningly along the road, to cover the others. Then this too started to run back. They ran for about a mile, stumbling along, their boots thudding on the road, until they came to the crossroads marking the intersection with the same Brest-Litovsk Alley where they had spent the previous night. The crossing was completely dead, and there wasn't another person in sight. Here Nai singled out three cadets.

"At the double, to Porevaya and Bogshchagovskaya Streets," he ordered the cadets, "and find out where our tloops are and what they're doing. If you come acloss any baggage wagons, carts or any other means of tlansport retleating in a disorganized way, seize them. If you meet with lesistance, thleaten them with weapons, and then, if necessaly, shoot them…"

The cadets disappeared at a run back to the left. Suddenly they came under fire from somewhere in front. The bullets ricocheted off the walls, and the shooting intensified. One cadet collapsed face down on the snow, reddening it with his blood. He was followed by another cadet, who slumped back from his machine gun with a groan. As Nai's men spread out they poured a rapid, constant hail of fire onto the shadowy groups of the enemy, who seemed to rise out of the ground as if by magic. The wounded cadets were picked up and bandaged. Knots seemed to have formed in Nai's cheekbones. He turned his body more and more often, trying to see what was happening far out on either flank. It was evident, just from the expression on his face, that he was waiting impatiently for the three cadets he had sent off into the City. Finally they arrived at a run, panting like hounds on the chase, breathing with a hoarse whistle. Nai drew himself up, his face darkening. The first cadet ran up to him and stood there in front of him, gasping for breath.

"Colonel, there was no sign of any of our troops not only on Shulyavka, but anywhere at all," the cadet said, catching his breath. "We heard machine-gun fire to our rear, and the enemy cavalry is now moving along from the far end of Shulyavka, apparently entering the City…"

At that instant the cadet's words were drowned out by Nai's deafening whistle.

The three carts rumbled into Brest-Litovsk Alley, then clattered along it, and from there down Fonarny, rolling and swaying in the potholes. The carts were fully loaded with the two wounded cadets, fifteen other armed and able-bodied men, and all three machine guns. Nai-Turs turned to face his lines of men and, in his idiosyncratic accent, gave the cadets a strange order they had never heard before in their lives.

Meanwhile the twenty-eight cadets in the third section of the First Infantry Detachment were idling away their time in the somewhat dilapidated but well-heated building of the former army barracks on Lvovskaya Street. The most interesting point about this inactivity was that the cadets' commander was none other than Nikolka Turbin. The detachment's commander, Staff Captain Bezrukov, together with two of his officers, both ensigns, had left that morning to go to headquarters, but had not returned. Nikolka – the most senior lance corporal present – was loafing about, now and again going up to look at the telephone.

This situation lasted until three o'clock. By now the cadets all had rather bleak expressions.

Then, at three o'clock, the telephone rang.

"Is that the third section?"

"Yes."

"Put the commander on the telephone."

"Who's speaking?"

"This is headquarters…"

"The commander has not returned."

"And who are you?"

"Lance Corporal Turbin."

"Are you the senior person there?"

"Yes, I am."

"Take your men and start implementing the plan."

And Nikolka took his twenty-eight men and led them along the street.

Alexei Vasilyevich Turbin slept the sleep of the dead right through to two o'clock in the afternoon. He woke up suddenly as if someone had doused him with water, glanced at the little clock on his bedside chair, saw that it was ten to two, and started to rush about the room. He tugged on his felt boots, and began stuffing things into his pockets, in his haste forgetting first one thing then another – matches, cigarette case, handkerchief, Browning and two cartridge clips – and tightened the belt on his greatcoat. Then he remembered something else, something that seemed to him to be both shameful and cowardly. Nonetheless, after a moment's hesitation, he went to his desk and took out his civilian doctor's passport. But as he was turning it over in his hands deciding whether or not to take it, he heard Yelena calling out to him and he put the passport down on the table and forgot about it.

"Listen, Yelena," Turbin said, tugging nervously at his belt. He had a nagging premonition of impending disaster, and he was distinctly unhappy at the thought that Yelena and Anyuta would be remaining alone in the large, empty apartment. "It can't be helped, I have to go. I don't suppose anything will happen to me. The battalion will not be going any farther than the outskirts of the City, and I will be somewhere or other that's safe. And let's pray that God will keep Nikolka safe too. I heard this morning that the situation has worsened a little, but let's hope we'll beat off Petlyura. Goodbye, goodbye…"

When he'd gone, Yelena walked about the empty sitting room, from the piano, with its colourful *Faust* music still standing open, to the door to Alexei's study, and back again. The parquet floor creaked under her feet. She looked very sad.

Standing on the corner of Vladimirskaya Street and his own winding street, Turbin hailed a cab. Sighing gloomily, the cabby agreed to take him, but only after naming a monstrously inflated price, making it clear he wasn't going to back down. Gritting his teeth, Turbin got into the sleigh and they set off in the direction of the museum. There was frost everywhere.

Alexei felt deeply anxious. As they travelled along he could hear distant bursts of machine-gun fire, coming from the direction of the Polytechnic; it sounded as if they were firing at the railway station. Turbin wondered what this might signify (he had slept through Bolbotun's midday incursion into the City). He turned to look at the pavements. Although there was a sense of confusion and anxiety, there were still quite a few people about.

"Stop… st…" shouted an inebriated voice.

"What's the meaning of this?" Turbin asked angrily.

The cabby pulled back on the reins with such force that Turbin was almost thrown onto his knees. An extremely red face could be seen swaying by the shaft, clinging onto the reins and trying to clamber along them to get to the driver's seat. The crumpled epaulettes of an ensign gleamed on his short tanned coat. From only a couple of feet away Turbin was almost overcome by the powerful reek of onion and illicit vodka. The ensign was holding a rifle in his unsteady hands.

"Tur... turn around," said the red-faced drunkard. "Tell your pass... passenger to get off..." The word "passenger" suddenly struck him as funny, and he giggled.

"What's the meaning of this?" Turbin repeated angrily. "Can't you see who I am? I'm on my way to report for duty. Please let go of the driver. Carry on!"

"No, you stay there," said the red-faced man menacingly. But then, suddenly, he blinked as he noticed Turbin's epaulettes. "Ah, a doctor, I see. In that case I'll come with you..."

"We aren't going your way... Carry on, driver!"

"Just a moment..."

"Carry on!"

The cabby, his head sunk into his shoulders, made as if to tug at the reins, but changed his mind, and gave the red-faced man a look that was both fearful and dark with anger. But the latter had moved away, his attention caught by the sight of an empty cab. As the empty cab tried unsuccessfully to move off, the man raised his rifle in both hands and threatened the cabby. The cabby froze on the spot, and the drunkard shambled towards him, stumbling and hiccupping.

"I knew I shouldn't have agreed to take you, even for five hundred," Turbin's cabby grumbled angrily, whipping his horse. "If I get shot in the back, where does that get me?"

Turbin maintained a gloomy silence.

"What a swine," he thought angrily. "It's people like him who bring shame on the whole enterprise."

The crossroads by the opera house were seething with bustle and activity. Two cadets were standing in the middle of a tramline guarding a machine gun. One of them was short and obviously frozen, with earmuffs and wearing a black greatcoat; the other was in grey uniform. Crowds of passers-by had gathered in little groups on the pavements like flies, looking with curiosity at the machine gun. At the chemist's on the corner, with the museum in sight, Turbin stopped the cab and paid the driver.

"I need more than that, Your Honour," the cabby insisted grimly. "If I'd known, I wouldn't have agreed to take you. Look what's going on!"

"No, that's all you're getting."

"Why have they dragged children into this?" said a woman standing nearby.

Only then did Turbin notice a large group of armed soldiers by the museum, swaying and growing in size. In among the folds of the greatcoats on the pavement he could dimly make out a number of machine guns. At that moment there was the furious rattle of a machine gun from the direction of Pechersk.

"What nonsense is this now?" wondered Turbin in confusion, and, quickening his pace, he crossed the road making for the museum.

"I'm not late, am I?… What a disgrace… they might think I've made off somewhere."

Crowds of ensigns and cadets, together with a few soldiers, were dashing around excitedly by the entrance to the museum and the broken side gates leading to the Alexandrovsky High School parade ground. The enormous glass windows in the doors shuddered and the doors groaned as the armed, dishevelled and excited cadets rushed into the circular white museum building with its pediment boasting the following inscription in gold letters:

"For the Enlightenment of the Russian People."

"Oh my God!" shouted Turbin involuntarily. "They've already gone!"

Standing lonely and abandoned, exactly where they had been the day before, the mortars gaped silently at Turbin.

"I don't understand a thing… what does it mean?"

Without knowing why, Turbin started running across the parade ground towards the mortars. They grew bigger as he approached, looking more and more threatening. And then, suddenly, he noticed the mortar on the end. He stopped, frozen to the spot: its breech mechanism was missing. He raced back across the parade ground and out again onto the street. Here the crowd had got even bigger, many people were shouting and bayonets could be seen poking up above people's heads.

"We have to wait for Kartuzov! That's what we must do!" boomed someone anxiously. An ensign walked in front of Turbin, carrying a yellow saddle with dangling stirrups.

"It's for the Polish Legion."

"Yes, but where is it?"

"God knows!"

"Everyone into the museum! Come on, into the museum!"

"To the Don!"

The ensign suddenly stopped and threw the saddle down on the pavement.

"Oh, to hell with it! They can all rot, for all I care!" he shouted furiously. "Those bloody staff officers!"

"What a catastrophe... Now I understand... That's awful: they must have gone into battle as infantry. Yes, yes, that must be it. Petlyura must have got here quicker than expected. There weren't any horses, so they set off with just their rifles, without the mortars... Oh, my God! I must get to Madame Anjou's quickly... Maybe I'll find out what's going on once I'm there... surely there'll still be someone there, won't there?"

Turbin slipped out of all the confusion and ran back towards the opera theatre, ignoring everything around him. A dry gust of wind blew along the asphalt path around the theatre, ruffling the edge of a half-torn poster on the wall of the theatre, by the darkened windows of the side entrance. *Carmen. Carmen.**

At last he was at Madame Anjou's. The cannon and the gold epaulettes in the windows had gone. A glowing light flickered fitfully in the windows. Was the place on fire? Turbin tried to push open the door; it jangled a little, but didn't open. He knocked cautiously. He knocked again. A dim grey figure appeared momentarily behind the glass door, opened it and Turbin went inside. Dumbfounded, he stared at the strange figure who was wearing a student's black greatcoat and a moth-eaten civilian cap with ear flaps pulled down over the crown of his head. The stranger's face seemed somehow familiar, but there was something weirdly disfigured about it. The stove was roaring away, consuming sheets of paper. The floor was littered with paper. After letting Turbin in, the stranger darted to the stove without saying a word and squatted down, the red glow from the fire playing on his face.

"Is it Malyshev? Yes, it is Colonel Malyshev," Turbin said to himself, recognizing who it was.

The colonel had lost his moustache. His upper lip was now blue and clean-shaven.

His hands spread out wide, Malyshev scooped up sheets of paper from the floor and put them on the fire.

"Aha," thought Turbin.

"What's happening? It's all over, isn't it?" he asked dully.

"Yes, it's all over," the colonel replied laconically. He jumped up and went quickly over to his desk, gave it a searching look and banged the drawers a few times, pulling them out and putting them back. Then he suddenly bent down, picked up the last lot of sheets of paper from the floor and stuffed them into the stove. Only then did he turn to Turbin and say, calmly and ironically: "Well, we've done our bit of fighting.

Enough!" He reached inside his coat and hastily pulled out his wallet, examining the documents inside. He then took two of them out, tore them in half and tossed them into the stove. All this time Turbin was staring at him. This wasn't the Colonel Malyshev that he knew at all. Instead, he saw in front of him the figure of a rather sturdy student, an amateur actor with puffy, pinkish-red lips.

"Doctor, what are you thinking of?" Malyshev said with a worried tone, pointing at Turbin's epaulettes. "Take them off at once. What are you doing here? Where have you come from? Don't you know anything?"

"I was late, Colonel," Turbin began to explain.

Malyshev gave him a cheerful grin. Then the smile suddenly disappeared, and he shook his head with an apologetic and anxious expression on his face.

"Oh my God, I was the one who put you in this spot! I was the one who told you to be back at this time... You've been at home all day, haven't you? Well, all right; let's not talk about that now. Let's just say you need to remove your epaulettes immediately, then run off and hide somewhere."

"Yes, but tell me what's going on, for goodness' sake!"

"What's going on?" echoed Malyshev, with an ironic laugh. "What's going on is that Petlyura's already in the City – in Pechersk, if not already on the Kreshchatik. The City's been taken." Malyshev suddenly grinned again, looking to one side. Then, again unexpectedly, he started talking as if he were the old Malyshev and not some amateur actor. "Headquarters have betrayed us. We should have dispersed as long ago as this morning but luckily, thanks to some good people, I was told all about it last night and managed to disband the battalion. Doctor, we haven't got time to waste; take those epaulettes off!"

"...But the museum, back there at the museum..."

Malyshev's face darkened.

"Nothing to do with me," he answered furiously. "Not my problem! Nothing's my problem any more. I was there not long ago, shouting and warning people to disperse. I can't do any more now. I've saved all my own men: I haven't sent them to be slaughtered, and I have saved them from a shameful fate!" Malyshev suddenly began shouting hysterically – clearly something had been coming to the boil inside him which could not be suppressed any longer. "Those damn generals!" he yelled, clenching his fists and making a threatening gesture. His face had gone purple.

From somewhere farther up the street came the crackle of machine-gun fire, and it seemed as if the large house next door was being hit.

Malyshev gave a start, and fell silent.

"Right, doctor, get going! Goodbye! Just run – but not out into the street; go out the back way and then through the courtyards. That way's still open. Quickly."

He shook the stunned Turbin's hand, turned sharply on his heels and ran off through the dark gap behind the partitions. Immediately everything went quiet in the shop. Outside, the machine gun had stopped firing.

Now he was alone. The paper in the stove was still alight. Turbin made his way to the door slowly and listlessly, despite Malyshev's exhortations to hurry. He fumbled for the latch and dropped it into the loop. Ignoring what Malyshev had said, he took his time over everything he did, moving around on sluggish legs, his mind blurred and apathetic. The paper in the fire was burning out, and the stove's cheerful flames had now become a dull red glow. Immediately the shop went much darker. In the grey shadows, the shelves clung to the walls. Turbin ran his eyes over them, dimly conscious that Madame Anjou's still smelt of perfume – faintly, maybe, but the scent was still definitely there.

Turbin's thoughts were milling around in total confusion, and he spent some time in pointless contemplation of the place where the smooth-shaven colonel had disappeared. Then, in the silence, the knot in his brain slowly unravelled, and the most important thread became transparently clear: Petlyura was here! "Peturra, Peturra," he repeated dully, grinning for no particular reason. He went up to the mirror that was hanging on the wall between the windows. It was covered with a layer of dust, like muslin.

The paper had now all been used up and the final little red tongue of fire flickered for a moment longer on the floor and then went out. Everything went dark.

"Petlyura... how ridiculous it all is... the country's now essentially a hopeless cause," Turbin muttered in the darkness. Then he suddenly remembered where he was. "What am I standing here dreaming for? They could be here any minute."

Then, just like Malyshev immediately before his departure, he hurriedly ripped off his epaulettes. The threads made a crackling sound as they came away, and he found himself holding two tarnished silver stripes from his tunic and two green ones from his greatcoat. He looked at them, turning them in his hands and wanting to tuck them away in his pockets as a keepsake. But realizing that this was dangerous, he changed his mind and decided to burn them. There was no lack of combustible material, even though Malyshev had burnt every single document. He scooped up an armful of silk scraps from the floor, stuffed them in the stove and set them alight. Once again, distorted shadows played on the walls and the floor, as Madame Anjou's establishment temporarily came to life. The silver stripes warped and buckled in the flames, bubbling as they swelled up, then turned black and shrivelled into nothing.

At that point a really serious thought occurred to Turbin: what should he do with the door? Leave it on the latch or not? What if one of the volunteers, who had been left behind just like him, should come running here looking for shelter? There wouldn't be anywhere to hide otherwise! He unfastened the latch. Then another thought seared through his brain: what about his passport? He clutched at one pocket, then another – nothing there! So that was it, damn it; he'd left it behind at home! That was awful! What if he were to bump into some of them? He would be wearing a grey greatcoat and they would ask who he was. Aha, a doctor, you say? Prove it! How stupidly absent-minded of him!

"Come on, get a move on," a voice whispered inside him.

Wasting no more time thinking, Turbin dashed through into the depths of the shop and, taking the same way out as Malyshev, ran out of the small door into a dark corridor, and from there into the yard at the back.

11

IN OBEDIENCE TO THE VOICE on the telephone and following the orders he had been given, Lance Corporal Nikolai Turbin led his group of twenty-eight cadets out onto the streets and right across the City. These orders brought Nikolka and his cadets to a completely empty crossroads. Although the crossroads seemed totally lifeless, there was a lot of gunfire. All around them – in the sky, on the roofs and walls – the crackle of machine-gun fire could be heard.

These crossroads were clearly where the enemy should have been, for they had been the final destination in the telephone message. But for the moment there was no enemy in sight, and Nikolka was a little uncertain what he should do now. His cadets – like their commander, looking a little pale but not lacking in courage – spread out in a line on the snow-covered street, all except for the machine-gunner, Ivashin, who squatted by his weapon on the side of the street. Raising their heads from the ground, the cadets looked warily ahead of them, waiting to see what exactly was about to happen.

Their leader meanwhile was so engrossed in thought that he seemed to have shrunk and become even paler. He was struck, first of all, by the absence at the crossroads of everything that the voice on the telephone had promised. He was supposed to be reinforcing a group of men from the Third Detachment who should have been there. But they weren't, and there was no trace of them at all.

Secondly, Nikolka was struck by the fact that the rattle of machine-gun fire could be heard not only in front of them, but also to their left and even, it seemed, behind them. Thirdly, he was afraid of being frightened, and constantly put himself to the test by asking: "Am I afraid?" "No, I'm not afraid," his inner voice would reply buoyantly. And feeling proud that the fact of his bravery had been confirmed in this way, Nikolka turned even paler. This pride turned into the thought that, if he were to be killed, then he would be buried to music. It would all be very simple: he imagined a white silk-lined coffin moving serenely down the street, carrying the body of Lance Corporal Turbin, killed in battle, with a noble expression on his waxlike face. It was a pity that crosses for bravery were no longer awarded, otherwise he would certainly be wearing a cross on his chest, as well as the ribbon of St George. Peasant women would be standing at the gate and asking: "Who are they burying, my dear?" "Lance Corporal Turbin." "Oh, what a handsome man…" And then the music. It is good to die in battle, people say. Just so long as you don't suffer. Thinking about the music and the medals helped some-what to compensate for his uncertainty regarding the enemy – an enemy who evidently had not obeyed the voice on the telephone and who was not going to turn up at all.

"We'll wait here," Nikolka said to the cadets, trying to make his voice sound as assured as possible, but without totally succeeding – there was something not quite right about the whole situation, and it had all become a little absurd. Where was the detachment? Where was the enemy? And it was strange that the shooting seemed to be coming from behind them.

And so the leader waited with his troops. Suddenly, in a little side street that led from the crossroads to the Brest-Litovsk highway, shots rang out and grey figures came pouring along the street in headlong flight.

They were rushing straight for Nikolka's cadets, their rifles pointing in all directions.

"Are we surrounded?" the thought flashed through Nikolka's mind, and he hesitated, not knowing what order to give. But the next moment he was able to make out the gold patches on the shoulders of some of those running towards him and he realized that they were on his side.

The tall, strapping, fur-capped cadets from the Constantine Military Academy, covered in sweat from their exertions, flung themselves down on one knee and fired two rounds, their rifle muzzles flashing faintly as they aimed down the street from which they had just emerged. Then they leapt up, flung down their rifles, and dashed off across the crossroads and past Nikolka's men. As they ran, they tore off their epaulettes, cartridge pouches and belts, tossing them down onto the flattened snow. As one large, well-built, grey-coated cadet ran past Nikolka he turned to his men and, gasping for breath, shouted out in a booming voice:

"Run, follow us! Save yourselves, if you can!"

Shocked at the sight of all this, the line of Nikolka's cadets began to stand up. Nikolka stood still for a moment, totally stupefied. Then, immediately, he took a grip on himself, one thought flashing through his brain like lightning: "This is my chance to become a hero." Then he gave a piercing shout:

"Don't dare stand up! Obey my orders!"

"What on earth are they doing?" Nikolka said to himself, enraged.

When they reached the other side of the crossroads, the twenty or so Constantine Academy cadets, now weaponless, dispersed down Fonarny Alley, some of them dashing into the first enormous gateway. The metal gates closed with a thunderous crash, and their boots could be heard clattering up the stairwell. A second group ran into the next gateway. The five remaining men continued to run, faster and faster, down Fonarny and disappeared into the distance.

Then one more fleeing figure, the final one with faint gold epaulettes on his coat, appeared on the crossroads. With a single sharp-eyed glance, Nikolka instantly recognized the figure of the commander of the second squad of the First Detachment, Colonel Nai-Turs.

"Colonel!" called out Nikolka, confused and yet at the same time elated. "Your men are fleeing in panic."

At this point something quite outrageous happened. Nai-Turs ran out onto the trampled snow of the crossroads, his greatcoat tucked up on both sides in the manner of a French infantryman. His battered service cap, held in place by a chinstrap, was perched on the back of his head. In his right hand he held a Colt pistol, the open holster dangling and banging on his hip. He had not shaved for some time and his bristly face bore a grim expression. His eyes were turned inwards, and when he came closer, the zigzag epaulettes of a hussar regiment were clearly visible on his shoulders. Nai-Turs ran up to Nikolka and, with one sweep of his free left hand, tore off first Nikolka's left epaulette and then the right. The waxed, good-quality threads holding the epaulettes in place snapped off with explosive force – in the case of the right-hand epaulette taking a piece of Nikolka's greatcoat with them. The movement was so forceful that Nikolka instantly realized just how strong Nai-Turs's hands were. Knocked backwards, Nikolka abruptly sat down on something soft, the something turning out to be the machine-gunner Ivashin, who leapt out from under him with a howl of protest. Then all hell broke loose, as the dumbfounded faces of Nikolka's cadets danced around in front of his eyes. Nikolka was able to retain his sanity only because Nai-Turs had acted so precipitately that he was too astonished to have time to do anything else. Turning to the scattered group of cadets, Nai-Turs yelled out an order in his strange, inimitable accent. Nikolka had the irrational feeling that a voice like that could be heard for several miles, and probably throughout the City.

"Cadets! Risten to me: tear off your epaurettes, cap badges and cartlidge pouches, and get lid of your weapons! Go down Fonarny, then take the back way to Lazezhaya Street and then on to Podor! To Podor! Tear up your identity papers as you go, then scatter and hide, terring anyone you meet to do the same!"

Then, waving his pistol in the air, Nai-Turs bawled out at the top of his voice, with the force of a cavalry bugle:

"Go down Fonarny! Only Fonarny – not any other way! Get to your homes and go into hiding! The fighting's over. Quickry!"

For a few moments the cadets were unable to collect their senses. Then they turned very pale. In front of Nikolka's eyes, Ivashin ripped off his epaulettes, flung his cartridge pouches onto the snow, and sent his rifle clattering along the raised verge of the pavement. Within thirty seconds, cartridge pouches and belts, together with someone's tattered service cap, lay abandoned on the crossroads. The cadets started running down Fonarny, darting into one or other of the backyards that led out onto Razyezhaya Street.

Nai-Turs returned his pistol to its holster with a flourish, ran to the machine gun by the pavement, crouched down beside it and turned it round so that it faced the way he had come. With his left hand he sorted out the cartridge belt. Then, from this position, he turned to Nikolka and yelled furiously:

"Are you deaf or something? Go on, lun!"

A strange, drunken feeling of ecstasy welled up from somewhere inside Nikolka, and his mouth turned instantly dry.

"I don't wish to, Colonel," he answered in a matter-of-fact voice and, squatting down on his haunches, grabbed the cartridge belt with both hands and started feeding it into the machine gun.

Then, in the distance, farther down the street from which the remaining men of Nai-Turs's detachment had emerged, several figures on horseback appeared. Nikolka and Nai-Turs could dimly make out that the horses were prancing along skittishly, and that the cavalrymen were holding the grey blades of swords in their hands. Nai-Turs cocked the trigger and sent a burst of machine-gun fire in their direction, then another, followed by a third, this time prolonged, burst. Instantly bullets started smashing into the roofs of houses on both sides of the street. Some more cavalrymen appeared, but then one of them darted off into a house, another's horse reared up extraordinarily high so that it almost reached the first floor, and several cavalrymen disappeared altogether. Then all the rest vanished as well, as if into the ground.

Nai-Turs released the trigger, shook his fist at the sky and shouted, his eyes blazing:

"My poor boys… those headquarters bastards!"

He turned to Nikolka and yelled in a voice that again sounded to Nikolka like a muted cavalry bugle:

"Crear off, you idiot! Crear off, I say!"

He looked back down the street again, making sure that all the cadets had disappeared. Then, looking along the crossroads to the distant street that ran parallel with the Brest-Litovsk highway, he shouted out in pain and in anger:

"Oh, damn it!"

Nikolka turned to look in the same direction and saw, far away on Cadet Street, by the unkempt snow-covered boulevard, dark lines of figures moving along, and then falling to the ground. Then, much closer, on the corner of Fonarny, right above his and Nai-Turs's heads, a sign saying:

BERTA YAKOVLEVNA PRINTZ-METALL
DENTAL SURGEON

The sign resounded with a clang, and somewhere on the other side of the gates, window panes shattered. Nikolka saw chunks of plaster leaping and bouncing along the pavement. He looked questioningly at Nai-Turs, wondering what the distant figures and the plaster signified. But the colonel reacted strangely, grinning inappropriately and leaping around on one leg while waving the other in the air, as if dancing a waltz. Then, suddenly, he was lying on the ground at Nikolka's feet. A black fog enveloped Nikolka's mind. Sobbing drily, without any tears, he bent down and tried to lift Nai-Turs up by his shoulders. Only then did he see the blood trickling through the colonel's left sleeve and his eyes staring at the sky.

"Colonel, sir, Colonel…"

"Corporal," Nai-Turs started to say, but then blood poured out of his mouth onto his chin, and his voice began to fade, weakening with every word, "stop being so damned heloic… I'm dying… Maro-Plovarnaya Street…"

He didn't want to explain any further. His lower jaw began to shudder, twitching convulsively three times as if he was suffocating, then stopped, and the colonel became as heavy as a bag of flour.

"So that's how people die, is it?" Nikolka thought. "It can't be: he was alive a moment ago. It seems it's not so terrible to die in battle. I wonder why I haven't been hit…"

DENT…URGEON

The sign overhead quivered and shook for a second time and, once again, there was the sound of glass shattering. Then the idiotic thought passed through Nikolka's confused brain that perhaps the colonel had simply fainted. He tried to pull him up, but to no avail. "Am I afraid?" he asked himself again, and he knew he felt hideously afraid. "But why? Why?" he wondered. But then he immediately realized that he was afraid because he was desperately sad and totally alone. If only Colonel Nai-Turs would get back up on his feet, then he wouldn't be afraid at all… But the colonel continued to lie there in front of him, completely motionless, unable to issue any commands, or to be aware of the large red puddle spreading by his sleeve, or of the plaster that was insanely breaking off and crumbling away on the wall ledges. No, Nikolka was afraid because he was totally alone. There weren't any cavalry galloping by at that moment, but it was clear that everybody was against him, and that he was totally on his own, the last one left… And it was loneliness that drove Nikolka from the crossroads. He crawled along on his stomach, propelling himself by his hands and arms – in the case of his right arm, by his elbow, as he was clutching Nai-Turs's Colt pistol in his palm. The fear hit him most strongly when he was a couple of yards from the corner of the street... "Any minute now, and I'll be hit in the leg, then I'll be unable to move and Petlyura's men will come riding up and hack me to pieces with their swords... terrible to be lying on the ground with people hacking at you... if there are any bullets in Nai-Turs's pistol, I'll fire at them... just a bit farther, one more push with the arms..." and Nikolka found himself round the corner in Fonarny Alley.

"How astonishing, extraordinarily astonishing I haven't been hit. It's nothing but a miracle, it's the Lord God working miracles," Nikolka thought as he stood up. "That's what a miracle is, then; I've experienced one for myself. Notre-Dame Cathedral. Victor Hugo. I wonder if anything's happened to Yelena? And what about Alexei? Clearly, once you have your epaulettes ripped off that spells disaster."

Nikolka leapt to his feet, up to his neck in snow. He put the Colt in his greatcoat pocket and dashed down the street until he met the first gaping gateway to the right. He ran into the echoing archway and out onto a gloomy, squalid little yard with some red-brick sheds on the right-hand side and a stack of logs on the left. Realizing that the way out was through the middle, he made a dash for it, slipping and sliding, and collided with someone in a sheepskin jacket. He could see him with total clarity: ginger beard and tiny little eyes, leaking hatred. A snub-nosed Nero in a sheepskin cap. As if taking part in some light-hearted game, the man seized hold of Nikolka with his left arm, while grabbing Nikolka's left hand with his other and twisting it behind his back. For several moments Nikolka was too shocked to move. "My God... he's got me... he hates me!... One of Petlyura's..."

"Got you, you little rat!" screeched the ginger-bearded man, pausing to gasp for breath. "Where do you think you're going? Stop!" he yelled. "Stop the cadets! Hold them, hold them! So you think you can take off your epaulettes so that people won't know who you are, do you, you little rat? Hold them!"

Filled from head to toe with an overwhelming sense of rage, Nikolka jerked his body down so abruptly that the belt on the back of his greatcoat snapped. Then he turned and, with unnatural force, freed himself from the clutches of the ginger-bearded man. Not seeing him for a moment, he turned and there he was again. He had no weapon, wasn't even a soldier, just the local caretaker. The rage that had been enveloping Nikolka's brain like a red blanket suddenly disappeared, to be replaced by an extraordinary sense of total control. He grinned like a young wolf, the wind and frost gushing into his hot body. He whipped the pistol from his pocket, thinking: "Let's hope there are some bullets, then I can kill the bastard." Then, when he did speak, his own voice seemed so strange and alien that he didn't recognize it.

"I'll kill you, you little snake," he shouted hoarsely, fingering the complex little Colt, and then instantly realized he had forgotten how to fire it. Seeing that Nikolka was armed, the ginger-bearded caretaker fell to his knees in horrified despair, miraculously transforming himself somehow from a Nero into a snake…

"Your Honour! Your…" he wailed.

All the same Nikolka would definitely have fired had he been able to, but the Colt remained silent. "Damn it, no bullets," he thought, his mind whirling. Shielding himself with his hand, the caretaker edged backwards and moved from a kneeling to a squatting position. Then he let out such a wail of anguish that it destroyed Nikolka. Unsure what he could do to close that huge gaping mouth framed in its copper-coloured beard, and in despair because his pistol had been unable to fire, Nikolka leapt onto the caretaker like a fighting cock and smashed the butt into the man's teeth, risking shooting himself as he did so. In a flash, Nikolka's rage dissipated. The caretaker jumped up and ran off back into the archway through which Nikolka had come. No longer wailing and out of his mind with terror, the caretaker ran off, slipping and stumbling on the ice. He turned once to look back and Nikolka could see that half of his beard was covered in blood. Then he disappeared. Nikolka dashed off in the opposite direction, past the little brick shed and towards the gate leading out onto Razyezhaya Street. There he stopped, overcome by despair. "That's it! I'm finished! I'm too late, and I'm trapped. And, my God, the gun doesn't fire!" He shook at the huge bolt and lock, but to no avail. He had to do something. The ginger-headed caretaker had locked the gate as soon as Nai-Turs's cadets had run through onto the street, leaving Nikolka confronting a completely insuperable obstacle in the form of a sheer metal barrier, totally without any footholds. He turned and glanced up at the sky, covered by extraordinarily dense and low-lying clouds, and saw a flimsy black ladder propped on a firewall leading up to the roof of a four-storey building. "Perhaps I could climb up that?" he thought, and immediately the graphic image of Nat Pinkerton* wearing a yellow jacket and with a red mask over his face clambering up just such a ladder flashed absurdly through his mind. "Nat Pinkerton, America, eh?... All right, I climb up it, and then what? I'll be sitting on the roof like some idiot and, in the meantime, the caretaker will have got hold of a group of Petlyura's men. That Nero's sure to give me away: he won't forgive me for smashing his teeth in."

And sure enough, he could hear the caretaker desperately shouting for help by the gate into Fonarny Alley, and then the clatter of horses' hooves. Nikolka realized what must have happened: Petlyura's cavalry had entered the City in a flanking movement, and had already reached Fonarny. So that's what Nai-Turs had been shouting about. But there was no going back down Fonarny now.

These thoughts came to him as he stood unaccountably on the stack of logs piled next to the brick shed, under the wall belonging to the adjacent house. Ripping his trousers and stumbling and falling on the icy logs shifting around under his feet, he made his way to the wall. He looked over the top into an identical yard to the one he was in. The two courtyards were so alike that he expected the ginger Nero in the sheepskin coat to leap out onto him again. But nobody leapt out. With a terrible hollow feeling in his stomach and his side he sat down on the ground. As he did so, his pistol jerked in his hand and a deafening shot rang out. At first he was astonished, but then he realized that the safety catch had been on all this time and that his sudden movement had released it. "That's a bit of luck!" he thought.

But the gate into Razyezhaya Street here was just like the other one, damn it: locked and impossible to climb. Right then, let's try the next wall. But, to his horror, he saw there were no logs by this one. Securing the safety catch, he put the pistol into his pocket. He clambered along a pile of broken bricks, and then started climbing up the sheer face of the wall like a fly, placing his feet into such tiny little nooks and crannies that normally wouldn't have accommodated even a small coin. With torn fingernails and his fingers covered in blood he clawed his way to the top of the wall. As he lay there on his stomach, he heard, behind him in the first yard, a piercing whistle and Nero's voice. And then, in front of him, in the third yard, he saw a woman's face, distorted with horror, looking at him from a darkened first-floor window – just for an instant – and then the face was gone. Tumbling off the wall he landed, as luck would have it, in a fortunately placed snowdrift, but he twisted his neck and felt a sharp pain at the top of his skull. His head ringing and with flashes in his eyes, he ran to the gate.

Absolute joy! This gate was locked as well, but that didn't matter: there was an elaborate metal railing on one side. Like a fireman Nikolka clambered up it and down onto the other side, finding himself in Razyezhaya Street. He saw that it was completely empty, not a soul about. "Just a few moments' rest, to catch my breath; otherwise my heart will burst," he thought, gulping air into his overheated body. "Ah, yes, my papers." He pulled a wad of dirty, oil-streaked papers out of his jacket pocket and tore them into pieces, scattering them all over the place like snowflakes. Behind him, from the direction of the crossroads where he had left Nai-Turs, a machine gun opened up, to be answered by machine-gun and rifle fire coming from in front of him, from the City. So that was it: there was fighting in the City centre and the City had been taken. Absolute disaster. Still breathing deeply, Nikolka brushed the snow off his body with both hands. What about the pistol? Should he throw that away too? Nai-Turs's pistol? No, not for one moment. He might be able to get through unscathed: they couldn't be everywhere at once, surely!

Panting heavily and feeling his legs weakening and giving way under him, Nikolka ran along the empty Razyezhaya Street and made his way without incident as far as the crossroads at the junction of two streets: Lubochitskaya, leading to Podol, and Lovskaya curving away towards the City centre. By the side of a pillar he saw a pool of blood and a pile of manure, together with two abandoned rifles and a blue student's cap. He hastily took off his fur cap, replacing it with the cap. It seemed rather too small for him, giving him an insolent, devil-may-care, non-military look – like some down-at-heel character who had been slung out of high school. Peering round the corner, he took an anxious glance down Lovskaya Street and saw a distant group of cavalry trotting along with dark blue patches on their fur caps. He could hear the crackle of rifle fire; there was clearly some trouble down there. So he darted down Lubochitskaya Street, where he saw his first live human being in the form of a woman running along the opposite pavement, a black-feathered hat perched on one side of her head and a grey bag swinging in her hand from which a cockerel was desperately trying to claw its way out and screeching with such force that the whole street could hear. "Peturra! Peturra!" it seemed to be shouting. Carrots were spilling out onto the pavement through a hole in the paper bag the woman was carrying. She was shouting and weeping as she ran, keeping close to the wall. Some well-to-do man whirled past, crossing himself furiously and shouting:

"Oh Christ, Jesus! Volodka! Volodka! Petlyura's coming!"

At the end of Lubochitskaya Street there were many people bustling and scurrying about, making quickly for the gates. Someone in a black coat, crazed with fear, dashed up to the gates, inserted his stick into the metal bars and snapped it in half.

Meanwhile, all this time, twilight had been coming on so fast that by now it had already arrived. When Nikolka turned off Lubochitskaya Street onto Volsky Hill the electric street lamp on the corner lit up and began to hiss faintly. The shutters of a little shop crashed shut, instantly hiding a pile of multicoloured boxes marked "soap powder". A cabby took a bend too sharply and crashed into a snowdrift overturning his sleigh, and started lashing out at his miserable horse with his whip. Nikolka dashed past a four-storey house with three entrances, all three of which were again and again being flung open. Someone in a sealskin fur collar rushed past Nikolka, yelling at the gate:

"Pyotr! Pyotr! Are you out of your mind? Close the gate! Close the gate!"

A door slammed shut in one of the entrances and a woman's voice yelled from the dark staircase inside:

"Petlyura's coming! Petlyura!"

The closer Nikolka came to Podol – the safe area that Nai-Turs had told him about – the greater the number of people who were dashing and bustling along the streets, but there seemed to be less fear, and not everyone was heading in the same direction as he was – some were moving towards him.

At the very top of the slope leading down to Podol a young cadet in a grey greatcoat with white epaulettes emblazoned with the gold letter V emerged solemnly from the entrance to a grey stone building. He had a button nose, and his eyes darted animatedly from side to side. A large rifle was slung over one shoulder. When the people who were scurrying by caught sight of this armed young man they scattered in all directions. But the cadet simply stood on the pavement and listened intently to the shooting coming from the Upper City with a knowing, inquisitive expression on his face. His nose twitched and he began to move off. Nikolka abruptly blocked his way, standing in the middle of the pavement and pressing right up against him.

"Get rid of that rifle and hide immediately," he whispered.

Alarmed, the cadet shuddered and took a step back. But then he clutched at his rifle threateningly. In a move born of experience Nikolka pushed and forced the cadet back into the entrance, between two doorways.

"Hide, I tell you," he repeated forcefully. "I'm a cadet. The situation's disastrous; Petlyura's taken the City."

"What do you mean? How's he taken the City?" the cadet asked, his mouth open, revealing a tooth missing in his left jaw.

"That's how," answered Nikolka, pointing in the direction of the Upper City. "Do you hear that? That's Petlyura's cavalry moving along the streets. I've only just managed to escape myself. Run home, hide your rifle, and warn everyone you see."

The cadet froze to the spot in the entrance, speechless. That was how Nikolka left him – he had no time to waste with people who were so slow on the uptake.

In Podol the sense of alarm was less, but there were still plenty of people on the move. Passers-by quickened their step, flinging back their heads to listen, while cooks hurried into entrances and gateways, wrapping themselves in grey shawls. The crackle of machine-gun fire from the Upper City was now constant. But at this twilight hour on 14th December, nowhere, neither in the distance nor close by, was there the sound of heavy artillery.

Nikolka still had a long way to go. By the time he had crossed Podol the streets had already become shrouded in twilight. The heavily falling snow, its flakes glistening in the lamplight, blanketed the sound of anxious people scurrying along. Here and there through the snow he glimpsed cheerful lights in shop windows. But not everywhere – some windows had already gone completely dark. The snow was beginning to settle more and more. When Nikolka finally arrived at the bottom of the steep slope of his street, St Alexei's Hill, and started to walk up it, he came across the following scene by the gateway to No. 7: two boys in grey knitted jackets and headgear had just tobogganed down from the top of the hill. One of them, as small and round as a ball and plastered with snow from head to foot, was sitting on the ground roaring with laughter. The other one, slightly older, a thin serious-looking lad, was untying the knot on his rope. Another lad, in a sheepskin coat, was standing by the gate, picking his nose. The sound of gunfire intensified, flaring up in various different places above them.

"Hey, Vaska, I really banged my bum back there, against a post!" the younger boy shouted.

"Look at them, tobogganing like that, without a care in the world," thought Nikolka in astonishment, and turned to the lad in the sheepskin coat.

"Can you please tell me," he asked softly, "what that shooting is up there?"

The lad took his finger out of his nose and said nasally:

"That's our boys giving the officers what for."

Nikolka looked at him mistrustfully, absent-mindedly fingering the pistol in his pocket.

"They're getting their own back on the officers," the older boy put in angrily. "Serves them right. There's only eight hundred of them in the entire City, and they've behaved like idiots. Petlyura's here now, and he's got a million men."

He turned and started pulling the toboggan back up the hill.

The cream-coloured curtain between the veranda and the small dining room was flung open immediately. The clock ticked on… *tonk tank…*

"Is Alexei back?" Nikolka asked Yelena.

"No," she replied, and burst into tears.

It was dark; the entire apartment was dark, except for a lamp shining in the kitchen where Anyuta was sitting weeping, her elbows propped on the table; she was weeping, naturally, for Alexei Vasilyevich. In Yelena's bedroom, the logs glowed in the fire, spitting out embers through the damper, emitting hot sparks that danced around for a moment on the floor. Having cried her heart out for Alexei, Yelena sat on a little stool, her cheek propped on her fist. Bathed in the red glow of the fire, Nikolka lay on the floor at her feet, his legs spread out like a pair of scissors.

This colonel… this Bolbotun. The Shcheglovs had been putting it about that afternoon that he was none other than Grand Duke Mikhail Alexandrovich.* Here, in the semi-darkness, in the glow of the fire, there was a general sense of despair. But what was the point of weeping for Alexei? Tears, of course, wouldn't help at all. He had been killed, there was no doubt about it. It was obvious: nobody was taking any prisoners. The fact that he hadn't come home meant that he had been killed, together with the rest of the battalion. The worst thing of all, so they said, was that Petlyura had over eight hundred thousand men, all hand-picked, elite troops. We had been betrayed and sent to our deaths…

But where had this terrifying army come from? It had appeared seemingly from nowhere, fashioned from the needle-sharp blue, twilight air, from the frost and the mist… mist… everywhere mist…

Yelena stood up and stretched out her hand.

"It's those Germans, damn them to hell. If God doesn't punish them, then He has no sense of justice. Surely they won't get away with what they've done, will they? No, they'll answer for it. They will suffer, just as we are suffering now, I know they will."

She repeated the words "they will" several times persistently, as if uttering a curse. The red light from the fire played on her face and neck, and her vacant eyes were dark with hatred. Yelena's outburst had reduced Nikolka, lying on the floor with his legs spread out, to a state of absolute gloom and despair.

"Maybe he's still alive," he said hesitantly. "After all, he is a doctor, isn't he? Maybe he's not dead, but in captivity somewhere."

"They'll be eating cats and killing each other, just like us," Yelena shouted, gesturing savagely at the fire.

"Oh my goodness..." thought Nikolka. "Bolbotun simply can't be a Grand Duke... eight hundred thousand men... that's just impossible, let alone a million... It's all nothing but mist and fog. We've been hit by really hard times now. And that clever so-and-so Talberg clearly got away from it all just in time. Look at the fire dancing on the floor. Surely there've been peaceful times and beautiful countries, haven't there? Paris, for example, or Louis with those little images on his hat, or Hugo's Clopin Trouillefou* crawling around the floor and warming himself in front of a fire just like this? And he was happy, even though he was a beggar. Nowhere has there ever been such a vile little snake as that ginger-headed caretaker Nero! All right: everybody hates us, I know, but he was just an unmitigated swine! Twisted my arm behind my back!"

Then suddenly there was the sound of heavy gunfire. Nikolka leapt up and started pacing up and down.

"Do you hear that? Do you hear that? Do you? Perhaps it's the Germans! Perhaps it's the Allies who've come to our aid! Who is it? Surely they can't be firing at the City if they've already taken it, can they?"

Yelena folded her arms on her chest and said:

"Nikol, there's no way I'm going to allow you to go out there. No way. I implore you not to go anywhere. Don't even think about it; it would be madness."

"I'd only want to go as far as the square by St Andrew's Church, just to see what's happening and to listen. You can see all of Podol from there."

"All right then, go. Go, if you want to leave me alone at such a time."

Nikolka stood there, embarrassed.

"All right, then I'll just go outside and listen in the backyard."

"And I'll come with you."

"But, Lenochka, what if Alexei should come back? You won't be able to hear the front doorbell."

"No, that's right, we won't. And it will be your fault."

"All right then, Lenochka, I give you my word that I'll keep to the yard; not a step beyond."

"Promise?"

"I promise."

"You won't go out of the gate? Or up the hill? You'll stay in the yard?"

"Word of honour."

"Well, off you go then."

On 14th December 1918 the City was covered in a blanket of thick snow. And this strange, totally unexpected gunfire started up at nine o'clock in the evening, lasting for no more than a quarter of an hour.

The snow had melted under Nikolka's collar, and he struggled against the temptation to climb up to the snow-covered hills above him. From up there it would have been possible to see not only Podol, but also part of the Upper City, the seminary, the tall buildings with their hundreds of rows of lights and the little houses on the hills with their icon lamps burning in the windows. But no one must break their word once they have given it, otherwise it is not possible to live on this earth. That was what Nikolka thought. At every threatening boom of distant gunfire he would pray: "Oh, Lord, please let it..."

But then the guns fell silent.

"Those were our guns," he said sorrowfully to himself. As he walked back from the gate he glanced in at the Shcheglovs' window next door. The little white curtain in the annexe window had been pulled back and he could see Maria Petrovna washing little Petka. The naked Petka was sitting in a tub weeping soundlessly, because some soap had got into his eyes. Maria Petrovna wrung out the sponge over Petka. There was some washing hanging on a line, and Maria Petrovna's large shadow moved back and forth by the line, bending under it from time to time. As Nikolka stood there shivering in his unbuttoned greatcoat, everything in the Shcheglov household seemed very warm and cosy.

In the deep snow, some five miles to the north of the City outskirts, a staff captain was sitting in a small abandoned watchman's hut that was totally buried in the white snow. On a little table there were some hunks of bread, a field telephone and a tiny three-wick lamp with a bulbous, blackened glass cover. A fire was burning in a little stove. The captain, a small man with a long, pointed nose, wore a greatcoat with a large collar. He was tearing to pieces and crumbling a hunk of bread with his left hand, while pressing the buttons on the telephone with his other. But there was no answer; the telephone seemed to have gone dead.

For a couple of miles round the captain there was nothing except pitch darkness and driving snow. The snow had formed into huge drifts.

After another hour of this the captain left the telephone in peace. Around nine o'clock in the evening he started snuffling.

"I'm going out of my mind," he suddenly said out loud. "There's nothing for it but to shoot myself."

At that moment, as if in reply, the telephone rang.

"Is that Battery No. 6?" asked a distant voice.

"Yes, yes," the captain answered, deliriously happy.

The distant, agitated voice seemed jubilant, even if a little muffled:

"Open fire immediately on the wooded area…" squawked the blurred voice at the other end of the line, "…everything you've got…" The voice broke off. "I have the feeling that…" At that point the line went dead again.

"Yes, I hear you, I hear you," the captain shouted into the receiver, baring his teeth in despair. There was a long pause.

"But I can't open fire," he said into the receiver. He had to speak, even though he was perfectly aware that he was talking into a total void. "All my men and my three ensigns have run off. I'm the only one left. Inform Post."

The captain sat there for another hour and then went outside. It was snowing and blowing hard. The four sullen and fearsome-looking guns were already covered in snow, with ridges forming on the muzzles and breechblocks. The captain jabbed around like a blind man in the cold whirling snow and the wail of the blizzard. In the darkness and the snow he stuck at the task for a long time, until he was finally able, through touch alone, to remove the first breechblock. At first he wanted to toss it down the well behind the watchman's hut, but then he thought better of it and went back into the hut. He came out again three more times to remove the remaining breechblocks, hiding them together with the potatoes in the little space under the floorboards. Then he extinguished the lamp and went out into the darkness. He walked for two hours, his feet sinking in the snow, totally invisible in the dark, until he reached the main road leading to the City. The dim light of an occasional street lamp could be seen. Under the first of these lamps a group of cavalrymen with tasselled caps killed him with their swords, taking his boots and watch.

In a dugout, three miles or so away, to the west of the watchman's hut, the same voice sprang to life on the end of the line:

"Open fire on the wooded area immediately. It seems that the enemy has slipped between us and into the City."

"Can you hear me? Are you there?" answered the dugout. "Find out from Post…" Sudden silence.

Without listening to the reply, the voice continued squawking:

"Rapid fire on the wooded area… on the cavalry…"

Then the line went totally dead.

Three officers with torches and three cadets in sheepskin coats clambered out of the dugout. A fourth officer and two more cadets were standing by a gun under a lamp that the blizzard was threatening to extinguish. Five minutes later and the guns started to leap around as they fired into the darkness. The crash and roar of the guns could be heard throughout the whole area, over a radius of twelve miles, reaching as far as No. 13 on St Alexei's Hill… O Lord, please let it…

Whirling through the blizzard, a cavalry squadron leapt out of the dark from behind the lamps and cut down all the cadets and the four officers. The battery commander, who had remained in the dugout by the telephone, shot himself through the mouth, his last words being:

"Those headquarters bastards… I can understand the Bolsheviks perfectly."

That night Nikolka switched on the ceiling light in his little corner room, and carved out a large cross on his door, using a penknife to scratch the following unsteady inscription:

"Col. Turs, 14th December 1918, 4 p.m."

He omitted the "Nai" just in case Petlyura's men should come searching the house.

He didn't want to sleep, afraid he might miss the front-door bell. He knocked on Yelena's wall and said:

CHAPTER 11

"Go ahead and sleep – I'll stay awake."

And immediately he fell into a deep sleep, lying fully dressed on the bed. But Yelena, on the other hand, stayed awake all night, waiting and waiting for the bell to ring. But it didn't ring; of their elder brother Alexei there was no sign.

A tired, shattered person needs to sleep. It was already eleven o'clock, but Nikolka slept on and on – in somewhat strange circumstances, I have to report: his boots were too tight, his belt was digging into his ribs, his collar was choking him and a nightmare was sinking its claws into his chest.

Nikolka had collapsed flat on his back onto the bed. His face had turned purple and he was whistling as he breathed in and out... A whistle!... Snow all around, and some cobweb or other... The cobweb was everywhere, damn it! More than anything he needed to break his way out of the cobweb, otherwise the blasted thing would get bigger and bigger until it reached his face. And it might well wrap itself around him so tightly that he wouldn't be able to get out at all! And then he'd suffocate. Through the strands of the web he could see nothing but the purest snow, as much snow as you could imagine, acres and acres of it! He had to make his way out to this snow as quickly as possible – someone seemed to be saying "Nikol" in an anguished voice. And then, just imagine, a cheery little bird seemed to get caught in the web as well, and started chirping... *tiki tiki... weeoo... weeoo... tiki tiki.* Damn it! He couldn't see the bird itself, but it was chirping and tweeting somewhere very close to him. And then there was the sound of someone weeping and moaning, and once again the voice shouting: "Nik! Nik! Nikolka!"

"Ugh!" Nikolka croaked, as he ripped the cobweb away and sat bolt upright, bedraggled and dishevelled, his belt buckle twisted to one side. His blond hair stood on end, as if someone had been ruffling it for a long time.

"Who is it? Who is it?" Nikolka asked in a terrified voice, not understanding a thing.

"Who, who, who, yes! Yes! *Feee teee! Fiooo! Feeyoo!*" the cobweb replied, and a mournful voice, trying hard to hold back the tears, said:

"Yes, with her lover!"

Terrified, Nikolka pressed up against the wall and stared at the apparition. It was wearing a brown army jacket, brown riding breeches and yellow-topped jockey's boots. Its clouded, mournful eyes looked out at the world from the deepest of sockets, framed by an improbably large close-shaven head. It was clearly young, this apparition, but the skin on its face was grey, like an old man's, and its teeth were crooked and yellow. It was carrying a large cage covered by a black shawl and an unsealed blue letter...

"I must still be asleep," Nikolka reasoned to himself and gestured with his hand, trying to dispel the apparition as he had with the cobweb, but his fingers became jammed extremely painfully in the bars of the cage. The bird in the cage immediately went berserk, screeching and shouting in fury.

"Nikolka," came Yelena's anxious voice from a long distance away.

"Oh, Lord Jesus Christ," thought Nikolka. "No, I am awake, after all, but have simply gone out of my mind. And I know why: I'm exhausted from all the fighting. My God! I'm already beginning to see things... and look at my fingers! My God! Alexei's not returned... yes, that's it... he's not returned... he's been killed... oh no, oh no, please, no!"

"With her lover, on the very same sofa," the apparition said in a tragic voice, "on which I used to read poetry to her."

The apparition turned towards the door, evidently addressing someone listening outside, but then it turned eagerly back towards Nikolka.

"Yes, on the very same sofa... They're sitting there now, embracing and kissing each other, after I signed promissory notes to the value of seventy-five thousand, signed like a gentleman without a moment's hesitation. For I always have been, and always will be a gentleman. Let them kiss each other!"

"Oh, no," thought Nikolka, his eyes rolling and a chill running up his spine.

"But, you must forgive me," said the apparition, emerging gradually from the shadowy substance of dream and assuming more and more the form of a real live person. "You probably don't fully understand what this is all about. So, please, take a look at this letter; it will explain everything. As a gentleman, I will not hide my disgrace from anybody."

At this, the stranger handed Nikolka a blue letter. In total shock, Nikolka took the letter, and began to read it, his lips moving. Undated, it was written on soft blue notepaper in large, sprawling and agitated handwriting.

My darling, darling Lenochka! Knowing what a kind-hearted person you are, I am sending him directly to you, as one of the family. I have sent you a telegram, but he'll be able to tell you all about it himself, poor boy. Lariosik has had a most terrible shock, and for a long *time I was afraid he wouldn't get over it. You remember he married Milochka Rubtsova a year ago? Well, she turned out to be a real snake in the grass! I implore you to take care of him and look after him as only you know how. I will send you a regular allowance for his upkeep. He has come to loathe Zhitomir,* and I totally understand why. I won't be writing again – I'm too upset – and the hospital train will be here very shortly. He'll be able to tell you everything. Fondest love and kisses to you and to Seryozha!*

The signature at the bottom was indecipherable.

"I brought the bird with me!" said the stranger with a sigh. "A bird is a man's best friend. Many people, it is true, wonder what's the point of having a bird in the house, but I'll only say that at least it doesn't do anybody any harm."

Nikolka liked this last idea very much. Content not to try to understand anything for the moment, he gently brushed his eyebrows with the mysterious letter, and began to get up from the bed, wondering whether it would be rude to ask the stranger his surname... "What an extraordinary turn of events," he thought.

"Is it a canary?" he asked.

"Yes, but what a canary!" the stranger exclaimed proudly. "Actually, it's not just any old canary – it's a genuine male canary. I've got fifteen of them back in Zhitomir. I took them over to Mama; she'll be able to feed them. That scoundrel would probably have broken their necks; he hates birds. Can I put it on your desk for now?"

"Go ahead," Nikolka answered. "So you're from Zhitomir, are you?"

"Yes," answered the stranger. "And just imagine, what a coincidence! I arrived at the same time as your brother."

"What brother?"

"What do you mean, 'What brother'? Your brother arrived at the same time as I did," the stranger said, astonished at the question.

"What brother?" Nikolka shouted plaintively. "What brother? From Zhitomir?!"

"Your older brother..."

"Nikolka! Nikolka!" Yelena's voice could be heard clearly, calling from the sitting room. "Illarion Larionych! Could you wake him up, please!"

"*Triki, triki, tweet, tweet,*" chirped the bird at the top of its voice.

Nikolka dropped the blue letter and flew like a bullet through the library into the dining room. There he froze to the spot, his arms stretched out wide.

On the sofa, under the clock, lay the motionless figure of Alexei Turbin wearing someone else's black coat with a torn lining and trousers. His face had a bluish pallor and his teeth were tightly clenched. Yelena bustled about nearby. Her dressing gown had fallen open, revealing her black stockings and lace underwear. She was clutching now at the buttons on Alexei's chest, and now at his hands. "Nikol! Nikol!" she shouted.

Three minutes later and Nikolka, his student's cap on the back of his head and his grey army coat unbuttoned, was running up St Alexei's Hill, panting heavily. "What if he's not there?" he muttered to himself. "What extraordinary goings-on with that strange man in his yellow boots! Mustn't ask Kuritsky under any circumstances… kit and cat!…" The canary song rattled around in his head deafeningly… *kiti, kiti, kot!*

An hour later, a bowl full of reddish water stood on the dining-room floor, together with pieces of red-stained cotton wool and fragments of the white dish which the stranger in the yellow-topped boots had swept off the sideboard as he was reaching for a glass. The fragments of the dish crunched underfoot as people ran and walked over them. Alexei, his face still pale but no longer bluish, lay flat on his back on the pillow. He had regained consciousness and was trying to say something. But the doctor, a man with a pointed beard and rolled-up sleeves, and wearing a pair of gold pince-nez, leant down over him and, wiping his bloodstained hands with pieces of gauze, said:

"Don't try to speak, doctor…"

Together, the two of them – Anyuta, wide-eyed and her face as white as chalk, and Yelena, her golden hair dishevelled – lifted Alexei up and took off his wet, bloodstained shirt with its sleeve cut open.

"You might as well cut off some more," the bearded doctor said. "It's no use to him now, anyway."

With scissors they cut Alexei's shirt into small shreds, revealing his thin, yellowish body and his left arm, which had been bandaged right up to the shoulder. The ends of splints poked out from above and below the bandage. Nikolka knelt down, carefully unbuttoned Alexei's trousers and took them off.

"Undress him completely and get him straight into bed," the bearded doctor said in his bass voice. Anyuta began pouring water onto his arms and hands from a jug, and the soap flakes dripped down into the basin. The stranger stood a little way off to one side, taking no part in the hustle and bustle, looking mournfully now at the shattered crockery and now, his face blushing, at the sight of the dishevelled

Yelena whose dressing gown had come completely undone. His eyes were moist with tears.

They all carried Alexei from the dining room to his own room. Even the stranger did his bit by putting his arms under Alexei's knees and bearing the weight of his legs.

In the sitting room Yelena offered the doctor some money, but he withdrew his hand.

"What are you thinking of, for goodness' sake?" he said. "Do you think I'd take money from a doctor? More importantly, he should really go to the hospital…"

"No, I can't," came Alexei's feeble voice from the next room. "I can't go to the hosp—"

"Be quiet, colleague," the doctor responded. "We can manage without you. But I understand, of course; God knows what's going on in the City at the moment." He nodded towards the window. "Hmm… maybe he's right; he can't go… Well then, we'll have to manage at home… I'll come again this evening."

"Is it serious, doctor?" Yelena asked anxiously.

The doctor stared down at his feet as if the diagnosis lay somewhere in the brilliant yellow of the parquet flooring. Then he grunted and stroked his beard.

"The bone's intact," he said. "Hmm… so are the major blood vessels… But the wound's bound to fester… strands of wool from his coat got into the wound… and he has a fever…" Having delivered these disjointed, arcane statements, the doctor raised his voice and said with greater assurance: "Complete rest… morphine, if he's in pain… I'll give him some myself this evening. Only liquids to eat… some bouillon soup… and make sure he doesn't talk too much…"

"Please, doctor, he would like you not to say anything to anyone."

The doctor glowered at Yelena, looking at her sideways, and growled: "Yes, I understand… How did this happen to him? Did he slip?"

Yelena merely gave a little sigh and spread her hands.

"Right then," the doctor said abruptly, and sidled like a bear out into the hallway.

Part Three

T HE DARK CURTAINS on the two windows in Alexei's little bed-room that looked onto the glassed-in veranda had been drawn. Yelena's head of golden hair shone in the dark room, mirrored by the pale indistinct blur that was Alexei's head and neck on the pillow. A wire from the plug snaked towards the chair, the pinkish light in the lamp with its little shade went on, and day had turned into night. Alexei gestured to Yelena to close the door.

"Warn Anyuta immediately she mustn't say anything…"

"Yes, all right, I know. Alyosha, try not to talk too much."

"Yes, I know… I'll talk quietly. Oh, if only I don't lose my arm!"

"Oh, Alyosha, lie still and be quiet… What about this woman's coat? Is it going to stay here for a bit?"

"Yes, yes. And on no account must Nikolka try to take it to her. Otherwise, out there, on the street… Do you hear? And, in general, for goodness' sake don't let him go anywhere!"

"May God bring her health and happiness," Yelena said sincerely and tenderly. "And they say there aren't any good people in this world…"

A faint patch of colour appeared on the sick man's cheekbones, and he glanced up at the low white ceiling. Then he turned to Yelena and asked, with a grimace:

"Ah, yes, and who, may I ask, is this dolt who's just appeared?"

Yelena leant forward in the pink glow of the lamp, and shrugged her shoulders.

"Well, you see, he's someone who turned up literally only a couple of minutes before you did. He's Seryozha's nephew from Zhitomir. You've heard the name Larion Surzhansky? Well, here he is, the famous Lariosik."

"And?"

"He's come here with a letter. There's been some trouble back there. He had just begun to tell me about it when she brought you here."

"And he has some bird or other with him, for Heaven's sake!"

Laughing, but with a look of horror on her face, Yelena leant down towards the bed.

"Never mind about the bird! He's asking if he can live here, with us. I don't know what to do."

"*Live* here?"

"Well, yes. But be quiet and lie still, please, Alyosha. In her letter his mother begs us to take him in; she adores this Lariosik of hers, you know… I've never seen such a clumsy fool as this Lariosik in my life. The first thing he does when he gets here is to smash all the crockery. The blue dinner service. There are only two plates left intact."

"So there we are. I don't know what to do any more."

The whispering continued for a long time in the pink glow of the lamplight. Some distance away, on the other side of the door and the curtains, the voices of Nikolka and the unexpected guest could be heard. Yelena wrung her hands, begging Alexei not to talk quite so much. In the dining room there was the crunch of broken china as the agitated Anyuta swept up the blue dinner service. In view of the fact that nobody had any idea what might be going on in the City and that therefore people would very possibly be coming to requisition rooms, and in view of the fact that they had no money and that someone would be paying for Lariosik's keep, they decided to let him stay. But on condition that he observed the rules of the Turbin household. As far as the bird was concerned, they agreed to have it for a trial period. If it should prove impossible to have it in the house, then it would have to leave, although its owner could remain. As for the dinner service, it was decided it would be best to forget all about it – it would have been in such appallingly bad taste to complain, and Yelena naturally couldn't mention it. They decided to allow Lariosik to sleep in the library, where they would put a bed with a spring mattress and a little table.

Yelena went into the dining room. Lariosik stood there sorrowfully, hanging his head and looking at the spot on the sideboard where the stack of twelve plates had been, an expression of absolute misery in his cloudy, light-blue eyes. Nikolka stood opposite them, his mouth open. He was clearly listening to every word Lariosik was saying. His eyes were full of an unbridled curiosity.

"There's no leather in Zhitomir," gabbled Lariosik. "None at all, you understand. At least, not the kind of leather I'm used to. I've asked round all the shoemakers, offering them any amount of money, but no use…"

Seeing Yelena come into the room, Lariosik turned pale and started moving shiftily, glancing down for some reason at the emerald hem on Yelena's dressing gown.

"Yelena Vasilyevna, I will go down to the shops at once, ask around, and you will have a new dinner service today. I don't know what to say. How can I apologize to you? I deserve the death penalty for what I did. I'm such a hopeless case," he said, turning to Nikolka. "I'll go down to the shops at once," he repeated to Yelena.

"I would really rather you didn't go to the shops, particularly since they'll be closed anyway. Let me ask you: do you really not know what's going on in the City?"

"Of course I know what's going on," Lariosik exclaimed. "I arrived on the hospital train, if you remember – as you know from the telegram."

"What telegram?" Yelena asked. "We haven't had any telegram."

"What?" Lariosik's mouth opened wide in astonishment. "Aha! I can see now," he said, turning to Nikolka, "why you're looking at me in such a puzzled way... But if you'll permit me... Mama certainly handed in a telegram with sixty-three words."

"Tsk... Sixty-three words!" Nikolka said, quite astonished at such news. "What a pity! But the telegraph service is working very poorly at the moment, you know. In fact, it's stopped altogether."

"So what will happen now?" Lariosik asked dejectedly. "Will I be able to stay with you?" He looked around the room helplessly, and it was immediately clear from his expression that he liked it at the Turbins very much and that he had no wish to go anywhere else.

"Everything's organized," answered Yelena with a friendly nod. "We agree to have you here, so you can stay and make yourself at home. But you can see what an unfortunate thing has happened to us..."

Lariosik became even more dejected. His eyes filled with tears.

"Yelena Vasilyevna!" he exclaimed emotionally. "Allow me to help you in any way you would like. I can do without sleep for three or four nights in a row if necessary, you know."

"Thank you, thank you very much."

"And now," Lariosik said, turning to Nikolka again, "might I trouble you for some scissors?"

Agog with astonishment and curiosity, Nikolka flew off somewhere and returned with a pair of scissors. Blinking rapidly, Lariosik grabbed his army jacket by one of its buttons and once again turned to Nikolka:

"Forgive me: do you think I could use your room for a moment?"

Once he was in Nikolka's room he took off his jacket, revealing an exceptionally dirty shirt underneath. With the scissors he made a cut in the lustrous black lining of his jacket and pulled out a thick yellow-and-green wad of money. Solemnly he carried the money into the dining room and put it down on the table in front of Yelena.

"Yelena Vasilyevna," he said, "I am pleased, with your permission, to be able to give you the money for my keep now."

"But why such a hurry?" Yelena said, blushing. "Perhaps we can wait a little…"

"No, no, Yelena Vasilyevna," Lariosik protested hotly. "Please accept the money from me now. I know full well just how important it is to have money at this time." As he was unwrapping the bundle, the photograph of a woman fell out onto the table. He picked it up hastily and put it in his pocket with a sigh. "Anyway, you'll be able to make better use of it. What will I need, apart from being able to buy some cigarettes for myself, and canary seed for the bird?"

For a moment Yelena forgot about Alexei's wound, and her eyes sparkled with pleasure – Lariosik's actions were so appropriate and thorough.

"It seems he's not such a dolt as I had first imagined," Yelena thought. "He's polite and conscientious, just a little eccentric. But I am devastated about the dinner service."

"What a character," Nikolka said to himself. The fact of Lariosik's quite miraculous appearance among them had totally driven any unhappy thoughts from his mind.

"There's eight thousand here," Lariosik said, pushing the bundle of money resembling fried eggs with onions across the table. "If it's not enough, we can do some recalculating, and I can get some more."

"No, no, that's perfect, we can talk about that later," said Yelena. "This is what I suggest you do now: I'll ask Anyuta to heat up the water and you can have a bath. But tell me, I still don't quite understand how you managed to get here." Yelena gathered up the money and put it into her enormous dressing-gown pocket.

Lariosik's eyes filled with horror as the memories flooded back.

"It was a nightmare!" he exclaimed, folding his arms across his chest like a Catholic at prayer. "I was on the train for nine days… no, sorry, was it ten?… Let me see… Sunday, yes, Monday… I was on the train from Zhitomir for eleven days!"

"Eleven days!" Nikolka shouted. "You see?" he said to Yelena reproachfully.

"Yes, eleven days... When we set out, the Hetman's troops were in charge of the train, but along the way Petlyura's men took it over. When we came to some station or other... let me think, what was its name?... Oh, never mind, it doesn't matter... they wanted to take me off the train and shoot me. Can you imagine? Petlyura's men had those fur caps with tassels..."

"Were they blue?" asked Nikolka, burning with curiosity.

"No, red... yes, they were red. Anyway, they started shouting at me, telling me to get off the train. 'We're going to shoot you immediately!' they said. They had decided that I must be an officer who had been hiding in the hospital train. But I'd only been able to get on the train because Mama knew Dr Kuritsky."

"Kuritsky?" Nikolka exclaimed knowingly. "Ah, yes, him... cat and kit... We know him."

"*Kiti, kot, kit, kot,*" trilled the little bird distantly from the other room.

"Yes, him. He'd been the one to bring the train to us in Zhitomir... Anyway, my God! Thinking that everything was lost I began to pray to God. And do you know what saved me? It was the bird! I told them that I wasn't an officer, but a professional bird breeder, and showed them my canary. At this, one of them gave me a wallop on the back of my head and said rudely: 'Get the hell out of here, birdman!' The insolent swine! As a gentleman, I would have killed him, but you yourselves can understand..."

"Yelen..." Turbin could be heard feebly calling from his bedroom. Yelena quickly got up and rushed off, without hearing the end of the story.

According to the calendar, on 15th December the sun sets at half-past three. Twilight therefore began to seep into the apartment from three o'clock. But at this hour the hands of the clock on Yelena's face pointed to half-past five, the most depressing and hopeless time of all. The hands were formed by the two sad folds at the corners of her mouth, stretching down to underneath her chin. Her eyes reflected her dejection and her determination to fight the disaster that now confronted them.

The clock hands on Nikolka's face pointed to a spiky, ridiculous twenty to one – his head was full of a sense of chaos and confusion deriving from the expressive, enigmatic words "Malo-Provalnaya Street" that had been uttered by a dying man on those war-torn crossroads the day before, words whose significance would need to be made clear as soon as possible in the very near future. The chaos and worry had been further increased by the totally unexpected arrival of the enigmatic and engrossing figure of Lariosik into their lives, together with the most monstrous, far-reaching circumstance of all: the capture of the City by Petlyura. Yes, Petlyura – that Petlyura! And yes, the City – our City! And what would happen there now was beyond the comprehension and grasp of even the most developed and educated minds. What was completely clear was, firstly, that a totally appalling catastrophe had taken place: all our troops had been taken unawares and slaughtered, their blood crying out in agony to the heavens. And secondly, those criminals at headquarters, the generals and staff officers, deserved nothing less than death. But apart from the horror of the situation, there was also a burning curiosity to find out what would actually happen. What would life be like for the seven hundred thousand people living in the City, who now found themselves in the hands of this mysterious person with such a fearsome and unattractive name, Petlyura? What sort of a person was he? And why was he who he was?... Yes, but even this had to take a back seat when compared with the most important point of all, the bloodiest and most terrible thing that had happened to Alexei... oh my God!... just horrible, I tell you. And, although, it is true, there had been no firm news, Myshlayevsky and Karas had most probably been killed as well.

Nikolka was sitting at the slippery and greasy kitchen table, breaking up blocks of ice into little pieces with a broad-bladed chopper. The ice blocks were either splitting apart easily with a crunch as they did so, or they were skidding out from under the chopper and flying all over the kitchen. Nikolka's fingers had become numb from cold. The bag of ice with its silvery top lay close to hand.

"Malo... Provalnaya..." Nikolka said to himself, his lips moving soundlessly. Images of Nai-Turs, the ginger-headed Nero and Myshlayevsky flashed through his mind. And no sooner had this last image – of Myshlayevsky in his torn overcoat – come to mind than the clock hands on the face of Anyuta, who was busy at the hot stove, her face expressing sad, confused dreams, began to show more and more clearly twenty-five to five – the time of depression and sorrow. Were those multicoloured eyes still alive? Would anyone ever hear that broad stride, those jingling spurs again?

"I need some ice," said Yelena, opening the door into the kitchen.

"Just coming," Nikolka answered hastily. He screwed on the top of the ice bag and dashed through into the other room.

"Anyuta, my love," said Yelena, "you'll make sure you won't say a word to anyone about the fact that Alexei's been wounded, will you?

If, God forbid, someone should find out which side he's been fighting on, we'll be in real trouble."

"Of course I won't say anything, Yelena Vasilyevna. I completely understand." Anyuta looked at Yelena, her eyes wide with anxiety. "Such terrible things going on in the City, Holy Mother of God! There I was, on Borichevy Tok, just walking along, when I saw two bodies lying there on the street without boots. And the blood! There was so much blood. A crowd had gathered around, just standing and looking. Somebody was saying that it was two officers who had been killed... they were just lying there, bare-headed... my legs gave way under me, and I nearly dropped my basket. Then I ran away."

Anyuta's shoulders shivered and twitched at the memory, and the frying pans slipped out of her hands, crashing onto the floor.

"Shh, shh, for goodness' sake," Yelena said, calming Anyuta down with her outstretched hands.

At three o'clock in the afternoon the clock hands on Lariosik's grey face stood at precisely twelve o'clock – the time when energy and strength are at their peak. Both hands had converged on midday, fusing and pointing straight upwards like a sword. This was because, after the disaster that had shattered Lariosik's tender heart in Zhitomir, and after his terrible eleven-day journey in the hospital train and everything that he had had to live through, he was finding life in the Turbin household extraordinarily pleasant. Exactly why this should have been the case, Lariosik was unable to explain for the moment, because he didn't know the precise reason for it himself.

The beautiful Yelena seemed to him to be particularly deserving of his respect and attention. And he liked Nikolka very much as well. Wishing to demonstrate this, Lariosik waited until Nikolka had stopped darting back and forth to Alexei's room. Then he helped him set up the narrow spring bed in the library.

"You have a very open and trustworthy face," Lariosik said politely, looking so attentively at Nikolka's open face that he didn't watch what he was doing with the complicated creaking bed, and it slammed shut, trapping Nikolka's hand between two of the folds. It was so painful that Nikolka let out a yell, which, although muffled, was sufficiently loud for Yelena to come rushing into the room. Large tears were involuntarily welling up in Nikolka's eyes, even though he was exerting every effort to stop himself from howling. Yelena and Lariosik grappled with the bed's complicated mechanism, eventually managing to release it and free Nikolka's numb, blue hand. Lariosik almost burst into tears himself when he saw the crumpled, mottled hand emerge.

"My God!" he said, screwing up his already dejected face. "What's the matter with me? I make such a mess of everything!... Does it really hurt? Please forgive me, for God's sake!"

Without saying anything, Nikolka ran into the kitchen, where Anyuta, as instructed, doused his hand with cold water from the tap.

When they had succeeded in snapping open and unfolding the devious patent bed and it had become clear that Nikolka's hand wasn't too badly damaged, Lariosik once again experienced an onrush of quiet pleasure at being somewhere where there were so many books. Apart from his love of birds, he had a passion for books. And here, on the open bookshelves, there were lines upon lines of one treasure after another. Along all four walls Lariosik could see books of every description – in green, red and gold bindings, yellow covers and black slip cases. The bed had been made up some time ago. Next to it stood a chair with a towel hanging on the back, and with all the usual male accessories on the seat – soap dish, cigarettes, matches and watch. And, propped up against the back of the chair there was a photograph of a mysterious woman. But Lariosik had eyes only for the library as he wandered around looking at the book-lined shelves, stopping every so often to squat down by the bottom-most shelves and to feast his eyes on the covers, not knowing which to take out first: *The Posthumous Papers of the Pickwick Club* or the 1871 issue of *The Russian Herald*. The hands on his face pointed to midday.

But with the onset of twilight the mood in the apartment became sadder and sadder. The clocks didn't once strike twelve, their hands standing silent, like gleaming swords wrapped in a flag of mourning.

The cause of all this sadness, the reason for the different times showing on the clock faces of all those who were an inseparable part of the dusty, rather old-fashioned comfort of the Turbin household, was a slender column of mercury. At three o'clock in Alexei's bedroom it had shown 39.6 degrees. Yelena turned pale when she saw it, and wanted to shake the thermometer down, but Alexei turned his head and, in a weak but insistent voice, asked her to show it to him. Silently and reluctantly she handed him the thermometer. He looked at it and gave a deep, heavy sigh.

By five o'clock he was lying in his bed with a grey, cold bag on his head, the pieces of ice melting and floating around in the bag. There was now some colour in his cheeks, and his eyes were shining and much improved.

"Thirty-nine point six... that's fine," he said licking his dry, parched lips. "So... Anything might happen... In any event, that's the end of my practice for a bit. Just so long as I don't lose my arm... otherwise..."

"Alyosha, do be quiet, please," said Yelena, tucking up the blanket round his shoulders. Turbin fell silent and closed his eyes. From the wound high up in his left armpit a dry, prickly heat had spread out and was crawling through his entire body. Every so often he would breathe in deeply, holding his breath until his head swam, but his feet had become unpleasantly cold. By the evening, when all the lamps had been lit and dinner for the three of them – Yelena, Nikolka and Lariosik – had long since passed in anxious silence, the column of mercury, miraculously swelling and rising from the dense silver bulb at the bottom of the thermometer, crept up to 40.2 degrees. And then, suddenly, in the pink glow of the bedroom, the despondency and anxiety began to dissipate and float away. This feeling of anxiety had come and squatted on the blanket in a great, grey lump, but now it had turned into yellowish strands, drifting around like seaweed in water. Any worry about the practice and any fear for the future were now forgotten, eliminated by the seaweed. The sharp pain in the left side of his chest dulled and became less mobile. The fever was replaced by shivering. Now and then the burning candle in his chest changed into an icy knife that twisted somewhere in his lung. Whenever this happened, Alexei would shake his head, toss away the ice bag and snuggle down deeper under the blanket. Then the pain in his chest would burst its boundaries, bringing on a spasm of such intensity that the wounded man would involuntarily start to moan in a weak, dry voice. And then, when the icy knife disappeared, giving way again to the hot candle, the heat flooded throughout his body, the sheet and the cramped space under the blanket. Then he would call out for water. Now Nikolka's, now Yelena's, and now Lariosik's face would appear out of the haze, bending down and listening. The eyes of all three seemed terribly alike, frowning and angry. The hands on Nikolka's face dropped immediately, pointing to half-past five precisely, just like Yelena's. Every other minute, Nikolka would go out into the dining room, where, for some reason, the lights seemed to be burning especially dully and hesitantly, and look at the clock. *Tonk... tonk...* wheezed the clock angrily and ominously, its hands pointing to nine o'clock, then to quarter-past nine, and then to half-past.

Then Nikolka would sigh deeply and wander off, like a sleepy fly, out of the dining room, across the hallway, past Alexei's bedroom and into the sitting room. From there he would go into the study and, pulling back the white curtains, look out through the balcony door onto the street... "Let's hope the doctor will find the courage to come..." The steep, winding street was emptier than it had been for many days, but things out there didn't look too awful. Now and then a cabby's sleigh scraped along the snow, but only very occasionally. He started to consider whether perhaps he'd have to go himself, and whether he'd be able to persuade Yelena.

"If he hasn't come by half-past ten, I'll go myself together with Larion Larionovich, while you stay here looking after Alyosha... No, please be quiet: you have the look of a cadet about you, don't you understand? And we can give Lariosik Alyosha's civilian clothes to wear... Anyway, he'll be left alone if he's with a woman."

Lariosik hastily expressed his willingness to sacrifice himself and to go alone, and then he went off to get into civilian clothes.

The icy knife had disappeared altogether, but the fever had intensified, exacerbated by the typhus, and in his fever Alexei began to have vague visions of someone totally unknown dressed in grey.

"Do you know, that man in grey must have turned a somersault!" Alexei said suddenly, sternly and distinctly, looking directly at Yelena. "Not very pleasant. Basically, they're all birds of course. They should be taken away and put in a warm larder, and they'd come to their senses there."

"What are you on about, Alyosha?" asked Yelena, frightened, leaning over him and feeling the heat from his face on hers. "Birds? What birds?"

In his black civilian clothes, Lariosik looked hunched and broader in the shoulders, with his yellow boots concealed under his trousers. Frightened, he looked around him disconsolately. Balancing on tiptoe, he ran out of the bedroom, through the hallway into the dining room, and then through the library and on into Nikolka's room. Here, his arms swinging importantly, he went quickly up to the cage on the desk and threw a black cloth over the top of it. But there had been no need: the bird had long since been asleep in the corner, curled up into a feathery ball and quite silent, unaware of the world's troubles. Lariosik firmly closed the door into the library, and then the door from the library into the dining room.

"Not pleasant at all, really nasty," Alexei said uneasily, looking into the corner of the room. "I shouldn't have shot him... No, listen..." He began to free his good arm from under the blanket. "It would be best to ask him to come and explain why he was dashing about like that, like an idiot. I take full responsibility, of course… It's all so hopeless and stupid…"

"Yes, of course it is," Nikolka said gravely, and Yelena hung her head. Alexei became agitated and tried to get up. But the sharp pain was too strong, and he groaned.

"Then get rid of it," he said angrily.

"Perhaps we should take the bird into the kitchen? I've covered it up, by the way, and it's quiet," Lariosik whispered anxiously to Yelena.

Yelena dismissed the idea with a wave of her hand. "No, no, that's not it…" Nikolka strode out decisively into the dining room. His hair was dishevelled. He looked at the clock: it was nearly ten. Anyuta appeared in the doorway.

"How is Alexei Vasilyevich?" she asked anxiously.

"Delirious," Nikolka answered, sighing deeply.

"Oh my goodness," Anyuta whispered. "Why doesn't that doctor come?"

Nikolka looked at her and went back into the bedroom. He bent down to Yelena's ear and began to whisper into it persuasively:

"It's your decision, but I would like to go and see if he's there. If he's not, then we need to get someone else. It's ten o'clock. And it's quite quiet outside."

"Let's wait until half-past ten," Yelena whispered in reply, shaking her head and wrapping her hands in her shawl. "It'll be difficult asking someone else. He'll come, I know he will."

Just after ten o'clock, totally absurdly, a large, heavy mortar appeared in the narrow little bedroom. What the hell was that about? Staying here any longer would be senseless! The mortar took up so much space between the walls that its left wheel was pressed up against the bed. He couldn't stay here; he'd have to clamber out through the heavy spokes, then arch his back in order to squeeze through the other, right-hand wheel with all his things, including God knows how much stuff hanging on his left arm. The weight of everything would pull the arm down to the ground, so that it would cut into his armpit like a tow rope. The mortar couldn't be removed, so the whole apartment had become a mortar room, as ordered, and when that slow-witted Colonel Malyshev and Yelena, who had now also become slow-witted, saw the wheels they wouldn't be able to do anything to get rid of the gun or even to remove the patient to more tolerable conditions, to somewhere where there were no mortars. Because of that blasted, heavy, cold object the apartment itself had become like a roadside inn. Then the doorbell started ringing... *rrring... rrring...* and visitors began to appear. He caught a glimpse of Colonel Malyshev carrying a whole pile of papers, looking ridiculous, like some Laplander in his cap with earmuffs and his gold epaulettes. When Alexei called out to him he disappeared down the barrel of the gun, only for Nikolka to come and start fussing about the place, incoherent and stupidly stubborn. Nikolka gave him something to drink, but instead of it being a cold stream of water from a fountain, it was something warm and disgusting, smelling as if it had come from a saucepan.

"Ugh... that's revolting... Stop it," he mumbled.

Nikolka raised his eyebrows in alarm, but he persisted clumsily. Several times Yelena changed into the dark and superfluous Lariosik, Seryozha's nephew. When she changed back again to being Yelena, she would run her fingers along his forehead, but without relieving the pain very much. Yelena's hands, usually so warm and deft, now felt like a rake, as she scraped away idiotically, doing everything irritating and unnecessary to poison the life of a peaceful man lying stuck in this damned weapon store. But she couldn't be responsible for the pole on which his wounded body had been placed, could she? Yet what was the matter with her? She was sitting on the end of the pole, which was beginning to revolve nauseatingly under her weight... Well, you try and live when a round pole is digging into your body! No, no, it's all so unbearable! And, as loudly as he could, although it actually came out quietly, he called out:

"Julia!"

But Julia didn't respond to the sick man's call, remaining in her old-fashioned room with the portrait of a man of the 1840s with gold epaulettes. And the grey figures who, together with the other Turbins, began parading round the apartment and the bedroom would have been the final straw for the wounded man, had it not been for the arrival of a large man – a persistent and very capable man – in gold-rimmed glasses. In honour of his appearance, one more light was added to the room in the form of a flickering wax candle in an old, black, heavy candlestick. The candle now glimmered on the table, now moved around Alexei, while the ugly figure of Lariosik flitted around the walls above, looking like a bat with clipped wings. The candle leant over sideways, dripping white wax. The little bedroom smelt strongly of iodine, spirit and ether. A chaotic jumble of glittering little boxes with lights in nickel-plated mirrors started to mount up on the table, together with piles of cotton wool – theatrical Christmas snow. The large man in the gold-rimmed glasses and with the warm hands injected something into Alexei's good arm, with miraculous results: within just a few minutes the grey figures had stopped their outrageous behaviour. The mortar was moved through the curtained window onto the veranda. Its black barrel didn't seem nearly so frightening now. He could now breathe more easily, because the huge wheel had gone away, and he didn't need to clamber between the spokes any longer. The candle went out, and the angular figure of Larion, Lariosik Surzhansky from Zhitomir, as black as coal, disappeared from the walls, while Nikolka's face became more normal and not so irritatingly obstinate – possibly because, thanks to the skill of the large man in the gold-rimmed glasses, the hands had stopped pointing so inexorably and despairingly straight downwards towards his pointed chin. The hands had now returned from indicating half-past five to twenty to five, and, although the time on the clock in the dining room did not correspond to this, its hands relentlessly moving ever onwards, the senile wheezing and grumbling had nonetheless been replaced by its familiar clear, weighty baritone... *tonk*! And the tower clock, just as in the magnificent toy castle of Louis XIV, chimed *bom... bom...* midnight... listen!... midnight... listen! The chimes sounded a warning note, combined with the pleasant, silvery clang of halberds. The sentries walked up and down on guard, for man has unwittingly brought towers, alarm bells and weapons into the world for one purpose only: to maintain peace among men and to preserve hearth and home. That is the reason he goes to war and, essentially, that is the only possible reason why he should ever do so.

And it was only in such peaceful circumstances that Julia – that self-centred, depraved, but seductive woman – agreed to appear. And appear she did, in black stockings, the edge of her black fur-lined boots illuminated briefly by the light brick of the steps, with the hasty clatter of her feet and the rustle of her dress accompanied by the tinkling sound of little bells playing a gavotte from where Louis XIV was basking surrounded by enchanting, exotic women in his sky-blue garden on the shores of a lake.

At midnight, Nikolka carried out some extremely important and very necessary tasks. First of all, he emerged from the kitchen with a dirty, moist rag and erased the following phrases from the side of the Shipwright of Saardam:

Long live Russia!
Long live autocracy!
Thrash Petlyura!

Then, with Lariosik's eager assistance, he accomplished an even more important task. From the drawer of the desk in Alyosha's room he carefully and silently took out Alyosha's Browning, together with its two magazines and the little box of ammunition that went with it. When he checked the contents of the box he found that six rounds had already been fired.

"Good for him," Nikolka whispered.

It would never have entered anyone's mind of course that Lariosik might be a traitor. No intelligent person, in general, could ever, on any account, be a supporter of Petlyura, and even less, in particular, a gentleman who had signed promissory notes to the value of seventy-five thousand, and who had sent telegrams containing sixty-three words... Both Alyosha's Browning and Nai-Turs's pistol were greased all over with engine oil and kerosene. Following Nikolka's example, Lariosik rolled up his sleeves, helping him with the greasing and packing everything away in a long, high-sided tin that had once contained caramels. They worked quickly, for any decent person who has taken part in a revolution knows full well that all powers that be, wishing to search people's houses, will always do so at night, between the hours of half-past two and quarter-past six in winter, and from midnight to four o'clock in summer. All the same, completion of the work was delayed, thanks to Lariosik who, wanting to acquaint himself with the workings of a ten-chambered pistol such as a Colt, placed the magazine in the wrong end. Removing it required considerable effort and a fair amount of grease. And then there was a second, unexpected hitch: the tin, which was lined with paraffin paper inside and sealed with strips of sticky insulating tape on the outside, and which contained the revolvers, Nikolka's and Alexei's epaulettes, Alexei's chevron and the photograph of Tsarevich Alexei, would not fit through the little window pane at the top – the only part of the window unsealed during the winter months.

The problem was how and where to hide it: they weren't all as stupid as Vasilisa. Just that afternoon Nikolka had hit on the idea of a possible hiding place. The wall of No. 13 was right next to their neighbours' wall at No. 11, with a gap of no more than a couple of feet. In No. 13 there were only three windows on this wall: one in Nikolka's corner room and two completely unnecessary ones in the library (it was dark anyway). In addition, downstairs in Vasilisa's larder there was a dark little window covered by a grating. And the wall of No. 11 was totally blank. Imagine a splendid little ravine about two feet in width, quite dark and invisible even from the street, and inaccessible to nearly everyone except possibly the odd enquiring little boy. And, indeed, as a boy, Nikolka had clambered into this space while playing cops and robbers, stumbling over the piles of bricks, remembering very well seeing a row of spikes running up the wall of No. 13 to the roof. Before No. 11 had been built, these spikes had very probably formed the support for a fire escape that had subsequently been taken down, but leaving them in place. When he had put his hand out of the window earlier that evening Nikolka had been able to locate a spike almost immediately. All very clear and simple so far. But now, the tin, tied both ways with top-quality triple cord – so called sugar-cane cord – with an already prepared loop, wouldn't go through the window.

"We're clearly going to have to open the entire window," Nikolka said, climbing down from the window sill.

Acknowledging Nikolka's quick-wittedness and resourcefulness, Lariosik set about unsealing the window. The swollen frames did not want to open, and the difficult operation took up a whole thirty minutes. But finally they succeeded in opening first one window and then the second, with a long, winding crack appearing in the glass on Lariosik's side.

"Turn the light out!" Nikolka ordered.

The light went out and a blast of freezing air gushed into the room. Nikolka leant out halfway into the black, icy space and attached the upper loop of the rope to a spike. And there was the tin hanging down perfectly well at the end of a two-foot rope. There was no way anybody could see it from the street, firstly because the firewall of No. 13 had been built at an oblique angle to the street, rather than at right angles, and secondly because there was a sign hanging high up on the wall advertising the dressmaker's business next door. You would only be able to see the tin if you climbed up into the gap. But nobody would be able to do that until the spring, because huge snowdrifts had piled up, blown in from the yard, forming an ideal barrier from the street side. But the best thing of all about it was that you didn't need to open the window to operate it. All you needed to do was to stick your arm out of the top pane and you could pull on the rope like a piece of string. Perfect!

The light was turned on again, and after softening the sealant left over by Anyuta from the autumn on the window sill, Nikolka resealed the main window. Even if, by some strange chance, someone were to find the tin, there would be a ready-made reply. "I'm sorry? Whose tin did you say? Aha, revolvers... the Tsarevich? Of course not! Don't know anything about it, not a thing. How the hell should I know who put it there? They must have climbed down from the roof and hung it there. There are all kinds of people about nowadays, aren't there? Well, then. We're peaceful people here; don't know anything about any tsarevich."

"Brilliantly done, I swear to God," said Lariosik.

How could it be otherwise? The thing was accessible, and yet at the same time outside the apartment.

It was three o'clock in the morning. Evidently, they wouldn't be receiving any visitors that night. With exhausted, drooping eyelids Yelena tiptoed into the dining room. It was Nikolka's turn to take over from her: Nikolka from three to six, and then Lariosik from six to nine.

They spoke in whispers.

"So that means it's typhus," Yelena whispered. "Bear in mind that Vanda has already been up to find out what's wrong with Alexei. I told her that it was possibly typhus... She almost certainly didn't believe me; she started rolling her eyes... She kept on asking how things were with us, where the others were, and whether anyone had been wounded. Not a word about the wound."

"No, absolutely not," Nikolka said, waving his arms around. "Vasilisa is the world's greatest coward! If it came to it, he would blurt out to all and sundry that Alexei had been wounded, just to protect himself."

"What a bastard," Lariosik said. "That's vile behaviour!"

Alexei lay in his room, his mind in a complete fog. After the injection his face had become absolutely calm, his features sharper and more refined. The soothing poison was now flowing through his blood, keeping guard over his body. The grey figures had stopped ordering everyone around as if they were in their own homes, and had gone about their own business, taking the mortar away with them for good. And even if some complete stranger did appear on the scene, he would nonetheless behave respectably, trying to communicate and connect with familiar objects and people who had always been a rightful part of the Turbin household. Colonel Malyshev appeared once again, but this time he sat in a chair for a bit, smiling away as if to say everything was fine and there was nothing to worry about, rather than scowling and muttering threateningly or stuffing the room with pieces of paper. He set fire to some documents, it is true, but he didn't dare lay a finger on Alexei's diploma or the photographs of his mother. And the fire that he used was a pleasant, blue-burning alcohol flame and, in any case, it was a comforting fire because it usually preceded an injection. Madame Anjou's doorbell rang frequently.

"*Rrring*," said Alexei, trying to convey the sound of the doorbell to whoever was sitting in the chair. They seemed to be taking turns to sit there: first it was Nikolka, then some Mongolian-looking stranger (because of the injection Alexei did not dare kick up a fuss), and then the melancholy, grey-haired, trembling figure of Maxim. "*Rrring...*" the patient repeated affectionately, attempting to create a live tableau from the shifting figures in front of him – a tortuously difficult task, but one that ended in a surprisingly happy, even if painful conclusion.

The dining-room clock moved rapidly on, its hands spinning round, and when the short, stubby hand approached five o'clock on the pale dial, Alexei fell into a semi-doze. Every so often he shifted his position, half-opening his eyes and muttering incoherently to himself.

"Up the stairs... up the stairs... I'm not going to make it up the stairs... Too weak, I'll fall... Goodness, she's walking fast... her boots... through the snow... I'll leave footprints... wolves... *Rrring... rrring!...*"

13

T HAT HAD BEEN THE LAST TIME Alexei had heard the doorbell ring, as he rushed out of the back entrance of Madame Anjou's boutique, situated Heaven knows where and smelling sweetly of perfume. The bell: that meant someone had just come into the shop. Perhaps it was someone just like him, someone on his side who had got lost and had been left behind. Or perhaps it was the enemy, chasing after him. Either way, to have returned to the boutique would have been impossible, an act of totally unnecessary heroism.

Down some slippery steps and Alexei was outside, in the yard. Here he heard with total clarity the sound of shooting coming from somewhere quite close, on the street leading down to the Kreshchatik. It wasn't very likely to be coming from the museum area. He realized now that he had clearly wasted too much time wrapped in gloomy contemplation in the dimly lit shop, and that Colonel Malyshev had been absolutely right in telling him that he needed to hurry. His heart was racing with anxiety.

As he looked around him, Alexei could now see that the long, endlessly high yellow building that housed Madame Anjou's was bordered by a huge yard that stretched as far as a low wall. Beyond the wall, the adjoining property belonged to the railway company. Screwing up his eyes and glancing round once again, he set off across the deserted yard, making straight for the wall. There was a gate in the wall that, to his great astonishment, was unlocked. He went through the gate and found himself in a horrible little yard, with the dark slits of windows on the railway company building staring at him unpleasantly. The building was clearly lifeless. He went under the echoing archway that cut through the building and out onto the street. The hands of the ancient clock on the tower of the building opposite indicated exactly four o'clock. It had already begun to grow dark. The street was completely empty. Filled with foreboding, Alexei looked round apprehensively, and set off down, rather than up, the street covered with a sprinkling of snow, towards the Golden Gate, towering in the middle of the wet, slushy square. A single pedestrian in a black coat ran towards him with a frightened expression on his face, and then disappeared.

Empty streets in general leave a very unpleasant impression, and this one in particular gnawed away at him, filling him with a nasty premonition. Frowning angrily, as he tried to make his mind up about what he should do next – he knew that he couldn't get home by flying through the air, and that, whatever happened, he had to keep going – he raised his greatcoat collar and moved off.

Then he realized partly why he was feeling so uneasy: it was the sudden absence of heavy gunfire. For the last two weeks it had been heard constantly, everywhere. But now the sky was quite quiet. And yet, on the other hand, somewhere down there on the Kreshchatik, he could clearly hear the intermittent crackle of rifle fire. He needed to turn left, away from the Golden Gate, into that alleyway, and from there, keeping close to the St Sophia Cathedral, quietly make his way along the back streets to St Alexei's Hill and home. If he had done that, everything would have turned out differently. But he didn't. There is this force in life that sometimes impels you to look down from a great height into an abyss. You're drawn towards the cold, towards the steep drop. And now, it was the thought of the museum that attracted him: he simply had to go and see what was happening there, even if only from a distance. And so, instead of turning off the square, he took ten quite unnecessary steps that brought him out onto Vladimirskaya Street. But once there, the alarm bells inside him immediately started to ring, and he could distinctly hear Malyshev's voice whispering to him to "run!". He looked to the right, where, in the distance, he could see the museum. He managed to see a section of white wall and the lowering cupolas, and some black figures flitting about in the distance. But that was all he had time to see.

Climbing up the steep Proreznaya Street from the Kreshchatik, which was veiled in a distant frosty haze, several figures in grey greatcoats were coming straight towards him, spread across the whole width of the street. They were only about thirty yards away. Alexei could tell immediately that they had been running for a long time and that they were exhausted. Some unaccountable inner instinct, rather than his eyes, told him that they were Petlyura's men.

"Trapped," said Malyshev's voice distinctly from the pit of his stomach.

At that point, several seconds seem to have disappeared from Alexei's life; he had no idea what happened during this time. He came to only when he found himself round the corner, on Vladimirskaya Street, his head hunched between his shoulders, his feet having carried him swiftly from the fateful corner on Proreznaya Street, just by the Marquise confectionery shop.

"That's right, just a bit farther, a bit farther…" he panted, the blood coursing through his temples.

Just a little bit farther without any noise from behind! If only he could turn himself into a knife blade, or simply merge into the wall. But come on!… Then the silence was broken and, inevitably, he heard them behind him again.

"Halt!" someone shouted hoarsely at Alexei's cold, retreating back.

"So this is it," said the voice from the pit of his stomach.

"Halt!" the voice repeated sharply.

Alexei glanced round and stopped as if frozen to the spot, struck by a sudden notion that he might be able to pass himself off as a peaceful citizen. "I'm just going about my business… Leave me alone," or words to that effect. From a distance of about fifteen yards, his pursuer quickly raised his rifle. As soon as Alexei turned to face him, the astonishment on his face visibly increased, and it seemed to Alexei that he had slanted, Mongolian eyes. A second pursuer burst round the corner and pulled back the bolt on his rifle. The expression on the first man's face changed from one of astonishment to one of malicious, unfathomable glee.

"Look what we have here, Petro! An officer!" he shouted in Ukrainian. As he said this, he looked like a hunter who had suddenly caught sight of a hare.

"What? How on earth could he know that?" The thought hammered away in Alexei's brain.

The second man's rifle suddenly turned into a small black hole, the size of a little coin. Alexei felt himself flying like an arrow along Vladimirskaya Street, aware that his felt boots were killing him. Above and behind him came a sound like a whip cracking in the air.

"Halt! Get him!" Another crack of the whip. "Get that officer!" The whole of Vladimirskaya Street resounded with the thunder of the pursuit. Two more shots zinged through the air.

To transform someone's rather weak and, in really difficult circumstances, useless brain into the cunning instinct of a wild animal, all you need do is to chase after him with guns and he'll turn into a cunning wolf. As Alexei rounded the corner of Malo-Provalnaya Street like a hunted wolf, he caught a glimpse behind him of the black muzzle of a rifle that suddenly turned into a pale, circular ring of fire. Putting on speed, he dashed into Malo-Provalnaya Street, taking a decision that changed his life for the second time in just five minutes.

His instinct told him that if someone chases after you stubbornly and persistently enough, keeping on your tail, they will catch you and, once having caught you, they will kill you. And they would kill him, because he was running away from them, because he was carrying no papers and because of his grey greatcoat and his revolver. And finally, they would kill him, because, having missed once, and then a second time, they would get him the third time. It was always the third time: that has been known since antiquity. In other words, this was the end. Another thirty seconds and his felt boots would give up the ghost. The end was inevitable, and that being so, his fear drained away from his body and legs and into the ground. But as he ran along, he began violently spitting out the feeling of icy rage that flooded up through his legs; his eyes became slits, just like a wolf's. Two grey-coated pursuers, followed by a third, leapt round the corner of Vladimirskaya Street, all three firing at once. Gritting his teeth, Alexei slowed and, without taking aim, fired back three times. Again he picked up speed, dimly seeing a shadowy black figure in front of him, flitting along right next to the wall by a drainpipe. Then he suddenly felt as if someone with wooden pincers was tugging at his left armpit, making him run strangely and unevenly, a little to one side.

He turned once again and loosed off three more shots, disciplining himself to stop at the sixth shot.

"The seventh is for me. Oh, my Nikolka! My lovely golden-haired Yelena! It's all over; they'll torture me and slice the epaulettes into my skin. The seventh bullet is for me."

Moving along sideways, he felt a strange sensation: the revolver in his right hand was pulling his arm down on that side, but his left arm seemed somehow heavier. He needed to stop and rest – he was, in any case, totally out of breath, and he'd arrived at the end of the line. Yet he somehow managed to reach the bend in the world's most fantastic street and get round the corner out of sight, where he had a moment's respite. But, farther on, it looked hopeless: all the gates were locked… that one there… and there, by that huge building… and there. The idiotic, comic proverb came into his head: "Only lose hope, my friend, when you've hit rock bottom."

That was when he saw her, like a miracle, by a dark, moss-covered fence in front of a line of trees fringing a garden. Half-slumped against the wall, she was stretching out her arms towards him melodramatically, her enormous eyes ablaze with terror.

"Hey, officer!" she shouted. "Here! This way!"

Slipping and sliding a little in his felt boots, and gulping hot air into his lungs, he staggered as quickly as he could towards the woman's outstretched arms. Drawn on by them, he practically fell through a narrow gateway in the black wooden wall. The situation was immediately transformed. The woman closed the gate and the lock snapped shut behind her. Alexei found himself looking right into the woman's eyes. He was dimly aware of blackness and an expression of active determination.

"Come on, run, this way… follow me," she whispered. She turned and started running along a narrow brick path, with Alexei slowly following. To his left he glimpsed some sheds, and then she turned again. To his right was what looked like a fairy-tale, white terraced garden. Then, right ahead of him, there was a low fence and another gate, through which the woman darted, with Alexei following, gasping for air. She slammed the gate shut, and Alexei caught a glimpse of a slender, black-stockinged leg, as she climbed agilely up some brick steps, the hem of her dress rustling. Pricking up his ears, he could hear the sounds of pursuit coming from the street behind them. Yes, there they were, just turning the corner, looking for him. "She might have saved me… might have saved me," he thought, "but I don't think I can make it… my heart…" On the very last step he suddenly fell down onto his left knee and left arm. Everything started spinning round. The woman bent down and lifted him up by his right arm.

"Just a bit farther!" she urged. With a trembling left hand she opened a third little gate and, dragging the stumbling Alexei through, set off again at a run along a little alleyway. "My goodness, what a labyrinth… That's just what I need now!" he thought vaguely. And then he was in the white garden, but now much higher up and well away from that fateful Provalnaya Street. As he felt the woman dragging him along, he was aware of the heat in his left side and arm. But the rest of his body was icy cold, including his heart, which had almost stopped beating. "She might have saved me, but this is the end… the absolute end… my legs are giving way." Under the snow he could dimly see some untouched virgin clumps of lilacs. Then there was a doorway, and a glass lantern hanging outside an ancient, snow-covered porch. He could hear the jingle of a key. Still keeping to his right-hand side, the woman used the last ounce of her strength to drag him towards the lantern. Then there was another jingle of keys, and they were in some gloomy place with a lived-in, rather musty smell. Here, above them in the gloom, a light shone very faintly, and the floor skidded sideways to the left under his feet… Green, poisonous-looking lights rimmed with fire flashed in front of his eyes, followed by total darkness, giving him an immediate sense of relief.

A row of worn brass knobs glinting in the dim, unsteady light. There was something cold trickling down his chest, enabling him to breathe more freely, but his arm inside his left sleeve felt ominously warm and lifelessly damp. "I'm wounded – that's what it is." Alexei was aware that he was lying on the floor, his head pressed painfully up against something hard and uncomfortable. The brass knobs he could see in front of him clearly belonged to a trunk. The cold sensation from the water she was splashing over him was so great he could scarcely breathe.

"For God's sake, drink some of this," he heard a faint, chesty voice say somewhere above his head. "Are you breathing? What do we do now?"

The glass knocked against his teeth as Alexei gulped down the icy-cold water. Now that she was close to him, squatting on the floor, he could see the woman's blond curls and dark, dark eyes. She put the glass down on the floor and, supporting him gently by the back of his head, started to lift him up.

"Is my heart still beating?" he wondered. "I'm coming back to life, it seems... Maybe I haven't lost too much blood. I have to fight this." Yes, his heart was beating, but unsteadily and too fast, as if it were tying itself in knots.

"Use whatever you like to cut everything off if you need to, but get a tourniquet on me quickly," he said weakly.

Her eyes wide, she tried to digest what he'd just said. Then, grasping what it was he wanted her to do, she leapt up and dashed to the cupboard and started pulling out heaps of material.

Biting his lip, Alexei thought: "There's not much sign of blood on the floor; with any luck, I've not lost too much." As he twisted and turned, she helped him take his greatcoat off. Then he sat up, trying to ignore his dizziness. She began to take off his jacket.

"Scissors," he said.

He found it difficult to talk as he was short of breath. With a swish of her black silk skirt the woman went off towards the doorway, where she took off her cap and fur coat. Then she came back and squatted down beside him again. With the scissors she cut clumsily and painfully into his sleeve, which was now sodden and sticky with blood, and freed him from his jacket, tearing the rest of it away. The left sleeve was soaked in dark-red blood from top to bottom. Blood started dripping onto the floor.

"Cut off as much as you like..."

Piece by piece the shirt came away. White-faced, his yellowish body naked to the waist and covered in blood, Alexei willed himself to stay alive, not allowing himself to fall down a second time. He gritted his teeth and felt around on his left shoulder with his right hand.

"The bone's not broken, thank God..." he said through his teeth. "Use a strip of something, or a bandage."

"I've got bandages," she said faintly, but eagerly. She went off somewhere and returned, tearing open a packet.

"There's no one else here," she said. "I'm by myself."

She sat down by him again. Alexei could see now where he'd been hit: it was a small, not very deep entrance wound, lying close to where the arm joined the body. There was a thin trickle of blood oozing from it.

"What about the other side?" he asked abruptly, almost casually, instinctively preserving the breath of life.

"There's a wound there as well," she answered with alarm.

"Tie the tourniquet above it... Yes, there... You'll save the arm."

Never before had he experienced such pain. Green circles, now merging into one, now intermingling with each other, danced in front of his eyes. He bit his lower lip.

As she pulled the bandage tight, he helped her with his teeth and his right hand. Together they bound the arm above the wound in a single painful, burning knot. The trickle of blood stopped immediately.

She now had to move him somehow. He got up onto his knees and put his right arm round her shoulder. She then helped him stand up on his weak, tottering legs and, with her taking the full weight of his body, they managed to get across the room. The low, old-fashioned room was shadowed in twilight. When she had sat him down on something soft and covered in dust, she turned and switched on a lamp with a cherry-coloured shade. He could make out a velvet pattern, the edge of a double-breasted frock coat and a yellowish-gold epaulette in a frame on the wall. Breathing heavily from all the excitement and her exertions, she reached her hands out towards Alexei and said:

"I have some brandy… Perhaps you should have some?… Some brandy?"

"Yes, immediately," he answered. And then he collapsed onto his right elbow.

The brandy seemed to help a little: at least now he felt that he was no longer at death's door and that he would be able to bear the pain gnawing away at his left shoulder. Kneeling down, the woman bandaged his wounded hand and then, reaching farther down to his feet, pulled off his felt boots. Then she brought him a pillow and a long Japanese robe embroidered with flowers and smelling sweetly of some age-old perfume.

"Lie down," she said.

Obediently he lay down. She placed the robe on top of him, followed by a blanket, and then stood by a narrow ottoman looking directly at him.

"You are a remarkable woman," he said, adding, after a pause: "I'll lie here for a bit, recover my strength, and then I'll get up and go home; I won't trouble you much longer."

His heart was full of anxiety and despair. "What about Yelena? My God, oh my God… and Nikolka? What did he die for? He must be dead…"

Without saying a word, she pointed towards the low window, hung with a curtain with pompons. In the distance he could clearly hear the sound of rifle shots.

"You'd be killed immediately, you can be sure of that," she said.

"In that case... I'm afraid... I'll put you in danger... What if they come looking?... My revolver... the blood... there, in my greatcoat," he said, licking his lips. His head was spinning lightly from the brandy and loss of blood. The woman's face became anxious, and she thought hard for a moment.

"No," she said decisively. "No; if they'd known where you were they would have been here a long time ago. It's such a maze around here that nobody would be able to trace where you'd gone. We ran through three different gardens. But, for now, I have some clearing up to do..."

He heard the splash of water, the rustle of some material and some clattering around in cupboards.

When she came back she had his Browning with her, holding it by the handle with just two fingers, as if it were red-hot.

"Is it loaded?" she asked.

Freeing his right hand from underneath the blanket, Alexei checked the safety catch.

"Just be careful with it," he replied. "Hold it only by the handle."

When she came back again she said with some embarrassment:

"Just in case they come... you ought to take off your breeches as well... they'll find you lying there, and I'll tell them that you're my husband and that you're unwell."

Grimacing and screwing up his eyes, he started to undo the buttons. Without hesitating, she came up to him, knelt down and, pulling off the breeches by the foot straps, took them away somewhere. She wasn't away from him for long. While she was gone he noticed an archway, indicating that there were essentially two rooms. The ceilings were so low that if a tall man were to stand on the tips of his toes he would be able to touch them with his hand. Beyond the archway, in the depths of the other room, it was dark, but there was the gleaming side of an old polished piano, and something else reflecting the light as well – it seemed to be the flowers of a rubber plant. And there was that glimpse of an epaulette again.

My God, the place was full of antiques! He was riveted by the sight of the epaulettes. The tallow candle in its candlestick gave off a peaceful light. There had been peace at one time, and now that peace was dead. Those years had gone for ever. Behind him there were more low windows, and another one to the side. What a strange little house! She was alone. Who was she? She had saved his life... There was no peace any longer... They were still shooting out there...

*

She came in carrying an armful of firewood which she dropped noisily into one corner of the stove.

"What are you doing? What's that for?" he asked angrily.

"I would have needed a fire in any case," she replied with the hint of a smile. "I heat the place myself..."

"Come here," Alexei said quietly. "You know, I haven't thanked you for... what you've done... But how can I thank you?" He reached out and took hold of her fingers. She responded by moving closer to him, and he kissed her slender hand twice. As if relieved of the shadow of anxiety, her face softened and lightened, and at that moment her eyes looked extraordinarily beautiful.

"If it hadn't been for you," he continued, "they would almost certainly have killed me."

"Yes, of course," she replied, "they would have done. But you killed one of them."

He raised his head.

"I did?" he asked, feeling weak and giddy again.

"M'hmm," she nodded approvingly, and looked at him anxiously and enquiringly. "Oh, that was so awful... they almost shot me too." She shivered.

"How did I kill someone?"

"Well, when they came rushing round the corner you started to fire, and one of them crashed to the ground.... Maybe you just wounded him... In any case you're a brave man... I thought I would faint... You ran on again for a bit and then fired again... Then you ran on again... You're clearly a captain, aren't you?"

"How did you know I was an officer? Why did you call out 'officer'?"

Her eyes shone.

"If someone has a cap badge, then you know these things, I think. Why did you take such a risk?"

"Cap badge? Oh my God... I... That was... I..." He suddenly remembered the doorbell ringing... the mirror covered in dust. "I took everything else off, but forgot about the cap badge! I'm not an officer; I'm a military doctor. My name is Alexei Vasilyevich Turbin. May I ask your name?"

"Julia Alexandrovna Reiss."

"Why are you alone?"

"My husband's not here at the moment," she answered, sounding a little strained and averting her eyes. "He's gone away. And his mother as well. I'm alone... *brrr*... It's cold," she added, after a pause. "I'll make the fire up right away."

Just as the wood started roaring away in the stove, the most violent headache came on. The wound in his arm seemed to have calmed down, but all the pain was now transferring itself to his head, beginning in his left temple, then spreading to the top and the back. A vein above his left eyebrow contracted, and an excruciating pain radiated in all directions. Julia Reiss knelt by the stove and stoked the fire. Wracked with pain, his eyes closing and opening, he looked across at her, her head flung back, her pale hand shielding it from the heat and her hair that seemed difficult to define. Ash-coloured, flecked with gold? Or golden-blond? But her eyes and both eyebrows were definitely as black as coal. Hard to decide whether the slightly irregular profile and aquiline nose were beautiful or not. Impossible to read the expression in her eyes. Fear, alarm, perhaps... maybe even some hidden vice... Yes, some vice, perhaps.

Kneeling there like that, bathed in the waves of heat, she seemed wonderfully attractive. His saviour.

Later that night, when the fire in the stove had long since died down, and when the fever in his arm and hand had begun to flare up again, someone started hammering a red-hot nail into the top of his head and set about destroying his brain. "I have a fever," he repeated to himself laconically. "Tomorrow I must get up and make my way home," he urged himself. The nail was destroying his brain, so that eventually any thoughts, even of Yelena, or Nikolka, or home, or Petlyura disappeared. He stopped caring about anything. Peturra... Peturra... All he wanted now was for the pain to stop.

In the early hours of the morning Julia Reiss came and sat by him. She was wearing a pair of soft, fur-lined slippers. Again, he put his arm round her neck and, although feeling very weak, managed to walk through the two little rooms of the apartment. Just before this she had gathered her strength and said:

"Try to get up, if you can. Don't pay any attention to me. I'll help you. Then you'll be able to lie down again properly... But, if you're not able to... then, of course..."

"No, I can do it, so long as you help me..."

Together, with her in the lead, they walked as far as the small entrance door of her mysterious little house and then back again. As he lay down, shivering, his teeth chattering from the cold, he felt the pain in his head taking pity on him and dying down.

"I swear I'll never forget this, what you're doing for me," he said. "You must go and sleep now."

"Shh… Let me stroke your head."

And then the vile, diffuse pain completely flowed out of his head, out of his temples and into her soft hands, and on through them and her body down into the floor, covered with a dusty, fluffy carpet, where the pain totally disappeared. Instead of pain, his entire body was now flooded with an even, delicious heat. When his arm grew numb and as heavy as cast iron, he didn't try to move it, but just closed his eyes and surrendered to the heat. He had no idea how long he lay there in that way. Maybe five minutes, maybe hours. But in any case he felt he could lie like that, bathed in fire, for a whole eternity. When he opened his eyes quietly, so as not to disturb the person sitting next to him, everything looked as before: the faint, even glow of the lamplight under the cherry-red shade, illuminating the room with its peaceful light, and the profile of the unsleeping woman next to him. Pouting her lips sadly like a child, she was looking out of the window. Swimming in heat, Alexei shifted his position and reached out to her.

"Come here, come closer," he said. His voice had become dry, weak and high-pitched. She turned to him, with a wary expression in her deeply shadowed eyes. He put his right arm round her neck, drew her to him, and kissed her on the lips. Her lips felt cold and sweet-tasting. She didn't seem surprised, but simply looked into his face even more enquiringly.

"Oh my goodness, you have such a fever," she said. "What are we going to do? We need to call a doctor, but I don't know if that's possible."

"No, that's not necessary," he said quietly. "A doctor won't be necessary. Tomorrow morning I'll get up and go home."

"But I'm so worried you'll get much worse," she whispered. "Then how will I be able to help you? Is it still bleeding?" She touched his bandaged arm so quietly he couldn't hear her doing so.

"No, you don't have to worry, I'll be all right. You go back to bed."

"No, I'm staying here," she said and stroked his hand. "Such a fever," she repeated.

Unable to restrain himself, he put his arm round her and drew her to him again. She didn't resist him. He drew her so close to him that she found herself leaning directly over him and then lying right next to him. Through the heat of his own feverish body he could clearly feel the warmth of her woman's body.

"Just keep still; don't move," she whispered, "and I'll stroke your head."

She stretched out by his side and he could feel her knees touching his. She began to stroke his head from his temple up to his hair and down again. He felt so good that he concentrated all his thoughts on not falling asleep.

And so he fell asleep. He slept for a long time, evenly and deeply. When he woke up, he was aware that he was floating along a warm river in a boat, that the pain had gone completely, and that, outside the window, the night was gradually getting paler and paler. Everywhere there was total silence, not only inside the little house, but throughout the City. A glassy light began to trickle in through the gaps in the curtains. The woman, warm and sad, was asleep next to Alexei. And once again he fell asleep.

That morning, at nine o'clock, a passing cabby picked up two fares from an empty Malo-Provalnaya Street – a pale-looking man wearing dark civilian clothes and a woman. The woman was solicitously supporting the man, who was holding onto her sleeve. She directed the driver to take them to St Alexei's Hill. There was no traffic on the Hill, except for a cab outside No. 13, from which a strange visitor to the house, carrying a suitcase, a parcel and a cage, had just emerged.

14

EVERYBODY HAD TURNED UP. Nobody had been killed, and they had all turned up the very next evening.

"It's him!" Anyuta's breast resounded with the realization, and her heart leapt around like Lariosik's bird. Somebody was outside the Turbins' apartment, standing in the yard and knocking cautiously at the snow-covered window. Anyuta pressed her face to the window, trying to see who it was. Yes, it was him... him all right, but without his moustache! Smoothing back her dark hair with both hands, Anyuta opened the door leading onto the porch, and then from the porch into the snowy yard. And there he was: Myshlayevsky, unbelievably close to her! The student coat with the fur collar, the service cap... no moustache, it was true... but the eyes, even in the semi-gloom of the porch, were instantly recognizable. The right eye, glittering green like a precious stone from the Urals, and the left, dark. And he had grown smaller…

With trembling hands Anyuta unhooked the latch. The yard and the bands of light from the kitchen door disappeared from view, as Anyuta became enveloped in Myshlayevsky's coat.

"Hello, Anyutochka…" whispered a voice that was so familiar. "You'll get cold… Is there nobody in the kitchen?"

"No, no one," Anyuta answered, not thinking what she was saying. She, too, was whispering for some reason. "He's kissing me… How sweet his lips have become," she thought in the seventh heaven of bliss. "You mustn't, Viktor Viktorovich," she whispered "Put me down… Yelena…"

"Never mind about Yelena," the voice whispered reproachfully, smelling of tobacco and eau de Cologne. "Really, Anyutochka…"

"Put me down, Viktor Viktorovich, or I'll scream, I swear I will," Anyuta said passionately, flinging her arms around Myshlayevsky's neck. "We've had a tragedy: Alexei Vasilyevich has been wounded."

The python set her down instantly.

"What do you mean, wounded? What about Nikol?"

"Nikol's fine, but Alexei Vasilyevich has been wounded."

A patch of light from the kitchen door.

When Yelena saw Myshlayevsky from the dining room she burst into tears and said:

"Vitka, you're alive! Thank God! But we've…" She started sobbing, and pointed towards Alexei's door. "He's got a temperature of forty… He's very badly wounded."

"Holy Mother of God," Myshlayevsky said, pushing his cap to the back of his head. "How on earth did he manage to get here?"

He turned to the figure by the table, bent over a bottle and some shiny boxes.

"Are you a doctor, may I ask?"

"Sadly, no," answered a faint, sad voice. "I'm not a doctor. Permit me to introduce myself: Larion Surzhansky."

The sitting room. The door into the hall was shut and the heavy drape over the door closed, so that the sound of voices would not disturb Alexei. Three people had just left his bedroom and driven away: the man with a pointed beard and wearing gold pince-nez, a second man, young and clean-shaven, and finally a third man, grey-haired, elderly and wise, in a heavy fur coat and a boyar's cap, a professor, Alexei's one-time teacher. Yelena had shown them to the door, her face set in stone. Everybody had been talking about the possibility of typhus, and now it was definite.

"It's not just the wound – it's typhus as well."

And the thermometer stood at forty, and then this "Julia" all the time. Feverish heat in the bedroom. Silence, interrupted by delirious muttering about some steps and the *rrring* of a doorbell...

"How do you do, kind sir?" Myshlayevsky whispered venomously in Ukrainian, placing his feet wide apart. Shervinsky turned beetroot red, and looked away. His black suit fitted him irreproachably: starched white shirt, bow tie and patent-leather boots. The papers in his pocket identified him as an "Artiste, Kramskoi Opera Studio". "Where are your epaulettes? Why aren't you wearing them?" continued Myshlayevsky. "Russian flags are flying on Vladimirskaya Street... There are two divisions of Senegalese troops in the port of Odessa, and there are Serbian billet officers in the City... Officers, go to the Ukraine and form your units... etc., etc. Why, you absolute—"

"Stop going on at me," Shervinsky protested. "It's not my fault, is it? What have I got to do with it? I nearly got killed myself. I was the last to leave headquarters, at midday precisely, when the first enemy units appeared in the City from Pechersk."

"Yes, you're such a hero," said Myshlayevsky. "But I trust that His Excellency, the Commander-in Chief, managed to leave earlier... Just like His Highness, the Hetman, God damn him to hell. I do so hope he's now somewhere safe; the motherland needs people like him. By the way, could you tell me perhaps their precise whereabouts?"

"Why do you want to know? What's it to you?"

"I'll tell you why." Myshlayevsky made a fist with his right hand and struck the palm of his left hand. "If I were to come across His Excellency and His Highness, I would grab one by the left leg and the other by the right, turn them upside down and bang their heads on the road until I got tired of it. And as for you and the rest of your headquarters gang, you should be drowned in a latrine..."

Shervinsky turned crimson.

"Hold on a minute, if you please," he said. "Calm down. Don't forget that the prince also left staff officers in the lurch. Two of his adjutants went with him, but the others he simply abandoned to their fates."

"Do you know that at this moment there are thousands of our troops sitting waiting in the museum, starving, with machine guns? Petlyura's men will crush them like bedbugs, no doubt about it. Do you know how Colonel Nai was killed? He was the only one…"

"Just leave me alone, please!" Shervinsky shouted, really angry now. "How dare you talk to me like that? I'm an officer, too, just like you, you know!"

"Gentlemen, please," intervened Karas between the two of them. "This is a completely pointless conversation. And why *are* you going on at him like that? Leave it, it's not getting anyone anywhere…"

"Shh, be quiet," Nikolka whispered dejectedly. "He'll hear us…"
Embarrassed, Myshlayevsky calmed down.

"All right, take it easy, Mr Baritone; I was simply… you know…"

"It's still a bit strange…"

"Gentlemen, please, be quiet…" Nikolka said, suddenly alerted to something, and stamped on the floor. Everyone started listening. Voices could be heard coming up from Vasilisa's apartment below them. They could dimly hear Vasilisa burst out laughing about something, a little hysterically, it seemed. Vanda shouted something in reply; she sounded elated. Then everything went quiet for a bit. Then the distant voices started up again.

"Well, what a surprise!" Nikolka said thoughtfully. "Vasilisa's got guests. Guests, at a time like this! Absolutely earth-shattering!"

"Yes, he's definitely a character, your Vasilisa," agreed Myshlayevsky.

It was around midnight when Alexei eventually went to sleep following his morphine injection. Yelena settled down in the chair by his bed. Meanwhile, in the sitting room, the others were holding a council of war.

It was decided that everybody should stay there for the night. Firstly, it was the middle of the night, and there would be no point in going anywhere, even if they did have valid papers. Secondly, it would be better for Yelena, because they would be there to help. And then, perhaps most importantly, it was better at such a time to be visiting rather than sitting at home. But, perhaps even more importantly, there was nothing they could do. And, moreover, if they stayed here, they could have a game of vint.*

"Do you play?" Myshlayevsky asked Lariosik.

Lariosik blushed and became flustered. Then everything came out in a rush to the effect that, yes, he did play vint, but only very, very badly… just so long as people didn't swear at him, as the tax inspectors had done in Zhitomir… that he'd been through such a difficult time, but that, here, at Yelena Vasilyevna's, he was really coming to life, as Yelena Vasilyevna was such an exceptional person and it was such a warm and cosy apartment, especially the cream-coloured curtains on every window, thanks to which he felt protected from the world outside... and this world outside, as you had to agree, was dirty, bloody and senseless...

"May I ask whether you write poetry?" Myshlayevsky enquired, looking intently at Lariosik.

"I do," Lariosik replied modestly, blushing.

"I see... Forgive me for interrupting you... Senseless, you were saying. Please go on..."

"Yes, senseless. And our wounded psyches look for peace precisely behind such cream-coloured curtains."

"You know, in so far as peace is concerned, I don't know about Zhitomir, but here, in the City, you probably won't find it... By the way, you'd better wet your whistle; you'll get very dry, otherwise. Do we have any candles? Brilliant. We'll put you down as dummy, in that case... When there are five people playing, it gets pretty dull."

"Nikolka plays like a dummy anyway," interposed Karas.

"Do you mind, Fedya? Who lost hands down last time? You were the one who revoked. Stop flinging mud about like that."

"But these cards are speckled blue, like Petlyura's caps..."

"...Yes, you're right when you say people really should live behind cream curtains. Poets always get laughed at for some reason."

"God forbid. Why did you take my question the wrong way? I have nothing against poets... although, it's true, I don't read any poetry..."

"Or anything else, apart from artillery manuals and the first fifteen pages of Roman law. When war breaks out on page sixteen, he stops reading..."

"That's a lie; you're not listening to me. What's your first name and patronymic? Larion Ivanovich?"

Lariosik explained that his name was Larion Larionovich, adding what pleasant company he was in, except that company wasn't really the right word, it was more like a friendly family, and that he would be very pleased if people simply called him "Larion", without any patronymic... unless, of course, anyone had any objection.

"He seems a nice chap," Karas whispered quietly to Shervinsky.

"Well, let's get going then... But why... He's lying: if you really want to know, I have read *War and Peace*. Now there's a book for you. I read it all the way through, and really enjoyed it. And why? Because it was written not by some halfwit, but by an artillery officer. Do you have a ten? You're with me, then... Karas is with Shervinsky... Nikolka, sit this one out."

"But please, for God's sake, don't swear at me," Lariosik begged nervously.

"Really, please, what do you take us for? A bunch of savages? I see what you mean about those awful Zhitomir tax inspectors; they've really put the fear of God into you... We play strictly according to the rules here."

"Absolutely; no need to worry at all," said Shervinsky, taking his seat.

"Two spades... Yes, he was some writer, that Lieutenant of Artillery Count Lev Nikolayevich Tolstoy... Shame he left the army... Pass... He would have made general... Owned an estate of course... You can write a novel out of sheer boredom... Nothing to do in the winter... Quite simple, when you have a country estate. No trumps..."

"Three diamonds," Lariosik said timidly.

"Pass," replied Karas.

"What are you on about? You play a really good game. You should be complimented, not sworn at. Right then, if you're saying three diamonds, I'll say four spades. I wouldn't object to the idea of going off to my country estate right now..."

"Four diamonds," Nikolka prompted Lariosik, glancing at his cards.
"Four? Pass."

"Pass."

In the flickering wax candlelight, and surrounded by clouds of cigarette smoke, the nervous Lariosik bought more cards. Myshlayevsky dealt everyone a card each, tossing them out of his hands like spent cartridges from a rifle.

"A low spade," he announced. "Well done!" he said encouragingly to Lariosik.

The cards flew out of Myshlayevsky's hands soundlessly, like maple leaves. Shervinsky laid his cards down neatly, while Karas threw his down fiercely – he wasn't having much luck. Lariosik laid his down calmly, each one accompanied by a sigh, as if establishing his identity.

"Aha, king on queen. So that's what you're up to, is it?" said Karas.

Myshlayevsky suddenly turned purple and hurled his cards down on the table, looking daggers at Lariosik.

"Why the hell did you have to go and trump my queen, Larion?!"
"That's great!" Karas laughed gleefully. "One down!"

Uproar broke out around the green baize table, setting the candles flickering. Nikolka started gesturing and shushing everyone and dashed to close the door and pull the curtains.

"I thought Fyodor Nikolayevich had the king," Lariosik tried to explain, mortified.

"How on earth could you think that?" said Myshlayevsky. In his efforts not to shout, he started hissing instead, making his voice sound even more threatening. "You'd bought the king yourself, and then passed it on to me, hadn't you? Eh? What a..." Myshlayevsky looked round at everyone. "Well, I don't know... He says he wants peace and quiet, does he? That's a funny way to go about it by trumping your own partner! It's a game of skill! It's not like poetry – you have to use your brains!"

"Wait a moment. Maybe Karas—"

"What do you mean 'maybe'? Maybe nothing: it was just stupidity. Forgive me, old man, people in Zhitomir might play like that, but this is something else entirely!... Don't take it out on me: Pushkin and Lomonosov* might have written poetry, but they'd never have done anything as stupid as that... Neither would Nadson,* for that matter."

"Calm down. Leave him alone; it could happen to anybody."

"I knew this would happen," Lariosik muttered. "I'm such an unlucky man."

"Ssh... Listen!"

The room suddenly became quiet. In the distance, many doors away, a bell rang in the kitchen. Then they heard the sound of footsteps and doors opening, and Anyuta appeared. Yelena's head disappeared into the hallway. Myshlayevsky drummed his fingers on the tablecloth and said:

"Seems a little early, doesn't it?"

"Yes, it does," replied Nikolka, considering himself to be a leading expert on the question of house-to-house searches.

"Shall I answer it?" Anyuta enquired anxiously.

"No, Anna Timofeyevna," Myshlayevsky answered. "Wait a moment." He got up from his chair with a grunt. "Don't bother; I'll go and do the answering."

"I'll go with you," said Karas.

"All right," Myshlayevsky said, and his face immediately took on the expression of a commander addressing his platoon. "I assume everything's all right through there... The doctor has typhus etc., etc. You, Lena, are the nurse... Karas, you're the doctor... no, a medical student... Quickly, into the bedroom... Have a syringe ready, or something. We're quite a crowd. Well, perhaps it won't matter."

The bell rang again, impatiently. Anyuta gave a start, and they all looked even graver.

"Plenty of time," said Myshlayevsky, producing from his trouser pocket a small black revolver that looked like a child's toy.

"That's not necessary, surely," said Shervinsky, with a frown. "I'm astonished at you; you might have been a bit more careful. What, you mean you walked through the streets with that in your pocket?"

"Stop worrying," Myshlayevsky answered politely and seriously. "It will be all right. Here, Nikolka, you take it. Go and stand by the back door or by the window. If it should turn out to be Petlyura's merry men, I'll cough, and you can ditch it outside, but make sure we'll be able to find it later. It's an expensive piece, and I've had it with me ever since Warsaw... Everything OK with you?"

"Absolutely fine," said the specialist Nikolka sternly and proudly, taking possession of the revolver.

"Right, then," said Myshlayevsky, jabbing his finger in Shervinsky's chest. "You, Mr Baritone, are just a visitor." Then, turning to Karas with the same gesture: "Karas, you're a medical student." Then, to Nikolka: "You're the sick man's brother." And, finally, to Lariosik: "Student lodger. Do you have some identification with you?"

"I have a tsarist passport and my Kharkov University student card," said Lariosik, his face growing pale.

"Hide the passport, and show them the university card."

Lariosik grabbed hold of the curtain over the door and ran off.

"All the rest is just rubbish – the women won't matter," went on Myshlayevsky. "Right, does everyone have their papers? Anything in your pockets that shouldn't be there?... Hey, Larion!... Someone ask him if he has a gun or anything."

"Hey, Larion!" shouted Nikolka from the dining room. "Do you have a gun?"

"Of course not, God forbid!" came Larion's shouted response.

The doorbell rang again, persistently and even more impatiently. It went on for a long time.

"Well, may God be with us," said Myshlayevsky, moving towards the door. Karas disappeared into Alexei's bedroom.

"They've set out a game of patience," Shervinsky said, and blew out the candles.

Three doors led into the Turbins' apartment. The first was from the hallway onto the staircase. The second was a glass door marking the limit of the Turbin property. Beyond this door there was a cold, dark passageway leading to the door to the Lisovichs' apartment on one side, and ending with the final door giving out onto the street.

There was the sound of doors banging and Myshlayevsky's voice shouting down below: "Who is it?"

Behind him, on the stairs, he sensed the presence of the others listening.

On the other side of the door a muffled voice said plaintively:

"I've been ringing and ringing! I have a telegram here for a Talberg-Turbin. Open the door."

"Well, maybe, maybe not," the thought flitted through Myshlayevsky's head, and he gave a sickly cough. One of the figures on the staircase disappeared. Myshlayevsky cautiously pulled open the bolt, turned the key and opened the door, leaving it on the chain.

"Give me the telegram," he said, standing sideways to the door so that it shielded him from whoever was outside. A hand in a grey coat thrust a small envelope round the door. The astonished Myshlayevsky saw that it really was a telegram.

"I need a signature," the voice behind the door said curtly.

Myshlayevsky gave a quick glance outside and saw that there was only one person there.

"Anyuta, Anyuta," he called out cheerfully, miraculously recovering from his bronchitis. "Can you get me a pencil?"

But instead of Anyuta, it was Karas who came running down the stairs with a pencil. Myshlayevsky scrawled the word "Tur" on a scrap of paper torn from the envelope and whispered to Karas:

"Give me twenty-five…"

Sound of the door slamming shut, followed by the key being turned.

Puzzled by all this, Myshlayevsky and Karas went back upstairs. Everyone gathered round while Yelena opened the square envelope and started to read out the telegram in a matter-of-fact tone.

"Lariosik hit by terrible misfortune stop Opera artiste Lipsky…"

"Oh my God," shouted Lariosik, his face the colour of beetroot. "It's from her!"

"Sixty-three words!" gasped Karas. "Look! It's covered all over in writing!"

"Oh, Lord," Yelena groaned. "What have I done? Please forgive me, Larion, for reading that out; I had completely forgotten about her!…"

"What happened?" asked Myshlayevsky.

"His wife's left him," Nikolka whispered in his ear. "A real scandal…"

Suddenly the whole apartment resounded with a terrible hammering on the glass door, as if they had been hit by a landslide. Anyuta screamed, and Yelena turned pale, leaning back against the wall. The hammering was so monstrously, ridiculously loud that even Myshlayevsky's face changed colour. Shervinsky, who had also turned pale, clutched at Yelena... A groan came from Alexei's bedroom.

"The doors!" Yelena shouted.

Forgetting about any strategic plan, Myshlayevsky, followed by Karas, Shervinsky and the deathly pale Lariosik, dashed down the stairs.

"It's something worse this time," muttered Myshlayevsky.

They suddenly saw a single, black figure silhouetted behind the glass door. The hammering abruptly ceased.

"Who's there?" Myshlayevsky bawled at the top of his voice, as if they were in a cavernous weapons store.

"For the love of God... for the love of God... open the door... It's me, Lisovich!" screamed the figure. "It's Lisovich!"

Vasilisa looked terrible... the hairs around his gleaming, pink bald patch were all standing on end... his tie was hanging to one side, and his jacket tails were flapping about like the doors of a ransacked cupboard. His eyes had a dulled, crazed expression, as if he'd been poisoned. Standing on the top step, he suddenly swayed and collapsed onto Myshlayevsky. Myshlayevsky grabbed hold of him, barely able to stop him falling. Then he himself sat down on the stairs, shouting out in a hoarse, distraught voice:

"Karas! Water!"

15

IT WAS EVENING, almost eleven o'clock. Because of the events in the City, the street outside, not very busy even at normal times, had quietened down significantly earlier than usual. Light snow was falling, the flakes floating around evenly outside the windows, and the branches of the acacia trees lining the pavement – which, in summer, blocked the light to the Turbins' windows – were now drooping more and more under the weight of the layers of snow.

It had started to snow at lunchtime, the prelude to a nasty, gloomy evening, characterized by unpleasant events and a sinking heart. For some reason the electricity had come on at only half-power, and Vanda had served up brains for dinner that evening. As a food, brains are pretty awful at the best of times, but Vanda's method of cooking them rendered them inedible. The brains had been preceded by soup, to which Vanda had added vegetable oil, and Vasilisa had got up from the table feeling depressed by the nagging thought he hadn't had anything to eat at all. That evening there had been a mass of things to do, all of them difficult and unpleasant. The dining-room table had been turned upside down and a bundle of Lebid-Yurchyk's banknotes lay on the floor.

"You're a fool," Vasilisa said to his wife.

Vanda's expression changed.

"I've known for a long time that you're a pig," she replied, "but your behaviour recently has been beyond the pale."

Vasilisa had had an acute desire to punch her so hard in the face that she would have been sent flying across the room, crashing into the edge of the sideboard. And then to hit her again and again with such force that her wretched, bony body would have been forced to admit defeat and keep quiet. After all, when all was said and done, he – Vasilisa – had become exhausted from working like an ox, and he absolutely demanded that he be obeyed in his own home. But he gritted his teeth and desisted from hitting her – attacking Vanda was by no means as safe an undertaking as might have been expected.

"Do as I tell you," he said through clenched teeth. "Can't you get it into your head that they could move the sideboard, and then what would happen? But, hiding the money like this, it would never occur to anybody. It's what everyone in the City does."

Vanda did as she was told, and they set to work together, pinning banknotes to the underside of the table.

Soon the entire underside of the table was covered in colourful banknotes so that it resembled a richly embroidered silk carpet.

His face flushed with blood, Vasilisa stood up with a grunt and surveyed the field of money spread out before him.

"But that's not very convenient," remarked Vanda. "Whenever I need any money, I'll have to turn the table upside down."

"So what if you do?" rasped Vasilisa. "Your hands won't drop off. Better to turn the table upside down than lose everything. Have you heard what's going on in the City? It's worse than the Bolsheviks. They're conducting searches everywhere apparently, looking for officers all the time."

At eleven o'clock Vanda brought the samovar out of the kitchen and turned off all the lights. Then she took out a paper bag from the sideboard with a piece of stale bread and a lump of green cheese. There was just one bulb alight in one of the chandelier's three holders, dimly illuminating the room with a feeble red glow.

Vasilisa chewed away at his piece of French roll, so irritated by the green cheese that he almost burst into tears, as if he were suffering from a gnawing toothache. As he bit into the nauseating powdery substance the crumbs spattered everywhere out of his mouth and onto his jacket and tie. Unaware of what was so upsetting him, Vanda gave her husband a wary look as he chewed away.

"I'm amazed how easily they get away with it," she said, pointing at the ceiling. "I was convinced one of them would be killed. But no, here they are, all back again, and the apartment is full of officers once more."

At any other time, Vanda's words would have made no impression on Vasilisa, but just at this moment, with his whole being wracked by gloom and depression, they seemed intolerably unfair.

"And I'm amazed at you," he replied, avoiding looking at her so as not to become too annoyed. "You know full well that, in essence, they've done the right thing. Somebody had to defend the City from those" – Vasilisa lowered his voice – "...bastards. And besides, you're wrong if you think they've got away with things so easily... I think he's..."

Vanda nodded, her eyes fixed on her husband.

"Yes, that's immediately what I thought myself... He's been wounded, of course..."

"Well, why are you so pleased about it? 'Got away with things', indeed!"

Vanda licked her lips.

"I'm not pleased about it; I'm simply saying they've 'got away' with things. But what if, God forbid, they should come here and ask you, as the chairman of the housing committee, who was upstairs, and whether they supported the Hetman? What would you say, I'd like to know?"

Vasilisa frowned.

"I would say he's a doctor," he said, averting his gaze. "But, anyway, what on earth do I know about it?"

"That's just the point, what—"

Just at that moment the bell rang in the hallway. Vasilisa's face turned pale, and Vanda turned her scrawny neck in the direction of the bell.

Vasilisa got up from his chair and said with a sniff:

"Do you know what? Why don't we run up and get the Turbins?"

But before Vanda had time to reply, the bell rang again.

"Oh my God!" Vasilisa said anxiously. "It's no good; we'll have to answer it."

With a frightened expression Vanda went with him. They opened the door leading out into the shared passageway. As Vasilisa went into the cold passageway, Vanda stood there watching him, her angular face expressing wide-eyed alarm. Above her, the electric bell in its shiny little cover rang a third time, importunately.

Vasilisa considered for a moment whether he might go and knock on the Turbins' glass doors. Maybe one of them might come out, and then it wouldn't all be quite so frightening. But he was afraid to do it. What if they said, "What are you knocking about? Something to hide, eh?" And he still nurtured the fleeting, though, admittedly, not very confident, hope that it wasn't them at all, but someone else.

"Who... is it?" he asked tremulously.

At once the bell rang again and a hoarse voice replied through the keyhole at the level of Vasilisa's stomach.

"Open up," shouted the keyhole in Ukrainian. "From headquarters. Stay where you are, or we'll shoot through the door."

"Oh my God..." moaned Vanda.

Vasilisa drew back the bolt and unhooked the heavy latch with lifeless hands. Mechanically he undid the chain.

"Get on with it!" ordered the keyhole unceremoniously.

The door opened, revealing a glimpse of a dark street, a grey sky, the edge of an acacia tree and snowflakes. When they came in there were only three of them, but it seemed to Vasilisa that there were many more.

"Why are you here... might I ask?"

"To search your apartment," replied the first of them in a wolfish voice, as he made straight for Vasilisa. The passageway revolved, and Vasilisa saw Vanda's heavily powdered face in the lit doorway.

"In that case, if you'll excuse me, please," said Vasilisa in a feeble, colourless voice, "might I ask if you have a warrant? I am a strictly law-abiding citizen... I have no idea why you've come here. There's nothing here... Nothing," he said, repeating the last word in Ukrainian, suddenly overcome by a desperate urge to speak the language.

"Well, we'll just have to see," the first man replied.

As the advancing men pushed Vasilisa back into his apartment, it all seemed to be happening like a dream. Everything about the first man appeared to Vasilisa to be wolf-like – his narrow face, his small, deep-set eyes, his grey skin, his straggling moustache and his unshaven, deeply furrowed cheeks. He had a strange squint, looking out at the world with a mistrustful expression, and even here, in this confined space, he gave the impression of something inhuman, of a creature used to loping through the snow and across fields. He spoke the terrifyingly incorrect mix of Russian and Ukrainian familiar to people from the Podol region – that area of the City, along the banks of the river Dnieper, where, in the summer, cranes whistle and swing back and forth alongside jetties, and scruffily dressed men unload watermelons from barges. On the wolf's head was a fur cap, with a scrap of blue material decorated with gold braid dangling down on one side.

The second man was a giant, almost as tall as Vasilisa's hallway ceiling. He was young, with the plump, ruddy, completely smooth cheeks of a jolly peasant woman. He wore a crumpled cap with moth-eaten earflaps, a grey army coat and a pair of dreadful-looking down-at-heel shoes on his improbably small feet.

The third man had a sunken nose, eaten away on one side by a suppurating scab, and an ancient, disfiguring scar on one lip. He was wearing an old officer's peak cap, with a red band and the trace of a badge, an old double-breasted army jacket with tarnished buttons, black trousers and bast shoes over thick, grey, government-issue socks. In the lamplight his face gave off two colours – waxy yellow and violet. The expression in his eyes was one of suffering combined with malice.

"We'll just have to see, won't we," the wolf repeated. "And we have a warrant."

As he said this, he reached into a trouser pocket and pulled out a crumpled piece of paper, which he thrust at Vasilisa. With his right eye he pierced right through Vasilisa to the core, while his left eye flicked over the trunks standing in the hallway.

The crumpled piece of paper, folded into four, was embossed with a Ukrainian stamp: "Headquarters First Cossack Company". Underneath it was the following notice, also in Ukrainian, scrawled in indelible pencil:

You are instructed to carry out a search of the apartment owned by Vasily Lisovich, No. 13, St Alexei's Hill. All resistance punishable by execution on the spot.

Chief of Staff Protsenko.
Adjutant Miklun.

In the lower left-hand corner there was an indecipherable blue stamp.

The flowered wallpaper danced in front of Vasilisa's eyes. While the wolf was reclaiming the document, he said:

"Please come in, but you won't find anything here…"

The wolf took a black, well-oiled Browning out of his pocket and pointed it at Vasilisa. Vanda gave a muffled scream. Then the disfigured man produced a large, threatening, gleaming pistol. Vasilisa seemed to shrink as he went weak at the knees and sank down towards the ground. At this point the electric light appeared to flare up, making the room much brighter and somehow cheerful.

"Who's here at the moment?" rasped the wolf.

"Nobody," Vasilisa answered, his lips white, "apart from me and the wife."

"Right lads, take a look, and be quick about it," said the wolf, turning to his colleagues. "No time to waste."

The giant immediately picked up one of the trunks and started shaking it as if it were a lightweight box, while the disfigured man darted over to the stove. The revolvers had disappeared. As the disfigured man knocked along the wall with his fists the black air vent opened, releasing a thin stream of warm air into the room.

"Any weapons?" the wolf asked.

"Word of honour... I ask you, why would I have a weapon?"

"No, no weapons here," Vanda's shadow confirmed in a single breath.

"Better to say now. Ever seen anyone being shot?" the wolf said with a meaningful expression.

"But where would I get a gun from, for Heaven's sake?"

One of them turned on the green lamp in the study. Irritated beyond measure, to the depths of his metallic soul, Alexander II looked down at the three men. In the green light, his head spinning ominously, Vasilisa had a premonition of what it feels like to have a fainting fit for the first time ever. All three of them immediately started examining the wallpaper. Casually, almost playfully, the giant hurled row after row of books off the shelves, and three pairs of hands began knocking along the wall. Tap, tap, tap, the wall echoed dully... and then, suddenly, there was a hollow sound as they came to the hidden safe. The wolf's eyes shone with glee.

"What did I tell you?" he whispered soundlessly. The giant stood on the leather of the armchair, ripping it with his heavy legs as he reached up almost to the ceiling. Something tore under his fingers, and he pulled the cover from the wall. A moment later, and the wolf was holding a paper-wrapped package in his hands. Vasilisa swayed and slumped against the wall. The wolf began to shake his head, continuing to shake it for a long time as he looked at the half-dead Vasilisa.

"So, you little rat," he said angrily, "what's all this then? 'You won't find anything here,' you said, you son of a bitch. You said there was nothing here, but you had money hidden in the wall. You ought to be shot!"

"Oh, no, please," Vanda screamed.

Vasilisa's reaction, however, was somewhat strange: he suddenly burst out in a fit of convulsive laughter. But the laughter was particularly horrific, as only his lips, nose and cheeks were laughing; his blue eyes expressed nothing but terror.

"But, sir, I've done nothing against the law. It's simply some money and some other stuff… money that I've earned… Besides, tsarist money is now useless…"

As Vasilisa said these words, he looked at the wolf as though the sight of him gave him an unnatural pleasure.

"You ought to be arrested," the wolf said accusingly, shaking the package and putting it into the bottomless pocket of his tattered coat. "Right lads, now for the drawers."

Vasilisa himself opened the drawers. A stream of papers, seals, stamps, postcards, pens and cigarette cases poured out. The green carpet and red tablecloth were littered with pieces of paper, the pieces rustling as they fell on the floor. The disfigured man upturned and emptied the wastepaper basket. They knocked on the sitting-room wall superficially, as if reluctantly. The giant ripped up the carpet and stamped on the floor, leaving intricate markings on the floor, like scorch marks. The electricity, which had gone on at nightfall, blazed merrily away, and the gramophone horn gleamed brightly. Vasilisa shuffled along after the three men, as he dragged himself around the apartment. He was possessed by a dulled sense of calm, and his thoughts were beginning to flow seemingly with greater coherence. And then, suddenly, chaos erupted in the bedroom, as sheets, blankets and an upturned mattress emerged, hunchbacked on two legs, from the mirrored wardrobe. The giant suddenly stopped in his tracks and glanced down with a shy, beaming smile: Vasilisa's new kid boots with the patent-leather toes were peeping out from under the ravaged bed. The giant grinned as he looked timidly at Vasilisa.

"Lovely-looking boots," he said in a high-pitched voice, "maybe they'll suit me. What do you think?"

Before Vasilisa could think up what to say in reply, the giant had bent down and gently picked up the boots. Vasilisa shuddered.

"They're kidskin boots, sir," he said, not thinking what he was saying.

The wolf turned to him, his squinting eyes full of bitterness and rage.

"Quiet, you poisonous little rat!" he said threateningly. "Quiet!" he repeated, suddenly becoming even more irritated. "You should just thank us that we haven't shot you for stacking away that treasure of yours, like some bandit or thief. You just keep your mouth shut," he continued, his eyes blazing and advancing directly on Vasilisa, who had gone totally pale. "You've been hoarding all this stuff, and stuffing your fat pink snout like a pig, and now you can see what good, honest folk are wearing on their feet, can't you! His feet are frostbitten, in shreds, as a result of rotting away in trenches while you were sitting at home playing the gramophone. You motherf—" the urge to box Vasilisa round the ears flickered momentarily in his eyes, but he restrained himself.

"What do you think you're doing?" Vanda screamed.

The wolf thought better of hitting someone in Vasilisa's position and simply jabbed him in the chest with his fist. Pale-faced, Vasilisa staggered backwards, feeling a sharp, anguished pain in his chest from the blow.

"So this is the revolution," the thought flashed through his pink, neat little head, "our wonderful revolution! They should all have been hanged a long time ago, but it's too late now."

"Try the boots on, Vasilko," the wolf said affectionately to the giant. The giant sat down on the spring mattress and took off his wretched pair of shoes. The boots didn't fit over the thick, grey socks. "Give him a pair of socks," the wolf ordered Vanda. She immediately bent down by the lower drawer of the yellow wardrobe and took out a pair of socks. The giant tossed his grey socks to one side, revealing his reddened toes and black scars where the frostbite had eaten away his feet, and pulled on the other pair. Yet even now the boots didn't go on easily, and the laces on the left boot snapped off. Then, smiling in delight like a child, he tied the ends together and stood up. And, suddenly, as these five strange individuals followed each other, step by step, around the apartment, it was as if something had snapped in the tense relationship that had become established among them. Everything was now much simpler. Captivated by the sight of the giant's boots, the disfigured man suddenly grabbed hold of a pair of Vasilisa's trousers hanging on a hook by the washbasin. The wolf looked suspiciously at Vasilisa one final time, to see if he was going to say anything, but both Vasilisa and Vanda kept quiet, walking around with huge round eyes, their faces totally white. The bedroom turned into something resembling a corner of a clothes shop. The disfigured man stood just in his striped, tattered underpants, examining Vasilisa's trousers in the light.

"Wool, not cheap," he said nasally. He sat down in a blue chair and began to pull on the trousers. The wolf exchanged his dirty army blouse for Vasilisa's grey jacket, and handed over some papers to

Vasilisa, saying: "Here, take these, mister, you may need them." Then he picked up a globe-shaped glass clock inscribed with large, black Roman figures from the table. When he put his coat on, the clock could be heard ticking away underneath.

"Clocks are necessary things – to be without a clock is like having no arms," the wolf remarked to the disfigured man. His attitude towards Vasilisa was softening all the time. "In the middle of the night you need to be able to see what the time is."

Then the three of them set off back through the sitting room and into the study. Vasilisa and Vanda followed them, walking together in silence. Once in the study, the wolf thought for a moment, his eyes looking in different directions, and then said to Vasilisa:

"We'd like a receipt, mister..." His brow was furrowed: something seemed to be worrying him.

"What did you say?" Vasilisa whispered.

"A receipt, saying you've given us this stuff," the wolf elucidated, looking down at his feet.

Vasilisa's expression changed, and a flush came into his cheeks.

"But, what... but I..." He wanted to shout "What, you want me to give you a receipt as well?" But, instead, he found himself saying: "But you're the ones who should be giving us a receipt, so to speak..."

"Why, you... you should be shot like a dog! You bloodsucker, you! I know what you're thinking! I know! If you had the power you'd crush us like insects, wouldn't you?! I can see I can't talk any sense into you. Put him up against the wall, lads. I'll give him what for..."

Agitated and angry, he pressed Vasilisa up against the wall, grabbing him by the throat. Vasilisa immediately turned a bright red colour.

"Stop!" shouted Vanda, horrified, grabbing the wolf's hand. "What are you doing?... Vasya, please, I beg you, do as they ask, write them a receipt..."

The wolf let go of the engineer's throat, and his coat collar snapped back into place, as if on a spring. Vasilisa had no idea himself how he came to be sitting on a chair. His hands were shaking. He tore off a sheet of paper and dipped his pen in the ink. Everything in the room went quiet – so quiet that you could hear the globe-shaped glass clock ticking in the wolf's pocket.

"What shall I write?" Vasilisa asked in a hoarse whisper.

The wolf thought for the moment, his eyes blinking.

"Write... 'By order of Cossack Company Headquarters... items... such and such... to the amount... given in total...'"

"'To the amount…'" Vasilisa croaked and immediately fell silent.

"'Handed over in course of the search. I renounce all further claims.' Then sign."

At this point Vasilisa gathered all his remaining strength and asked, averting his eyes:

"But who shall I say I've given these things to?"

The wolf gave Vasilisa another suspicious look, but restrained his anger and simply sighed.

"Write, 'Having received… all items received by Nemolyaka,'" he paused for a moment, looking at the disfigured man, "'by Kirpaty and Hetman Uragan.'"

Staring with glazed eyes at the piece of paper, Vasilisa wrote down what was being dictated to him. When he had finished, he wrote "Vasilis" at the bottom, instead of his usual signature, and handed the document to the wolf. The wolf took the sheet of paper and examined it.

Just then there was a distant crash as the glass doors at the top of the staircase banged shut, followed by the sound of footsteps and Myshlayevsky's booming voice.

The expression on the wolf's face darkened immediately. His colleagues started shifting about. The wolf's face turned red and he hissed at everyone to keep quiet. He drew his Browning out of his pocket and pointed it at Vasilisa, who gave a pathetic grin. Then they heard the bolt, latch and chain on the door being slammed shut. This was followed by more footsteps, and the sound of men laughing. Then the glass door banged shut again, followed by the sound of receding footsteps, and everything went quiet. The disfigured man went out into the hallway, put his ear to the door and listened. On his return, he exchanged meaningful glances with the wolf, and all three of them went out into the hallway, keeping close to each other. Once in the hallway, the giant wiggled his toes in his tight boots and said:

"It's going to be cold."

He put on Vasilisa's galoshes.

The wolf turned to Vasilisa and said softly, his eyes darting around:

"Right, my friend… Not a word about any of this. If you tell anybody we were here, our lads will come and give you a good going-over. Stay here, in the apartment, until tomorrow morning, or there'll be trouble."

"We're sorry," whined the man with the broken nose.

The ruddy-cheeked giant said nothing, but simply looked timidly at Vasilisa, glancing happily with one eye at his gleaming galoshes. They went quickly out of Vasilisa's apartment, jostling each other as they tiptoed along the passageway to the outside door. With a rattle of bolts, the door opened to reveal the dark sky outside. Then Vasilisa closed the bolts again, his hands numb from cold. His head was spinning and, for a moment, everything seemed like a dream. His heartbeat slowed and then started to race. Vanda was in the hallway, sobbing. She slumped down onto the trunk, banging her head against the wall, large tears rolling down her face.

"Oh my God! What was all that about?... My God, oh my God, Vasya! In broad daylight! What was going on?"

Vasilisa stood in front of her, shaking like a leaf, his face distorted.

"Vasya," Vanda shouted, "they weren't from headquarters or the Cossacks at all, were they? Vasya! They were just a bunch of thieves!"

"Yes, I know, I know," Vasilisa muttered, his arms flung wide in despair.

"My God!" Vanda continued in the same vein. "We've got to go this minute, this instant, and report what's happened, so they can be arrested! Arrested! All our things! All of them! Why didn't someone, someone?..." She started shaking, and slid down from the trunk onto the floor, burying her face in her hands. Her hair was dishevelled and her blouse had become unbuttoned at the back.

"Yes, but go where?" Vasilisa asked.

"Where do you think? To army headquarters and the City authorities, of course! To report what's happened. As quickly as possible. What's happened to us?"

Vasilisa stood still for a moment, and then made a dash for the door. He flew up the stairs and started hammering at the glass door.

Everyone, apart from Shervinsky and Yelena, crowded into Vasilisa's apartment. Lariosik, his face white, stood in the doorway. Myshlayevsky stood with his legs apart, looking at the down-at-heel shoes and rags abandoned by the mysterious visitors.

"Your things have gone for good," he said, turning to Vasilisa. "They were just a bunch of thieves. You should thank God you're still alive. To tell you the truth, I'm astonished you got off so lightly."

"My God... Look what they've done to us!" Vanda exclaimed.

"They threatened to kill me!"

"Just be thankful they didn't carry out their threat. It's the first time I've seen anything like it."

"Yes, very neatly done," Karas agreed quietly.

"So, what should I do now?" Vasilisa asked, his voice faltering. "Go somewhere and complain? But where?... Viktor Viktorovich, tell me what to do, for God's sake."

Myshlayevsky grunted and thought for a moment.

"I advise you not to go anywhere," he said. "In the first place, they'll never be caught... that's the first thing," he continued, holding up his long finger. "In the second place—"

"But, Vasya, you remember they said they'd kill you if you told the authorities, don't you?"

"No, that's rubbish," said Myshlayevsky frowning. "Nobody's going to kill you, but the point is they won't be caught, and nobody's going to try and catch them. And, in the second place..." – he held up a second finger – "you'll have to report what it was they took from you... Pre-revolutionary money, wasn't it? Well, if that's what you tell them at headquarters, or wherever, they'll possibly come round and search your apartment a second time."

"Yes, that's very possible," confirmed Nikolka, as the leading search specialist among them.

Vasilisa, dishevelled, drenched by the water that had been poured over him to revive him, hung his head, while Vanda quietly burst into tears and leant back against the lintel. Everyone felt sorry for them. Lariosik stood by the doorway, sighing deeply and rolling his glazed eyes.

"So, that's it: we all have our particular grief to bear," he whispered.

"What weapons did they have?" asked Nikolka.

"My God! Two of them had revolvers, and the third... Vasya, did the third have anything with him?"

"There were just two of them with revolvers," Vasilisa repeated dully.

"What kind of revolvers? Did you notice?" enquired Nikolka in a businesslike tone.

"How should I know?" sighed Vasilisa. "I'm not an expert in such things. One was large and black, and the other was small and black, on a chain."

"Yes, a chain," Vanda confirmed with a sigh.

Nikolka frowned, and looked at Vasilisa, cocking his head to one side like a bird. He stood still for a moment, then he stirred uneasily and made quickly for the door. Lariosik dragged himself after him, but before he could reach the dining room he heard the sound of breaking glass coming from Nikolka's room, followed by a howl from Nikolka himself. Lariosik dashed into the brightly lit room. A blast of cold air was coming from the open upper window pane, as well as from the huge gaping hole that Nikolka had made with his knees as he had jumped down from the window sill in despair. His eyes had a wild look.

"No, it can't be!" Lariosik shouted, waving his arms in the air. "Pure witchcraft!"

Nikolka rushed out of the room, through the library and into the kitchen, where the dumbfounded Anyuta shouted at him as he sped by: "Nikol, hey, Nikol! Where are you going without your hat? Lord, what's happened now?" But he dashed on through the porch and out into the yard. Crossing herself, Anyuta put the porch door on the latch, ran back into the kitchen, and glued herself to the window, but Nikolka had instantly disappeared from sight.

He turned sharply to his left, ran down for a bit, and stopped by the snowdrift, blocking the entrance to the gap between the two houses. The snowdrift was totally free of footprints or any marks. "I don't understand," Nikolka muttered to himself in despair, and plunged unhesitatingly into the snowdrift. He felt he would suffocate. After a long time battling and scraping his way through the snow, spitting and snorting, he finally broke through the barrier. Covered in snow from head to toe, he clambered out into the narrow, desolate gap between the walls. When he looked up, he could see the brightly lit window (the fateful window belonging to his room), the black tips of the spikes and the sharp shadows they cast onto the wall, but no tin. In the faint hope that the rope might have snapped, Nikolka fell to his knees again and again, rummaging around in the rubble. But there was still no tin.

Suddenly, it was as if a bright light came on in his head. "Aha!" he cried, and crawled on farther towards the fence between the gap and the street. When he reached the fence he felt around with his fingers, causing the planks to separate and forming a dark hole gaping out onto the street. Now he understood! Yes, that was it: they had removed several planks in the fence, got through into the gap, and had even tried to climb into Vasilisa's apartment, through his larder. But they had found a grille over the window.

Still covered in snow, Nikolka returned to the kitchen without saying a word.

"Lord!" exclaimed Anyuta. "Let me at least brush the snow off you."

"Just leave me alone, for God's sake," answered Nikolka, and went through into the rest of the apartment, rubbing his numb hands on his trousers. "Larion, just hit me, will you!" he said. Larion blinked and rolled his eyes.

"What is it, Nikolasha?" he said. "Why are you in such a state?" He timidly began to run his hands up and down Nikolka's back, brushing the snow off with his sleeve.

"Leaving aside the fact that Alyosha will rip my head off – if, that is, as I pray to God, he recovers," continued Nikolka, "the most important thing is Nai-Turs's pistol. It would be better if I'd been killed, for Heaven's sake! This is God's punishment for making fun of Vasilisa. I feel sorry for Vasilisa, but don't you see? That was the pistol they used on him – although it would have been easy enough to rob him without the help of any revolver. That's the sort of person he is. My God, what a business! Larion, get some paper; we need to seal up the window."

That night Nikolka, Myshlayevsky and Lariosik climbed up out of the gap with nails, an axe and a hammer, and boarded up the fence with a number of short planks. Nikolka himself drove the long, thick nails into the planks with such furious energy that their sharp points emerged on the other side. A little later, the three of them went out onto the veranda with candles and climbed up through the cold storeroom into the attic. Once up there, above their apartment, they crashed and clambered about everywhere, bending down between the warm pipes and the washing, and blocked up the dormer window.

When he learnt about the goings-on in the attic, Vasilisa started showing the keenest interest in their actions, and joined them as they clambered about between the rafters, expressing his approval of everything that Myshlayevsky was doing.

"What a pity you couldn't have warned us," said Nikolka, his candle dripping wax. "You could have sent Vanda Mikhaylovna to us by the back entrance."

"I don't think so, my friend," replied Myshlayevsky. "Once they were in the apartment, things were pretty desperate. Do you imagine they wouldn't have defended themselves, if attacked? Of course they would! You'd have had a bullet in your belly before you'd got into the apartment. And there you'd be – a dead man! Yes, dead! But letting them in the apartment in the first place – that's a different matter."

"But they threatened to shoot us through the door, Viktor Viktorovich," Vasilisa said in an impassioned voice.

"They would never have fired," Myshlayevsky replied, hammering away. "Not under any circumstances; shooting would have attracted the attention of the whole street."

Later on that night, Karas was to be found luxuriating in the Lisovich's apartment, like Louis XIV. This had been preceded by the following conversation:

"But they won't come back tonight, for Heaven's sake!" Myshlayevsky had said.

"No, no, please, we beg you," Vanda and Vasilisa had said on the staircase, interrupting each other. "Please, we implore you, either you or Fyodor Nikolayevich! It wouldn't cost you anything. Vanda Mikhaylovna will bring us all tea. We'll make you up a comfortable bed. We beg you, tonight and tomorrow as well! We must have another man with us in the apartment!"

"I won't sleep at all otherwise," agreed Vanda, wrapping herself in her angora shawl.

"I've got some brandy – that will keep us warm," said Vasilisa in an unexpectedly jaunty tone.

"Go on, Karas, you go," said Myshlayevsky.

So Karas was now having a fine old time. As might be expected, the brains-and-vegetable-oil soup had been merely the outward symptoms of the loathsome disease of miserliness with which Vasilisa had infected his wife. Yet, in actual fact, delights known only to Vanda lay hidden in the depths of the apartment. On the dining-room table appeared a jar of pickled mushrooms, slices of veal, cherry jam and a genuine, first-class bottle of Shustov's brandy,* with a bell on the label. Karas poured out a glass for Vanda Mikhaylovna.

"Not a full glass," Vanda cried.

Giving in to Karas with a despairing gesture, Vasilisa also drank a glass.

"Don't forget, Vasya, it's not good for you," Vanda tenderly pointed out.

Following Karas's authoritative pronouncement that brandy couldn't possibly harm anyone, and that it was even given, with milk, to anaemics, Vasilisa drank a second glass. A blush appeared on his cheeks, and sweat on his brow. After five glasses Karas was in an exceptionally good mood. "Feed her up a bit, and she wouldn't be at all bad," he thought, looking at Vanda.

Then Karas praised the layout of the Lisovich's apartment, and started discussing the possibility of an alarm system that connected with the Turbins' apartment; one ring would mean the kitchen, two the hallway. Anything at all, and the alarm would ring upstairs. And then, there you are, it would be Myshlayevsky going to the door. Now that would be quite a different matter.

And Karas continued to extol the apartment's virtues, pointing out how comfortable and well-furnished it was. Just one thing, however: it was cold.

That night Vasilisa himself brought in some logs and stoked up the stove in the sitting room. Undressing, Karas lay down on the ottoman between two luxurious sheets, feeling very comfortable and contented. Then Vasilisa appeared in his shirt and braces, sat down in the chair, and said:

"You know, I can't seem to sleep. Would you mind if we chatted for a bit?"

The stove started to burn low. The rotund figure of Vasilisa, now much calmer, sat in the chair, sighing the whole time as he talked.

"Just think, Fyodor Nikolayevich. In the course of a single evening, everything that I've earned with the sweat of my brow has disappeared into the pockets of those scoundrels, taken from me by force. But don't think I don't agree with the revolution! No, not at all! I perfectly understand the historical reasons that brought it about."

The crimson light from the fire played on Vasilisa's face and on the buckles of his braces. Karas lay there, feeling magnificently relaxed from the brandy, and began to doze off, trying to maintain an expression of polite interest on his face.

"But you do agree with me, don't you, that here in Russia, this admittedly most backward of countries, the revolution has already degenerated into chaotic anarchy? Look at what's been happening: in the course of just two years we have been deprived of any legal protection, of even our minimal human and civil rights. The English say—"

"Ah yes, the English... They, of course..." Karas mumbled, feeling as if a cushioned wall was beginning to separate him from Vasilisa.

"But, in this country, 'a man's home is his castle' is totally meaningless if, in your own apartment, with all doors and windows locked and bolted, no one can guarantee that people such as that gang of crooks who were here this evening will not come in and take all that you possess, and maybe even your life!"

"We'll put alarms on your shutters as well," Karas said sleepily and not entirely convincingly.

"But surely, Fyodor Nikolayevich, my dear fellow, it's not just a question of an alarm system! No alarm system can put a stop to the corruption and decadence that is now infecting the hearts of human beings. All right, an alarm system has particular benefits, but what if it goes wrong?"

"Then we'll mend it," Karas replied, feeling immensely happy.

"But surely you can't build your entire life on an alarm system and those revolvers of yours. That's missing the point. I'm speaking now in general terms, I'm generalizing, so to speak, from a specific instance. The point is that the most important thing has been lost: respect for property. And once that's happened, then everything's finished. If that's the case, then we're all dead. I'm instinctively a democrat, one of the people. My father was a simple foreman on the railway. I've earned everything you see here – everything that that bunch of thieves took away with them; it's all been my handiwork, no one else's. And, believe me, I have never stood on guard defending the old regime. On the contrary! Let me tell you a secret: I am a Constitutional Democrat, but when I see with my own eyes the way everything is going I become more and more angry and more and more convinced that only one thing can save us…" Karas, wrapped in his soft, cushioned little world, was aware of the voice sinking to a whisper… "Autocracy. Yes, sir… the most rigorous dictatorship that it is possible to imagine… autocracy."

"Goodness, listen to him going on," Karas thought blissfully. "Hmm, yes… autocracy… that's complicated. Hmm…" he said, speaking through cotton wool.

"Blah, blah, blah… habeas corpus… blah, blah, blah," the voice droned on through the layer of cotton wool. "Blah, blah, they're wrong if they think, and when they maintain, that such a state of affairs can carry on for many years. No! It won't survive for long, and it would be laughable to think that—"

"Long live Fort Ivangorod," Vasilisa was suddenly interrupted by the voice of one of Karas's former commanders, now dead.

"And long live Ardagan and Kars,"* Karas responded through the mist.

And, through the mist, came the sound of Vasilisa's polite, watery laughter.

"Long may they live!" sang the jubilant voices in Karas's head.

16

"LONG MAY HE LIVE! Long may he live!" sang the nine basses in Tomashevsky's famous choir.

"Lo-o-o-ng…" echoed the crystal voices of the descants, and the voice of the soprano soared up to the very dome of the cathedral.

"Look! Look! It's Petlyura himself!"

"Look, Ivan!"

"No, you idiot… Petlyura's already outside, in the square."

In the choir lofts hundreds of heads crowded together, shoving and pushing each other, hanging down over the balustrade between the ancient pillars adorned with dark-coloured frescos. Excitedly pushing their way forward towards the balustrade, jostling and crushing each other, people were trying to look down into the depths of the cathedral, but their progress was barred by three lines of densely packed heads, like rows of yellow apples. Down there, in the airless depths of the cathedral, a thousand heads rocked and swayed backwards and forwards like a wave, while just above them floated a haze of sweat, steam and incense, together with the lampblack from hundreds of candles and from the heavy, chained icon lamps. The massive grey-blue curtain creaked as it was drawn along the rails, hiding the central doors of the iconostasis made from fretted, twisting, age-old metal that was as dark and as gloomy as the rest of St Sophia Cathedral. Tongues of flames from the candles in the chandeliers spluttered and swayed as the threads of smoke drifted upwards. They were running out of air. In the side-chapel, by the altar, there was an unbelievable commotion. Gold chasubles and fluttering stoles were pouring out of the side-altar doors and along the worn granite slabs. Violet-coloured headdresses were emerging from round cardboard boxes and banners were swaying from side to side as they were being taken down from the walls. From somewhere in the depths of the building the fearsome bass of Archdeacon Serebryakov was roaring away. A headless, armless, hunched chasuble hovered for a moment above the crowd and then plunged down into it. One sleeve of a quilted cassock rose into the air, followed by the other. People were waving check handkerchiefs and knotting them into plaits.

"Father Arkady, you need to cover your cheeks more; there's a very fierce frost outside. Come on, let me help you."

The banners dipped as they passed under the doorway, as if belonging to a defeated army. Brown faces and mysterious golden words floated along, fringes scraping the ground.

"Make way!"

"Goodness! Where are they going?"

"Manka, watch out! You'll be crushed!"

"What's all this about?" in a bass whisper. "The Ukrainian People's Republic?"

"God knows." Again in a whisper.

"Anybody not a priest will be some bigwig or other."

"Look out!"

"Long may he live!" The voices of the choir rang out once more, filling the entire cathedral. The corpulent, purple-faced Tomashevsky extinguished a greasy wax candle and replaced his tuning fork in his pocket. The main body of the choir, wearing brown gold-braided surplices down to their ankles, the swaying boy trebles with their blond hair – so blond it almost made them look as if they were bald – and the equine heads of the basses, Adam's apples bobbing, streamed down from the dark, gloomy choir lofts. An avalanche of people gushed noisily down the steps, like water down a drain, the crowd getting thicker and thicker, pushing and shoving each other along.

Surplices emerged from the side-chapel, their owners' faces bandaged as if they were suffering from toothache, their eyes looking anxious beneath their mauve, toylike headgear. The small, frail figure of Father Arkady, the cathedral dean, wearing his mitre sparkling with semi-precious stones above his grey checked scarf, floated along in the stream of people. His eyes had a look of despair and his sparse little beard was quivering.

"There's going to be a procession round the cathedral. Get a move on, Mitka."

"Shh! Where do you think you're going? You're getting in the priests' way."

"So what! Serves them right!"

"These Orthodox! I ask you! A child's been crushed to death."

"I don't understand a thing."

"If you don't understand anything then you should go home; you shouldn't be here at all."

"Someone's taken my purse!"

"Of course! What do you expect? They're all socialists. Isn't that what I've been saying all along? What have the priests got to do with it?"

"I'm sorry!"

"Give the priests a bit of money and they'll say a Mass for the Devil himself!"

"Why don't we go to the market right now and smash in some of the Yids' shops? Just the right moment to do it."

"I don't speak the same language as you."

"A woman is being suffocated... She can't breathe!"

"Aargh!"

The crowds swirled out of the colonnaded side areas and down from the choir lofts, step by step, shoulder to shoulder, unable to turn round, as they made their way towards the doors. On the ancient frescos brown-painted, fat-legged buffoons of uncertain antiquity pranced along the walls playing their pipes. The crowds, half-suffocated, half-intoxicated by carbon dioxide, smoke and incense, streamed towards all the doors in a cacophony of sound. The whole time a woman could be heard shrieking in pain. Pickpockets in black mufflers worked through the crowd, efficiently and skilfully slipping their virtuoso hands in between the compacted lumps of human flesh. The crowd swished and rustled along, their feet scraping on the stone slabs.

"Oh my God!"

"Jesus Christ... Holy Mother of God..."

"I'm sorry I came. What's going on, anyway?"

"I hope you get crushed, you pig..."

"My watch, my silver watch... Please, dear brothers and sisters... I only bought it yesterday."

"Looks like they've said their last Mass here."

"What language was the service in, for goodness' sake? Didn't understand a word."

"God's language, grandma."

"The use of Moscow Russian is strictly forbidden."

"What's that? What are you saying? That we can't use our own Orthodox language any more?"

"Someone's pulled her earrings off, tearing away half her ear."

"Cossacks! Stop that man! He's a Bolshevik, a Bolshevik spy!"

"This isn't Russia any longer, my good man."

"Look over there... Those tassels! Look, Marusya, those soldiers with the braided caps!"

"I'm feeling... feeling... faint."

"The woman's feeling faint."

"Everyone's feeling faint, old girl. The whole nation's feeling terrible. Hey, stop pushing like that! You'll poke my eyes out. You've all gone mad, you horrible creatures!"

"Go back to Russia! Get out of the Ukraine!"

"There ought to be police cordons here, Ivan Ivanovich, like there were for the 1912 celebration. Do you remember? Ah, yes..."

"So you want that bloody Nicholas back again, do you? We know, we all know, what's going on in that head of yours."

"Get away from me, for Christ's sake! I'm not touching you."

"God, if only we could get out of here now... I need some air!"

"I won't make it; I'm going to die."

The crowd pushed their way out of the main entrance, spinning and turning, hats flying, people crossing themselves amid a buzz of sound. The religious procession, all in silver and gold, crushed and confused, was streaming out from a second side door, where two panes of glass had been smashed. Flashes of gold in the black mêlée of people and vestments, headdresses and mitres rose into the air, church banners dipped as they passed under the windows, then straightened up again as they floated on.

There was a severe frost. The City was wreathed in smoke. The cathedral square resonated constantly with the sound of thousands of tramping feet. The frosty haze hung in the frozen air, drifting up towards the bell tower. The great St Sophia bell in the main tower boomed out, trying to drown the terrible, howling chaos below. The smaller bells were yelping away, without harmony or form, competing with each other, as if Satan himself had climbed up into the bell tower in a surplice and amused himself by adding to the general din. Through the dark lancet windows of the multi-storeyed bell tower, which had once warned of the imminent arrival of the slit-eyed Tatars, the small bells could be seen thrashing about and howling like fierce dogs on a chain. The frost crunched underfoot and smoked in the air. Souls were softened, primed for repentance, as the black hordes poured across the square.

Despite the fierce frost, a group of mendicant friars, their heads either bared like ripe pumpkins, or with a sparse covering of orange hair, was already sitting cross-legged along the stone path leading to the great stairwell of the old St Sophia bell tower, and singing in their nasal voices.

A group of blind minstrels were tugging at people's heartstrings with a forlorn song about Judgement Day, their tattered peaked caps lying upturned at their feet, ready to receive the greasy banknotes that fell into them like leaves, landing on top of the tattered notes already waiting for them at the bottom of the caps.

> "Oh, when we come to the end of time,
>   that dreadful hour of Judgement Day..."

Wrested, squeaking from the yellow-toothed banduras with their crooked necks, the harrowing, heart-rending sounds drifted up from the hard, frosty ground.

"My brothers and sisters, have mercy on me, on my poverty. Give alms, for the love of Christ."

"You run on, to the square, Fedosei Petrovich; otherwise we'll be late."

"There's going to be an open-air service."

"There'll be a procession."

"They're going to pray for the victory of the revolutionary Ukrainian People's Army."

"But what victory? They've already won, haven't they?"

"Yes, and they'll win again!"

"There'll be a campaign."

"Where to?"

"To Moscow."

"Which Moscow?"

"The usual one."

"They won't manage it."

"What did you say? Say that again? Hey, lads, listen to what this chap's saying!"

"I didn't say anything."

"Arrest him! Stop, thief!"

"You run on, Marusya, through those gates. We shan't get through this way. Petlyura's on the square, they say. Let's go and see him."

"Petlyura's in the cathedral, you idiot."

"You're the idiot. He's there, people are saying, on the square, riding a white horse."

"Hurrah for Petlyura! Long live the People's Republic of Ukraine!"

"*Bong... bong... bong,*" thundered the bells.

"Have pity on a poor orphan, good people, brothers and sisters in Christ... on a blind man... on a cripple..."

Dressed all in black, a legless man in leather-patched trousers, looking like a broken-backed beetle, was pulling himself along the trampled snow between people's feet. The crippled and deformed, with sores on their knees, blue from the cold, moved among the crowd, their heads shaking as though suffering from a debilitating tic or paralysis. Some, affecting blindness, rolled the whites of their eyes. Heartstrings were tugged as people were reminded of poverty, deceit, despair and the unending savagery of life on the steppes. Groaning and creaking like unoiled wheels, the lyres of the cursed and condemned howled out their refrain.

"Come back, my child, you'll get lost..."

Unkempt old women, shivering from the cold, hobbled about on sticks, thrusting out their desiccated, parchment-like hands, whining:

"Kind, beautiful sir! May God grant you health!"

"Have pity, miss, on an old woman, a poor orphan."

"My darling, God will take care of you…"

Beggar women, people wearing kaftans and caps with ear muf-flers, peasants in sheepskin caps, rosy-cheeked young girls, retired government officials with little paunches, nimble-footed young boys, Cossacks in army coats, in caps with tassels and crowns of different colours – blue, red, green, magenta – with gold and silver piping, and gold tassels from the fringes of coffin covers – everyone was stream-ing into the cathedral square like a dark tide, just as the cathedral doors were disgorging fresh waves of people. Heartened by being in the open air, the procession gathered strength, regrouped and closed ranks, moving off in a tight orderly line of heads in checked scarves, mitres and headdresses, hatless deacons with long, flowing manes of hair, monks in skullcaps, sharp-pointed crosses on gilded poles, banners depicting Christ the Saviour as well as the Virgin Mary and child, and carved, forged, gold and crimson icons covered in Slavonic lettering.

In the form now of a grey cloud with a snakelike belly moving through the City, now of dark-brown turbulent rivers of people pouring through the ancient streets – Petlyura's innumerable forces were making their way to the cathedral square for the parade.

The first to arrive, carving their way through the black river of people, with a crash of gleaming cymbals and a blast of trumpets shattering the frost, were the densely packed ranks of the Blue Division.

Then, dressed in their blue jackets and in their showy astrakhan cocked caps with blue tops, came the Galicians. Two blue-and-yellow standards, propped between bared sabres, followed immediately behind the massed ranks of the brass band and, behind the flags, jauntily marching with measured tread on the crystalline snow, came rank upon rank of soldiers, wearing uniforms of a good-quality, albeit German cloth. The first battalion was followed by lines of troops in long, black, belted cloaks, wearing helmets and parading their bristling bayonets in a dense brown thicket.

Then came Cossack rifle regiments, in their countless numbers, wearing ragged grey uniforms, followed by battalion after battalion of Haydamak Cossack infantrymen,* with the dashing regimental, battalion and company commanders prancing along on horseback between each battalion. Confident, triumphant march tunes crashed through the air like gold in the multicoloured river of the parade.

The infantry were followed by the cavalry regiments, the men rising and falling in their saddles as they trotted gently along. The eyes of the delighted crowd were dazzled by the sight of the crumpled, battered fur caps, with their blue, green and red tops and gold tassels. The lances, looped onto the cavalrymen's right hands, jigged up and down like needles. In among the cavalrymen the standards waved cheerfully, and the horses of the commanders and the buglers were impelled forward by the triumphant sound of the music. As round as a ball, the large, jolly figure of Bolbotun rode ahead of his company, offering up his low forehead, gleaming with grease, and his chubby, radiant cheeks to the frost. His chestnut mare, her bloodshot eyes rolling, champing at the bit and dribbling foam, kept rearing up as it tried to shake off the sixteen-stone weight of the colonel. His curved sabre clattered in its scabbard as he dug gently into her nervous, steep-sided flanks with his spurs.

"Our leaders are with us,
are one with us, as brothers!"

sang the brave haydamaks in chorus as they trotted and bounced along, their colourful cap tassels bobbing.

Next to ride past, with its tattered yellow-and-blue standard fluttering, and accompanied by accordions, was the regiment of the dark-skinned, moustached Colonel Kozyr-Leshko. The colonel was in a bad mood as he lashed out at the rump of his stallion with his whip. He had good reason to be angry: Nai-Turs's rifles had fired at his best platoons that foggy morning on the Brest-Litovsk highway, and the regiment that trotted along was depleted in numbers and therefore reduced in size.

Kozyr was followed by the brave cavalrymen of the victorious Black Sea Hetman Mazeppa Troop. The glorious name of the Hetman – the man who had almost defeated Tsar Peter the Great at the battle of Poltava* – was set out in gleaming gold letters on the blue silk standard.

The crowds of people pressed against the grey-and-yellow walls of the houses, surging forward and climbing onto advertisement hoardings. Small boys clambered up lamp-posts, sitting on the crosspieces, standing on rooftops, whistling and cheering.

"Hurrah! Hurrah!" people cheered from the pavements.

The flat disks of faces peered out in huge numbers from behind balcony doors and windows.

Cabbies were standing unsteadily on the boxes of their sleighs, waving their whips in the air.

"They said they were just a rabble... Some rabble! Hurrah!"

"Hurrah! Long live Petlyura! Glory to our Leader!"

"Hurrah!"

"Manya, look, look! There he is, Petlyura himself, on the grey... Look! Look how handsome he is!"

"No, madam, you're wrong... That's just a colonel."

"Really? So where's Petlyura then?"

"He's at the palace receiving the French emissaries who've come from Odessa."

"Don't be idiotic, mister! What emissaries?"

"They say Petlyura's in Paris, Pyotr Vasilyevich. Just imagine that!"

"That's some rabble for you! There must be millions of them."

"Well, where's Petlyura then? So, my friends, where is he? We only want just one look at him."

"Petlyura, madam, is now on the square reviewing the parade."

"Nothing of the sort. He's in Berlin, being presented to the president, on the occasion of the signing of the federal agreement."

"What president?! What do you think you're doing mister, spreading such provocative rubbish?"

"He's being presented to the president in Berlin... on the occasion..."

"Did you see that... did you see? Looking so important... going past along Rylsky Alley in a carriage. Six horses."

"But they don't really believe in the Orthodox church, do they?"

"I'm not saying they do, I'm not saying they don't... I'm saying he rode past, that's all. Look at the facts yourself."

"The fact is that the priests are saying Mass right now."

"He'll be in a stronger position with the priests on his side..."

"Petlyura, Petlyura, Petlyura!..."

Following the ten cavalry regiments came an endless column of artillery, with the fearsome rumble of heavy wheels and the rattle of limbers. The gun carriages carried large blunt-snouted mortars and compact howitzers rolled along. Cheerful, contented gun crews sat on the limbers with triumphant expressions, while the cavalrymen themselves looked calm and sedate. The carriages were pulled by large, big-rumped, well-fed horses fourteen hands high, and smaller, hard-working peasant horses, looking like pregnant fleas. A troop of light mountain artillery trotted nimbly past, the small cannon bouncing along with their gallant crews.

"So, there's your so-called fifteen thousand for you... What lies we were told! Fifteen thousand... bandits... chaos... and look what we have! Good Lord, you'd never count them all! Another battery... and another... and another."

His birdlike nose thrust into the collar of his student coat, Nikolka felt himself being shoved and pushed around by the crowd, until he finally managed to worm his way into a small niche in the wall where he was able to stand his ground. The niche was already occupied by a jolly peasant woman in felt boots who said cheerfully:

"You hang on to me, my lad, and I'll hang on to the wall, and we should be all right."

"Thanks," Nikolka muttered dejectedly into his frozen collar. "I'll hold on to this hook."

"But where's Petlyura?" the woman babbled on. "Oh, I'd so love to see Petlyura. They say he's such a handsome man."

"Yes," growled Nikolka indeterminately, muffled in his sheepskin. "Such a handsome man..."

"Another gun battery, damn it..." he thought. "Now I understand..."

"He was here just now, people say, riding by in a car... Didn't you see him?"

"He's in Vinnitsa," Nikolka pronounced in a dry, sepulchral voice, moving his frozen toes around in his boots. "Why the hell didn't I wear my felt boots in such a frost," he thought.

"Look, look, Petlyura!"

"That's not Petlyura – that's just the commander of the bodyguard."

"Petlyura has taken up residence in Belaya Tserkov. That will be the capital now."

"So does that mean he won't be coming to the City, may I ask?"

"He'll come in his own good time."

"So that's it. I see..."

Clang, clang, clang. From St Sophia Square came the muffled sound of Turkish drums. Four fearsome-looking armoured cars rolled along the street, swaying from side to side under the weight of their heavy turrets, machine guns poking out threateningly through the slits in their sides. But none of the armoured cars contained the rosy-cheeked, enthusiastic Strashkevich. His cheeks no longer rosy, but a dirty waxen colour, he was now lying quite still at the spot where he had fallen, right by the gates of Mariinsky Park in Pechersk. There was a little hole in his forehead, and another one, still caked with blood, behind his ear. The enthusiastic lieutenant's bare feet were poking up out of the snow, and his glassy eyes were staring straight up into the sky through the bare branches of a maple tree. Around him everything was very quiet – there wasn't a soul in the park, and only the occasional person in the street. The sound of the music coming from St Sophia did not reach as far as the park, and the lieutenant's face was therefore perfectly calm.

The armoured cars hooted as they sliced through the crowd of people and rolled off towards where Bogdan Khmelnitsky* was sitting, his mace pointing to the north-east, black against the sky. The great bell was still sending oily waves of sound reverberating around the snow-covered hills and city rooftops, the drums were still beating somewhere in the thick of the crowd and small boys were clambering excitedly up onto the hooves of black Bogdan's horse. Following the armoured cars, a line of lorries thundered down the street, snow chains clanking, carrying girls wearing brightly coloured skirts under their sheepskin jackets and straw wreaths on their heads, and lads in blue, baggy Ukrainian trousers. They were standing on the running boards, singing quietly but melodiously.

Then, suddenly, shots rang out on Rylsky Alley. Just before this, screams from some peasant women had whirled around in the crowd. Someone had started running and yelling:

"This is so terrible!"

Then someone had started shouting, hurriedly, spluttering hoarsely:

"I know who those people are! Stop them! They're officers... officers... I saw their epaulettes!"

Several men rushed out from one of the platoons of the 10th Rada Company, waiting its turn to join the parade, and burst into the crowd grabbing hold of someone. Women shrieked. The person they had grabbed, Captain Pleshko, started protesting in a weak, distraught voice:

"I'm not an officer; I'm nothing of the sort. Not at all. How dare you? I work in a bank."

Next to him, they seized someone else, a man with a pale face who said nothing but who fought to get free.

Then people started dashing down the alleyway, as if from a burst bag, jostling each other. Struck dumb with horror, everybody joined in the rush. Behind them they left a completely empty space, quite white except for the black spot of an abandoned cap. Then, in the alleyway, there was a flash and a bang as Captain Pleshko, who had denied himself thrice, paid for his curiosity towards parades. He lay face down by the small front garden of the St Sophia Cathedral residence, his arms outstretched. Then the second man to have been caught, the silent one, fell at his feet, his face crashing into the pavement. Immediately the cymbals waiting on the corner of the square crashed out, the crowd surged back, and the orchestra struck up its thunderous roar once more. "Quick march!" roared a triumphant voice, and the Rada cavalry company marched onto the square, their tassels gleaming.

Then, suddenly, quite unexpectedly, in the gap between the cathedral domes the layer of grey cloud parted and the sun broke through the mist and gloom. The sun was so large that nobody in the Ukraine had ever seen anything that size before, and it was completely blood-red. As the distant globe fought to pierce through the layer of cloud, it sent streaks of clotted blood and plasma flowing out from its surface. The main dome of St Sophia became bathed in blood-red sunlight, casting a strange shadow onto the square below, making Bogdan appear violet and the milling crowd even darker, denser and more confused. And then men in grey coats wearing belts with ropes and bayonets were seen climbing up the steep, black granite wall on a ladder, in an attempt to scrape away the inscription. But it was a hopeless task: the bayonets slipped and slithered away from the granite. And in his fury Bogdan tore his steed away from the cliff at a gallop, trying to fly away from those people who were clinging onto his hooves and weighing him down. His face, turned directly towards the red globe of the sun, expressed his rage, his mace still pointing into the distance.

At that moment a man was raised high up onto the slippery, icy fountain opposite Bogdan, above the humming, milling crowd of people. The man was wearing a dark coat with a fur collar but, despite the frost, he had removed his cap and was holding it in his hands. The square continued to hum and buzz like an anthill, but the bells of St Sophia had now fallen silent, and the bands had marched off, disappearing down various frosty streets. A huge crowd gathered at the bottom of the fountain.

"Hey, Petka, who's that they've lifted up?"

"Looks like Petlyura."

"Petlyura's giving a speech…"

"What nonsense… That's just any old speaker…"

"Marusya, look, a speaker…"

"He's going to read out a declaration…"

"No, he's going to read one of the Universals."*

"Long live the free Ukraine!"

The man who had been lifted up gave an inspired glance over and above the forest of a thousand heads towards the place in the sky where the sun's disc had become even more evident, bathing the crosses in a thick, red gold. With a wave of his arm he shouted in a weak voice:

"Long live the people!"

"Petlyura… Petlyura."

"What are you talking about? That's not Petlyura!"

"What's Petlyura doing up on a fountain?"

"Petlyura's in Kharkov."

"Petlyura's just gone into the palace for a banquet."

"Nonsense – there won't be any banquet."

"Long live the people!" repeated the man on the fountain, a lock of blond hair drooping onto his forehead.

"Shh!"

The fair-haired man's voice grew stronger, and it was now clearly audible above the racket and crunching of feet, the droning and hum, and the sound of the drums in the distance.

"Did you see Petlyura?"

"Yes! Just a moment ago!"

"Oh, you lucky man! What's he like?"

"Black, upturned moustache, just like the Kaiser Wilhelm, and in a helmet. There he is, there, look, Marya Fyodorovna, he's riding past us now… Look!"

"Why are you talking such provocative nonsense? That's the chief of the fire service."

"Petlyura's in Belgium, madam."

"Why has he gone to Belgium?"

"To conclude an agreement with the Allies."

"No, that's not it. He's just gone this minute to the parliament with his escort."

"What for?"

"For the oath."

"He's gone to swear an oath?"

"Why would he need to do that? They're going to swear an oath of allegiance to him."

"Well, I would rather die" – in a whisper – "than swear an oath of allegiance to him."

"Well, you won't have to… Women will be left alone."

"Yids won't be left alone, that's for certain."

"Neither will officers. They'll have their guts ripped from them."

"So will the landlords. Down with them all!"

"Shh!"

The fair-haired orator, with a determined expression in his eyes but also one of unspeakable grief, pointed towards the sun.

"Did you hear that, brothers and comrades?" he said. "The Cossacks singing 'Our leaders are with us, with us like brothers'? With us! Yes, with us!" And the man took his cap and started striking himself on his chest sporting an enormous scarlet bow, billowing like a wave. "Our leaders are with the people, they were born of the people, and they will die with them. They froze with them in the snow during the siege of the City, they played their valorous part in the capture of the City, and the red flag is now flying over all the buildings..."

"Hurrah!"

"What 'red flag'? What does he mean? It's yellow and blue."

"The Bolsheviks' flag is red."

"Shh! Hurrah!"

"And his Ukrainian is pretty awful."

"Comrades! A new task now awaits you: to sustain and strengthen our new independent republic, for the benefit of all workers, for those who work in the factories and those who work on the land. Only those who have shed their blood and sweat for our motherland will have the right to possess it!"

"That's right! Hurrah!"

"Did you hear? He addressed us as 'comrades'... Wonders will never cease."

"Shh! Be quiet!"

"And so, fellow citizens, on the glorious occasion of our people's victory," the orator said, beginning to use less and less Ukrainian, his eyes shining, as he stretched out his hands more and more passionately towards the sky, "let us swear an oath that we will not lay down our arms until the red flag – the symbol of freedom – is flying above all the workers of the world."

"Hurrah! Hurrah!... 'The Inter—'"

"Shut up, Vaska! Have you gone off your head?"

"Shchur, what on earth are you thinking of? Keep quiet!"

"But I swear I can't stay silent, damn it, Mikhail Semyonovich."

Arise, ye damned of the Earth...*

The Onegin-like black sideboards disappeared into the thick beaver collar, leaving only his eyes gleaming in the direction of an excited cyclist who had been crushed in the crowd of people... eyes that were uncannily similar to those of the dead Ensign Shpolyansky, who had died on the night of 14th December. A hand in a yellow glove reached out and pulled Shchur's hand down.

"All right, all right, I'll keep quiet," Shchur muttered, his eyes boring into the fair-haired man's face. The speaker had by now fully captured the attention of the people in the front of the crowd.

"Long live the soviets of workers', peasants' and Cossack deputies!" he shouted. "Long live..."

The sun suddenly disappeared, and the cathedral and its domes were cast into shadow. The faces of both Bogdan and the speaker, the lock of blond hair bouncing up and down on his forehead, were clearly delineated.

A gasp went through the crowd.

"...the soviets of workers', peasants' and Red Army deputies. Workers of the world, unite!"

"What's that? What did he say? Hurrah!"

At the back of the crowd a few men, accompanied by one high-pitched resonant voice, began singing: "When I die..."*

"Hurrah!" came a triumphant shout from another part of the crowd.

And then, suddenly, there was a whirlwind of commotion in yet another section of the crowd.

"Seize him! Seize him!" shouted a cracked male voice, in an unpleasant whine. "Seize him! It's sheer provocation! He's a Bolshevik! You Russian scum! Get him! You heard what he was saying..."

Someone's hands flashed in the air. The speaker leant to one side, then his legs and stomach disappeared, followed by his head, now in a cap.

"Seize him!" piped a thin tenor voice in response to the first. "He's spreading lies. Get him, lads, get him, everyone..."

"Ha! Wait! Who's that you've got there? Who is it? That's not the one!"

The owner of the high-pitched voice pushed through the crowd to the fountain, waving his arms about as if he were landing a large slippery fish. But muddle-headed Shchur, in his weather-beaten jacket and fur cap, stood in front of him, twisting and turning, and yelling: "Seize him!"

"Hey, stop him!" he suddenly barked. "He's taken my watch!"

A woman in the crowd screamed out as someone kicked her.

"Whose watch? Where? You're lying; you won't get away!"

Someone standing behind the owner of the high-pitched voice grabbed him by the belt and held on to him, while a large, cold fist connected with his nose and lips in a punch of considerable weight.

"Ouch!" the high-pitched voice yelled, its owner turning deathly pale, sensing that his head was bare and that his hat had disappeared. At that instant he received a second massive blow to the face, and someone bawled up to the skies:

"I've got him, the thief, the pickpocket, the son of a bitch. Give him what for!"

"What are you doing?" howled the high-pitched voice. "Why are you hitting me? It wasn't me! It wasn't me! It's the Bolshevik you need. Ouch!" he yelled again.

"Oh, my God, my God, Marusya, let's get out of here now! What's going on?"

In the crowd, right by the fountain, there was a mad scrum of people swirling around. One man was being beaten up, another was howling, and people were scattering everywhere, but the main thing was that the fair-haired orator had disappeared. Somebody was dragged out of the middle of it all, but he turned out to be the wrong man: the orator had had a black cap, whereas this one was wearing a fur cap. And, within three minutes, the pandemonium had died down of its own accord as if it had never existed: a new speaker had been found who had been lifted up onto the edge of the fountain and a crowd of people, soon some two thousand strong, were surging forward from all directions and forming a central nucleus to listen to him.

In the snow-covered alleyway by the small front garden, now abandoned by the inquisitive public who had gone off to follow the parade, Shchur could contain himself no longer and abruptly sat down on the pavement roaring with laughter.

"Oh, this is incredible," he roared, clutching at his stomach. He was heaving with convulsive laughter, his white teeth gleaming. "I'll die from laughing, like a hyena. Did you see how hard they were hitting him, for goodness' sake?"

"Come on, Shchur, get a move on," said his companion, the unknown man in a beaver collar, the spitting image of the famous dead ensign and chairman of the Magnetic Triolet Society, Shpolyansky.

"All right, in a minute," Shchur said, starting to get to his feet.

"Give me a cigarette, Mikhail Semyonovich," said Shchur's other companion, a tall man in a black coat. He had tilted his fur cap onto the back of his head, a lock of fair hair hanging down over his forehead. He was breathing heavily and puffing and panting, as if he were too warm in spite of the frost.

"So, have you had enough?" the unknown man asked affectionately. He turned back the hem of his coat and, taking out a small gold cigarette case, offered the fair-haired man an untipped German cigarette. The fair-haired man lit up, shielding the light with his hands. It was only when he had exhaled that he gave a sigh of relief.

Then all three of them quickly set off and disappeared round the corner.

Two figures in student uniforms came hurrying out from the square into the small alleyway. One of them was short in stature, but well-built and neat-looking, in shining rubber galoshes. The other was tall, broad-shouldered, his legs like a pair of compasses, with each stride measuring almost two yards.

Both of them had their collars turned up right to the brims of their peaked caps, and the tall one even had a scarf covering his smooth-shaven mouth – clearly because of the frost. As if obeying a single command, both figures turned their heads to look at the body of Captain Pleshko and the body of the other man lying face downwards, his knees spread out in opposite directions, and then both walked on without saying a word.

Then, as the two of them were turning into Zhitomirskaya Street from Rylsky, the tall one turned to his shorter companion and said in a hoarse tenor voice:

"So, did you see that then? I'm asking you: did you see it?"

"I shall never forget it as long as I live," the tall man continued, striding out along the street. "I'll always remember it."

The smaller man walked behind him without saying anything.

"We need to thank them for teaching us a lesson. If ever I come across that swine… that hetman…" – a hiss of derision could be heard coming from behind the scarf – "I'll…" and the tall man delivered himself of a fearsome first-class expletive that seemed to go on for ever. When they came out onto Bolshaya Zhitomirskaya Street, they found their way blocked by the procession that was making its way to the watchtower in the old part of the City. Strictly speaking, the route from the cathedral square was direct and uncomplicated, but Vladimirskaya Street was blocked off by the cavalry squadrons, which had still not been able to disperse after the parade, and so the procession, like everyone else, had to make a diversion.

The procession was headed by a group of young boys, running along, leapfrogging and emitting piercing whistles. They were followed by a man in a tattered, unbuttoned coat, without a hat. He was walking on the trampled snow, his eyes rolling with an expression of horror and despondency. His face was covered in blood, and tears were pouring down his cheeks. His wide mouth was open and he was crying out in a thin, hoarse voice, in a mixture of Russian and Ukrainian.

"You have no right to do this! I am a well-known Ukrainian poet. My name is Gorbolaz, and I have written an anthology of Ukrainian poetry. I will complain to the chairman of the Rada* and to the minister. It is an absolute disgrace – beyond words!"

"Give him what for, the pickpocketing bastard!" people were shouting from the pavements.

Sobbing in despair and looking all around himself, the man shouted: "It was me who tried to detain the Bolshevik provocateur..."

"What? What's all this?"

"Who's he talking about?"

"Someone tried to kill Petlyura."

"Well? And?"

"He shot at our leader, the son of a bitch."

"But he's a Ukrainian."

"He's not a Ukrainian, he's a swine," a bass voice growled. "He's stolen someone's purse."

The boys whistled derisively.

"What are you saying? By what right?"

"They've caught a Bolshevik provocateur. Kill him on the spot, the scum."

The excited crowd crept up behind the poor man. There was a glimpse of a fur cap with a gold-braided tassel and the tips of two rifles. One person, a multicoloured belt fastened tightly round his waist, started shambling alongside the man covered in blood, mechanically punching him on the neck from time to time, whenever he started to cry out particularly loudly. The hapless man, not knowing what to do any more, walked along, every so often breaking into violent but soundless sobbing and then falling silent again.

The two students let the procession go by. When it had disappeared, the tall man seized his smaller companion by the arm and started whispering in malicious glee:

"Serves him right – just what was needed. Well, I'll tell you one thing, Karas: the Bolsheviks are brilliant – I mean it, absolutely brilliant. That's the way to do things! Did you see how neatly they managed to spirit that speaker away? And they're bold operators. I admire them for that – for their boldness, damn them."

233

But the smaller man simply answered quietly:

"If we don't get a drink this minute, I'll hang myself."

"That's an idea, a great idea," responded the tall man enthusiastically. "How much money have you got?"

"Two hundred."

"And I've got one hundred and fifty. Let's go to Tamara's and get a couple of bottles…"

"It's closed."

"She'll open up for us."

The two of them turned onto Vladimirskaya Street, and walked on until they came to a two-storeyed house with a sign saying "Groceries". Next to it was another sign: "Cellar. Tamara's Castle". They dived down some steps and began knocking cautiously on the glass double door.

17

THROUGHOUT THE LAST THREE DAYS, during which events had crashed down on his family like rocks, Nikolka had had one cherished aim in life, an aim connected with the mysterious final words uttered by the man stretched out in the snow. This aim he had now achieved, but in order for it to be realized, he had had to dash about the City before the start of the parade, visiting no fewer than nine addresses. And although, while he was rushing about, he lost heart in the whole enterprise many, many times, each time he picked himself up and carried on, finally achieving what he had set out to do.

In a small house on the very edge of the City, on Litovskaya Street, he managed to locate someone who had served in the second company of their detachment and to find out Nai-Turs's address, first name and patronymic.

For two hours Nikolka tried to battle his way through the stormy waves of people, in an attempt to get across St Sophia Square. But it had proved quite impossible to cross the square – out of the question! So the frozen Nikolka had spent about another half-hour freeing himself from the claws of the crowd in order to return to his starting point – Mikhaylovsky Monastery. Then he had the plan of going down Kostelnaya Street, after which, with a big detour, he could carry on down to the Kreshchatik and, from there, make his way onto Malo-Provalnaya Street along the low-lying back alleyways. But that turned out to be impossible as well! As with everywhere in the City, dense columns of troops were snaking up Kostelnaya Street on their way to join the parade. So he took an even longer and more circuitous route and found himself totally alone, on Vladimir Hill. He ran along the park terraces and avenues, making his way between the walls of white snow, finding himself at times in sections of the park where the snow wasn't so deep. From the terraces he could look across the ocean of snow to the Imperial Park on the opposite hills, and then farther to the left, to the unending Chernigov plains stretching away in utter winter stillness beyond the Dnieper, lying white and proud in its icy banks.

Everything was utterly peaceful and still, but at that moment Nikolka had no time for peace or stillness. Fighting his way through the snow, he climbed up one terrace after another, occasionally noting with some astonishment that here and there there were tracks in the snow: people clearly ventured onto the hill even in the middle of winter.

Finally he was able to make his way down an avenue where, with a sigh of relief, he saw that there were no troops on the Kreshchatik, and he made straight for the cherished spot: No. 21, Malo-Provalnaya Street. This was the address he was looking for, an unwritten address that had become firmly lodged in his brain.

Nikolka felt both excited and shy. "Who shall I ask, and how best to put it? I'm in the dark here..." He rang the doorbell of an annexe, nestling at the bottom of a garden terrace. For a long time nobody came to the door, but finally he could hear the sound of shuffling footsteps, and the door was opened a fraction on a chain. A woman's face in a pince-nez peered round the door.

"What is it?" she asked abruptly from the gloom of the hallway.

"Can you tell me, please, does the Nai-Turs family live here?"

The woman's face adopted a completely unwelcoming expression, and her pince-nez glittered at him hostilely.

"There's nobody called Turs here," she said in a low voice.

Nikolka blushed. He felt embarrassed and sad.

"This is apartment no. 5?"

"Well, yes," the woman answered reluctantly and suspiciously. "Tell me what it is you want."

"I was told that the Turs family lives here..."

More of the woman's face emerged from behind the door as she took a quick glance around the garden to see if there was anybody with Nikolka. She was so close he could clearly see her full double chin.

"Yes, but tell me what it is you want."

Nikolka sighed and, glancing behind him, said:

"I've come here about Felix Felixovich... I have some information about him."

The expression on the woman's face changed abruptly.

"And you are?"

"A student."

"Wait here a moment," she said, and slammed the door. The footsteps died away.

A minute and a half later the click of heels could be heard as someone approached the door. The door opened wide and Nikolka was able to go in. The hallway was illuminated with light coming from the sitting room, and Nikolka was able to see the side of a comfortable armchair and then the woman in the pince-nez. He took off his cap and suddenly saw another woman standing in front of him. She was small and thin, bearing traces of a faded beauty on her face. Indefinite, insignificant signs – her forehead, possibly, or the colour of her hair – gave Nikolka to understand that she was Nai's mother, and he was horrified, wondering how he would be able to break the news. When the woman looked at him steadily, her eyes bright with curiosity, he found himself at even more of a loss. There was someone else standing next to her – a younger woman, also seemingly with Nai's features.

"Well then, what is it you have to tell us?" the mother asked insistently.

Nikolka clutched at his cap, looked at her and said:

"I... I..."

The thin lady, the mother, gave him an angry, apparently hostile look and suddenly yelled so loudly that the glass in the door behind him shook:

"Felix has been killed!"

She clenched her fists, waving them in front of Nikolka's face, and shouted:

"He's been killed... did you hear that, Irina? Felix has been killed."

Nikolka's eyes glazed over with fear. "My God! I haven't even said anything yet!" he thought despairingly. The large lady in the pince-nez quickly shut the door behind Nikolka and ran up to the mother, seized her by the shoulders and whispered:

"Shh, Maria Frantsevna, my dear, shh."

Then bending close to Nikolka she asked: "Perhaps it's not true?... Oh, Lord... Please tell us... Is it really true?"

But he was unable to say anything. He simply looked ahead of him in despair, aware once more of the side of the armchair.

"Shh, Maria Frantsevna, shh, my dear... They'll hear us, for goodness' sake... It is the will of God," the large woman babbled.

Nai-Turs's mother collapsed onto the floor on her back, shouting:

"Four years! Four years! I've been waiting and waiting." The younger woman, standing behind Nikolka, quickly went over to her mother and helped her up from the floor. Nikolka wanted to help her, but he unaccountably suddenly broke into a fit of sobbing, unable to stop.

The curtains had been drawn across the windows, and the room lay in semi-gloom. There was utter silence in the room, pervaded by the unpleasant smell of medicine.

Eventually, the silence was broken by the younger woman, clearly Nai's sister. She turned away from the window and went up to Nikolka. He got up from the armchair, still clutching his cap, which he had found impossible to put down in such terrible circumstances.

Absent-mindedly smoothing down a lock of her dark hair, Nai's sister asked, her mouth contorted with sorrow:

"How did he die?"

"He died..." Nikolka answered, summoning up his most natural voice. "He died... I'd like you to know that he died the death of a hero... a real hero... He'd sent away all his cadets in good time, at the very last moment, but he himself... but he himself stayed where he was and covered their retreat with rifle fire." All the time he was telling them this, Nikolka was in tears. "We came under machine-gun fire and I was nearly killed as well," he continued, still crying. "There were only the two of us left, and he shouted at me, trying to drive me away, firing from his machine gun... The enemy's cavalry was coming at us from every angle – we had fallen into a trap. Literally, from every angle."

"But perhaps he was just wounded?"

"No," he answered firmly, wiping his eyes, nose and mouth with a dirty handkerchief. "No, he was killed. I was able to feel him; he had been hit in the head and chest."

The room became even darker. Maria Frantsevna had fallen silent and there was no sound coming from the next room. The three of them remained in the sitting room, huddling together and whispering to each other: Nai's sister, Irina, the large lady in the pince-nez, Lydia Pavlovna – Nikolka had learnt that she was the landlady of the apartment – and Nikolka himself.

"I don't have any money with me," he whispered. "But, if necessary, I can go and get some straight away, and then we can set off."

"I can give you some money immediately," Lydia Pavlovna boomed. "The money's not important. But just make sure you're successful. Irina, you mustn't say a word to her about any of this… I really don't know what to do…"

"I'll go with him," whispered Irina. "And we will be successful. Why don't you just tell her that his body is lying in the barracks, and that we need permission to see him?"

"Yes, yes… that's a good idea."

The large lady crept quietly into the next room where her voice could be heard whispering reassuringly.

"Come now, Maria Frantsevna, why don't you lie down, for the love of Christ? They're going right now to sort everything out. That cadet said he was lying in some barracks."

"What, on bare boards?" she asked in a resonant and still hostile (or so it seemed to Nikolka) voice.

"No, no Maria Frantsevna, he's in a chapel, a chapel…"

"Perhaps he's still lying on those crossroads, with dogs gnawing at his body."

"Maria Frantsevna, please, don't say such things… Just try to stay calm, I beg you."

"Mama has not been her normal self these last three days," Nai's sister whispered, again smoothing back the lock of hair on her forehead, her eyes focused on a distant spot, somewhere beyond Nikolka. "But now everything else has become unimportant."

"I'm going with them," they heard from the next room.

Nai's sister jumped up and ran through to the next room.

"Mama, you're not going with them. You're not. The cadet will refuse to help us if you go. He could be arrested. Just stay there, where you are, I beg you…"

"Oh, Irina, Irina…" the mother continued. "He's been killed, and what are you doing about it? Tell me, what? And what will I do now that Felix has been killed? Killed… Lying in the snow… Just think…" And she burst out sobbing again, with the bed creaking beneath her. Then the voice of the landlady could be heard:

"Maria Frantsevna, my darling, try to be brave…"

"Oh Lord, oh my God," cried Nai's sister, running quickly through the sitting room. Nikolka sat there, wrapped in horror and despair. "What if we don't find him?" he thought. "What then?"

Nikolka stopped outside the most horrible doorway of all. Despite the frost the most terrible, foul stench was coming through the doors.

"Perhaps you should wait here," he said to Irina. "There's such a foul smell through there you'll probably feel ill."

Irina looked at the green door, then at Nikolka.

"No," she answered, "I'm coming with you."

Nikolka pulled the handle of the heavy door and they went in. At first everything was completely dark. Then they gradually began to make out endless rows of empty coat hooks, lit dimly by a ceiling lamp.

Nikolka turned anxiously to look at his companion, but she seemed to be all right, walking along next to him. It was just that her face was pale, and she was frowning. She was frowning in a way that reminded him of Nai-Turs. The similarity was only passing – Nai had had a straightforward, masculine face, as if sculpted in metal, whereas she was a beautiful woman, cast more perhaps in the foreign mould rather than the Russian. An astonishing, extraordinary young woman.

The smell, whose effect on Irina Nikolka had so feared, was everywhere. Everything smelt – the floors, the walls, the wooden coat hooks. The stench was so terrible that you could even see it. The walls seemed thick and sticky with grease, the coat hooks were glistening and everywhere there was the stench of rotting flesh. Although you could very quickly get used to the smell, it was better not to look at anything or, indeed, think about anything. That was the most important thing: not to think, otherwise you would realize what the smell signified. There was a brief glimpse of a medical student in a coat; then he was gone. Beyond the coat hooks on the left, a door creaked open and someone in boots emerged. Nikolka looked at him and then quickly averted his gaze, to avoid looking too closely at his jacket. The jacket, as well as the man's hands, were glistening like one of the coat hooks.

"What do you want?" the man asked brusquely.

"We've come on a matter that… We really need to see the person in charge here," Nikolka said. "We need to find a particular person who's been killed. Could he be here, do you think?"

"Who is this person?" the man asked mistrustfully.

"He was killed here, on a city street, three days ago."

"Ah, I see, a cadet or an officer?... Caught by the Cossacks. What was he exactly?"

Not wanting to say that Nai-Turs was an officer, Nikolka simply said: "Well, yes, he was killed too..."

"He was an officer, mobilized by the Hetman," Irina said, going up to the man. "Nai-Turs."

Clearly uninterested in who Nai-Turs might have been, the man gave Irina a sideways glance and answered her, coughing and spitting on the floor:

"I don't really know what I can do. It's past working hours now and there's nobody here. The other janitors have gone home. It will be difficult to find him, very difficult. The bodies have been taken down to the cellars. Difficult, very difficult..."

Irina Nai undid her bag, took out a banknote and held it out to the janitor. Nikolka turned away, afraid that, if the man were honest, he would demur. But he accepted the money.

"Thank you, miss," said the janitor, clearly much more cheerful now. "We'll be able to find him – we'll just need permission. If the professor agrees, you can pick up the body."

"But where is the professor?" Nikolka asked.

"He's here, but he's busy. I don't know... should I tell him you're here?"

"Yes, yes please, tell him at once," Nikolka said. "I'll be able to recognize the dead man immediately."

"I can do that for you," the janitor said, and led them up some steps and into a corridor where the stench was even more unbearable. Then along the corridor, then left into another corridor where the smell was less intense and where it was a little lighter because of the glass ceiling. Here the doors on both side of the corridor were painted white. The janitor stopped at one of these doors and knocked. Then, removing his cap, he went in. The corridor was quite quiet, and light filtered through the roof. In a distant corner of the corridor it was beginning to grow dark. The janitor came out and said:

"Come this way."

Nikolka went in, followed by Irina. He took off his cap. Looking around the huge room, he was struck first of all by the black stains on the glistening curtains, and the patch of intensely bright light falling onto the table illuminating a black beard, a haggard, wrinkled face and a hooked nose. Finding all this depressing, he looked round at the walls. Endless rows of shelves gleamed in the semi-gloom, and he could just make out monstrous-looking objects, dark and yellow, like fearsome Chinese. A little farther off he saw a tall man in a priestlike leather apron and black gloves. He was bending down over a long table on which stood a row of microscopes, like cannon, their mirrors gleaming white and gold in the light of a low lamp, under a green shade.

"What do you want?" asked the professor.

Nikolka realized that the man with the beard and the haggard face must be the professor, and that the other, smaller man in the leather apron was an assistant.

Nikolka coughed, his eyes fixed on the brilliant patch of light emanating from the strangely curved lamp, on the tobacco-stained fingers and on the terrible, revolting-looking object lying in front of the professor – someone's neck and chin, consisting of veins and tendons, pierced and threaded through with scores of gleaming hooks and scissors...

"Are you relatives?" asked the professor. His voice sounded dull and muffled, a voice that corresponded to his lined face and his beard. He looked up and peered at Irina Nai and at her fur coat and boots.

"I'm his sister," she replied, trying not to look at the object lying in front of the professor.

"You see, Sergei Nikolayevich, how difficult this all is? This isn't the first time... Anyway, it's possible he's not here any more. Have the bodies been taken to the general mortuary?"

"Possibly," the tall man replied, tossing an instrument to one side.

"Fyodor!" shouted the professor.

"No, you go that way... you mustn't come this way... I'll go myself," Nikolka said shyly.

"It's not really for you, miss," the janitor agreed. "Why don't you wait here?" he added.

Nikolka took the janitor to one side, gave him two more banknotes, and asked him to find her a clean chair to sit on. The janitor, puffing away at his pipe with its home-made tobacco, produced a chair from a small room with a green lamp and some skeletons.

"You're not a doctor, are you, sir? Doctors get used to all this straight away," said the janitor, opening a large door, and switching on a light on the glass ceiling. There was a strong smell in the room, containing row upon row of gleaming zinc tables. They were empty. Somewhere a tap was dripping into a sink. The stone floor rang under their feet. Finding it difficult to cope with the smell that no doubt must have always pervaded the room, Nikolka walked along trying to keep his mind a blank. He followed the janitor through the doors at the other end into a totally dark corridor. Here the janitor lit a small lamp, and they went on a little farther. The janitor threw back a heavy bolt, opened a metal door and again flicked a switch. In the corners of the room stood huge cylinders, reaching up towards the ceiling and bulging with lumps and pieces of human flesh, strips of skin, fingers and fragments of shattered bones. Nikolka swallowed hard and averted his eyes.

"Take a sniff of this, sir," said the janitor.

Nikolka closed his eyes, and eagerly inhaled a lungful of unbearably strong sal ammoniac from a bottle.

As if half-asleep and screwing up his eyes, Nikolka was aware of Fyodor's glowing pipe and the sweet smell of cheap tobacco. After fiddling for a long time with the lock of the lift door, Fyodor managed to open it, and they took their places on the lift platform. Fyodor pulled a handle and the lift started to descend, creaking as it went. Down below they were met by a blast of icy-cold air. The lift came to a halt. They went into a huge mortuary. Nikolka could dimly make out something that he had never seen before in his life: row upon row of naked human corpses lying one next to the other like stacks of wood, emitting an unbearable stench in spite of the sal ammoniac. Particularly noticeable were the protruding soles of their feet, some rigid, some flopping sideways. The hair on women's heads was fluffed up and dishevelled, and their breasts were crushed, creased and bruised.

"I'll turn them over now, and you'll be able to see," the janitor said, bending over the first corpse. He grabbed hold of a woman's foot and she flopped onto the floor as if on oil. She seemed horribly beautiful to Nikolka, lying there glistening like a witch. Her eyes were wide open and she seemed to be looking straight at Fyodor. Nikolka managed only with some difficulty to take his eyes away from the scar encircling her body like a red ribbon and to look elsewhere. He felt quite sick and his head spun at the thought they would have to be turning over all these sticky, slippery bodies.

"Wait, there's no need to go on," he said feebly to Fyodor, putting the bottle of sal ammoniac in his pocket. "There he is, I've found him. Up there... there."

Balancing carefully so as not to slip onto the floor, Fyodor immediately climbed up, grabbed Nai-Turs by the head and gave it a sharp tug. A flat-chested, broad-hipped woman lay on Nai's stomach, a cheap little comb on the back of her hair gleaming dully like a fragment of broken glass. In a single easy movement Fyodor pulled the comb out and dropped it into the pocket of his apron. Then he gripped Nai under the arms and pulled him out from the general pile. Nai's head lolled back, his sharp unshaven chin pointing upwards, and one hand flopped down towards the ground.

Fyodor didn't drop Nai casually onto the ground as he had the woman, but, holding him under his arms and bending his now slack body, turned him to face Nikolka, his feet touching the floor.

"Take a good look," he said. "Is this the one? We don't want to make a mistake..."

Nikolka looked Nai straight in the eyes. Nai's wide-open eyes looked back at Nikolka with a glassy, uncomprehending stare. On his left cheek there was a barely perceptible touch of green, and there were large stains, probably of congealed blood, marking his chest and stomach.

"Yes, it's him," said Nikolka.

Continuing to hold Nai under the arms Fyodor dragged him onto the lift platform and laid him down at Nikolka's feet. The corpse lay there, its arms flung out wide and its chin pointing upwards. Fyodor got onto the lift, pulled the lever and they started to move back up.

That evening, in the chapel, all Nikolka's wishes were fulfilled and, although he still felt unbearably sad, his conscience was completely calm. The light was turned on in the bare, gloomy chapel attached to the anatomical theatre. In the corner of the room the lid had been placed on the coffin of some unknown person, so that such an unpleasant neighbour should not disturb Nai's peace and calm. It even seemed that Nai himself started to look out at the world from his coffin with a more cheerful expression.

Nai's body had been washed by the good-humoured and talkative attendants. He was now clean and wearing his army coat without epaulettes, with a wreath on his brow and with three candles at the head of his coffin, and, most importantly of all, with his colourful ribbon of St George which Nikolka had himself placed onto his cold and clammy chest under his shirt. Seeing the three candles, Nai's old mother turned her trembling head towards Nikolka and said:

"That is my son. Thank you."

When he heard this, Nikolka burst into tears again and went out of the chapel into the snow. All around him, above the yard of the anatomical theatre, lay the night and the snow, and overhead the Milky Way and the stars, like crosses.

ALEXEI TURBIN STARTED TO DIE during the afternoon of 22nd December. The day was snowy and overcast, and full of the spirit of the imminent arrival of Christmas. This was reflected above all in the shine of the parquet floor in the sitting room – the result of the combined efforts of Anyuta, Nikolka and Lariosik moving quietly about the room the day before. There was a similar spirit of Christmas in the holders of the icon lamps which Anyuta had polished with her own hands. And, finally, there was the smell of pine needles and a radiant display of greenery in the corner by the passage from *Faust*, lying seemingly forever forgotten above the open piano keys...

Please, I beg you, for my sister's sake...

Moving a little unsteadily, Yelena had come out of Alexei's room at about midday and had gone quietly through the sitting room, where Karas, Myshlayevsky and Lariosik were sitting in complete silence. They all remained perfectly still, avoiding looking at her face as she walked through. Yelena went into her own room and closed the door, the heavy curtain falling into place and lying still.

Myshlayevsky stirred.

"So," he said in a hoarse whisper, "the commander did a good job, except that he didn't do so well by Alyosha."

Karas and Lariosik had nothing to add to this. Lariosik blinked, dark-violet shadows lining his cheeks.

"Oh, damn it..." Myshlayevsky added. He stood up and, swaying from side to side, made his way to the door. Then he stopped in indecision, and gestured in the direction of Yelena's door. "Listen, chaps, why don't you keep an eye on her... Otherwise, maybe..."

He shifted from one foot to the other and went into the library, where the sound of his footsteps died down. A little while later his voice could be heard again, together with some strangely plaintive sounds emanating from Nikolka's room.

"She's in tears, Nikol," Lariosik whispered with a despairing sigh. He tiptoed up to Yelena's door and bent down to the keyhole, but was unable to see anything. He glanced round helplessly at Karas, making questioning gestures. Karas went up to the door, hesitated for a moment, and then tapped quietly on the door with his fingernail.

"Yelena Vasilyevna, Yelena Vasilyevna," he said quietly.

"Don't worry, I'm all right," Yelena's muffled voice could be heard from the other side of the door, "but don't come in."

Karas moved away from the door, as did Lariosik. They both returned to their places, to their chairs under the Saardam stove, and fell quiet.

There was nothing that the Turbin family, or those closely connected to them, could do in Alexei's room; with the three men already there, the room was cramped enough as it was. One of them was the golden-eyed bearlike figure, the second was the trim figure of a young, clean-shaven man, looking more like a guardsman than a doctor, and finally, the third was the grey-haired professor. It was his expert knowledge that had revealed both to him and the other Turbins the unwelcome news as soon as he had appeared on 16th December. Realizing at once what was wrong, he had said there and then that Alexei had typhus. And straight away the bullet wound under the left shoulder had become less significant. It was he who, an hour ago, had gone out with Yelena into the sitting room where, in answer to her persistent questioning – reflected not just in what she said but in the expression of her dry eyes and cracked lips – he had told her that there was little hope, adding, as he looked directly into Yelena's eyes with his own experienced and therefore all-pitying eyes, "very little hope". Everyone, including Yelena, knew very well what that meant: that there was no hope at all and that, therefore, Alexei was dying. After this, Yelena had gone into Alexei's bedroom and stood there for a long time looking at his face. And it was then that she realized that there was, indeed, no hope. She didn't need the expertise of the kind, grey-haired, old professor to tell her that Alexei was clearly dying.

He lay there, still in a fever, but the fever was fitful, seemingly liable to disappear at any moment. His face was already beginning to take on a strangely waxen sheen, and the shape of his nose was changing, becoming thinner, with the especially striking curved part exhibiting an aura of hopelessness. Yelena's feet grew cold standing there, and for a moment she was overcome by the sense of depression and gloom pervading the purulent, camphor-ridden air in the room, but this soon passed.

Something sank in Alexei's chest like a stone, and he started to whistle as he breathed in, trying to force a stream of clammy air into his lungs.

He had long ago fallen unconscious, and he was totally unaware of what was going on around him. For a little while Yelena stood there looking at him. Then the professor touched her hand and whispered:

"You go, Yelena Vasilyevna. We can do everything here now."

Yelena obediently left the room. But the professor in fact didn't really do anything other than to take off Alexei's gown, wipe his hands with balls of moist cotton-wool, and look once more at his face. The folds of his lips and nose were beginning to take on a bluish tinge.

"It's hopeless," the professor said, speaking very quietly into the ear of his clean-shaven colleague. "You stay here, by his side, Doctor Brodovich."

"Shall I give him camphor?" Brodovich asked in a whisper.

"Yes, yes."

"By injection?"

"No." The grey-haired professor thought for a moment, looking out of the window. "Give him three grams immediately. And then more frequently thereafter." After another moment's thought he added: "Telephone me at my clinic in case things come to a head." As the professor whispered this he took great care to ensure that Alexei, even through the fog of delirium, couldn't hear what he was saying. "And, in any event, if nothing has happened, I'll come immediately when I've finished my lecture."

Every year, for as long as the Turbins could remember, the icon lamps had been lit at dusk on 24th December and, later that evening, the sitting room had begun to bask in the warm glow of the twinkling lights on the green fir-tree branches. But now, this time, the treacherous bullet wound and the wheezing typhus had thrown everything into confusion, bringing everything forward, including the lighting of the icon lamps. Closing the door into the dining room, Yelena went up to her bedside table, took out some matches, stood on a chair and lit the light in the heavy icon lamp hanging on a chain in front of the large-framed icon. The flame flared up brightly, turning the halo above the dark head of the Virgin Mary into gold, and her eyes adopted a welcoming expression. The head, inclined to one side, looked down on Yelena. Outside, through the two square frames of the windows, it was a white, soundless December day, and the flickering tongue of flame in the corner of the room created a sense of the approaching festival. Yelena climbed down from the chair, threw her shawl off her shoulders and went down on her knees. She rolled back the edge of the carpet to reveal an open space of gleaming parquet flooring, and silently bowed down to the ground.

Myshlayevsky walked through the dining room, followed by Nikolka, his eyelids puffy from tears. They stood in Alexei's room for a moment, and then returned to the dining room, where Nikolka said to the others with a deep intake of breath:

"He's dying."

"Do you think we should call a priest?" Myshlayevsky asked. "What do you think, Nikol? What if he should… without confession?"

"We need to tell Lena first," Nikolka answered anxiously. "We can't do it without her. And anyway, she might not be able to cope with it…"

"But what does the doctor say?" asked Karas.

"What is there to say?" Myshlayevsky mumbled. "There's nothing more to be said."

They spent a long time whispering anxiously among themselves, the pale-faced, confused Lariosik sighing audibly the whole time. Once again they called in to see Doctor Brodovich. He glanced out into the hallway, lit a cigarette, and whispered that it was the final death agony, and that of course it would be possible to summon a priest – he didn't mind, since the sick man was unconscious and therefore it couldn't do any harm.

"Silent confession…"

They continued whispering among themselves, but without deciding whether to summon a priest. They knocked on Yelena's door, but she answered them through the door in a muffled voice: "Leave me for a bit… I'll come out in a minute." So they went away again.

From her kneeling position Yelena looked up mistrustfully at the jagged halo crowning the dark face with the clear eyes and, stretching out her arms, whispered:

"You have sent us too much grief all at once, Holy Mother of God. In the space of just one year you have destroyed a family. What for? You have taken our mother away from us, and I no longer have a husband. He's gone for ever – that I can understand, understand only too clearly. But now you are taking our eldest away. What for? How will Nikol and I manage alone, just the two of us? Just look around and see what's happening to us, just look… Holy Mother of God, please, I beg you, take pity on us. All right, we might certainly be bad people, but why are you punishing us in this way?"

She bowed down again, eagerly pressing her forehead to the floor. Then she crossed herself and, stretching out her arms, started to pray once more:

"In you alone is there hope, Virgin Mother. In you alone. Pray for us to your son, pray to the Lord God, that He send us a miracle…"

Yelena's whispering became more and more passionate. At times she stumbled over words, but her prayers continued in an unbroken stream. She prostrated herself on the floor with greater and greater frequency, tossing her head to sweep back the lock of hair that escaped from her comb and fell into her eyes. As the daylight faded in the square frames of the windows, the white falcon too disappeared, and the tinkling of the gavotte as the clock struck three went unnoticed. Also completely unheard was the appearance of the one to whom Yelena had been praying through the intercession of the dark Virgin Mary. There He was, standing barefoot by the open tomb, risen and merciful. Yelena's breast expanded, a red blush suffused her cheeks, and her eyes, brimming over with dry, tearless weeping, were filled with light. She bowed down, pressing her forehead and cheek against the floor, and then, reaching out with all her soul, she moved as fast as she could to the icon lamp, no longer aware of the hard floor beneath her knees. The light of the lamp swelled up, and the dark face, framed by the halo, clearly came to life, as the Virgin's eyes drew from Yelena fresh streams of more and more words. Outside in the street, as well as within the rest of the apartment, there was total silence, and the daylight was disappearing with incredible speed, as another vision arose within the room: a heavenly vault filled with a hard, glassy light, strangely unfamiliar red-and-yellow sandy outcrops, olive trees and the heart of a temple filled with cold and a dark, centuries-old silence.

"Holy Mother of God," Yelena whispered in the glow of the lamp, "pray to Him. There He is. What would it cost you? Have mercy on us… have mercy. Your days, your festival, are fast approaching. Alexei, perhaps, will still be able to do good in the world, and I will pray to you to forgive us our sins. I agree that Sergei should not return… If you have taken him from me, then so be it, but please don't punish us with Alexei's death… We are all guilty of bloodshed, but please don't punish us in this way. Please don't. He is here, your Son…"

The lamp started to flicker, and one long ray of light reached out towards Yelena's eyes. Then, as she looked at the Virgin Mary's face framed by its golden coif, she watched in bewilderment as the lips parted and the eyes adopted a preternatural expression. Her heart burst with such a feeling of terror and such a rush of intoxicated joy that she fell to the floor, this time without rising.

*

The alarm spread throughout the apartment like a dry wind, as somebody ran on tiptoe through the dining room. Someone else tapped on Yelena's door whispering: "Yelena... Yelena..." Wiping her cold, clammy forehead with the back of her hand and tossing back the curl of hair from her eyes, Yelena got up from the floor, no longer looking at the shining icon in the corner, but blankly straight ahead of her, like some wild person. Then she went to the door with a heart that had turned into steel. Without waiting for permission, the door crashed open of its own accord to reveal Nikolka standing framed by the heavy curtain. He looked at her with horror-struck eyes. He was gasping for breath.

"Yelena... you have to... don't worry... please don't worry... please come... it seems..."

Doctor Alexei Turbin, as waxen-looking as a broken, crumpled candle in someone's sweaty hands, lay there, his sharp chin pointing towards the ceiling, his bony hands with their unclipped fingernails protruding from under the blanket. His body was swimming in clammy sweat, and his glistening, desiccated chest could be seen rising and falling under his shirt. Then his head dropped, and he buried his chin in his chest. His lips parted to reveal his yellowing teeth, and he half-opened his eyes. The expression in his eyes was still partly concealed by a quivering, ragged curtain of fog and delirium, but here and there patches of light could be glimpsed through the darkness. Then, in an extremely weak, thin and hoarse voice he said:

"It's the crisis, Brodovich. Will I pull through this?... Aaah."

The lamp that Karas was holding in his shaking hands illuminated the sunken bed and the crumpled folds of the sheets. With a hand that was not entirely steady, the clean-shaven doctor grasped a piece of flesh on Alexei's arm and inserted a little needle. Small beads of sweat had formed on the doctor's forehead. He was agitated and shaken.

19

PETURRA. His sojourn in the City had lasted for forty-seven days. The January of 1919, ice-bound and powdered with snow, had flown past the Turbins, and now February had erupted in the form of a blizzard.

On 2nd February, a dark figure with a shaven head covered by a black silk cap moved through the Turbins' apartment. This was Alexei Turbin himself, risen from the dead. He had changed considerably. Two deep lines had appeared on his face, at the corners of his mouth, seemingly for ever. His complexion was waxen and his eyes were shadowed and sunken, with a permanently gloomy and unsmiling expression.

Just as forty-seven days previously, Alexei stood in the sitting room, his face pressed against the window, listening. And, just as then, when he had looked out of the window and seen the snow falling and lights blazing in the sky as in an opera, he could hear the distant, muffled sound of gunfire. Grimacing painfully, he leant his full weight on his stick and looked out onto the street. He noticed that, by some magic, the days had got longer and that there was more light outside, despite the raging blizzard that was sending millions of snowflakes cascading through the air.

Under the silk cap, his head was beset with thoughts – grim and cheerless, but always lucid. His head seemed to him to be a light and empty vessel, as if it were some alien box sitting on his shoulders, so that these thoughts appeared to be coming from somewhere outside him, in a sequence that they themselves had determined. He was quite happy to be alone, standing looking out of the window...

"Peturra..." he thought. "By no later than tonight it will all be over, and Peturra will have gone... But was he here at all? Or have I dreamt it all? I don't know – impossible to prove one way or the other. I like Lariosik very much. He doesn't get in our way as a family at all; in fact, we need him here. I need to thank him for taking such care of me... But what about Shervinsky? God knows. It's never easy with women. Yelena's absolutely bound to get involved with him. But what's so good about him, apart from his voice? Yes, he has a marvellous voice, but surely, when all's said and done, it's possible to listen to someone's voice without getting married to them, isn't it? But, in any case, it doesn't matter. So what does matter then? Yes, it was Shervinsky who was saying that they have red stars on their fur caps. I suppose all hell will probably break loose in the City, won't it? Yes, very probably... So later tonight... The troop transports are probably already moving along the streets... Nevertheless, I'm going; I'll go in the daytime... and I'll take... *Rrring.* Grab him! I'm a murderer. No, I'm not: I fired at someone in the heat of battle. Or maybe I just wounded him... Who does she live with? Where is her husband? *Rrring.* Malyshev. Where is he now? Disappeared off the face of the earth. And what about Maxim... and Alexander I?"

As all these thoughts were streaming through his head, he was interrupted by the doorbell. Everybody had gone into the City, hastily completing their items of business while it was still light, and there was nobody in the apartment except for Anyuta.

"If that's a patient for me, Anyuta, show him in."

"All right, Alexei Vasilyevich."

Somebody climbed the stairs behind Anyuta, took off his mohair coat in the hall and went into the sitting room.

"Please come this way," Alexei said.

A scrawny-looking young man with a yellowish face and wearing an army jacket got up from his chair. There was a glazed, concentrated look in his eyes. Alexei, now in his white doctor's gown, stood aside for him to pass and showed him through to his study.

"Please sit down. How can I help you?"

"I have syphilis," the visitor said in a hoarse voice, looking straight at Alexei, with a gloomy expression.

"Have you been having treatment?"

"Yes, I have, but it's been rather poor and slapdash. Not much help, really."

"Who sent you to me?"

"The priest at St Nicholas the Good, Father Alexander."

"Who did you say?"

"Father Alexander."

"What, do you know him?"

"I have been to him for confession, and talking with the saintly old man has brought me considerable spiritual relief," the visitor explained, looking out at the sky. "Treatment wasn't for me. Or so I thought: God was punishing me for my terrible sins, and I had to endure it patiently. But the priest persuaded me that this was incorrect. And so I did as he told me."

Alexei made a thorough examination of the man's pupils and then proceeded to test his reflexes. But the owner of the mohair coat's pupils turned out to be quite normal – just full of a dark melancholy.

"So," Alexei said, laying down his hammer, "you're evidently a religious person."

"Yes, I think about God and pray to Him day and night. He is my only refuge and comforter."

"That's wonderful of course," Alexei replied, looking his patient straight in the eye, "and I respect that. But this is my advice: while you are being treated, put such persistent thoughts about God to one side. It seems they're becoming something of an *idée fixe* with you. And in your condition that's harmful. You need fresh air, exercise and sleep."

"I pray at night."

"No, you need to change that habit and reduce the time you spend praying. It will simply tire you out, and you need rest."

The man submissively lowered his eyes.

He undressed and waited, naked, for Alexei to examine him.

"Have you taken cocaine?"

"Among all the other revolting habits I used to succumb to, yes. But not any more."

"What if he's a crook?" Alexei wondered. "Perhaps he's having me on. Goodness only knows. I'll need to make sure that none of the fur coats in the hall have disappeared."

Alexei took the hammer and drew a question mark on the man's chest with the handle. The white mark turned red.

"You must stop getting carried away by questions of a religious nature. And in general you need to stop burdening yourself with all these oppressive thoughts. Please get dressed. Tomorrow I'll begin injecting you with mercury, and then, in a week's time, you'll have your first blood transfusion."

"All right, doctor."

"And no cocaine. Or alcohol. Or women..."

"I have given up women and all poisons. And all nasty people," said the man, buttoning up his shirt. "The evil genius of my life, the precursor of the Antichrist, has gone to the city of the Devil."

"My dear chap, please stop all that stuff," Alexei groaned. "Otherwise you'll find yourself in a psychiatric hospital. What is this Antichrist you're talking about?"

"I'm talking about his precursor, Mikhail Semyonovich Shpolyansky, the man with the black sideburns and the eyes of a snake. He has gone to the kingdom of the Antichrist in Moscow to raise the alarm and to lead a host of fallen angels to this City to punish it for the sins of its inhabitants. Just like Sodom and Gomorrah..."

"By the 'fallen angels' you mean the Bolsheviks, I suppose? Well, I agree. Nonetheless, you must stop all that stuff. You will take bromide, one tablespoon three times a day."

"He may still be young, but he's as depraved as any thousand-year-old devil. He incites women to debauchery and young men to commit sinful acts, and the trumpets of war of the legions of evil are already sounding, and above the fields the face of Satan can be seen behind them."

"Trotsky, you mean?"

"Yes, that is the name he has adopted. But his real name is Abaddon in Hebrew and Apollyon in Greek – that is to say, the destroyer."*

"Seriously, I'm telling you, if you don't stop all this, you'll need to look out; it's becoming a mania with you."

"No, doctor, I'm perfectly normal. How much do you charge for your sacred work?"

"Please! Why do you keep on using this word 'sacred'? I don't see anything particularly sacred in the work I do. I charge the usual fee for a course of treatment, like everybody else. If you wish to become a patient of mine, you'll need to leave a deposit."

"Very good."

The man unbuttoned his army jacket.

"Perhaps you don't have very much money," Alexei muttered, looking at the threadbare knees on the man's trousers. "No, he's not a crook," he thought. "Just deranged."

"No, doctor, the money can be found. You are bringing solace to mankind in your own way."

"And sometimes with great success. Don't forget to take the bromide correctly."

"But total solace, dear doctor, will come only when we've arrived up there," the man said passionately, pointing towards the white ceiling. "But just at this moment a time of suffering is upon us, the like of which no one has ever seen before. And it will be with us very soon."

"I am most grateful to you for that information; I have suffered enough already."

"Oh no, doctor, you mustn't talk too soon," the man muttered as he was putting on his mohair coat in the hall. "For as it has been written: 'And the third angel poured out his vial upon the rivers and fountains of waters; and they became blood.'"

"Now where have I heard that before?" Alexei wondered to himself. "Oh, yes, of course: when I had that heartfelt talk with the priest. And now they've found each other... That's wonderful."

"My sincere advice to you is to read the Book of Revelation less. I repeat: it's harmful. My very best wishes. Six o'clock tomorrow, please. Anyuta, please show this gentleman out."

"Please accept this... I really would like the person who saved my life to have something to remember me by... This bracelet belonged to my late mother..."

"But why? You don't need to do this... I don't want you to..." said Julia Reiss, trying to push Alexei away, but he persisted and fastened the dark, heavy, metal bracelet around her pale wrist. Julia's hand, all of her indeed, now seemed even more beautiful than ever. The pink glow on her cheeks was visible, even in the semi-gloom.

Unable to restrain himself any longer, Alexei put his right arm round Julia, pulled her towards him and kissed her several times on her cheek. As he was doing this his weak hand dropped his stick which clattered onto the floor by the legs of the table.

"You must go," Julia whispered, "it's time to go. There are troop transports on the streets already. Make sure you stay safe."

"You are so dear to me," Alexei whispered. "May I come to see you again?"

"Yes, please come."

"Tell me, why are you alone, and whose is this photograph on the table, the dark-looking man with the sideburns?"

"That's my cousin," she answered, lowering her eyes.

"What is his surname?"

"Why do you want to know?"

"You saved my life... I just want to know."

"I see: because I saved your life, that means you have the right to know things? His name is Shpolyansky."

"Is he here?"

"No, he's gone away... to Moscow. You're being very inquisitive."

Something stirred deep within Alexei and he stood there for a long time looking at the black sideburns and dark eyes. An unpleasant thought gnawed away at him more persistently than any others as he studied the forehead and lips of the chairman of the Magnetic Triolet. But he couldn't bring it into focus... Precursor. That unfortunate man in the mohair coat. What was it that was troubling him, gnawing away at him? What did it have to do with him, anyway? Fallen angels... Oh, it didn't matter... just so long as he could come here again, to this strange, peaceful little house with its portrait of the man with the gold epaulettes.

"You must go. It's time."

"Nikol? Is that you?"

The brothers came face to face with each other on the lowest terrace of the mysterious garden by the other little house. Nikolka seemed somehow embarrassed, as if he'd been caught red-handed.

"Ah, Alyosha! I've been to see the Nai-Turs family," he explained, looking as if he had been caught on a fence trying to steal apples.

"Well, that was kind of you. Is his mother still alive?"

"Yes, and his sister too. You see, Alyosha… Well, anyway…"

Alexei gave his brother a sideways glance and didn't subject him to any more questions.

The brothers walked half the way home in silence. Then Alexei said:

"It seems that Peturra threw us together onto Malo-Provalnaya Street, doesn't it, Nikol? Oh well, we'll be coming here quite a lot in that case. But who knows what will come of it all, eh?"

Nikolka's attention was immediately engaged by this cryptic utterance. Taking his cue, he asked:

"What about you, Alyosha? Have you been seeing someone, too, on Malo-Provalnaya?"

But Alexei merely mumbled a reply and, raising his coat collar, disappeared inside it. For the rest of the way home he didn't say another word.

On this important and historic day everybody – Myshlayevsky, Karas and Shervinsky – was having dinner at the Turbins. It was the first time they had all sat down together for a meal since Turbin had returned home wounded. And everything was as it usually was, with one exception: there were no gloomy-looking sultry roses on the table, since the shattered Marquise confectionery shop no longer existed and had vanished into the unknown, to a place where, no doubt, Madame Anjou also lay at peace. And nobody sitting at the table was wearing epaulettes, all epaulettes having turned to dust and been blown away by the blizzard.

Everybody was listening to Shervinsky open-mouthed – even Anyuta who was leaning against the door, having joined them from the kitchen.

"What kind of stars?" Myshlayevsky asked morosely.

"Small, in the form of hat badges, five-pointed," Shervinsky answered, "on their fur caps. There's a whole mass of them coming, they say… In a word, they'll be here at midnight…"

"At midnight, you say? How can you be so precise?"

But before Shervinsky had time to answer there was a ring on the doorbell and Vasilisa appeared.

Bowing to the left and to the right, and shaking everyone's – particularly Karas's – hand warmly, Vasilisa went straight to the piano, his boots squeaking. With a beaming smile, Yelena held out her hand to him and, with a peculiar little hop, he kissed it. "Well, I never," thought

Nikolka, "Vasilisa seems to have become much nicer since that money was taken from him. Perhaps," he continued in philosophical vein, "money stops people from being nice. Take this room, for example: nobody has any money and everybody's nice."

Vasilisa thanks them all most humbly, but he doesn't want any tea. Splendid, all splendid... *tee, hee.* How snug it all is here, despite the appalling things going on. He thanks them all most humbly again, but no, thank you. Vanda Mikhaylovna's sister has come to stay with them from the country, and he has to go back downstairs very soon. He's come to give Yelena Vasilyevna a letter, found just a minute ago in the letterbox by the front door. "Considered it my duty to bring it to you. My deepest respects to you all." With another little hop, Vasilisa took his leave.

Yelena took the letter off to her bedroom.

"Can it really be a letter from abroad? I know about such letters: as soon as you pick up the envelope, you know what's inside. And how did it get here? There's no post at all at the moment. Even letters sent from Zhitomir to the City only get here if brought especially by someone. How stupid, how absurd everything's become in this country! After all, the trains are still running, so I wonder why letters can't travel the same way, and why they get lost. But this one got through. Don't worry: a letter like this will make it, will find the right address. War... Warsaw. Warsaw. But the handwriting isn't Talberg's. I don't like this: my heart's beating so fast."

Although there was a shade on the lamp, everything suddenly became so unpleasant in Yelena's bedroom, as if someone had ripped the colourful silk off the shade causing the harsh light to shine directly into her eyes and creating a general sense of chaos. Her face changed, taking on the appearance of the ancient Virgin Mary in her fretted frame. Her lips were trembling, but forming into folds of contempt. Her mouth was twitching. Tearing the envelope she took the sheet of grey, lined notepaper out and placed it in the pool of light.

...I have only just learnt that you have separated from your husband. The Ostroumovs saw Sergei Ivanovich at the embassy. He was on his way to Paris, together with the Hertz family; they say he's getting married to Lydia Hertz; strange how this chaos is affecting everything. I'm sorry you didn't leave the City as well. I'm sorry for all of you, trapped in the peasants' clutches. They seem to be saying in the newspapers here that Petlyura is advancing on the City. We hope the Germans will stop him...

Crashing and thumping through the walls and door, draped with the curtain portraying Louis XIV, Nikolka's march resounded mechanically in Yelena's head. Louis was smiling, one arm thrust out, holding his cane, entwined with ribbons. Someone rapped on the door with the handle of a stick and Alexei came in. Seeing his sister's expression, he made the same face and asked:

"From Talberg?"

Feeling ashamed and depressed, Yelena said nothing for a moment. But then, suddenly, she came to and pushed the sheet of notepaper across the table towards him. "From Olya... in Warsaw..." He ran his eyes along the lines until the end, and then went back and read the opening again: "Dear Lenochka, I don't know if this will reach you..."

Many different colours were reflected on his face. The general shade was saffron, his cheekbones were pinkish and his eyes were, at first, light blue, but then turning black.

"I can't tell you what pleasure it would give me," he said, through gritted teeth, "to give him such a belt on his ugly mug..."

"Who?" asked Yelena, wrinkling her nose, onto which the tears were beginning to drip.

"Myself," said Doctor Turbin, beside himself with shame, "for allowing myself to embrace him that time."

Yelena burst into tears.

"Do me a favour, will you?" he continued. "Send that horrible object there to the Devil," he said, jabbing at the photograph on the table with the handle of his stick. Sobbing, Yelena handed the photograph to him. In a flash he had pulled the photograph of Sergei Ivanovich from its frame and ripped it into pieces. Yelena started howling like a peasant woman, her shoulders shaking as she pressed herself into Alexei's starched shirt front. Out of the corner of her eye she looked with a sense of superstitious terror at the brown icon, in front of which the lamp in its gold holder was still burning.

"Yes, I prayed to you... and I know I set conditions... Well, please don't be angry with me... Don't be angry, Holy Mother of God," thought the superstitious Yelena. Alexei became alarmed.

"Shh... Not so loud... They'll hear you, and that wouldn't help."

But no one in the sitting room had heard anything. Nikolka had just finished crashing out the 'Two-Headed Eagle' march on the piano, and everyone was laughing.

G REAT AND TERRIBLE was the Year of Our Lord 1918, but the
year 1919 was still more terrible.

On the night of 2nd February, at the entrance to the Chain Bridge
across the river Dnieper, two men were dragging someone across the
snow in a black, torn overcoat, his bloodstained face covered in bruises.
Beside them ran a Cossack sergeant hitting him over the head with a
ramrod. At every blow the bloodstained man's head jerked back, but
he had stopped yelling and was now simply moaning. As the ramrod
lashed with considerable force into the torn overcoat the man would
respond to every blow with an "uff... aah".

"You Yiddish bastard!" the sergeant yelled, incensed with fury. "You're
going to be taken to those stacks and shot! I'll teach you to skulk about
the place! I'll teach you! What were you doing, hiding behind those
stacks? You spy!..."

But the bloodstained man did not answer the enraged sergeant. Then
the sergeant ran a little way in front, and the two others jumped aside
to avoid the swish of the descending glittering rod. Without calculating
the strength of the blow, the sergeant smashed the rod into the man's
head with the force of a lightning bolt. Something cracked, and this
time there was no response from the man. His head lolled back and,
thrusting out one arm, he slumped over from his knees to one side
and, with a wide sweep, he flung his other arm back as if he wanted
to scoop up as much as possible of the trampled and dung-covered
ground around him. His fingers formed into a crook and he started
scrabbling at the dirty snow. Then he just lay there in a dark puddle,
twitching several times, and finally went still.

Above the victim, at the entrance to the bridge, an electric lamp
hissed, and all around him scuttled the frightened shadows of Cossacks
with their tasselled caps. Above was the black vault of the sky, shining
with a myriad of twinkling stars.

And at the very moment that the man lying on the ground died, the
star of Mars in the frozen heights above the outskirts of the City suddenly exploded with a deafening roar, spattering fire. And, following
the star, the black distances on the far bank of the Dnieper leading to

far-off Moscow also erupted in a prolonged, heavy crash of thunder. And then a second star exploded, but this time lower down, right above the roofs of the houses buried under the snow.

And immediately the Blue Haydamak Division set off from the bridge and trotted into the City, continuing through the City and out of sight for ever. Behind them raced the frozen horses of Kozyr-Leshko's unit like a pack of wolves, followed by a bouncing field kitchen. Then the entrance to the bridge was empty, as if nobody had been there. Only the congealing corpse of the black-coated Jew remained, together with the trampled mounds of snow and the piles of horse dung.

And the corpse was the only witness to the fact that Peturra had not been just a myth, that he really had been there... *rrring... clang...* the guitar and the Turk... the metal lamp on Bronnaya... girls' plaits, whirling snow, gunshot wounds, wolves howling at night-time, the frost... Yes, it had all really happened.

Look, there's Grisha, he's off to work...
But his boots are torn! He's gone berserk...

But why had it happened? What was it all for? Nobody can tell. But will anyone pay for all the bloodshed?

No. No one.

The snow will simply thaw, the green Ukrainian grass will spring up and plait the earth, the fresh, lush shoots will sprout, and the heat will shimmer over the fields. But, of all that blood, not a trace will remain. Blood is cheap in those dark red fields, and no one will ever pay for it.

No one.

Since the early evening the tiles on the Saardam stove had glowed with heat, and all the stoves had been kept warm until deep into the night. All the inscriptions on the Shipwright of Saardam had been washed off, except for the remains of one:

...Len... have a ticket for Aid...

The house on St Alexei's Hill, the house crowned by its general's cap of snow, had long since been wrapped in a warm sleep. Dreams flitted among the curtains and flickered in the shadows. Outside, the frozen night became more and more dominant as it floated over the earth.

The stars danced, shrinking and expanding, and especially high in the sky was the red five-pointed star of Mars.

Alexei slept in his bedroom, his dream hovering above him like an indistinct painting. The hallway floated by, swaying as it went, and the Emperor Alexander I was setting light to the battalion papers in the stove. Julia went by, beckoning to him and laughing, shadows flitted past, and people shouted "Grab him! Grab him!"

There were people firing at him soundlessly, and he was trying to run away from them, but his feet stuck to the pavement on Malo-Provalnaya Street, and Alexei died in his sleep. He woke up with a groan and heard Myshlayevsky snoring in the sitting room, and the gentle whistle of Karas's and Lariosik's breathing from the library. Becoming fully awake, he wiped the sweat from his brow, smiling to himself as he reached out for his watch.

It said three o'clock.

"They must have gone by now... Peturra too... and he'll never come back."

And then he fell asleep again.

The night blossomed as it moved towards morning. The house slept on, buried under its shaggy mantle of snow. Tossing and turning, Vasilisa slept in the cold sheets, warming them with his emaciated body. He was having an absurd, circular dream. In the dream it was as if there hadn't been any revolution at all; it had all been nonsensical rubbish. A vague, indeterminate feeling of happiness washed over him. And then, in his dream, it was summer, and he had just bought an allotment in which vegetables sprang up instantaneously. The beds were full of cheerful little green shoots, through which cucumbers peeked out like little figs. Vasilisa stood there in a pair of canvas trousers, scratching his stomach and watching the enchanting sunset.

Then he dreamt of his globe-shaped clock that had been stolen from him. He wanted to feel sad because of the clock, but the sun was shining so pleasantly that he was unable to feel sad.

And then, at this precise moment, when everything was so pleasant, several round, pink piglets flew into the allotment and immediately started rooting up the vegetable beds with their little round snouts. The earth spewed up into the air like fountains. Vasilisa picked up a stick from the ground and prepared to chase the piglets away, but they suddenly turned into fearsome-looking animals with sharp fangs. They rushed towards him, jumping several feet into the air as they did so, because they had springs inside them. Vasilisa howled with terror in his sleep. Then a huge black doorpost crashed down on the piglets and they disappeared into the ground, and Vasilisa emerged from his dream to find himself in his damp, dark bedroom.

The night continued to blossom. The spirit of sleep flew on over the City like some nebulous white bird, passing by the cross of St Vladimir until it reached the other side of the river Dnieper where, at the very dead of night, it floated along the railway track. When it reached Darnitsa it stopped and began hovering above the station. On track no. 3 an armoured train stood waiting. The grey gun platforms were armour-plated, right down to the wheels. The locomotive loomed up into the sky in a dark mass of multi-faceted metal, red-hot fire spilling out from its belly onto the rails, so that from the side it looked as if its womb was overflowing with incandescent coals. It was quietly and ominously hissing away to itself, something was oozing from its sides and its blunt snout was silently pointed at the forests lying along the bank of the Dnieper. On the last gun platform a broad muzzle wrapped in a cover pointed up into the blue-black sky, aimed directly at the midnight cross some eight miles away.

The station was frozen in horror. It moved into the darkness head-on, and it shone with the eyes of little yellow lights, still reeling from the thunder of the evening's events. Despite the late hour, its platforms were bustling with people. There were three bright lights showing in the small, yellow telegraph building, and through the windows the constant clatter of telegraph machines could be heard. Despite the biting frost, the figures of people wrapped up in fur coats down to their knees, in greatcoats and black jackets, ran up and down the platform. On a side track behind the armoured train a troop train waited patiently, its carriage doors slamming with a resounding echo.

By the locomotive of the armoured train and the metal sides of the first armoured car, a man in a long greatcoat, tattered felt boots and a sharp-pointed domed hat was patrolling back and forth like a pendulum. He held his rifle in his hands tenderly as if he were a tired mother cradling a baby. In the dim lamplight, the sharp black outline of a soundless bayonet kept pace with him as he moved up and down between the rails. The man was extremely tired and frozen to the bone. The wooden fingers of his blue, cold hands dug around in vain, seeking shelter in the torn sleeves of his coat. His eyes stared out from under snow-covered eyelashes and the ragged white fringe of his hood, framing his mouth, encrusted with frost. His languorous, light-blue eyes were glazed with suffering and lack of sleep.

The man walked up and down methodically, his bayonet lowered, thinking only about one thing: how soon his hour of frozen torture could end, and he would be able to leave this brutal cold behind and go inside, into the heavenly warmth of the carriage and its hissing pipes, and into the crowded space of his compartment where he could flop onto his narrow bunk and sprawl out, sticking to it like glue. Up and down the man's shadow moved, from the fiery glow of the armoured locomotive belly to the dark side of the first armoured car until he reached the black sign saying "Armoured Train *Proletarian*".

Now increasing in size, now hunching up like some hideous monster, but always retaining its sharply pointed tip, the shadow carved its way through the snow with its black bayonet. Behind him the blue lights of the lamps hung in the air. On the platform there were two blue moons that teased rather than warmed. The man looked everywhere for a fire, but without success. Clenching his teeth, and abandoning any hope of ever warming his toes by simply wiggling them around, he fixed his gaze on the stars. The easiest star for him to look at was Mars, shining in the sky above the edge of the City. And as he looked upwards, his eyes encompassing distances of millions and millions of miles, he never for an instant let the vibrant red star out of his sight. It was five-pointed and clearly alive as it expanded and contracted. At times, overcome by exhaustion, the man stopped and lowered the butt of his rifle onto the snowy ground and, within the space of a moment, fell transparently asleep. Yet although he was asleep, the black wall of the armoured train and the sounds of the station remained with him as he slept. But they were joined by other sounds, and the vault of the sky expanded into something vast, sparkling and glittering with an abundance of vibrant red stars. His heart instantly flooded with happiness. Then a strange, unknown man in chain mail appeared on horseback and floated up towards him in a friendly sort of way. The black armoured train was on the verge of disappearing from his dream, it seemed, to be replaced by a village, buried deep in snow – the village of Malye Chugry. The man was standing on the edge of the village, and the other man, the one on horseback coming towards him, was his fellow villager and neighbour.

"Zhilin?" the man's brain asked silently, without using his lips. And immediately he heard the grim voice of the guard hammering away inside him with the words: "Sentry… post… you'll freeze to death."

With a totally superhuman effort the man grabbed his rifle, slung it on his arm, and staggered on his way again, struggling through the snow.

Back and forth, back and forth. The vast, glittering, sleepy vault disappeared, and the frozen world was once more clothed in the familiar, blue, silky sky, pierced by the black, sinister shape of a gun barrel. Reddish Venus twinkled, and from time to time the star on the man's chest would reflect the light coming from the blue moon of the station lamp. This star was small, and also five-pointed.

The spirit of sleep spun uneasily around as it flew along the river Dnieper, passing over the lifeless jetties and dropping down over Podol, where the lights had long since gone out. Everyone was asleep. Only in a three-storey stone building on the corner of Volynskaya Street, in the librarian's apartment, a room that was as narrow and as cramped as the cheapest room in the cheapest hotel, the blue-eyed Rusakov sat by a lamp with a humpbacked glass shade. In front of him lay a hefty book in a yellow leather binding. His eyes were moving slowly and solemnly across the lines:

And I saw the dead, small and great, stand before God; and the books were opened: and another book was opened, which is *the book* of life: and the dead were judged out of those things which were written in the books, according to their works.

And the sea gave up the dead which were in it; and death and hell delivered up the dead which were in them: and they were judged according to their works.

[…]

And whosoever was not found written in the book of life was cast into the lake of fire.

[…]

And I saw a new heaven and a new earth: for the first heaven and the first earth were passed away; and there was no more sea.

The more he read this extraordinary book,* the more his mind became like a shining sword, piercing the darkness.

Disease and suffering now appeared unimportant to him, lacking all substance. His illness fell away, like the scabby bark from a forgotten tree that has been felled in the forest. He saw the blue, bottomless mist of the centuries, the endless corridor of the millennia. And, instead of fear, he felt awe and the wisdom of submissiveness. He felt at peace, and it was in this state of peace that he arrived at the words:

[...] tears from their eyes; and there shall be no more death, neither sorrow, nor crying, neither shall there be any more pain: for the former things are passed away.

The dense fog lifted and Lieutenant Shervinsky appeared to Yelena. His prominent eyes had a knowing smile.

"I am a demon," he said, clicking his heels, "but Talberg's not coming back to you. So I'm going to sing to you..."

And he drew out of his pocket an enormous tinsel star and pinned it onto her left breast. The fog of sleep swirled around him and, through the clouds, his face appeared like that of a brightly painted doll. He started to sing piercingly, not in his normal real-life voice:

"We shall live, we shall live!"

"But death will come, and we shall die..." sang Nikolka, coming into the room.

He had a guitar in his hands, but his neck was covered in blood, and a yellow wreath with little icons hung round his forehead. Yelena's immediate thought was that he was going to die, and she burst out sobbing. Then, in the middle of the night, she woke up shouting:

"Nikolka, oh Nikolka!"

And she lay there for a long time, sobbing, listening to the murmuring of the night.

And the night floated on.

And, finally, young Petka Shcheglov, from the annexe next door to the Turbins, had a dream.

Petka was a little boy, and therefore he was not interested in the Bolsheviks, or Petlyura, or the Devil. And he dreamt a dream that was as simple and as joyful as the sun itself.

He dreamt he was walking along a large, green meadow, on which there was a glittering diamond globe, larger than Petka. Whenever adults try to run in their dreams, they find that their feet stick to the ground; they groan and thrash about, attempting to free themselves from the swamplike ground. Children's feet, on the other hand, are skittish and free. Petka ran up to the diamond globe and, laughing and catching his breath from happiness, grasped it with both hands. The globe showered Petka with sparkling droplets. That was the whole of his dream. He burst out laughing from happiness in the middle of the night. And from somewhere behind the stove a cricket joined in, chirping happily. Petka began to dream other dreams, all of them joyful and simple, and the cricket sang and sang in reply from its hiding place in a crack in the wall, behind the bucket, bringing the sleepy, murmuring family night to life.

The final night flowed on. During its second half, the entire blue, heavy vault of the sky – God's curtain cradling the earth – was a mass of stars. So many stars that it seemed as if, in the infinity lying beyond this blue curtain, an all-night Mass were being celebrated in front of the royal gates of a cathedral. The lights had been lit on the altar, and they had started shining through the curtain in the form of crosses, clusters and squares. Above the river Dnieper, and above the sinful, bloodstained and snow-covered earth, loomed the dark, sombre mass of the midnight cross of St Vladimir. From a distance it seemed as if the crosspiece had merged with the vertical and had disappeared, transforming the cross into a sharp, threatening sword.

But it is not to be feared. Everything will pass – suffering, torment, blood, hunger and plague. The sword will disappear, but the stars will remain when even the shadows of our bodies and of our deeds no longer remain on this earth. There is not a single person who does not know this. Why then do we not wish to direct our gaze towards them? Why?

Moscow
1923–24

Note on the Text

The text used for this translation is taken from M.A. Bulgakov, *Sobraniye sochinenii*, vol. 2 (St Petersburg: Azbuka-Klassika, 2002).

Notes

p. 3, The novel is dedicated to Lyubov Yevgenyevna Belozerskaya (1895–1987), Mikhail Bulgakov's second wife. They were married from 1924 to 1932.

p. 5, *The Captain's Daughter*: A historical novel of 1836, written by Alexander Pushkin (1799–1837) and set at the time of the Pugachov Rebellion (1773–75).

p. 7, *returned home... to the City*: Bulgakov refers to the Ukrainian capital Kiev throughout *The White Guard* as "the City".

p. 7, *St Alexei's Hill*: There is no such street in Kiev, although there is a St Andrew's Hill, on which Bulgakov himself lived, at No. 13. All other names of streets, alleyways, squares, districts and suburbs in the novel correspond with reality, with the exception of 'Malo-Provalnaya Street' (see note to p. 121).

p. 8, *The Shipwright of Saardam*: *The Shipwright of Saardam* (*Saardamskii plotnik*, 1849) is a novel by P.R. Furman (1816–65), centred on Peter the Great's visit to Holland in 1697. The name is used throughout to refer to the tiled Dutch stove.

p. 8, *Alexei Mikhaylovich*: Tsar Alexei I of Russia (r. 1645–76).

p. 9, *Natasha Rostova*: Natasha Rostova, the heroine of Tolstoy's *War and Peace* (1865–69).

p. 10, *And the third angel... blood*: Book of Revelation 16:4.

p. 11, *A sketch of Momus's face*: Momus, the Greek god of ridicule and satire.

p. 11, *Thrash Petlyura*: Semyon Vasilyevich Petlyura (in Ukrainian, Symon Vasylyovych Petlyura, 1879–1926) was the head of the Ukrainian state for two years from December 1918.

p. 12, *Aida*: An opera of 1871 by the Italian composer Giuseppe Verdi (1813–1901).

p. 12, *The day of Borodino*: The battle of Borodino was the turning point of Napoleon's disastrous invasion of Russia, taking place on 7th September 1812.

p. 12, *Abram Pruzhiner*: This was to become the title of a long poem written in 1971 by Naum Korzhavin (b. 1925), relating to the Kiev pogrom of 1919.

p. 12, *25th October 1917*: the date, according to the Julian (Old Style) Calendar, marking the Bolsheviks' seizure of power in St Petersburg.

p. 14, *Christmas Eve*: An opera of 1895 by Nikolai Rimsky-Korsakov (1844–1908), after Nikolai Gogol's (1809–52) short story of the same name, from his collection *Evenings on a Farm Near Dikanka*.

p. 14, *Svyatoshin*: A suburb of Kiev, now known as Svyatoshino.

p. 15, *the Hetman's money*: The Hetman (leader), referred to as such throughout the novel, was Pavlo Petrovych Skoropadsky (1873–1945), the head of the Ukrainian state from April to December 1918, whereupon he was ousted by Petlyura.

p. 15, *The Gentleman from San Francisco*: A short story written in 1915 by Ivan Bunin (1870–1953).

p. 20, *the Belgrade Hussars*: There was no such unit in the Russian army.

p. 21, *God-bearers straight out of Dostoevsky*: In Dostoevsky's novel *The Devils* (1871–72), the Russians are referred to as God's chosen people.

p. 22, *Tamara's Castle*: A wine cellar in Kiev.

p. 26, *Ignaty Perpillo, Ukrainian Grammar*: A fictionalized reference to Terpilo, P., *Ukrainska Hramatyka* (*Ukrainian Grammar*, Kiev, 1918).

p. 27, *I'll be able to get to the Don*: The river Don area in southern Russia was the focal point for the White forces commanded by General Denikin (see note below) during the Russian civil war (1917–21).

p. 27, *Denikin was my divisional commander*: Anton Ivanovich Denikin (1872–1947), one of the foremost generals of the White movement during the Russian civil war.

p. 28, *the ginger-bearded... Valentin sings*: The reference is to the leading baritone role in the 1859 opera *Faust* by Charles Gounod (1818–93).

p. 29, *SWR*: An acronym for South-Western Railways, the company operating in the north-central region of Ukraine.

p. 30, *the Kreshchatik*: The main street in the centre of Kiev.

p. 32, *Taras Bulba*: The Cossack hero of the eponymous historical novel written in 1842 by Nikolai Gogol (1809–52).

p. 32, *Karbovantsy*: The karbovanets was the unit of Ukrainian currency during the period 1917–20. It was twice later reinstated during the periods 1942–45 and 1992–96.

p. 32, *Order of St Stanislav*: One of the Russian imperial orders of chivalry, awarded for services to the state.

p. 32, *Goncharov and Dostoevsky*: The two Russian authors Ivan Alexandrovich Goncharov (1812–91) and Fyodor Mikhaylovich Dostoevsky (1821–81).

p. 32, *Brockhaus and Efron*: An encyclopedic dictionary in thirty-five volumes, published in St Petersburg and Leipzig, 1890–1906.

p. 33, *Order of Anna*: As with the Order of St Stanislav, the Order of Anna was yet another imperial Russian order of chivalry, awarded for services to the state.

p. 33, *Einem biscuit boxes*: Named after the Moscow biscuit manufacturer Einem. In the Soviet period the factory was renamed "Red October".

p. 35, *the humorous newspaper The Devil's Plaything*: A fictionalized version of the satirical newspaper *The Devil's Pepper Pot* (*Chortova perechnitsa*), first published in St Petersburg in 1918, and continuing publication into the early 1920s.

p. 35, *Rodzyanko'll be our president*: Mikhail Vladimirovich Rodzyanko (1859–1924), Russian politician and one of the founders and leaders of the Octobrist Party.

p. 36, *Prince Belorukov*: A fictionalized name for Prince Alexander Nikolayevich Dolgorukov (1873–1948), the Commander-in-Chief of the Hetman's armed forces.

p. 37, *where are the Senegalese troops then?*: Senegalese troops formed part of the French expeditionary force that landed in Odessa in 1918 to support the Whites in the civil war.

p. 38, *Alexandrovsky Imperial High School*: The name given in 1911 to Kiev High School No. 1, where Bulgakov himself was a student from 1901 to 1909.

p. 39, *Trotsky*: Lev Davidovich Trotsky (1879–1940, born Leyba Davidovich Bronstein), Bolshevik politician and People's Commissar for Military and Naval Affairs during the civil war.

p. 40, *The Tsar is dead*: Tsar Nicholas II, together with his wife, five children and a few members of the Imperial household, was executed by the Bolsheviks on 17th July 1918 in Yekaterinburg.

p. 41, *Kaiser Wilhelm*: Kaiser Wilhelm II (1859–1941), the last German Emperor, who abdicated on 9th November 1918.

p. 41, *Monsieur Gilliard*: Pierre Gilliard (1879–1962), Swiss tutor to the children of Tsar Nicholas II.

p. 42, *He will never be forgiven for abdicating at Dno*: Tsar Nicholas II signed the manifesto announcing his abdication at the railway station of Dno on 2nd March 1917.

p. 42, *All-mighty, all-powerful, / Reign over us*: Lines from the opening verse of the tsarist national anthem, composed in 1833 by Alexei Fyodorovich Lvov (1799–1870).

p. 43, *Russia can be sustained... a performance of Paul I*: A reference to the historical drama by Dmitry Sergeyevich Merezhkovsky (1865–1941), written in 1908. Myshlayevsky's line is a paraphrase of General Talyzin's statement in Act 4, Sc. 1, that "Russia alone, like an unflinching colossus, stands, and the foundation of that colossus is the Orthodox faith and autocracy".

p. 45, *like Liza from The Queen of Spades*: A short story (1834) by Alexander Pushkin (1799–1837).

p. 47, *For a Russian, the concept of honour is merely an unnecessary burden*: The quotation is from Dostoevsky's *The Devils*.

p. 48, *the Zaporozhian Cossacks*: Ukrainian Cossacks who lived below the rapids of the river Dnieper.

p. 48, *the Chersonese*: The region comprising the Crimea and the ancient city of Chersonesos (alternatively, Corsun).

p. 49, *the gigantic figure... on the top of Vladimir Hill*: The statue, more than twenty metres high, was erected in 1853 to commemorate Prince Vladimir the Great of Kiev (c.958-1015), who converted Kievan Rus to Christianity in 988.

p. 50, *the bottles of wonderful Abrau champagne*: Abrau is a major wine-producing area in southern Russia, famous for its sparkling wines.

p. 51, *nobody had any idea... new Poland was*: Poland was proclaimed an independent state on 7th November 1918.

p. 56, *Field Marshall Eichhorn, was assassinated*: Hermann von Eichhorn (1848–1918) was at the time of his assassination the supreme German commander of Army Group Kiev and the German military governor of Ukraine.

p. 61, *Galicia*: A historical region of Eastern Europe, now straddling the border region between Ukraine and Poland.

p. 62, *Quos vult perdere, dementat*: "Those whom [God/the god] wishes to destroy [He/he] drives mad" (Latin). A neo-Latin maxim of uncertain origin, with some variants including the insertion of 'Deus' ['God'] or 'Iuppiter' ['Jupiter'], making the subject explicit.

p. 65, *Thief of Tushino*: The horse bears the nickname given to False Dmitry II (d.1610), the second of three pretenders to the Russian throne claiming to be Tsarevich Dmitry Ivanovich, the son of Tsar Ivan IV (the Terrible).

p. 66, *those killed at Perekop*: The reference is to the fierce battles that took place on the Perekop peninsula in the Crimea in 1920, which led to the destruction of the White forces under General Wrangel.

p. 68, *Henryk Sinkiewicz*: Polish journalist and novelist (1846–1916).

p. 68, *Colonel Toropets*: A fictionalized portrayal of Yevgeny Mikhaylovich Konovalets (in Ukrainian, Yevhen Mykhaylovych Konovalets, 1891–1938), a native of Galicia who enlisted in the Austro-Hungarian army in 1914, was captured by the Russians, and subsequently entered the service of first the Ukrainian Rada and then Petlyura.

p. 68, *the writer Vinnichenko*: Vladimir Kirillovich Vinnichenko (in Ukrainian, Volodymyr Kyrylovych Vynnychenko, 1880–1951) was a Ukrainian writer and head of the Directorate (the Ukrainian provisional state committee) under Petlyura, from December 1918 to February 1919.

p. 75, *Alexander Fyodorovich Kerensky*: Alexander Fyodorovich Kerensky (1881–1970), prime minister in the Russian Provisional Government between the February and October revolutions of 1917.

p. 78, *Colonel Bolbotun*: A fictionalized portrayal of the real-life Pyotr Fyodorovich Bolbochan (in Ukrainian, Petro Fedorovych Bolbochan, 1883–1919), a colonel in the Ukrainian army.

p. 82, *Lensky and Onegin*: Characters from Alexander Pushkin's novel in verse *Eugene Onegin* (1823–31).

p. 87, *Emperor Alexander*: Alexander I (1777–1825), known as Alexander the Blessed, emperor of Russia from 1801 to 1825.

p. 91, *the Order of St George*: One of the Russian imperial orders of chivalry.

p. 96, *Notes of the Fatherland and Library for Reading*: Notes of the Fatherland (*Otechestvennye zapiski*), a Russian monthly literary journal published in St Petersburg from 1818 to 1884; *Library for Reading* (*Biblioteka dlya chteniya*), a Russian monthly magazine published in St Petersburg from 1834 to 1865.

p. 107, *Colonel Kozyr-Leshko*: A fictionalized portrayal of the Cossack leader Kozyr-Zirka.

p. 118, *Sh'ma Yisrael*: "Hear, O Israel" (Hebrew). The opening words of a section of the Torah that is a centrepiece of the morning and evening Jewish prayer services.

p. 120, *Shpolyansky*: The figure of Mikhail Shpolyansky is based on the Russian literary critic and writer Viktor Borisovich Shklovsky (1893–1984).

p. 121, *Malo-Provalnaya Street*: The actual name is Malopodvalnaya Street.

p. 124, *like Marcel's in Les Huguenots*: An opera of 1836, composed by Giacomo Meyerbeer (1791–1864), with a libretto by Eugène Scribe (1791–1861) and Émile Deschamps (1791–1871).

p. 128, *Alexandra Fyodorovna*: Alexandra Fyodorovna (1872–1918), born Princess Alix of Hesse, the wife of Tsar Nicholas II.

p. 128, *one of Tsar Alexander II's ministers, Milyutin*: Count Dmitry Alexeyevich Milyutin (1816–1912), Minister of War under Tsar Alexander II.

p. 137, *Carmen*: An opera of 1875, composed by Georges Bizet (1838–75) and based on the novel of the same name by Prosper Mérimée (1803–70).

p. 147, *Nat Pinkerton*: Nat Pinkerton, a fictional Russian detective and the hero of many adventures, originally derived from the stories of the American writer Alan Pinkerton (1819–94).

p. 152, *Grand Duke Mikhail Alexandrovich*: The younger brother of Tsar Nicholas II, executed by the Bolsheviks on 13th June 1918.

p. 153, *Hugo's Clopin Trouillefou*: A character from Victor Hugo's novel *The Hunchback of Notre-Dame* (1831).

p. 159, *Zhitomir*: A city in north-west Ukraine.

p. 194, *vint*: A Russian card game similar to bridge, sometimes known as "Russian whist".

p. 197, *Lomonosov*: Mikhail Vasilyevich Lomonosov (1711–65), a Russian academician and poet.

p. 197, *Nadson*: Semyon Yakovlevich Nadson (1862–87), a Russian poet.

p. 214, *Shustov's brandy*: A distillery founded by Nikolai Shustov in Moscow in 1863.

p. 216, *Long live Fort Ivangorod... Ardagan and Kars*: Three forts symbolizing for Karas, in his inebriated condition, the heroism and strength of the Russian armed forces. By the end of the civil war, Russia had ceded all three: Ivangorod to Estonia, and Ardagan and Kars to Turkey.

p. 222, *Haydamak Cossack infantrymen*: The term "haydamaks" originally referred to paramilitary bands of peasants and Cossacks operating in Ukraine in the 18th century.

p. 223, *the battle of Poltava*: The decisive victory of Peter the Great over Charles XII of Sweden on 27th June 1709.

p. 226, *Bogdan Khmelnitsky*: Bogdan Zinovy Mikhaylovich Khmelnitsky (in Ukrainian, Bohdan Zynovy Mykhaylovych Khmelnytsky, *c.*1595–1657), Hetman of the Zaporozhian Cossacks (see first note to p. 48). The monument to him, on his black charger, was erected on Sofia Square in the centre of Kiev in 1888.

p. 227, *one of the Universals*: The Universal declarations were the statements of independence proclaimed by the Rada (see note to p. 233) in 1917.

p. 229, *Arise, ye damned of the Earth*: The opening words of 'The Internationale' (1871), adopted by the Second International as its official anthem in 1889.

p. 230, *When I die*: The opening words of the poem 'The Will' by Ukraine's national poet, Taras Shevchenko (1814–61).

p. 233, *the chairman of the Rada*: The Rada was the revolutionary parliament of Ukraine in 1917–18

p. 253, *But his real name is… the destroyer*: Abaddon and Apollyon are, respectively, the Hebrew and Greek names for the "angel of the bottomless pit" – see Book of Revelation 9:11.

p. 263, *this extraordinary book*: The reference is to the Book of Revelation. The quotations in this section are from 20:12–15 and 21:1–4.

Extra Material

on

Mikhail Bulgakov's

The White Guard

Mikhail Bulgakov's Life

Mikhail Afanasyevich Bulgakov was born in Kiev – then in the Russian Empire, now the capital of independent Ukraine – on 15th May 1891. He was the eldest of seven children – four sisters and three brothers – and, although born in Ukraine, his family were Russians, and were all members of the educated classes – mainly from the medical, teaching and ecclesiastical professions. His grandfathers were both Russian Orthodox priests, while his father lectured at Kiev Theological Academy. Although a believer, he was never fanatical, and he encouraged his children to read as widely as they wished, and to make up their own minds on everything. His mother was a teacher and several of his uncles were doctors.

In 1906 his father became ill with sclerosis of the kidneys. The Theological Academy immediately awarded him a full pension, even though he had not completed the full term of service, and allowed him to retire on health grounds. However, he died almost immediately afterwards.

Every member of the Bulgakov family played a musical instrument, and Mikhail became a competent pianist. There was an excellent repertory company and opera house in Kiev, which he visited regularly. He was already starting to write plays which were performed by the family in their drawing room. He was a conservative and a monarchist in his school days, but never belonged to any of the extreme right-wing organizations of the time. Like many of his contemporaries, he favoured the idea of a constitutional monarchy as against Russian Tsarist autocracy.

A few years after her first husband's death, Mikhail's mother married an uncompromising atheist. She gave the children supplementary lessons in her spare time from her own teaching job and, as soon as they reached adolescence, she encouraged them to take on younger pupils to increase the family's meagre income. Mikhail's first job, undertaken when he was still at school, was as a part-time guard and ticket inspector on the local railway, and he continued such part-time employment when he entered medical school in Kiev in 1911.

He failed the exams at the end of his first year, but passed the resits a few months later. However, he then had to repeat his entire second year; this lack of dedication to his studies was possibly due to the fact that he was already beginning to write articles for various student journals and to direct student theatricals. Furthermore, he was at this time courting Tatyana Lappa, whom he married in 1913. She came from the distant Saratov region, but had relatives in Kiev, through whom she became acquainted with Bulgakov. He had already begun by this time to write short stories and plays. Because of these distractions, Bulgakov took seven years to complete what was normally a five-year course, but he finally graduated as a doctor in 1916 with distinction.

War   In 1914 the First World War had broken out, and Bulgakov enlisted immediately after graduation as a Red Cross volunteer, working in military hospitals at the front, which involved carrying out operations. In March 1916 he was called up to the army, but was in the end sent to work in a major Kiev hospital to replace experienced doctors who had been mobilized earlier. His wife, having done a basic nursing course by this time, frequently worked alongside her husband.

In March 1917 the Tsar abdicated, and the Russian monarchy collapsed. Two forces then began to contend for power – the Bolsheviks and the Ukrainian Nationalists. Although not completely in control of Ukraine, the latter declared independence from the former Tsarist Empire in February 1918, and concluded a separate peace deal with Germany. The Germans engineered a coup, placed their own supporters at the helm in Ukraine and supported this puppet regime against the Bolsheviks, the now deposed Nationalists and various other splinter groups fighting for their own causes. The Government set up its own German-supported army, the White Guard, which provided the background for Bulgakov's novel of the same name. The Bolsheviks ("The Reds"), the White Guard ("The Whites") and the Ukrainian Nationalists regularly took and retook the country and Kiev from each other: there were eighteen changes of government between the beginning of 1918 and late 1919.

Early in this period Bulgakov had been transferred to medical service in the countryside around the remote town of Vyazma, which provided him with material for his series of short stories

A Young Doctor's Notebook. Possibly to blunt the distress caused to him by the suffering he witnessed there, and to cure fevers he caught from the peasants he was tending, he dosed himself heavily on his own drugs, and rapidly became addicted to morphine. When his own supplies had run out, he sent his wife to numerous pharmacies to pick up new stocks for imaginary patients. When she finally refused to acquiesce in this any further, he became abusive and violent, and even threatened her with a gun. No more mention is made at any later date of his addiction, so it is uncertain whether he obtained professional help for the problem or weaned himself off his drug habit by his own will-power.

He returned to Kiev in February 1918 and set up in private practice. Some of the early stories written in this period show that he was wrestling with problems of direction and conscience: a doctor could be pressed into service by whichever faction was in power at that moment; after witnessing murders, torture and pogroms, Bulgakov was overwhelmed with horror at the contemporary situation. He was press-ganged mainly by the right-wing Whites, who were notoriously anti-Semitic and carried out most of the pogroms.

Perhaps as a result of the suffering he had seen during his enforced military service, he suffered a "spiritual crisis" – as an acquaintance of his termed it – in February 1920, when he gave up medicine at the age of twenty-nine to devote himself to literature. But things were changing in the literary world: Bulgakov's style and motifs were not in tune with the new proletarian values which the Communists, in the areas where they had been victorious, were already beginning to inculcate. The poet Anna Akhmatova talked of his "magnificent contempt" for their ethos, in which everything had to be subordinated to the creation of a new, optimistic mentality which believed that science, medicine and Communism would lead to a paradise on earth for all, with humanity reaching its utmost point of development.

Turning to Literature

He continued to be pressed into service against his will. Although not an ardent right-winger, he had more sympathy for the Whites than for the Reds, and when the former, who had forced him into service at the time, suffered a huge defeat at the hands of the Communists, evidence suggests that Bulgakov would rather have retreated with the right-wing faction, and maybe even gone into emigration, than have to work for the victorious Communists. However, he was prevented from doing this as just at this time he became seriously ill with typhus, and so remained behind when the Whites fled. Incidentally, both his brothers had fled abroad, and were by this time living in Paris.

From 1920 to 1921 Bulgakov briefly worked in a hospital in the Caucasus, where he had been deployed by the Whites, who finally retreated from there in 1922. Bulgakov, living in the town of Vladikavkaz, produced a series of journalistic sketches, later collected and published as *Notes on Shirt Cuffs*, detailing his own experiences at the time, and later in Moscow. He avowedly took as his model classic writers such as Molière, Gogol and particularly Pushkin, and his writings at this time attracted criticism from anti-White critics, because of what was seen as his old-fashioned style and material, which was still that of the cultured European intellectuals of an earlier age, rather than being in keeping with the fresh aspirations of the new progressive proletarian era inaugurated by the Communists. The authorities championed literature and works of art which depicted the life of the masses and assisted in the development of the new Communist ethos. At the time, this tendency was still only on the level of advice and encouragement from the Government, rather than being a categorical demand. It only began to crystallize around the mid-1920s into an obligatory uncompromising line, ultimately leading to the repression, under Stalin, of any kind of even mildly dissident work, and to an increasingly oppressive state surveillance.

In fact, although never a supporter of Bolshevism as such, Bulgakov's articles of the early 1920s display not approval of the Red rule, but simply relief that at last there seemed to be stable government in Russia, which had re-established law and order and was gradually rebuilding the country's infrastructure. However, this relief at the new stability did not prevent him producing stories satirizing the new social order; for instance, around this time he published an experimental satirical novella entitled *Crimson Island*, purporting to be a novella by "Comrade Jules Verne" translated from the French. It portrayed the Whites as stereotypical monsters and was written in the coarse, cliché-ridden agitprop style of the time – a blatant lampoon of the genre.

But by 1921, when he was approaching the age of thirty, Bulgakov was becoming worried that he still had no solid body of work behind him. Life had always been a struggle for him and his wife Tatyana, but he had now begun to receive some money from his writing and to mix in Russian artistic circles. After his medical service in Vladikavkaz he moved to Moscow, where he earned a precarious living over the next few years, contributing sketches to newspapers and magazines, and lecturing on literature. In January 1924 he met the sophisticated, multilingual Lyubov Belozerskaya, who was the wife of a journalist. In comparison with her, Tatyana seemed provincial and uncultured. They started a relationship, divorced their respective partners, and were entered in the local registers as married in late spring 1924, though the exact date of their marriage is unclear.

Between 1925 and 1926 Bulgakov produced three anthologies of his stories, the major one of which received the overall title *Diaboliad*. This collection received reasonably favourable reviews. One compared his stories in *Diaboliad* to those of Gogol, and this was in fact the only major volume of his fiction to be published in the USSR during his lifetime. According to a typist he employed at this time, he would dictate to her for two or three hours every day, from notebooks and loose sheets of paper, though not apparently from any completely composed manuscript.

But in a review in the newspaper *Izvestiya* of *Diaboliad* and some of Bulgakov's other writings in September 1925, the Marxist writer and critic Lev Averbakh, who was to become head of RAPP (the Russian Association of Proletarian Writers) had already declared that the stories contained only one theme: the uselessness and chaos arising from the Communists' attempts to create a new society. The critic then warned that, although Soviet satire was permissible and indeed requisite for the purposes of stimulating the restructuring of society, totally destructive lampoons such as Bulgakov's were irrelevant, and even inimical to the new ethos.

The Government's newly established body for overseeing literature subsequently ordered *Diaboliad* to be withdrawn, although it allowed a reissue in early 1926. By April 1925, Bulgakov was reading his long story *A Dog's Heart* at literary gatherings, but finding it very difficult to get this work, or anything else, published. In May 1926, Bulgakov's flat was searched by agents of OGPU, the precursor of the KGB. The typescript of *A Dog's Heart* and Bulgakov's most recent diaries were confiscated; the story was only published in full in Russian in 1968 (in Germany), and in the USSR only in 1987, in a literary journal.

In 1926 Bulgakov had written a stage adaptation of the story, but again it was only produced for the first time in June 1987, after which it became extremely popular throughout the USSR.

The White Guard   Between 1922 and 1924 Bulgakov was engaged in writing his first novel, ultimately to be known as *The White Guard*. The publishing history of this volume – which was originally planned to be the first part of a trilogy portraying the whole sweep of the Russian Revolution and Civil War – is extremely complex, and there were several different redactions. The whole project was very important to him, and was written at a period of great material hardship. By 1925 he was reading large sections at literary gatherings. Most of the chapters were published as they were produced, in literary magazines, with the exception of the ending, which was banned by the censors; pirated editions, with concocted endings, were published abroad. The novel appeared finally, substantially rewritten and complete, in 1929 in Paris, in a version approved by the author. Contrary to all other Soviet publications of this period, which saw the events of these years from the point of view of the victorious Bolsheviks, Bulgakov described that time from the perspective of one of the enemy factions, portraying them not as vile and sadistic monsters, as was now the custom, but as ordinary human beings with their own problems, fears and ideals.

It had a mixed reception; one review found it inferior to his short stories, while another compared it to the novelistic debut of Dostoevsky. It made almost no stir, and it's interesting to note that, in spite of the fact that the atmosphere was becoming more and more repressive as to the kind of artistic works which would be permitted, the party newspaper *Pravda* in 1927 could write neutrally of its "interesting point of view from a White-Guard perspective".

First Plays   Representatives of the Moscow Arts Theatre (MAT) had heard Bulgakov reading extracts from his novel-in-progress at literary events, realized its dramatic potential, and asked him to adapt the novel for the stage. The possibility had dawned on him even before this, and it seems he was making drafts for such a play from early 1925. This play – now known as *The Days of the Turbins* – had an extremely complicated history. At rehearsals, Bulgakov was interrogated by OGPU. MAT forwarded the original final version to Anatoly Lunacharsky, the People's Commissar for Education, to verify whether it was sufficiently innocuous politically for them to be able to stage it. He wrote back declaring it was rubbish from an artistic point of view, but as far as subject matter went there was no problem. The theatre seems to have agreed with him as to the literary merit of the piece, since they encouraged the author to embark on an extensive revision, which would ultimately produce a radically different version.

During rehearsals as late as August 1926, representatives of OGPU and the censors were coming to the theatre to hold lengthy negotiations with the author and director, and to suggest alterations. The play was finally passed for performance, but only at MAT – no productions were to be permitted anywhere else. It was only allowed to be staged elsewhere, oddly enough, from 1933 onwards, when the party line was being enforced more and more rigorously and Stalin's reign was becoming increasingly repressive. Rumour had it that Stalin himself had quite enjoyed the play when he saw it at MAT in 1929, regarded its contents as innocuous, and had himself authorized its wider performances.

It was ultimately premiered on 26th October 1926, and achieved great acclaim, becoming known as "the second Seagull", as the first performance of Chekhov's Seagull at MAT in 1898 had inaugurated the theatre's financial and artistic success after a long period of mediocrity and falling popularity. This was a turning point in the fortunes of MAT, which had been coming under fire for only performing the classics and not adopting styles of acting and subject matter more in keeping with modern times and themes. The play was directed by one of the original founders of MAT, Konstantin Stanislavsky, and he authorized a thousand-rouble advance for the playwright, which alleviated somewhat the severe financial constraints he had been living under.

The play received mixed reviews, depending almost entirely on the journal or reviewer's political views. One critic objected to its "idealization of the Bolsheviks' enemies", while another vilified its "petit-bourgeois vulgarity". Others accused it of using means of expression dating from the era of classic theatre which had now been replaced in contemporary plays by styles – often crudely propagandistic – which were more in tune with the Soviet proletarian ethos. The piece was extremely popular, however, and in spite of the fact that it was only on in one theatre, Bulgakov could live reasonably well on his share of the royalties.

At this time another Moscow theatre, the Vakhtangov, also requested a play from the author, so Bulgakov gave them *Zoyka's Apartment*, which had probably been written in late 1925. It was premiered on 28th October, just two days after *The Days of the Turbins*. The theatre's representatives suggested a few textual (not political) changes, and Bulgakov first reacted with some irritation, then acknowledged he had been overworked and under stress, due to the strain of the negotiations with OGPU and the censors over *The Days of the Turbins*.

Various other changes had to be made before the censors were satisfied, but the play was allowed to go on tour throughout the Soviet Union. It is rather surprising that it was permitted, because, in line with party doctrine, social and sexual mores were beginning to become more and more puritanical, and the play brought out into the open the seamier side of life which still existed in the workers' paradise. Zoyka's apartment is in fact a high-class brothel, and the Moscow papers had recently reported the discovery in the city of various such establishments, as well as drug dens. The acting and production received rave reviews, but the subject matter was condemned by some reviewers as philistine and shallow, and the appearance of scantily clad actresses on stage was excoriated as being immoral.

The play was extremely successful, both in Moscow and on tour, and brought the author further substantial royalties. Bulgakov was at this time photographed wearing a monocle and looking extremely dandified; those close to him claimed that the monocle was worn for genuine medical reasons, but this photograph attracted personal criticism in the press: he was accused of living in the past and being reactionary.

Perhaps to counteract this out-of-touch image, Bulgakov published a number of sketches in various journals between 1925 and 1927 giving his reminiscences of medical practice in the remote countryside. When finally collected and published posthumously, they were given the title *A Young Doctor's Notebook*. Although they were written principally to alleviate his financial straits, the writer may also have been trying to demonstrate that, in spite of all the criticism, he was a useful member of society with his medical knowledge.

Censorship   Bulgakov's next major work was the play *Escape* (also translated as *Flight*), which, according to dates on some of the manuscript pages, was written and revised between 1926 and 1928. The script was thoroughly rewritten in 1932 and only performed in the USSR in 1957. The play was banned at the rehearsal stage in 1929 as being not sufficiently "revolutionary", though Bulgakov claimed in bafflement that he had in fact been trying to write a piece that was more akin to agitprop than anything he'd previously written.

Escape is set in the Crimea during the struggle between the Whites and Reds in the Civil War, and portrays the Whites as stereotypical villains involved in prostitution, corruption and terror. At first it seems perplexing that the piece should have been banned, since it seems so in tune with the spirit of the times, but given Bulgakov's well-known old-fashioned and anti-Red stance, the play may well have been viewed as in fact a satire on the crude agitprop pieces of the time.

The year 1929 was cataclysmic both for Bulgakov and for other Soviet writers: by order of RAPP (Russian Association of Proletarian Writers) *Escape*, *The Days of the Turbins* and *Zoyka's Apartment* had their productions suspended. Although, with the exception of *Zoyka*, they were then granted temporary runs, at least until the end of that season, their long-term future remained uncertain.

Bulgakov had apparently started drafting his masterpiece *The Master and Margarita* as early as 1928. The novel had gone through at least six revisions by the time of the writer's death in 1940. With the tightening of the party line, there was an increase in militant, politically approved atheism, and one of the novel's major themes is a retelling of Christ's final days, and his victory in defeat – possibly a response to the atheism of Bulgakov's time. He submitted one chapter, under a pseudonym, to the magazine *Nedra* in May 1929, which described satirically the intrigues among the official literary bodies of the time, such as RAPP and others. This chapter was rejected. Yevgeny Zamyatin, another writer in disfavour at the time, who finally emigrated permanently, stated privately that the Soviet Government was adopting the worst excesses of old Spanish Catholicism, seeing heresies where there were none.

In July of that year Bulgakov wrote a letter to Stalin and other leading politicians and writers in good standing with the authorities, asking to be allowed to leave the USSR with his wife; he stated in this letter that it appeared he would never be allowed to be published or performed again in his own country. His next play, *Molière*, was about problems faced by the French playwright in the period of the autocratic monarch

Louis XIV; the parallels between the times of Molière and the Soviet writer are blatant. It was read in January 1930 to the Artistic Board of MAT, who reported that, although it had "no relevance to contemporary questions", they had now admitted a couple of modern propaganda plays to their repertoire, and so they thought the authorities might stretch a point and permit Bulgakov's play. But in March he was told that the Government artistic authorities had not passed the piece. MAT now demanded the return of the thousand-rouble advance they had allowed Bulgakov for *Escape*, also now banned; furthermore the writer was plagued by demands for unpaid income tax relating to the previous year. None of his works were now in production.

Help from Stalin

On Good Friday Bulgakov received a telephone call from Stalin himself promising a favourable response to his letter to the authorities, either to be allowed to emigrate, or at least to be permitted to take up gainful employment in a theatre if he so wished. Stalin even promised a personal meeting with the writer. Neither meeting nor response ever materialized, but Bulgakov was shortly afterwards appointed Assistant Director at MAT, and Consultant to the Theatre of Working Youth, probably as a result of some strings being pulled in high places. Although unsatisfactory, these officially sanctioned positions provided the writer with some income and measure of protection against the torrent of arbitrary arrests now sweeping through the country.

Yelena
Shilovskaya

Although there was now some stability in Bulgakov's professional life, there was to be another major turn in his love life. In February 1929 he had met at a friend's house in Moscow a woman called Yelena Shilovskaya; she was married with two children, highly cultured, and was personal secretary at MAT to the world-famous theatre director Vladimir Nemirovich-Danchenko. They fell in love, but then did not see each other again for around eighteen months. When they did meet again, they found they were still drawn to each other, divorced their partners, and married in October 1932. She remained his wife till his death, and afterwards became the keeper of his archives and worked tirelessly to have his works published.

Over the next few years Bulgakov wrote at least twice more to Stalin asking to be allowed to emigrate. But permission was not forthcoming, and so Bulgakov would never travel outside the USSR. He always felt deprived because of this and sensed something had been lacking in his education. At this time, because of his experience in writing such letters, and because of his apparent "pull" in high places, other intellectuals such as Stanislavsky and Anna Akhmatova were asking for his help in writing similar letters.

While working at MAT, Bulgakov's enthusiasm quickly waned and he felt creatively stifled as his adaptations for the stage of such classic Russian novels as Gogol's *Dead Souls* were altered extensively either for political or artistic reasons. However, despite these changes, he also provided screenplays for mooted films of both *Dead Souls* and Gogol's play *The Government Inspector*. Once again, neither ever came to fruition. There were further projects at this time for other major theatres, both in Moscow and Leningrad, such as an adaptation of Tolstoy's novel *War and Peace* for the stage. This too never came to anything. In May 1932 he wrote: "In nine days' time I shall be celebrating my forty-first birthday... And so towards the conclusion of my literary career I've been forced to write adaptations. A brilliant finale, don't you think?" He wrote numerous other plays and adaptations between then and the end of his life, but no new works were ever produced on stage.

Things appeared to be looking up at one point, because in October 1931 *Molière* had been passed by the censors for production and was accepted by the Bolshoi Drama Theatre in Leningrad. Moreover, in 1932, MAT had made a routine request to be allowed to restage certain works, and to their surprise were permitted to put *Zoyka's Apartment* and *The Days of the Turbins* back into their schedules. This initially seemed to herald a new thaw, a new liberalism, and these prospects were enhanced by the dissolution of such bodies as RAPP, and the formation of the Soviet Writers' Union. Writers hitherto regarded with suspicion were published.

However, although *Molière* was now in production at the Leningrad theatre, the theatre authorities withdrew it suddenly, terrified by the vituperative attacks of a revolutionary and hard-line Communist playwright, Vsevolod Vishnevsky, whose works celebrated the heroic deeds of the Soviet armed forces and working people and who would place a gun on the table when reading a play aloud.

Bulgakov was then commissioned to write a biography of Molière for the popular market, and the typescript was submitted to the authorities in March 1933. However, it was once again rejected, because Bulgakov, never one to compromise, had adopted an unorthodox means of telling his story, having a flamboyant narrator within the story laying out the known details of Molière's life, but also commenting on them and on the times in which he lived; parallels with modern Soviet times were not hard to find. The censor who rejected Bulgakov's work suggested the project should only be undertaken by a "serious Soviet historian". It was finally published only in 1962, and was one of the writer's first works to be issued posthumously. It is now regarded as a major work, both in content and style.

Acting   In December 1934 Bulgakov made his acting debut for MAT as the judge in an adaptation of Dickens's *Pickwick Papers*, and the performance was universally described as hilarious and brilliant. However, though he obviously had great acting ability, he found the stress and the commitment of performing night after night a distraction from his career as a creative writer. He was still attempting to write plays and other works – such as *Ivan Vasilyevich*, set in the time of Ivan the Terrible – which were rejected by the authorities.

At about this time, Bulgakov proposed a play on the life of Alexander Pushkin, and both Shostakovich and Prokofiev expressed an interest in turning the play into an opera. But then Shostakovich's opera *Lady Macbeth of Mtsensk* was slaughtered in the press for being ideologically and artistically unsound, and Bulgakov's play, which had not even gone into production, was banned in January 1936.

Molière, in a revised form, was passed for performance in late 1935, and premiered by MAT in February 1936. However, it was promptly savaged by the newspaper *Pravda* for its "falsity", and MAT immediately withdrew it from the repertoire. Bulgakov, bitterly resentful at the theatre's abject capitulation, resigned later in the year, and swiftly joined the famous Moscow Bolshoi Opera Theatre as librettist and adviser. In November 1936, in just a few hours he churned out *Black Snow* (later to be called *A Theatrical Novel*), a short satire on the recent events at MAT.

Play on Stalin   In mid-1937 he began intensive work on yet another redaction of *The Master and Margarita*, which was finally typed out by June 1938. Soon afterwards, he started work on a play about Stalin, *Batum*. The dictator, although in the main disapproving of the tendency of Bulgakov's works, still found them interesting, and had always extended a certain amount of protection to him. Bulgakov had started work in 1936 on a history of the

USSR for schools and, although the project remained fragmentary, he had gathered a tremendous amount of material on Stalin for the project, which he proposed to incorporate in his play. It is odd that this ruthless dictator and Bulgakov – who was certainly not a supporter of the regime and whose patrician views seemed to date from a previous era – should have been locked in such a relationship of mutual fascination.

Although MAT told him that the play on Stalin would do both him and the theatre good in official eyes, Bulgakov, still contemptuous of the theatre, demanded that they provide him with a new flat where he could work without interruption from noise. MAT complied with this condition. He submitted the manuscript in July 1939, but it was turned down, apparently by the dictator himself.

Bulgakov was devastated by this rejection, and almost *Illness and Death* immediately began to suffer a massive deterioration in health. His eyesight became worse and worse, he developed appalling headaches, he grew extremely sensitive to light and often could not leave his flat for days on end. All this was the first manifestation of the sclerosis of the kidneys which finally killed him, as it had killed his father. When he could, he continued revising *The Master and Margarita*, but only managed to finish correcting the first part. He became totally bedridden, his weight fell to under fifty kilograms, and he finally died on 10th March 1940. The next morning a call came through from Stalin's office – though not from the leader himself – asking whether it was true the writer was dead. On receiving the answer, the caller hung up with no comment. Bulgakov had had no new work published or performed for some time, yet the Soviet Writers' Union, full of many of the people who had pilloried him so mercilessly over the years, honoured him respectfully. He was buried in the Novodevichy Cemetery, in the section for artistic figures, near Chekhov and Gogol. Ultimately, a large stone which had lain on Gogol's grave, but had been replaced by a memorial bust, was placed on Bulgakov's grave, where it still lies.

After the Second World War ended in 1945, the country *Posthumous* had other priorities than the publication of hitherto banned *Publications and* authors, but Bulgakov's wife campaigned fearlessly for his *Reputation* rehabilitation, and in 1957 *The Days of the Turbins* and his play on the end of Pushkin's life were published, and a larger selection of his plays appeared in 1962. A heavily cut version of *The Master and Margarita* appeared in a specialist literary journal throughout 1966–67, and the full uncensored text in 1973. Subsequently – especially post-Glasnost – more and more works of Bulgakov's were published in uncensored redactions, and at last Western publishers could see the originals of what they had frequently published before in corrupt smuggled variants. Bulgakov's third wife maintained his archive, and both she and his second wife gave public lectures on him, wrote memoirs of him and campaigned for publication of his works. Bulgakov has now achieved cult status in Russia, and almost all of his works have been published in uncensored editions, with unbiased editorial commentary and annotation.

Mikhail Bulgakov's Works

It is difficult to give an overall survey of Bulgakov's works, which, counting short stories and adaptations, approach a total of almost one hundred. Many of these works exist in several versions, as the author revised them constantly to make them more acceptable to the authorities. This meant that published versions – including translations brought out abroad – were frequently not based on what the author might have considered the "definitive" version. In fact to talk of "definitive versions" with reference to Bulgakov's works may be misleading. Furthermore, no new works of his were published after 1927, and they only began to be issued sporadically, frequently in censored versions, from 1962 onwards. Complete and uncut editions of many of the works have begun to appear only from the mid-1990s. Therefore the section below will contain only the most prominent works in all genres.

Themes   Despite the wide variety of settings of his novels – Russia, the Caucasus, Ukraine, Jerusalem in New Testament times and the Paris of Louis XIV – the underlying themes of Bulgakov's works remain remarkably constant throughout his career. Although these works contain a huge number of characters, most of them conform to certain archetypes and patterns of behaviour.

Stylistically, Bulgakov was influenced by early-nineteenth-century classic Russian writers such as Gogol and Pushkin, and he espoused the values of late-nineteenth-century liberal democracy and culture, underpinned by Christian teachings. Although Bulgakov came from an ecclesiastical background, he was never in fact a conventional believer, but, like many agnostic or atheistic Russian nineteenth-century intellectuals and artists, he respected the role that the basic teachings of religion had played in forming Russian and European culture – although they, and Bulgakov, had no liking for the way religions upheld obscurantism and authority.

Some works portray the struggle of the outsider against society, such as the play and narrative based on the life of Molière, or the novel *The Master and Margarita*, in which the outsider persecuted by society and the state is Yeshua, i.e. Jesus. Other works give prominent roles to doctors and scientists, and demonstrate what happens if science is misused and is subjected to Government interference. Those works portraying historical reality, such as *The White Guard*, show the Whites – who were normally depicted in Communist literature as evil reactionaries – to be ordinary human beings with their own concerns and ideals. Most of all, Bulgakov's work is pervaded by a biting satire on life as he saw it around him in the USSR, especially in the artistic world, and there is frequently a "magical realist" element – as in *The Master and Margarita* – in which contemporary reality and fantasy are intermingled, or which show the influence of Western science fiction (Bulgakov admired the works of H.G. Wells enormously).

Bulgakov's major works are written in a variety of forms, including novels, plays and short stories. His first novel, *The White Guard*, was written between 1922 and 1924, but it received numerous substantial revisions later. It was originally conceived as the first volume of a trilogy portraying the entire sweep of the post-revolutionary Civil War from a number of different points of view. Although this first and only volume was criticized for showing events from the viewpoint of the Whites, the third volume would apparently have given the perspective of the Communists. Many chapters of the novel were published separately in literary journals as they appeared. The ending – the dreams presaging disaster for the country – never appeared, because the journal it was due to be printed in, *Rossiya*, was shut down by official order, precisely because it was publishing such material as Bulgakov's. Different pirate versions, with radically variant texts and concocted endings, appeared abroad. The novel only appeared complete in Russian, having been proofread by the author, in 1929 in Paris, where there was a substantial émigré population from the Tsarist Empire/USSR.

The major part of the story takes place during the forty-seven days in which the Ukrainian Nationalists, under their leader

The White Guard

Petlyura, held power in Kiev. The novel ends in February 1919, when Petlyura was overthrown by the Bolsheviks. The major protagonists are the Turbins, a family reminiscent of Bulgakov's own, with a similar address, who also work in the medical profession: many elements of the novel are in fact autobiographical. At the beginning of the novel, we are still in the world of old Russia, with artistic and elegant furniture dating from the Tsarist era, and a piano, books and high-quality pictures on the walls. But the atmosphere is one of fear about the future, and apprehension at the world collapsing. The Turbins' warm flat, in which the closely knit family can take refuge from the events outside, is progressively encroached on by reality. Nikolka Turbin, the younger son, is still at high school and in the cadet corps; he has a vague feeling that he should be fighting on the side of the Whites – that is, the forces who were against both the Nationalists and Communists. However, when a self-sacrificing White soldier dies in the street in Nikolka's arms, he realizes for the first time that war is vile. Near the conclusion of the novel there is a family gathering at the flat, but everything has changed since the beginning of the book: relationships have been severed, and there is no longer any confidence in the future. As the Ukrainian Nationalists flee, they brutally murder a Jew near the Turbins' flat, demonstrating that liberal tolerant values have disintegrated. The novel ends with a series of sinister apocalyptic dreams – indeed the novel contains imagery throughout from the Biblical Apocalypse. These dreams mainly presage catastrophe for the family and society, although the novel ends with the very short dream of a child, which does seem to prefigure some sort of peace in the distant future.

The Life of Monsieur de Molière

The Life of Monsieur de Molière is sometimes classed not as a novel but as a biography. However, the treatment is distinctive enough to enable the work to be ranked as semi-fictionalized. Bulgakov's interpretative view of the French writer's life, rather than a purely historical perspective, is very similar to that in his play on the same theme. The book was written in 1932, but was banned for the same reasons which were to cause problems later for the play. Molière's life is narrated in the novel by an intermediary, a flamboyant figure who often digresses, and frequently comments on the political intrigues of the French author's time. The censors may have felt that the description of the French writer's relationship to an autocrat might have borne too many similarities to Bulgakov's relationship to Stalin.

The book was only finally published in the USSR in 1962, and is now regarded as a major work.

Although he had written fragmentary pieces about the theatre before, Bulgakov only really settled down to produce a longer work on the theme – a short, vicious satire on events in the Soviet theatre – in November 1936, after what he saw as MAT's abject capitulation in the face of attacks by Communists on *Molière*. *A Theatrical Novel* was only published for the first time in the Soviet Union in 1969. There is a short introduction, purporting to be by an author who has found a manuscript written by a theatrical personage who has committed suicide (the reason for Bulgakov's original title, *Notes of the Deceased*; other mooted titles were *Black Snow* and *White Snow*). Not only does Bulgakov take a swipe at censorship and the abject and pusillanimous authorities of the theatre world, but he also deals savagely with the reputations of such people as the theatre director Stanislavsky, who, despite his fame abroad, is depicted – in a thinly veiled portrait – as a tyrannical figure who crushes the individuality and flair of writers and actors in the plays which he is directing. The manuscript ends inconclusively, with the dead writer still proclaiming his wonder at the nature of theatre itself, despite its intrigues and frustrations; the original author who has found the manuscript does not reappear, and it's uncertain whether the point is that the theatrical figure left his memoirs uncompleted, or whether in fact Bulgakov failed to finish his original project.

The Master and Margarita is generally regarded as Bulgakov's masterpiece. He worked on it from 1928 to 1940, and it exists in at least six different variants, ranging from the fragmentary to the large-scale narrative which he was working on at the onset of the illness from which he died. Even the first redaction contains many of the final elements, although the Devil is the only narrator of the story of Pilate and Jesus – the insertion of the Master and Margarita came at a later stage. In 1929 the provisional title was *The Engineer's Hoof* (the word "engineer" had become part of the vocabulary of the Soviet demonology of the times, since in May and June 1928 a large group of mining engineers had been tried for anti-revolutionary activities, and they were equated in the press to the Devil who was trying to undermine the new Soviet society). The last variant written before the author's death was completed around mid-1938, and Bulgakov began proofreading and revising it, making numerous

A Theatrical Novel

The Master and Margarita

corrections and sorting out loose ends. In his sick state, he managed to revise only the first part of the novel, and there are still a certain number of moot points remaining later on. The novel was first published in a severely cut version in 1966–67, in a specialist Russian literary journal, while the complete text was published only in 1973. At one stage, Bulgakov apparently intended to allow Stalin to be the first reader of *The Master and Margarita*, and to present him with a personal copy.

The multi-layered narrative switches backwards and forwards between Jerusalem in the time of Christ and contemporary Moscow. The Devil – who assumes the name Woland – visits Moscow with his entourage, which includes a large talking black cat and a naked witch, and they cause havoc with their displays of magic.

In the scenes set in modern times, the narrative indirectly evokes the atmosphere of a dictatorship. This is paralleled in the Pilate narrative by the figure of Caesar, who, although he is mentioned, never appears.

The atheists of modern Moscow who, following the contemporary party line, snigger at Christ's miracles and deny his existence, are forced to create explanations for what they see the Devil doing in front of them in their own city.

There are numerous references to literature, and also to music – there are three characters with the names of composers, Berlioz, Stravinsky and Rimsky-Korsakov. Berlioz the composer wrote an oratorio on the theme of Faust, who is in love with the self-sacrificing Margarita; immediately we are drawn towards the idea that the persecuted writer known as the Master, who also has a devoted lover called Margarita, is a modern manifestation of Faust. Bulgakov carried out immense research on studies of ancient Jerusalem and theology, particularly Christology. The novel demands several readings, such are the depths of interconnected details and implications.

Days of the Turbins   Apart from novels, another important area for Bulgakov to channel his creative energy into was plays. *The Days of the Turbins* was the first of his works to be staged: it was commissioned by the Moscow Arts Theatre in early 1925, although it seems Bulgakov had already thought of the possibility of a stage adaptation of *The White Guard*, since acquaintances report him making drafts for such a project slightly earlier. It had an extremely complex history, which involved numerous rewritings after constant negotiations between the writer, theatre, secret police and censors. Bulgakov did not want to leave any elements of the novel out, but on his reading the initial manuscript at the Moscow Arts Theatre it was found to be far too long, and so he cut out a few of the minor characters and pruned the dream sequences in the novel. However, the background is still the same – the Civil War in Kiev after the Bolshevik Revolution. The family are broadly moderate Tsarists in their views, and therefore are anti-Communist but, being ethnically Russian, have no sympathy with the Ukrainian Nationalists either, and so end up fighting for the White Guards. Their flat at the beginning is almost Chekhovian in its warmth, cosiness and air of old-world culture, but by the end one brother has been killed in the fighting and, as the sounds of the 'Internationale' offstage announce the victory of the Communists, a feeling of apprehension grips the family as their world seems to be collapsing round them. The final lines of the play communicate these misgivings (Nikolka: "Gentlemen, this evening is a great prologue to a new historical play." / Studzinsky: "For some a prologue – for others an epilogue."). The final sentence may be taken as representing Bulgakov's fear about the effect the Communist takeover might have on the rest of his own career.

The Soviet playwright Viktor Nekrasov, who was in favour of the Revolution, commented that the play was an excellent recreation of that time in Kiev, where he had also been participating in the historic events on the Bolshevik side – the atmosphere was all very familiar, Nekrasov confirmed, and one couldn't help extending sympathy to such characters as the Turbins, even if they were on the other side: they were simply individuals caught up in historical events.

At around the time of the writing of *The Days of the Turbins*, another Moscow theatre, the Vakhtangov, requested a play from Bulgakov, so he provided them with *Zoyka's Apartment*, which had been first drafted in late 1925. Various alterations had to be made before the censors were satisfied. At least four different texts of *Zoyka* exist, the final revision completed as late as 1935; this last is now regarded as the authoritative text, and is that generally translated for Western editions.

Zoyka's Apartment

The setting is a Moscow apartment run by Zoyka; it operates as a women's dress shop and haute-couturier during the day, and becomes a brothel after closing time. At the time the play was written, various brothels and drug dens had been unearthed by the police in the capital, some run by Chinese nationals. Bulgakov's play contains therefore not only easily recognizable political and social types who turn up for a session with the scantily clad ladies, but also stereotypical Chinese drug dealers and addicts. Zoyka is however treated with moral neutrality by the author: she operates as the madam of the brothel in order to raise money as fast as possible so that she can emigrate abroad with her husband, an impoverished former aristocrat, who is also a drug addict. In the final act the ladies and clients dance to decadent Western popular music, a fight breaks out and a man is murdered. The play ends with the establishment being raided by "unknown strangers", who are presumably government inspectors and the police. At this point the final curtain comes down, so we never find out the ultimate fate of the characters.

The Crimson Island   In 1924 Bulgakov had written a rather unsubtle short story, *The Crimson Island*, which was a parody of the crude agitprop style of much of the literature of the time, with its stereotypical heroic and noble Communists, and evil reactionaries and foreigners trying to undermine the new Communist state, all written in the language of the person in the street – often as imagined by educated people who had no direct knowledge of this working-class language. In 1927 he adapted this parody for the stage. The play bears the subtitle: *The Dress Rehearsal of a Play by Citizen Jules Verne in Gennady Panfilovich's theatre, with music, a volcanic eruption and English sailors: in four acts, with a prologue and an epilogue*. The play was much more successful than the story. He offered it to the Kamerny ["Chamber"] Theatre, in Moscow, which specialized in mannered and elegant productions, still in the style of the late 1890s; it was passed for performance and premiered in December 1928, and was a success, though some of the more left-wing of the audience and critics found it hard to swallow. However, the critic Novitsky wrote that it was an "interesting and witty parody, satirizing what crushes artistic creativity and cultivates slavish and absurd dramatic characters, removing the individuality from actors and writers and creating idols, lickspittles and panegyrists". The director of the play, Alexander Tairov, claimed that the work was meant to be self-criticism of the falsity and crudeness of some revolutionary work. Most reviews found it amusing and harmless, and it attracted good audiences. However, there were just a few vitriolic reviews; Stalin himself commented that the production of such a play underlined how reactionary the Kamerny Theatre still was. The work was subsequently banned by the censor in March 1929.

The Crimson Island takes the form of a play within a play: the prologue and epilogue take place in the theatre where the play is to be rehearsed and performed; the playwright – who, although Russian, has taken the pen name Jules Verne – is progressive and sensitive, but his original work is increasingly censored and altered out of all recognition. The rest of the acts show the rewritten play, which has now become a crude agitprop piece. The play within *Crimson Island* takes place on a sparsely populated desert island run by a white king and ruling class, with black underlings. There is a volcano rumbling in the background, which occasionally erupts. The wicked foreigners are represented by the English Lord and Lady Aberaven, who sail in on a yacht crewed by English sailors who march on singing 'It's a Long Way to Tipperary'. During the play the island's underlings stage a revolution and try unsuccessfully to urge the English sailors to rebel against the evil Lord and Lady. However, they do not succeed, and the wicked aristocrats sail away unharmed, leaving the revolutionaries in control of the island.

Bulgakov's play *Escape* (also translated as *Flight*), drafted between 1926 and 1928, and completely rewritten in 1932, is set in the Crimea during the conflicts between the Whites and Reds in the Civil War after the Revolution.

Escape

The Whites – who include a general who has murdered people in cold blood – emigrate to Constantinople, but find they are not accepted by the locals, and their living conditions are appalling. One of the women has to support them all by resorting to prostitution. The murderous White general nurses his colleagues during an outbreak of typhus, and feels he has expiated some of his guilt for the crimes he has committed against humanity. He and a few of his colleagues decide to return to the USSR, since even life under Communism cannot be as bad as in Turkey. However, the censors objected that these people were coming back for negative reasons – simply to get away from where they were – and not because they had genuinely come to believe in the Revolution, or had the welfare of the working people at heart.

Molière   Molière was one of Bulgakov's favourite writers, and some aspects of his writing seemed relevant to Soviet reality – for example the character of the fawning, scheming, hypocritical anti-hero of *Tartuffe*. Bulgakov's next play, *Molière*, was about problems faced by the French playwright during the reign of the autocratic monarch Louis XIV. It was written between October and December 1929 and, as seen above, submitted in January 1930 to the Artistic Board of MAT. Bulgakov told them that he had not written an overtly political piece, but one about a writer hounded by a cabal of critics in connivance with the absolute monarch. Unfortunately, despite MAT's optimism, the authorities did not permit a production. In this piece the French writer at one stage, like Bulgakov, intends to leave the country permanently. Late in the play, the King realizes that Molière's brilliance would be a further ornament to his resplendent court, and extends him his protection; however, then this official attitude changes, Molière is once again an outcast, and he dies on stage, while acting in one of his own plays, a broken man. The play's original title was *The Cabal of Hypocrites*, but it was probably decided that this was too contentious.

Bliss   A version of the play *Bliss* appears to have been drafted in
and   1929, but was destroyed and thoroughly rewritten between then
Ivan Vasilyevich   and 1934. Bulgakov managed to interest both the Leningrad Music Hall Theatre and Moscow Satire Theatre in the idea, but they both said it would be impossible to stage because of the political climate of the time, and told him to rewrite it; accordingly he transferred the original plot to the time of Tsar Ivan the Terrible in the sixteenth century, and the new play, entitled *Ivan Vasilyevich*, was completed by late 1935.

The basic premise behind both plays is the same: an inventor builds a time machine (as mentioned above, Bulgakov was a great admirer of H.G. Wells) and travels to a very different period of history: present-day society is contrasted starkly with the world he has travelled to. However, in *Bliss*, the contrasted world is far in the future, while in *Ivan Vasilyevich* it is almost four hundred years in the past. In *Bliss* the inventor accidentally takes a petty criminal and a typically idiotic building manager from his own time to the Moscow of 2222: it is a utopian society, with no police and no denunciations to the authorities. He finally returns to his own time with the criminal and the building manager, but also with somebody from the future who is fed up with the bland and boring conformity of such a paradise

(Bulgakov was always sceptical of the idea of any utopia, not just the Communist one).

Ivan Vasilyevich is set in the Moscow of the tyrannical Tsar, and therefore the contrast between a paradise and present reality is not the major theme. In fact, contemporary Russian society is almost presented favourably in contrast with the distant past. However, when the inventor and his crew – including a character from Ivan's time who has been transported to the present accidentally – arrive back in modern Moscow, they are all promptly arrested and the play finishes, emphasizing that, although modern times are an improvement on the distant past, the problems of that remote period still exist in contemporary reality. For all the differences in period and emphasis, most of the characters of the two plays are the same, and have very similar speeches.

Even this watered-down version of the original theme was rejected by the theatres it was offered to, who thought that it would still be unperformable. It was only premiered in the Soviet Union in 1966. Bulgakov tried neutering the theme even further, most notably by tacking on an ending in which the inventor wakes up in his Moscow flat with the music of Rimsky-Korsakov's popular opera *The Maid of Pskov* (set in Ivan the Terrible's time) wafting in from offstage, presumably meant to be from a radio in another room. The inventor gives the impression that the events of the play in Ivan's time have all been a dream brought on by the music. But all this rewriting was to no avail, and the play was never accepted by any theatre during Bulgakov's lifetime.

Adam and Eve

In January 1931 Bulgakov signed a contract with the Leningrad Red Theatre to write a play about a "future world"; he also offered it, in case of rejection, to the Vakhtangov Theatre, which had premiered *Zoyka's Apartment*. However, it was banned even before rehearsals by a visiting official from the censor's department, because it showed a cataclysmic world war in which Leningrad was destroyed. Bulgakov had seen the horror of war, including gas attacks, in his medical service, and the underlying idea of *Adam and Eve* appears to be that all war is wrong, even when waged by Communists and patriots.

The play opens just before a world war breaks out; a poison gas is released which kills almost everybody on all sides. A scientist from the Communist camp develops an antidote, and wishes it to be available to everybody, but a patriot and a party official want it only to be distributed to people from their homeland. The Adam of the title is a cardboard caricature of a well-meaning but misguided Communist; his wife, Eve, is much less of a caricature, and is in love with the scientist who has invented the antidote. After the carnage, a world government is set up, which is neither left- nor right-wing. The scientist and Eve try to escape together, apparently to set up civilization again as the new Adam and Eve, but the sinister last line addressed to them both is: "Go, the Secretary General wants to see you." The Secretary General of the Communist Party in Russia at the time was of course Stalin, and the message may well be that even such an apparently apolitical government as that now ruling the world, which is supposed to rebuild the human race almost from nothing, is still being headed by a dictatorial character, and that the proposed regeneration of humanity has gone wrong once again from the outset and will never succeed.

The Last Days

In October 1934 Bulgakov decided to write a play about Pushkin, the great Russian poet, to be ready for the centenary of his death in 1937. He revised the original manuscript several times, but submitted it finally to the censors in late 1935. It was passed for performance, and might have been produced, but just at this time Bulgakov was in such disfavour that MAT themselves backtracked on the project.

Bulgakov, as usual, took an unusual slant on the theme: Pushkin was never to appear on stage during the piece, unless one counts the appearance at the end, in the distance, of his body being carried across stage after he has been killed in a duel. Bulgakov believed that even a great actor could not embody the full magnificence of Pushkin's achievement, the beauty of his language and his towering presence in Russian literature, let alone any of the second-rate hams who might vulgarize his image in provincial theatres. He embarked on the project at first with a Pushkin scholar, Vikenty Veresayev. However, Veresayev wanted everything written strictly in accordance with historical fact, whereas Bulgakov viewed the project dramatically. He introduced a few fictitious minor characters, and invented speeches between other characters where there is no record of what was actually said. Many events in Pushkin's life remain unclear, including who precisely engineered the duel between the army officer d'Anthès and the dangerously liberal thinker Pushkin, which resulted in the writer's death: the army, the Tsar or others? Bulgakov, while studying all the sources assiduously, put his own gloss and interpretation on these unresolved issues. In the end, Veresayev withdrew from the project in protest. The play was viewed with disfavour by critics and censors, because it implied that it may well have been the autocratic Tsar Nicholas I who was behind the events leading up to the duel, and comparison with another autocrat of modern times who also concocted plots against dissidents would inevitably have arisen in people's minds.

The Last Days was first performed in war-torn Moscow in April 1943, by MAT, since the Government was at the time striving to build up Russian morale and national consciousness in the face of enemy attack and invasion, and this play devoted to a Russian literary giant was ideal, in spite of its unorthodox perspective on events.

Commissioned by MAT in 1938, *Batum* was projected as a play about Joseph Stalin, mainly concerning his early life in the Caucasus, which was to be ready for his sixtieth birthday on 21st December 1939. Its first title was *Pastyr* ["The Shepherd"], in reference to Stalin's early training in a seminary for the priesthood, and to his later role as leader of his national "flock". However, although most of Bulgakov's acquaintances were full of praise for the play, and it passed the censors with no objections, it was finally rejected by the dictator himself.

Batum

Divided into four acts, the play covers the period 1898–1904, following Stalin's expulsion from the Tiflis (modern Tbilisi) Seminary, where he had been training to be an Orthodox priest, because of his anti-government activity. He is then shown in the Caucasian town of Batum organizing strikes and leading huge marches of workers to demand the release of imprisoned workers, following which he is arrested and exiled to Siberia. Stalin escapes after a month and in the last two scenes resumes the revolutionary activity which finally led to the Bolshevik Revolution under Lenin. Modern scholars have expressed scepticism as to the prominent role that Soviet biographers of Stalin's time ascribed to his period in Batum and later, and Bulgakov's play, although not disapproving of the autocrat, is objective, and far from the tone of the prevailing hagiography.

Varying explanations have been proposed as to why Stalin rejected the play. Although this was probably because it portrayed the dictator as an ordinary human being, the theory has been advanced that one of the reasons Stalin was fascinated by Bulgakov's works was precisely that the writer refused to knuckle under to the prevailing ethos, and Stalin possibly wrongly interpreted the writer's play about him as an attempt to curry favour, in the manner of all the mediocrities around him.

One Western commentator termed the writing of this play a "shameful act" on Bulgakov's part; however, the author was now beginning to show signs of severe ill health, and was perhaps understandably starting at last to feel worn down both mentally and physically by his lack of success and the constant struggle to try to make any headway in his literary career, or even to earn a crust of bread. Whatever the reasons behind the final rejection of *Batum*, Bulgakov was profoundly depressed by it, and it may have hastened his death from the hereditary sclerosis of the kidneys which he suffered from.

Bulgakov also wrote numerous short stories and novellas, the most significant of which include 'Diaboliad', 'The Fatal Eggs' and *A Dog's Heart*.

Diaboliad   'Diaboliad' was first published in the journal *Nedra* in 1924, and then reappeared as the lead story of a collection of stories under the same name in July 1925; this was in fact the last major volume brought out by the author during his lifetime in Russia, although he continued to have stories and articles published in journals for some years. In theme and treatment the story has reminiscences of Dostoevsky and Gogol.

The "hero" of the tale, a minor ordering clerk at a match factory in Moscow, misreads his boss's name – Kalsoner – as *kalsony*, i.e. "underwear". In confusion he puts through an order for underwear and is sacked. It should be mentioned here that both he and the boss have doubles, and the clerk spends the rest of the story trying to track down his boss through an increasingly nightmarish bureaucratic labyrinth, continually confusing him with his double; at the same time he is constantly having to account for misdemeanours carried out by his own double, who has a totally different personality from him, and is a raffish philanderer. The clerk is robbed of his documents and identity papers, and can no longer prove who he is – the implication being that his double is now the real him, and that he doesn't exist any longer. Finally, the petty clerk, caught up in a Kafkaesque world of bureaucracy and false appearances, goes mad and throws himself off the roof of a well-known Moscow high-rise block.

The Fatal Eggs   'The Fatal Eggs' was first published in the journal *Nedra* in early 1925, then reissued as the second story in the collection *Diaboliad*, which appeared in July 1925. The title in Russian contains a number of untranslatable puns. The major one is that a main character is named "Rokk", and the word "rok" means "fate" in Russian, so "fatal" could also mean "belonging to Rokk". Also, "eggs" is the Russian equivalent of "balls", i.e. testicles, and there is also an overtone of the "roc", i.e. the giant mythical bird in the *Thousand and One Nights*. The theme of the story is reminiscent of *The Island of Doctor Moreau* by H.G. Wells. However, Bulgakov's tale also satirizes the belief of the time, held by both scientists and journalists, that science would solve all human problems, as society moved towards utopia. Bulgakov was suspicious of such ideals and always doubted the possibility of human perfection.

In the story, a professor of zoology discovers accidentally that a certain ray will increase enormously the size of any organism or egg exposed to it – by accelerating the rate of cell multiplication – although it also increases the aggressive tendencies of any creatures contaminated in this manner. At the time, chicken plague is raging throughout Russia, all of the birds have died, and so there is a shortage of eggs. The political activist Rokk wants to get hold of the ray to irradiate eggs brought from abroad, to replenish rapidly the nation's devastated stock of poultry. The professor is reluctant, but a telephone call is received from "someone in authority" ordering him to surrender the ray. When the foreign eggs arrive at the collective farm, they look unusually large, but they are irradiated just the same. Soon Rokk's wife is devoured by an enormous snake, and the country is plagued by giant reptiles and ostriches which wreak havoc. It turns out that a batch of reptile eggs was accidentally substituted for the hens' eggs. Chaos and destruction ensue, creating a sense of panic, during which the professor is murdered. The army is mobilized unsuccessfully, but – like the providential extermination of the invaders by germs in Wells's *The War of the Worlds* – the reptiles are all wiped out by an unexpected hard summer frost. The evil ray is destroyed in a fire.

A Dog's Heart was begun in January 1925 and finished the following month. Bulgakov offered it to the journal *Nedra*, who told him it was unpublishable in the prevailing political climate; it was never issued during Bulgakov's lifetime. Its themes are reminiscent of *The Island of Doctor Moreau, Dr Jekyll and Mr Hyde* and *Frankenstein*.

In the tale, a doctor, Preobrazhensky ["Transfigurative", or "Transformational"] by name, transplants the pituitary glands

A Dog's Heart

and testicles from the corpse of a moronic petty criminal and thug into a dog (Sharik). The dog gradually takes on human form, and turns out to be a hybrid of a dog's psyche and a criminal human being. The dog's natural affectionate nature has been swamped by the viciousness of the human, who has in his turn acquired the animal appetites and instincts of the dog. The monster chooses the name Polygraf ["printing works"], and this may well have been a contemptuous reference to the numerous printing presses in Moscow churning out idiotic propaganda, appealing to the lowest common denominator in terms of intelligence and gullibility. The new creature gains employment, in keeping with his animal nature, as a cat exterminator. He is indoctrinated with party ideology by a manipulative official, and denounces numerous acquaintances to the authorities as being ideologically unsound, including his creator, the doctor. Although regarded with suspicion and warned as to his future behaviour, the doctor escapes further punishment. The hybrid creature disappears, and the dog Sharik reappears; there is a suggestion that the operation has been reversed by the doctor and his faithful assistant, and the human part of his personality has returned to its original form – a corpse – while the canine characteristics have also reassumed their natural form. Although the doctor is devastated at the evil results of his experiment, and vows to renounce all such researches in future, he appears in the last paragraph already to be delving into body parts again. The implication is that he will never be able to refrain from inventing, and the whole sorry disaster will be repeated ad infinitum. Again, as with 'The Fatal Eggs', the writer was voicing his suspicion of science and medicine's interference with nature, and his scepticism as to the possibility of utopias.

Notes on Shirt Cuffs

From 1920 to 1921, Bulgakov worked in a hospital in the Caucasus, where he produced a series of sketches detailing his experiences there. The principal theme is the development of a writer amid scenes of chaos and disruption. An offer was made to publish an anthology of the sketches in Paris in 1924, but the project never came to fruition.

A Young Doctor's Notebook

A Young Doctor's Notebook was drafted in 1919, then published mainly in medical journals between 1925–27. It is different in nature from Bulgakov's most famous works, being a first-person account of his experiences of treating peasants in his country practice, surrounded by ignorance and poverty, in a style reminiscent of another doctor and writer, Chekhov. Bulgakov learns by experience that often in this milieu what he has learnt in medical books and at medical school can seem useless, as he delivers babies, treats syphilitics and carries out amputations. The work is often published with *Morphine*, which describes the experience of a doctor addicted to morphine. This is autobiographical: it recalls Bulgakov's own period in medical service in Vyazma, in 1918, where, to alleviate his distress at the suffering he was seeing, he dosed himself heavily on his own drugs and temporarily became addicted to morphine.

Select Bibliography

Biographies:

Drawicz, Andrzey, *The Master and the Devil*, tr. Kevin Windle (New York, NY: Edwin Mellen Press, 2001)

Haber, Edythe C., *Mikhail Bulgakov: The Early Years* (Cambridge, MS: Harvard University Press, 1998)

Milne, Lesley, *Mikhail Bulgakov: A Critical Biography* (Cambridge: Cambridge University Press, 1990)

Proffer, Ellendea, *Bulgakov: Life and Work* (Ann Arbor, MI: Ardis, 1984)

Proffer, Ellendea, *A Pictorial Biography of Mikhail Bulgakov* (Ann Arbor, MI: Ardis, 1984)

Wright, A. Colin, *Mikhail Bulgakov: Life and Interpretation* (Toronto, ON: University of Toronto Press, 1978)

Letters, Memoirs:

Belozerskaya-Bulgakova, Lyubov, *My Life with Mikhail Bulgakov*, tr. Margareta Thompson (Ann Arbor, MI: Ardis, 1983)

Curtis, J.A.E., *Manuscripts Don't Burn: Mikhail Bulgakov: A Life in Letters and Diaries* (London: Bloomsbury, 1991)

Vozdvizhensky, Vyacheslav, ed., *Mikhail Bulgakov and his Times – Memoirs, Letters*, tr. Liv Tudge (Moscow: Progress Publishers, 1990)